TALES OF OLD JAPAN

THE RÔNINS INVITE KÔTSUKÉ NO SUKÉ TO PERFORM HARA-KIRI

TALES OF OLD JAPAN

by A. B. MITFORD (Lord Redesdale)

WITH ILLUSTRATIONS

drawn and cut on wood by Japanese artists

CHARLES E. TUTTLE COMPANY
Rutland, Vermont & Tokyo, Japan

Representatives

Continental Europe: BOXERBOOKS, INC., *Zurich*

Australasia: BOOK WISE (AUSTRALIA) PTY. LTD.
104-108 Sussex Street, Sydney 2000

*Published by the Charles E. Tuttle Company, Inc.
of Rutland, Vermont and Tokyo, Japan
with editorial offices at
Suido 1-chome, 2-6
Bunkyo-ku, Tokyo, Japan*

Library of Congress Catalog Card No. 66-25436

International Standard Book No. 0-8048-1160-1

*First Tuttle edition, 1966
Eleventh printing, 1983*

PRINTED IN JAPAN

PUBLISHER'S FOREWORD

THE valuable lessons to be gleaned from this book of the history of Japan and toward the understanding of the people and things Japanese provoked this reprinting of A. B. Mitford's popular work.

By far it is the best anthology of its kind on Japanese literature. Adding credence to its authority and acceptability, Robert Louis Stevenson cited Mitford's collection of true stories, legends, fairy tales, etcetera, in an article the famous author wrote entitled, "Books Which Have Influenced Me."

First published nearly a century ago in 1871, *Tales of Old Japan* was written by Algernon Bertram Freeman-Mitford, First Baron Redesdale during his tenure (1866–70) as Attache to Japan. The diplomat-author arrived in the country only just over a decade following the opening of isolationist Japan's seaports, initiated by the entry of American Commodore Matthew Calbraith Perry and his "Black Ships" at Shimoda in 1854.

In addition to learning about Japan through the reflection of its literature, Mitford's work contains valuable chronicled records on his own eye-witness report as one of the first foreigners to ever participate in a *hara kiri* ritual, and his delvings into the religious teachings of Japan in his day.

PREFACE.

In the Introduction to the story of the Forty-seven Rônins, I have said almost as much as is needful by way of preface to my stories.

Those of my readers who are most capable of pointing out the many shortcomings and faults of my work, will also be the most indulgent towards me; for any one who has been in Japan, and studied Japanese, knows the great difficulties by which the learner is beset.

For the illustrations, at least, I feel that I need make no apology. Drawn, in the first instance, by one Ôdaké, an artist in my employ, they were cut on wood by a famous wood-engraver at Yedo, and are therefore genuine specimens of Japanese art. Messrs. Dalziel, on examining the wood blocks, pointed out to me, as an interesting fact, that the lines are cut with the grain of the wood, after the manner of Albert Dürer and some of the old German masters,—a process which has been abandoned by modern European wood-engravers.

It will be noticed that very little allusion is made in these Tales to the Emperor and his Court. Although I searched diligently, I was able to find no story in which they played a conspicuous part.

Another class to which no allusion is made is that of the Gôshi. The Gôshi are a kind of yeomen, or bonnet-lairds, as they would be called over the border, living on their own land, and owning no allegiance to any feudal lord. Their rank is inferior to that of the Samurai, or men of the military class, between whom and the peasantry they hold a middle place. Like the Samurai, they wear two swords, and are in many cases prosperous and wealthy men, claiming a descent more ancient than that of many of the feudal Princes. A large number of them are enrolled among the Emperor's body-guard; and these have played a conspicuous part in the recent political changes in Japan, as the most conservative and anti-foreign element in the nation.

With these exceptions, I think that all classes are fairly represented in my stories.

The feudal system has passed away like a dissolving view before the eyes of those who have lived in Japan during the last few years. But when they arrived there it was in full force, and there is not an incident narrated in the following pages, however strange it may appear to Europeans, for the possibility and probability of which those most competent to judge will not vouch. Nor, as many a recent event can prove, have heroism, chivalry, and devotion gone out of the land altogether. We may deplore and inveigh against the Yamato Damashi, or Spirit of Old Japan, which still breathes in the soul of the Samurai, but we cannot withhold our admiration from the self-sacrifices which men will still make for the love of their country.

The two first of the Tales have already appeared in the *Fortnightly Review,* and two of the Sermons, with a portion of the Appendix on the subject of the Hara-Kiri, in the pages of the *Cornhill Magazine.* I have to thank the editors of those periodicals for permission to reprint them here.

LONDON, *January* 7, 1871.

CONTENTS

CONTENTS

LIST OF ILLUSTRATIONS

TALES OF OLD JAPAN

THE FORTY-SEVEN RÔNINS

THE books which have been written of late years about Japan, have either been compiled from official records, or have contained the sketchy impressions of passing travellers. Of the inner life of the Japanese, the world at large knows but little : their religion, their superstitions, their ways of thought, the hidden springs by which they move—all these are as yet mysteries. Nor is this to be wondered at. The first Western men who came in contact with Japan—I am speaking not of the old Dutch and Portuguese traders and priests, but of the diplomatists and merchants of eleven years ago—met with a cold reception. Above all things, the native Government threw obstacles in the way of any inquiry into their language, literature, and history. The fact was that the Tycoon's Government—with whom alone, so long as the Mikado remained in seclusion in his sacred capital at Kiôto, any relations were maintained—knew that the Imperial purple with which they sought to invest their chief must quickly fade before the strong sunlight which would be brought upon it so soon as there should be European linguists capable of examining their books and records. No opportunity was lost of throwing dust in the eyes of the new-comers, whom, even in the most trifling details, it was the official policy to lead astray. Now, however, there is no cause for concealment; the *Roi Fainéant* has shaken off his sloth, and his *Maire du Palais*, together, and an intelligible Government, which need not fear scrutiny from abroad, is the result: the records of the country being but so many proofs of the Mikado's title to power, there is no reason for keeping up any show of mystery. The path of inquiry is open to all; and although there is yet much to be learnt, some knowledge has been attained, in which it may interest those who stay at home to share.

The recent revolution in Japan has wrought changes social as well as political; and it may be that when, in addition to the advance which has already been made, railways and telegraphs shall have connected the principal points of the Land of Sunrise, the old Japanese, such as he was and had been for centuries when we found him eleven short years ago, will have become extinct. It has appeared to me that no better means could be chosen of preserving a record of a curious and fast disappearing civilization, than the translation of some of the most interesting national legends and histories, together with other specimens of literature bearing upon the same subject. Thus the Japanese may tell their own tale, their translator only adding here and there a few words of heading or tag to a chapter, where an explanation or amplification may seem necessary. I fear that the long and hard names will often make my tales tedious reading, but I believe that those who will bear with the difficulty will learn more of the character of the Japanese people than by skimming over descriptions of travel and adventure, however brilliant. The lord and his retainer, the warrior and the priest, the humble artisan and the despised Eta or pariah, each in his turn will become a leading character in my budget of stories; and it is out of the mouths of these personages that I hope to show forth a tolerably complete picture of Japanese society.

Having said so much by way of preface, I beg my readers

to fancy themselves wafted away to the shores of the Bay of Yedo—a fair, smiling landscape: gentle slopes, crested by a dark fringe of pines and firs, lead down to the sea; the quaint caves of many a temple and holy shrine peep out here and there from the groves; the bay itself is studded with picturesque fisher-craft, the torches of which shine by night like glow-worms among the outlying forts; far away to the west loom the goblin-haunted heights of Oyama, and beyond the twin hills of the Hakoné Pass—Fuji-Yama, the Peerless Mountain, solitary and grand, stands in the centre of the plain, from which it sprang vomiting flames twenty-one centuries ago.[1] For a hundred and sixty years the huge mountain has been at peace, but the frequent earthquakes still tell of hidden fires, and none can say when the red-hot stones and ashes may once more fall like rain over five provinces.

In the midst of a nest of venerable trees in Takanawa, a suburb of Yedo, is hidden Sengakuji, or the Spring-hill Temple, renowned throughout the length and breadth of the land for its cemetery, which contains the graves of the Forty-seven Rônins,[2] famous in Japanese history, heroes

[1] According to Japanese tradition, in the fifth year of the Emperor Kôrei (286 B.C.), the earth opened in the province of Omi, near Kiôto, and Lake Biwa, sixty miles long by about eighteen broad, was formed in the shape of a *Biwa*, or four-stringed lute, from which it takes its name. At the same time, to compensate for the depression of the earth, but at a distance of over three hundred miles from the lake, rose Fuji-Yama, the last eruption of which was in the year 1707. The last great earthquake at Yedo took place about fifteen years ago. Twenty thousand souls are said to have perished in it, and the dead were carried away and buried by cartloads; many persons, trying to escape from their falling and burning houses, were caught in great clefts, which yawned suddenly in the earth, and as suddenly closed upon the victims, crushing them to death. For several days heavy shocks continued to be felt, and the people camped out, not daring to return to such houses as had been spared, nor to build up those which lay in ruins.

[2] The word *Rônin* means, literally, a "wave-man;" one who is tossed about hither and thither, as a wave of the sea. It is used to designate persons of gentle blood, entitled to bear arms, who, having become separated from their feudal lords by their own act, or by dismissal, or by fate, wander about the country in the capacity of somewhat disreputable knights-errant, without ostensible means of living, in some cases offering themselves for hire to new masters, in others supporting themselves by pillage; or who, falling a grade in the social scale, go into trade, and become simple wardsmen. Sometimes

of Japanese drama, the tale of whose deeds I am about to transcribe.

On the left-hand side of the main court of the temple is a chapel, in which, surmounted by a gilt figure of Kwanyin, the goddess of mercy, are enshrined the images of the forty seven men, and of the master whom they loved so well. The statues are carved in wood, the faces coloured, and the dresses richly lacquered; as works of art they have great merit—the action of the heroes, each armed with his favourite weapon, being wonderfully life-like and spirited. Some are venerable men, with thin, grey hair (one is seventy-seven years old); others are mere boys of sixteen. Close by the chapel, at the side of a path leading up the hill, is a little well of pure water, fenced in and adorned with a tiny fernery, over which is an inscription, setting forth that "This is the well in which the head was washed; you must not wash your hands or your feet here." A little further on is a stall, at which a poor old man earns a pittance by selling books, pictures, and medals, commemorating the loyalty of the Forty-seven; and higher up yet, shaded by a grove of stately trees, is a neat inclosure, kept up, as a signboard announces, by voluntary contributions, round which are ranged forty-eight little tombstones, each decked with evergreens, each with its tribute of water and incense for the comfort of the departed spirit. There were forty-seven Rônins; there are forty-eight tombstones, and the story of the forty-eighth is truly characteristic of Japanese ideas of honour. Almost touching the rail of the graveyard is a more imposing

---

it happens that for political reasons a man will become Rônin, in order that his lord may not be implicated in some deed of blood in which he is about to engage. Sometimes, also, men become Rônins, and leave their native place for a while, until some scrape in which they have become entangled shall have blown over; after which they return to their former allegiance. Now-a-days it is not unusual for men to become Rônins for a time, and engage themselves in the service of foreigners at the open ports, even in menial capacities, in the hope that they may pick up something of the language and lore of Western folks. I know instances of men of considerable position who have adopted this course in their zeal for education.

THE WELL IN WHICH THE HEAD WAS WASHED

monument under which lies buried the lord, whose death his followers piously avenged.

And now for the story.

At the beginning of the eighteenth century there lived a daimio, called Asano Takumi no Kami, the Lord of the castle of Akô, in the province of Harima. Now it happened that an Imperial ambassador from the Court of the Mikado, having been sent to the Shogun[1] at Yedo, Takumi no Kami and another noble called Kamei Sama were appointed to receive and feast the envoy; and a high official, named Kira Kôtsuké no Suké, was named to teach them the proper ceremonies to be observed upon the occasion. The two nobles were accordingly forced to go daily to the castle to listen to the instructions of Kôtsuké no Suké. But this Kôtsuké no Suké was a man greedy of money; and as he deemed that the presents which the two daimios, according to time-honoured custom, had brought him in return for his instruction, were mean and unworthy, he conceived a great hatred against them, and took no pains in teaching them, but on the contrary rather sought to make laughing-stocks of them. Takumi no Kami, restrained by a stern sense of duty, bore his insults with patience; but Kamei Sama, who had less control over his temper, was violently incensed, and determined to kill Kôtsuké no Suké.

One night when his duties at the castle were ended, Kamei Sama returned to his own palace, and having summoned his councillors[2] to a secret conference, said to them: "Kôtsuké

---

[1] The full title of the Tycoon was Sei-i-tai-Shogun, "Barbarian-repressing Commander-in-chief." The style Tai Kun, Great Prince, was borrowed, in order to convey the idea of sovereignty to foreigners, at the time of the conclusion of the Treaties. The envoys sent by the Mikado from Kiôto to communicate to the Shogun the will of his sovereign, were received with Imperial honours, and the duty of entertaining them was confided to nobles of rank. The title Sei-i-tai-Shogun was first borne by Minamoto no Yoritomo, in the seventh month of the year 1192 A.D.

[2] Councillor, lit. "elder." The councillors of daimios were of two classes; the Karô, or "elder," an hereditary office, held by cadets of the Prince's family, and the Yônin, or "man of business," who was selected on account of his merits. These "councillors" play no mean part in Japanese history.

no Suké has insulted Takumi no Kami and myself during our service in attendance on the Imperial envoy. This is against all decency, and I was minded to kill him on the spot; but I bethought me that if I did such a deed within the precincts of the castle, not only would my own life be forfeit, but my family and vassals would be ruined: so I stayed my hand. Still the life of such a wretch is a sorrow to the people, and to-morrow when I go to Court I will slay him: my mind is made up, and I will listen to no remonstrance." And as he spoke his face became livid with rage.

Now one of Kamei Sama's councillors was a man of great judgment, and when he saw from his lord's manner that remonstrance would be useless, he said: "Your lordship's words are law; your servant will make all preparations accordingly; and to-morrow, when your lordship goes to Court, if this Kôtsuké no Suké should again be insolent, let him die the death." And his lord was pleased at this speech, and waited with impatience for the day to break, that he might return to Court and kill his enemy.

But the councillor went home, and was sorely troubled, and thought anxiously about what his prince had said. And as he reflected, it occurred to him that since Kôtsuké no Suké had the reputation of being a miser he would certainly be open to a bribe, and that it was better to pay any sum, no matter how great, than that his lord and his house should be ruined. So he collected all the money he could, and, giving it to his servants to carry, rode off in the night to Kôtsuké no Suké's palace, and said to his retainers: "My master, who is now in attendance upon the Imperial envoy, owes much thanks to my Lord Kôtsuké no Suké, who has been at so great pains to teach him the proper ceremonies to be observed during the reception of the Imperial envoy. This is but a shabby present which he has sent by me, but he hopes that his lordship will condescend to accept it, and commends himself to his lordship's favour." And, with these words, he produced a thousand ounces of silver for Kôtsuké no Suké, and a hundred ounces to be distributed among his retainers.

When the latter saw the money, their eyes sparkled with pleasure, and they were profuse in their thanks; and begging the councillor to wait a little, they went and told their master of the lordly present which had arrived with a polite message from Kamei Sama. Kôtsuké no Suké in eager delight sent for the councillor into an inner chamber, and, after thanking him, promised on the morrow to instruct his master carefully in all the different points of etiquette. So the councillor, seeing the miser's glee, rejoiced at the success of his plan; and having taken his leave returned home in high spirits. But Kamei Sama, little thinking how his vassal had propitiated his enemy, lay brooding over his vengeance, and on the following morning at daybreak went to Court in solemn procession.

When Kôtsuké no Suké met him, his manner had completely changed, and nothing could exceed his courtesy. "You have come early to Court this morning, my Lord Kamei," said he. "I cannot sufficiently admire your zeal. I shall have the honour to call your attention to several points of etiquette to-day. I must beg your lordship to excuse my previous conduct, which must have seemed very rude; but I am naturally of a cross-grained disposition, so I pray you to forgive me." And as he kept on humbling himself and making fair speeches, the heart of Kamei Sama was gradually softened, and he renounced his intention of killing him. Thus by the cleverness of his councillor, was Kamei Sama, with all his house, saved from ruin.

Shortly after this, Takumi no Kami, who had sent no present, arrived at the castle, and Kôtsuké no Suké turned him into ridicule even more than before, provoking him with sneers and covert insults; but Takumi no Kami affected to ignore all this, and submitted himself patiently to Kôtsuké no Suké's orders.

This conduct, so far from producing a good effect, only made Kôtsuké no Suké despise him the more, until at last he said haughtily: "Here, my Lord of Takumi, the ribbon of my sock has come untied; be so good as to tie it up for me."

Takumi no Kami, although burning with rage at the affront, still thought that as he was on duty he was bound to obey, and tied up the ribbon of the sock. Then Kôtsuké no Suké, turning from him, petulantly exclaimed : " Why, how clumsy you are ! You cannot so much as tie up the ribbon of a sock properly ! Any one can see that you are a boor from the country, and know nothing of the manners of Yedo." And with a scornful laugh he moved towards an inner room.

But the patience of Takumi no Kami was exhausted ; this last insult was more than he could bear.

" Stop a moment, my lord," cried he.

" Well, what is it ? " replied the other. And, as he turned round, Takumi no Kami drew his dirk, and aimed a blow at his head; but Kôtsuké no Suké, being protected by the Court cap which he wore, the wound was but a scratch, so he ran away ; and Takumi no Kami, pursuing him, tried a second time to cut him down, but, missing his aim, struck his dirk into a pillar. At this moment an officer, named Kajikawa Yosobei, seeing the affray, rushed up, and holding back the infuriated noble, gave Kôtsuké no Suké time to make good his escape.

Then there arose a great uproar and confusion, and Takumi no Kami was arrested and disarmed, and confined in one of the apartments of the palace under the care of the censors. A council was held, and the prisoner was given over to the safeguard of a daimio, called Tamura Ukiyô no Daibu, who kept him in close custody in his own house, to the great grief of his wife and of his retainers ; and when the deliberations of the council were completed, it was decided that, as he had committed an outrage and attacked another man within the precincts of the palace, he must perform *hara kiri*, —that is, commit suicide by disembowelling; his goods must be confiscated, and his family ruined. Such was the law. So Takumi no Kami performed *hara kiri*, his castle of Akô was confiscated, and his retainers having become Rônins, some of them took service with other daimios, and others became merchants.

Now amongst these retainers was his principal councillor, a man called Oishi Kuranosuké, who, with forty-six other faithful dependants, formed a league to avenge their master's death by killing Kôtsuké no Suké. This Oishi Kuranosuké was absent at the castle of Akô at the time of the affray, which, had he been with his prince, would never have occurred; for, being a wise man, he would not have failed to propitiate Kôtsuké no Suké by sending him suitable presents; while the councillor who was in attendance on the prince at Yedo was a dullard, who neglected this precaution, and so caused the death of his master and the ruin of his house.

So Oishi Kuranosuké and his forty-six companions began to lay their plans of vengeance against Kôtsuké no Suké; but the latter was so well guarded by a body of men lent to him by a daimio called Uyésugi Sama, whose daughter he had married, that they saw that the only way of attaining their end would be to throw their enemy off his guard. With this object they separated and disguised themselves, some as carpenters or craftsmen, others as merchants; and their chief, Kuranosuké, went to Kiôto, and built a house in the quarter called Yamashina, where he took to frequenting houses of the worst repute, and gave himself up to drunkenness and debauchery, as if nothing were further from his mind than revenge. Kôtsuké no Suké, in the meanwhile, suspecting that Takumi no Kami's former retainers would be scheming against his life, secretly sent spies to Kiôto, and caused a faithful account to be kept of all that Kuranosuké did. The latter, however, determined thoroughly to delude the enemy into a false security, went on leading a dissolute life with harlots and winebibbers. One day, as he was returning home drunk from some low haunt, he fell down in the street and went to sleep, and all the passers-by laughed him to scorn. It happened that a Satsuma man saw this, and said: "Is not this Oishi Kuranosuké, who was a councillor of Asano Takumi no Kami, and who, not having the heart to avenge his lord, gives himself up to women and wine? See how he lies drunk in the public street! Faithless beast! Fool and craven! Unworthy the name of a Samurai!"[1]

And he trod on Kuranosuké's face as he slept, and spat upon him; but when Kôtsuké no Suké's spies reported all this at Yedo, he was greatly relieved at the news, and felt secure from danger.

One day Kuranosuké's wife, who was bitterly grieved to see her husband lead this abandoned life, went to him and said: "My lord, you told me at first that your debauchery was but a trick to make your enemy relax in watchfulness. But indeed, indeed, this has gone too far. I pray and beseech you to put some restraint upon yourself."

"Trouble me not," replied Kuranosuké, "for I will not listen to your whining. Since my way of life is displeasing to you, I will divorce you, and you may go about your business; and I will buy some pretty young girl from one of the public-houses, and marry her for my pleasure. I am sick of the sight of an old woman like you about the house, so get you gone—the sooner the better."

So saying, he flew into a violent rage, and his wife, terror-stricken, pleaded piteously for mercy.

"Oh, my lord! unsay those terrible words! I have been your faithful wife for twenty years, and have borne you three children; in sickness and in sorrow I have been with you; you cannot be so cruel as to turn me out of doors now. Have pity! have pity!"

"Cease this useless wailing. My mind is made up, and you must go; and as the children are in my way also, you are welcome to take them with you."

When she heard her husband speak thus, in her grief she sought her eldest son, Oishi Chikara, and begged him to plead for her, and pray that she might be pardoned. But nothing would turn Kuranosuké from his purpose, so his wife was sent away, with the two younger children, and

[1] *Samurai*, a man belonging to the *Buké* or military class, entitled to bear arms.

THE SATSUMA MAN INSULTS OISHI KURANOSUKÉ

went back to her native place. But Oishi Chikara remained with his father.

The spies communicated all this without fail to Kôtsuké no Suké, and he, when he heard how Kuranosuké, having turned his wife and children out of doors and bought a concubine, was grovelling in a life of drunkenness and lust, began to think that he had no longer anything to fear from the retainers of Takumi no Kami, who must be cowards, without the courage to avenge their lord. So by degrees he began to keep a less strict watch, and sent back half of the guard which had been lent to him by his father-in-law, Uyésugi Sama. Little did he think how he was falling into the trap laid for him by Kuranosuké, who, in his zeal to slay his lord's enemy, thought nothing of divorcing his wife and sending away his children! Admirable and faithful man!

In this way Kuranosuké continued to throw dust in the eyes of his foe, by persisting in his apparently shameless conduct; but his associates all went to Yedo, and, having in their several capacities as workmen and pedlars contrived to gain access to Kôtsuké no Suké's house, made themselves familiar with the plan of the building and the arrangement of the different rooms, and ascertained the character of the inmates, who were brave and loyal men, and who were cowards; upon all of which matters they sent regular reports to Kuranosuké. And when at last it became evident from the letters which arrived from Yedo that Kôtsuké no Suké was thoroughly off his guard, Kuranosuké rejoiced that the day of vengeance was at hand; and, having appointed a trysting-place at Yedo, he fled secretly from Kiôto, eluding the vigilance of his enemy's spies. Then the forty-seven men, having laid all their plans, bided their time patiently.

It was now mid-winter, the twelfth month of the year, and the cold was bitter. One night, during a heavy fall of snow, when the whole world was hushed, and peaceful men were stretched in sleep upon the mats, the Rônins determined that no more favourable opportunity could occur for carrying out their purpose. So they took counsel together, and, having divided their band into two parties, assigned to each man his post. One band, led by Oishi Kuranosuké, was to attack the front gate, and the other, under his son Oishi Chikara, was to attack the postern of Kôtsuké no Suké's house; but as Chikara was only sixteen years of age, Yoshida Chiuzayémon was appointed to act as his guardian. Further it was arranged that a drum, beaten at the order of Kuranosuké, should be the signal for the simultaneous attack; and that if any one slew Kôtsuké no Suké and cut off his head he should blow a shrill whistle, as a signal to his comrades, who would hurry to the spot, and, having identified the head, carry it off to the temple called Sengakuji, and lay it as an offering before the tomb of their dead lord. Then they must report their deed to the Government, and await the sentence of death which would surely be passed upon them. To this the Rônins one and all pledged themselves. Midnight was fixed upon as the hour, and the forty-seven comrades, having made all ready for the attack, partook of a last farewell feast together, for on the morrow they must die. Then Oishi Kuranosuké addressed the band, and said :—

"To-night we shall attack our enemy in his palace ; his retainers will certainly resist us, and we shall be obliged to kill them. But to slay old men and women and children is a pitiful thing ; therefore, I pray you each one to take great heed lest you kill a single helpless person." His comrades all applauded this speech, and so they remained, waiting for the hour of midnight to arrive.

When the appointed hour came, the Rônins set forth. The wind howled furiously, and the driving snow beat in their faces ; but little cared they for wind or snow as they hurried on their road, eager for revenge. At last they reached Kôtsuké no Suké's house, and divided themselves into two bands ; and Chikara, with twenty-three men, went round to the back gate. Then four men, by means of a ladder of ropes which they hung on to the roof of the porch, effected an entry into the courtyard; and, as they saw signs that all the inmates of the house were asleep, they went into the porter's lodge where the guard slept, and, before the latter had time to recover from their astonishment, bound them. The terrified guard prayed hard for mercy, that their lives might be spared; and to this the Rônins agreed on condition that the keys of the gate should be given up; but the others tremblingly said that the keys were kept in the house of one of their officers, and that they had no means of obtaining them. Then the Rônins lost patience, and with a hammer dashed in pieces the big wooden bolt which secured the gate, and the doors flew open to the right and to the left. At the same time Chikara and his party broke in by the back gate.

Then Oishi Kuranosuké sent a messenger to the neighbouring houses, bearing the following message:—" We, the Rônins who were formerly in the service of Asano Takumi no Kami, are this night about to break into the palace of Kôtsuké no Suké, to avenge our lord. As we are neither night robbers nor ruffians, no hurt will be done to the neighbouring houses. We pray you to set your minds at rest." And as Kôtsuké no Suké was hated by his neighbours for his covetousness, they did not unite their forces to assist him. Another precaution was yet taken. Lest any of the people inside should run out to call the relations of the family to the rescue, and these coming in force should interfere with the plans of the Rônins, Kuranosuké stationed ten of his men armed with bows on the roof of the four sides of the courtyard, with orders to shoot any retainers who might attempt to leave the place. Having thus laid all his plans and posted his men, Kuranosuké with his own hand beat the drum and gave the signal for attack.

Ten of Kôtsuké no Suké's retainers, hearing the noise, woke up; and, drawing their swords, rushed into the front room to defend their master. At this moment the Rônins, who had burst open the door of the front hall, entered the same room. Then arose a furious fight between the two parties, in the midst of which Chikara, leading his men through the garden, broke into the back of the house; and Kôtsuké no Suké, in terror of his life, took refuge, with his wife and female servants, in a closet in the verandah; while the rest of his retainers, who slept in the barrack outside the house, made ready to go to the rescue. But the Rônins who had come in by the front door, and were fighting with the ten retainers, ended by overpowering and slaying the latter without losing one of their own number; after which, forcing their way bravely towards the back rooms, they were joined by Chikara and his men, and the two bands were united in one.

By this time the remainder of Kôtsuké no Suké's men had come in, and the fight became general; and Kuranosuké, sitting on a camp-stool, gave his orders and directed the Rônins. Soon the inmates of the house perceived that they were no match for their enemy, so they tried to send out intelligence of their plight to Uyésugi Sama, their lord's father-in-law, begging him to come to the rescue with all the force at his command. But the messengers were shot down by the archers whom Kuranosuké had posted on the roof. So no help coming, they fought on in despair. Then Kuranosuké cried out with a loud voice: "Kôtsuké no Suké alone is our enemy; let some one go inside and bring him forth dead or alive!"

Now in front of Kôtsuké no Suké's private room stood three brave retainers with drawn swords. The first was Kobayashi Héhachi, the second was Waku Handaiyu, and the third was Shimidzu Ikkaku, all good men and true, and expert swordsmen. So stoutly did these men lay about them that for a while they kept the whole of the Rônins at bay, and at one moment even forced them back. When Oishi Kuranosuké saw this, he ground his teeth with rage, and shouted to his men: "What! did not every man of you swear to lay down his life in avenging his lord, and now are you driven back by three men? Cowards, not fit to be spoken to! to die fighting in a master's cause should be the noblest ambition of a retainer!" Then turning to his own son Chikara, he said, "Here, boy! engage those men, and if they are too strong for you, die!"

Spurred by these words, Chikara seized a spear and gave battle to Waku Handaiyu, but could not hold his ground, and backing by degrees, was driven out into the garden, where he missed his footing and slipped into a pond; but as Handaiyu, thinking to kill him, looked down into the pond, Chikara cut his enemy in the leg and caused him to fall, and then crawling out of the water despatched him. In the meanwhile Kobayashi Héhachi and Shimidzu Ikkaku had been killed by the other Rônins, and of all Kôtsuké no Suké's retainers not one fighting man remained. Chikara, seeing this, went with his bloody sword in his hand into a back room to search for Kôtsuké no Suké, but he only found the son of the latter, a young lord named Kira Sahioyé, who, carrying a halberd, attacked him, but was soon wounded and fled. Thus the whole of Kôtsuké no Suké's men having been killed, there was an end of the fighting; but as yet there was no trace of Kôtsuké no Suké to be found.

Then Kuranosuké divided his men into several parties and searched the whole house, but all in vain; women and children weeping were alone to be seen. At this the forty-seven men began to lose heart in regret, that after all their toil they had allowed their enemy to escape them, and there was a moment when in their despair they agreed to commit suicide together upon the spot; but they determined to make one more effort. So Kuranosuké went into Kôtsuké no Suké's sleeping-room, and touching the quilt with his hands, exclaimed, "I have just felt the bed-clothes and they are yet warm, and so methinks that our enemy is not far off. He must certainly be hidden somewhere in the house." Greatly excited by this, the Rônins renewed their search. Now in the raised part of the room, near the place of honour, there was a picture hanging; taking down this picture, they saw that there was a large hole in the plastered wall, and on thrusting a spear in they could feel nothing beyond it. So one of the Rônins, called Yazama Jiutarô, got into the hole, and found that on the other side there was a little courtyard, in which there stood an outhouse for holding charcoal and firewood. Looking into the outhouse, he spied something white at the further end, at which he struck with his spear, when two armed men sprang out upon him and tried to cut him down, but he kept them back until one of his comrades came up and killed one of the two men and engaged the other, while Jiutarô entered the outhouse and felt about with his spear. Again seeing something white, he struck it with his lance, when a cry of pain betrayed that it was a man; so he rushed up, and the man in white clothes, who had been wounded in the thigh, drew a dirk and aimed a blow at him. But Jiutarô wrested the dirk from him, and clutching him by the collar, dragged him out of the outhouse. Then the other Rônin came up, and they examined the prisoner attentively, and saw that he was a noble-looking man, some sixty years of age, dressed in a white satin sleeping-robe, which was stained by the blood from the thigh-wound which Jiutarô had inflicted. The two men felt convinced that this was no other than Kôtsuké no Suké, and they asked him his name, but he gave no answer, so they gave the signal whistle, and all their comrades collected together at the call; then Oishi Kuranosuké, bringing a lantern, scanned the old man's features, and it was indeed Kôtsuké no Suké; and if further proof were wanting, he still bore a scar on his forehead where their master, Asano Takumi no Kami, had wounded him during the affray in the castle. There being no possibility of mistake, therefore, Oishi Kuranosuké went down on his knees, and addressing the old man very respectfully, said:

" My lord, we are the retainers of Asano Takumi no Kami. Last year your lordship and our master quarrelled in the palace, and our master was sentenced to *hara kiri*, and his family was ruined. We have come to-night to avenge him, as is the duty of faithful and loyal men. I pray your lordship to acknowledge the justice of our purpose. And now, my lord, we beseech you to perform *hara kiri*. I myself shall have the honour to act as your second, and when, with all humility, I shall have received your lordship's head, it is my intention to lay it as an offering upon the grave of Asano Takumi no Kami."

Thus, in consideration of the high rank of Kôtsuké no Suké, the Rônins treated him with the greatest courtesy, and over and over again entreated him to perform *hara kiri*. But he crouched speechless and trembling. At last Kuranosuké, seeing that it was vain to urge him to die the death of a nobleman, forced him down, and cut off his head with the same dirk with which Asano Takumi no Kami had killed himself. Then the forty-seven comrades, elated at having accomplished their design, placed the head in a bucket, and prepared to depart; but before leaving the house they carefully extinguished all the lights and fires in the place, lest by any accident a fire should break out and the neighbours suffer.

As they were on their way to Takanawa, the suburb in which the temple called Sengakuji stands, the day broke; and the people flocked out to see the forty-seven men, who, with their clothes and arms all blood-stained, presented a terrible appearance; and every one praised them, wondering at their valour and faithfulness. But they expected every moment that Kôtsuké no Suké's father-in-law would attack them and carry off the head, and made ready to die bravely sword in hand. However, they reached Takanawa in safety, for Matsudaira Aki no Kami, one of the eighteen chief daimios of Japan, of whose house Asano Takumi no Kami had been a cadet, had been highly pleased when he heard of the last night's work, and he had made ready to assist the Rônins in case they were attacked. So Kôtsuké no Suké's father-in-law dared not pursue them.

At about seven in the morning they came opposite to the palace of Matsudaira Mutsu no Kami, the Prince of Sendai, and the Prince, hearing of it, sent for one of his councillors and said: "The retainers of Takumi no Kami have slain their lord's enemy, and are passing this way; I cannot sufficiently admire their devotion, so, as they must be tired and hungry after their night's work, do you go and invite them to come in here, and set some gruel and a cup of wine before them."

So the councillor went out and said to Oishi Kuranosuké: "Sir, I am a councillor of the Prince of Sendai, and my master bids me beg you, as you must be worn out after all you have undergone, to come in and partake of such poor refreshment as we can offer you. This is my message to you from my lord."

"I thank you, sir," replied Kuranosuké. "It is very good of his lordship to trouble himself to think of us. We shall accept his kindness gratefully."

So the forty-seven Rônins went into the palace, and were feasted with gruel and wine, and all the retainers of the Prince of Sendai came and praised them.

Then Kuranosuké turned to the councillor and said, "Sir, we are truly indebted to you for this kind hospitality; but as we have still to hurry to Sengakuji, we must needs humbly take our leave." And, after returning many thanks to their hosts, they left the palace of the Prince of Sendai and hastened to Sengakuji, where they were met by the abbot of the monastery, who went to the front gate to receive them, and led them to the tomb of Takumi no Kami.

And when they came to their lord's grave, they took the head of Kôtsuké no Suké, and having washed it clean in a well hard by, laid it as an offering before the tomb. When they had done this, they engaged the priests of the temple to come and read prayers while they burnt incense: first Oishi Kuranosuké burnt incense, and then his son Oishi Chikara, and after them the other forty-five men performed the same ceremony. Then Kuranosuké, having given all the money that he had by him to the abbot, said :—

"When we forty-seven men shall have performed *hara kiri*, I beg you to bury us decently. I rely upon your kindness. This is but a trifle that I have to offer; such as it is, let it be spent in masses for our souls!"

And the abbot, marvelling at the faithful courage of the men, with tears in his eyes pledged himself to fulfil their wishes. So the forty-seven Rônins, with their minds at rest, waited patiently until they should receive the orders of the Government.

At last they were summoned to the Supreme Court, where the governors of Yedo and the public censors had assembled; and the sentence passed upon them was as follows: "Whereas, neither respecting the dignity of the city nor fearing the Government, having leagued yourselves together to slay your enemy, you violently broke into the house of Kira Kôtsuké no Suké by night and murdered him, the sentence of the Court is, that, for this audacious conduct, you perform *hara kiri*." When the sentence had been read, the forty-seven Rônins were divided into four parties, and handed over to the safe keeping of four different daimios; and sheriffs were sent to the palaces of those daimios in whose presence the Rônins were made to perform *hara kiri*. But, as from the very beginning they had all made up their minds that to this end they must come, they met their death nobly; and their corpses were carried to Sengakuji, and buried in front of the tomb of their master, Asano Takumi no Kami. And when the fame of this became noised abroad, the people flocked to pray at the graves of these faithful men.

Among those who came to pray was a Satsuma man, who, prostrating himself before the grave of Oishi Kuranosuké, said: "When I saw you lying drunk by the roadside at Yamashina, in Kiôto, I knew not that you were plotting to avenge your lord; and, thinking you to be a faithless man, I trampled on you and spat in your face as I passed. And now I have come to ask pardon and offer atonement for the insult of last year." With those words he prostrated himself again before the grave, and, drawing a dirk from his girdle, stabbed himself in the belly and died. And the chief priest of the temple, taking pity upon him, buried him by the side of the Rônins; and his tomb

THE TOMB OF THE RÔNINS

still remains to be seen with those of the forty-seven comrades.

This is the end of the story of the forty-seven Rônins.

A terrible picture of fierce heroism which it is impossible not to admire. In the Japanese mind this feeling of admiration is unmixed, and hence it is that the forty-seven Rônins receive almost divine honours. Pious hands still deck their graves with green boughs and burn incense upon them; the clothes and arms which they wore are preserved carefully in a fire-proof store-house attached to the temple, and exhibited yearly to admiring crowds, who behold them probably with little less veneration than is accorded to the relics of Aix-la-Chapelle or Trèves; and once in sixty years the monks of Sengakuji reap quite a harvest for the good of their temple by holding a commemorative fair or festival, to which the people flock during nearly two months.

A silver key once admitted me to a private inspection of the relics. We were ushered, my friend and myself, into a back apartment of the spacious temple, overlooking one of those marvellous miniature gardens, cunningly adorned with rockeries and dwarf trees, in which the Japanese delight. One by one, carefully labelled and indexed boxes containing the precious articles were brought out and opened by the chief priest. Such a curious medley of old rags and scraps of metal and wood! Home-made chain armour, composed of wads of leather secured together by pieces of iron, bear witness to the secrecy with which the Rônins made ready for the fight. To have bought armour would have attracted attention, so they made it with their own hands. Old moth-eaten surcoats, bits of helmets, three flutes, a writing-box that must have been any age at the time of the tragedy, and is now tumbling to pieces; tattered trousers of what once was rich silk brocade, now all unravelled and befringed; scraps of leather, part of an old gauntlet, crests and badges, bits of sword handles, spear-heads and dirks, the latter all red with rust, but with certain patches more deeply stained

as if the fatal clots of blood were never to be blotted out : all
these were reverently shown to us. Among the confusion and
litter were a number of documents, yellow with age and much
worn at the folds. One was a plan of Kôtsuké no Suké's
house, which one of the Rônins obtained by marrying the
daughter of the builder who designed it. Three of the
manuscripts appeared to me so curious that I obtained
leave to have copies taken of them.

The first is the receipt given by the retainers of Kôtsuké
no Suké's son in return for the head of their lord's father,
which the priests restored to the family, and runs as
follows :—

"MEMORANDUM :—
"ITEM. ONE HEAD.
"ITEM. ONE PAPER PARCEL.

"The above articles are acknowledged to have been received.

" Signed, $\begin{cases} \text{SAYADA MAGOBEI.} & (Loc.\ sigill.) \\ \text{SAITÔ KUNAI.} & (Loc.\ sigill.) \end{cases}$

" To the priests deputed from the Temple Sengakuji,
    " His Reverence SEKISHI,
    " His Reverence ICHIDON."

The second paper is a document explanatory of their
conduct, a copy of which was found on the person of each of
the forty-seven men :—

"Last year, in the third month, Asano Takumi no Kami, upon the occa-
sion of the entertainment of the Imperial ambassador, was driven, by the
force of circumstances, to attack and wound my Lord Kôtsuké no Suké in the
castle, in order to avenge an insult offered to him. Having done this without
considering the dignity of the place, and having thus disregarded all rules of
propriety, he was condemned to *hara kiri*, and his property and castle of
Akô were forfeited to the State, and were delivered up by his retainers to the
officers deputed by the Shogun to receive them. After this his followers were
all dispersed. At the time of the quarrel the high officials present prevented
Asano Takumi no Kami from carrying out his intention of killing his enemy,
my Lord Kôtsuké no Suké. So Asano Takumi no Kami died without having
avenged himself, and this was more than his retainers could endure. It is
impossible to remain under the same heaven with the enemy of lord or father;
for this reason we have dared to declare enmity against a personage of so
exalted rank. This day we shall attack Kira Kôtsuké no Suké, in order to
finish the deed of vengeance which was begun by our dead lord. If any

honourable person should find our bodies after death, he is respectfully requested to open and read this document.

"15th year of Genroku.   12th month.

"Signed, OISHI KURANOSUKÉ, Retainer of Asano
Takumi no Kami, and forty-six others." [1]

The third manuscript is a paper which the Forty-seven Rônins laid upon the tomb of their master, together with the head of Kira Kôtsuké no Suké :—

"The 15th year of Genroku, the 12th month, and 15th day. We have come this day to do homage here, forty-seven men in all, from Oishi Kuranosuké down to the foot-soldier, Terasaka Kichiyémon, all cheerfully about to lay down our lives on your behalf. We reverently announce this to the honoured spirit of our dead master. On the 14th day of the third month of last year our honoured master was pleased to attack Kira Kôtsuké no Suké, for what reason we know not. Our honoured master put an end to his own life, but Kira Kôtsuké no Suké lived. Although we fear that after the decree issued by the Government this plot of ours will be displeasing to our honoured master, still we, who have eaten of your food, could not without blushing repeat the verse, 'Thou shalt not live under the same heaven nor tread the same earth with the enemy of thy father or lord,' nor could we have dared to leave hell and present ourselves before you in paradise, unless we had carried out the vengeance which you began. Every day that we waited seemed as three autumns to us. Verily, we have trodden the snow for one day, nay, for two days, and have tasted food but once. The old and decrepit, the sick and ailing, have come forth gladly to lay down their lives. Men might laugh at us, as at grasshoppers trusting in the strength of their arms, and thus shame our honoured lord ; but we could not halt in our deed of vengeance. Having taken counsel together last night, we have escorted my Lord Kôtsuké no Suké hither to your tomb. This dirk,[2] by which our honoured lord set great store last year, and entrusted to our care, we now bring back. If your noble spirit be now present before this tomb, we pray you, as a sign, to take the dirk, and, striking the head of your enemy with it a second time, to dispel your hatred for ever. This is the respectful statement of forty-seven men.'

The text, "Thou shalt not live under the same heaven with the enemy of thy father," is based upon the Confucian books. Dr. Legge, in his "Life and Teachings of Confucius,"

[1] It is usual for a Japanese, when bent upon some deed of violence, the end of which, in his belief, justifies the means, to carry about with him a document, such as that translated above, in which he sets forth his motives, that his character may be cleared after death.

[2] The dirk with which Asano Takumi no Kumi disembowelled himself, and with which Oishi Kuranosuké cut off Kôtsuké no Suké's head.

p. 113, has an interesting paragraph summing up the doctrine of the sage upon the subject of revenge.

"In the second book of the 'Le Ke' there is the following passage :—'With the slayer of his father a man may not live under the same heaven ; against the slayer of his brother a man must never have to go home to fetch a weapon ; with the slayer of his friend a man may not live in the same State.' The *lex talionis* is here laid down in its fullest extent.   The 'Chow Le' tells us of a provision made against the evil consequences of the principle by the appointment of a minister called 'The Reconciler.'   The provision is very inferior to the cities of refuge which were set apart by Moses for the manslayer to flee to from the fury of the avenger.   Such as it was, however, it existed, and it is remarkable that Confucius, when consulted on the subject, took no notice of it, but affirmed the duty of blood-revenge in the strongest and most unrestricted terms.   His disciple, Tsze Hea, asked him, 'What course is to be pursued in the murder of a father or mother ?'   He replied, 'The son must sleep upon a matting of grass with his shield for his pillow ; he must decline to take office ; he must not live under the same heaven with the slayer.   When he meets him in the market-place or the court, he must have his weapon ready to strike him.'   'And what is the course in the murder of a brother ?'   'The surviving brother must not take office in the same State with the slayer ; yet, if he go on his prince's service to the State where the slayer is, though he meet him, he must not fight with him.'   'And what is the course in the murder of an uncle or cousin ?'   'In this case the nephew or cousin is not the principal.   If the principal, on whom the revenge devolves, can take it, he has only to stand behind with his weapon in his hand, and support him.'"

I will add one anecdote to show the sanctity which is attached to the graves of the Forty-seven.   In the month of September 1868, a certain man came to pray before the grave of Oishi Chikara.   Having finished his prayers, he deliberately performed *hara kiri*,[1] and, the belly wound not being mortal, despatched himself by cutting his throat.   Upon his person were found papers setting forth that, being a Rônin and without means of earning a living, he had petitioned to be allowed to enter the clan of the Prince of Chôshiu, which he looked upon as the noblest clan in the realm ; his petition having been refused, nothing remained for him but to die, for to be a Rônin was hateful to him, and he would serve no

---

[1] A purist in Japanese matters may object to the use of the words *hara kiri* instead of the more elegant expression *Seppuku*.   I retain the more vulgar form as being better known, and therefore more convenient.

other master than the Prince of Chôshiu: what more fitting place could he find in which to put an end to his life than the graveyard of these Braves? This happened at about two hundred yards' distance from my house, and when I saw the spot an hour or two later, the ground was all bespattered with blood, and disturbed by the death-struggles of the man.

THE LOVES OF GOMPACHI AND KOMURASAKI

Within two miles or so from Yedo, and yet well away from the toil and din of the great city, stands the village of Meguro. Once past the outskirts of the town, the road leading thither is bounded on either side by woodlands rich in an endless variety of foliage, broken at intervals by the long, low line of villages and hamlets. As we draw near to Meguro, the scenery, becoming more and more rustic, increases in beauty. Deep shady lanes, bordered by hedgerows as luxurious as any in England, lead down to a valley of rice fields bright with the emerald green of the young crops. To the right and to the left rise knolls of fantastic shape, crowned with a profusion of Cryptomerias, Scotch firs and other cone-bearing trees, and fringed with thickets of feathery bamboos, bending their stems gracefully to the light summer breeze. Wherever there is a spot shadier and pleasanter to look upon than the rest, there may be seen the red portal of a shrine which the simple piety of the country folk has raised to Inari Sama, the patron god of farming, or to some other tutelary deity of the place. At the eastern outlet of the valley a strip of blue sea bounds the horizon; westward are the distant mountains. In the foreground, in front of a farm-house, snug-looking, with its roof of velvety-brown thatch, a troop of sturdy urchins, sun-tanned and stark naked, are frisking in the wildest gambols, all heedless of the scolding voice of the withered old grandam who sits spinning and minding the house, while her son and his wife are away toiling at some outdoor labour. Close at our feet runs a stream of pure water, in which a group of countrymen are washing the vegetables which they will presently shoulder and carry off to sell by auction in the suburbs of Yedo. Not the least beauty of the scene consists in the wondrous clearness of an atmosphere so transparent that the most distant outlines are scarcely dimmed, while the details of the nearer ground stand out in sharp, bold relief, now lit by the rays of a vertical sun, now darkened under the flying shadows thrown by the fleecy clouds which sail across the sky. Under such a heaven, what painter could limn the lights and shades which flit over the woods, the pride of Japan, whether in late autumn, when the russets and yellows of our own trees are mixed with the deep crimson glow of the maples, or in spring-time, when plum and cherry trees and wild camellias—giants, fifty feet high—are in full blossom?

All that we see is enchanting, but there is a strange stillness in the groves; rarely does the song of a bird break the silence; indeed, I know but one warbler whose note has any music in it, the *uguisu*, by some enthusiasts called the Japanese nightingale—at best, a king in the kingdom of the blind. The scarcity of animal life of all descriptions, man and mosquitoes alone excepted, is a standing wonder to the traveller; the sportsman must toil many a weary mile to get a shot at boar, or deer, or pheasant; and the plough of the farmer and the trap of the poacher, who works in and out of season, threaten to exterminate all wild creatures; unless, indeed, the Government should, as they threatened in the spring of 1869, put in force some adaptation of European game-laws. But they are lukewarm in the matter; a little hawking on a duck-pond satisfies the cravings of the modern Japanese sportsman, who knows that, game-laws or no game-laws, the wild fowl will never fail in winter; and the days are long past when my Lord the Shogun used to ride forth with a mighty company to the wild places about Mount Fuji, there camping out and hunting the boar, the deer, and the wolf, believing that in so doing he was fostering a manly and military spirit in the land.

There is one serious drawback to the enjoyment of the

beauties of the Japanese country, and that is the intolerable affront which is continually offered to one's sense of smell; the whole of what should form the sewerage of the city is carried out on the backs of men and horses, to be thrown upon the fields; and, if you would avoid the overpowering nuisance, you must walk handkerchief in hand, ready to shut out the stench which assails you at every moment.

It would seem natural, while writing of the Japanese country, to say a few words about the peasantry, their relation to the lord of the soil, and their government. But these I must reserve for another place. At present our dealings are with the pretty village of Meguro.

At the bottom of a little lane, close to the entrance of the village, stands an old shrine of the Shintô (the form of hero-worship which existed in Japan before the introduction of Confucianism or of Buddhism), surrounded by lofty Cryptomerias. The trees around a Shintô shrine are specially under the protection of the god to whom the altar is dedicated; and, in connection with them, there is a kind of magic still respected by the superstitious, which recalls the waxen dolls, through the medium of which sorcerers of the middle ages in Europe, and indeed those of ancient Greece, as Theocritus tells us, pretended to kill the enemies of their clients. This is called *Ushi no toki mairi*, or "going to worship at the hour of the ox,"[1] and is practised

---

[1] The Chinese, and the Japanese following them, divide the day of twenty-four hours into twelve periods, each of which has a sign something like the signs of the Zodiac:—

Midnight until two in the morning is represented by the rat.

2 a.m.	until	4 a.m.	,,	,,	ox.
4 a.m.	,,	6 a.m.	,,	,,	tiger.
6 a.m.	,,	8 a.m.	,,	,,	hare.
8 a.m.	,,	10 a.m.	,,	,,	dragon.
10 a.m.	,,	12 noon	,,	,,	snake.
12 noon	,,	2 p.m.	,,	,,	horse.
2 p.m.	,,	4 p.m.	,,	,,	ram.
4 p.m.	,,	6 p.m.	,,	,,	ape.
6 p.m.	,,	8 p.m.	,,	,,	cock.
8 p.m.	,,	10 p.m.	,,	,,	hog.
10 p.m.	,,	Midnight	,,	,,	fox.

by jealous women who wish to be revenged upon their faithless lovers.

When the world is at rest, at two in the morning, the hour of which the ox is the symbol, the woman rises; she dons a white robe and high sandals or clogs; her coif is a metal tripod, in which are thrust three lighted candles; around her neck she hangs a mirror, which falls upon her bosom; in her left hand she carries a small straw figure, the effigy of the lover who has abandoned her, and in her right she grasps a hammer and nails, with which she fastens the figure to one of the sacred trees that surround the shrine. There she prays for the death of the traitor, vowing that, if her petition be heard, she will herself pull out the nails which now offend the god by wounding the mystic tree. Night after night she comes to the shrine, and each night she strikes in two or more nails, believing that every nail will shorten her lover's life, for the god, to save his tree, will surely strike him dead.

Meguro is one of the many places round Yedo to which the good citizens flock for purposes convivial or religious, or both; hence it is that, cheek by jowl with the old shrines and temples, you will find many a pretty tea-house, standing at the rival doors of which Mesdemoiselles Sugar, Wave of the Sea, Flower, Seashore, and Chrysanthemum are pressing in their invitations to you to enter and rest. Not beautiful these damsels, if judged by our standard, but the charm of Japanese women lies in their manner and dainty little ways, and the tea-house girl, being a professional decoy-duck, is an adept in the art of flirting,—*en tout bien tout honneur*, be it remembered; for she is not to be confounded with the frail beauties of the Yoshiwara, nor even with her sisterhood near the ports open to foreigners, and to their corrupting influence. For, strange as it seems, our contact all over the East has an evil effect upon the natives.

In one of the tea-houses a thriving trade is carried on in the sale of wooden tablets, some six inches square, adorned with the picture of a pink cuttlefish on a bright blue ground. These are ex-votos, destined to be offered up at the Temple of Yakushi Niurai, the Buddhist Æsculapius, which stands opposite, and concerning the foundation of which the following legend is told.

In the days of old there was a priest called Jikaku, who at the age of forty years, it being the autumn of the tenth year of the period called Tenchô (A.D. 833), was suffering from disease of the eyes, which had attacked him three years before. In order to be healed from this disease he carved a figure of Yakushi Niurai, to which he used to offer up his prayers. Five years later he went to China, taking with him the figure as his guardian saint, and at a place called Kairetsu it protected him from robbers and wild beasts and from other calamities. There he passed his time in studying the sacred laws both hidden and revealed, and after nine years set sail to return to Japan. When he was on the high seas a storm arose, and a great fish attacked and tried to swamp the ship, so that the rudder and mast were broken, and the nearest shore being that of a land inhabited by devils, to retreat or to advance was equally dangerous. Then the holy man prayed to the patron saint whose image he carried, and as he prayed, behold the true Yakushi Niurai appeared in the centre of the ship, and said to him :—

"Verily, thou hast travelled far that the sacred laws might be revealed for the salvation of many men ; now, therefore, take my image, which thou carriest in thy bosom, and cast it into the sea, that the wind may abate, and that thou mayest be delivered from this land of devils."

The commands of the saints must be obeyed, so with tears in his eyes, the priest threw into the sea the sacred image which he loved. Then did the wind abate, and the waves were stilled, and the ship went on her course as though she were being drawn by unseen hands until she reached a safe haven. In the tenth month of the same year the priest again set sail, trusting to the power of his patron saint, and reached the harbour of Tsukushi without mishap. For three years he prayed that the image which he had cast away might be restored to him, until at last one night he was warned in a dream that on the sea-shore at Matsura Yakushi Niurai would appear to him. In consequence of this dream he went to the province of Hizen, and landed on the sea-shore at Hirato, where, in the midst of a blaze of light, the image which he had carved appeared to him twice, riding on the back of a cuttlefish. Thus was the image restored to the world by a miracle. In commemoration of his recovery from the disease of the eyes and of his preservation from the dangers of the sea, that these things might be known to all posterity, the priest established the worship of Tako Yakushi Niurai ("Yakushi Niurai of the Cuttlefish"), and came to Meguro, where he built the Temple of Fudô Sama,[1] another Buddhist divinity. At this time there was an epidemic of small-pox in the village, so that men fell down and died in the street, and the holy man prayed to Fudô Sama that the plague might be stayed. Then the god appeared to him, and said :—

"The saint Yakushi Niurai of the Cuttlefish, whose image thou carriest, desires to have his place in this village, and he will heal this plague. Thou shalt, therefore, raise a temple to him here that not only this small-pox, but other diseases for future generations, may be cured by his power."

Hearing this, the priest shed tears of gratitude, and having chosen a piece of fine wood, carved a large figure of his patron saint of the cuttlefish, and placed the smaller image inside of the larger, and laid it up in this temple, to which people still flock that they may be healed of their diseases.

Such is the story of the miracle, translated from a small ill-printed pamphlet sold by the priests of the temple, all the decorations of which, even to a bronze lantern in the middle of the yard, are in the form of a cuttlefish, the sacred emblem of the place.

What pleasanter lounge in which to while away a hot day could a man wish for, than the shade of the trees borne by the hill on which stands the Temple of Fudô Sama? Two

[1] Fudô, literally "the motionless:" Buddha in the state called Nirvana.

jets of pure water springing from the rock are voided by spouts carved in the shape of dragons into a stone basin enclosed by rails, within which it is written that "no woman may enter." If you are in luck, you may cool yourself by watching some devotee, naked save his loin-cloth, performing the ceremony called *Suigiyô*; that is to say, praying under the waterfall that his soul may be purified through his body. In winter it requires no small pluck to go through this penance, yet I have seen a penitent submit to it for more than a quarter of an hour on a bitterly cold day in January. In summer, on the other hand, the religious exercise called *Hiyakudo*, or "the hundred times," which may also be seen here to advantage, is no small trial of patience. It consists in walking backwards and forwards a hundred times between two points within the sacred precincts, repeating a prayer each time. The count is kept either upon the fingers or by depositing a length of twisted straw each time that the goal is reached; at this temple the place allotted for the ceremony is between a grotesque bronze figure of Tengu Sama ("the Dog of Heaven"), the terror of children, a most hideous monster with a gigantic nose, which it is beneficial to rub with a finger afterwards to be applied to one's own nose, and a large brown box inscribed with the characters *Hiyaku Do* in high relief, which may generally be seen full of straw tallies. It is no sinecure to be a good Buddhist, for the gods are not lightly to be propitiated. Prayer and fasting, mortification of the flesh, abstinence from wine, from women, and from favourite dishes, are the only passports to rising in office, prosperity in trade, recovery from sickness, or a happy marriage with a beloved maiden. Nor will mere faith without works be efficient. A votive tablet of proportionate value to the favour prayed for, or a sum of money for the repairs of the shrine or temple, is necessary to win the favour of the gods. Poorer persons will cut off the queue of their hair and offer that up; and at Horinouchi, a temple in great renown some eight or nine miles from Yedo, there is a rope about two inches and a half in diameter, and about six fathoms long, entirely made of human hair so given to the gods; it lies coiled up, dirty, moth-eaten, and uncared for, at one end of a long shed full of tablets and pictures, by the side of a rude native fire-engine. The taking of life being displeasing to Buddha, outside many of the temples old women and children earn a livelihood by selling sparrows, small eels, carp, and tortoises, which the worshipper sets free in honour of the deity, within whose territory cocks and hens and doves, tame and unharmed, perch on every jutty, frieze, buttress, and coigne of vantage.

But of all the marvellous customs that I wot of in connection with Japanese religious exercises, none appears to me so strange as that of spitting at the images of the gods, more especially at the statues of the Ni-ô, the two huge red or red and green statues which, like Gog and Magog, emblems of strength, stand as guardians of the chief Buddhist temples. The figures are protected by a network of iron wire, through which the votaries, praying the while, spit pieces of paper, which they had chewed up into a pulp. If the pellet sticks to the statue, the omen is favourable; if it falls, the prayer is not accepted. The inside of the great bell at the Tycoon's burial-ground, and almost every holy statue throughout the country, are all covered with these outspittings from pious mouths.[1]

Through all this discourse about temples and tea-houses, I am coming by degrees to the goal of our pilgrimage—two old stones, mouldering away in a rank, overgrown graveyard hard by, an old old burying-ground, forgotten by all save those who love to dig out the tales of the past. The key is kept by a ghoulish old dame, almost as time-worn and mildewed as the tomb over which she watches. Obedient to our call, and looking forward to a fee ten times greater than any native would give her, she hobbles out, and, opening the

---

[1] It will be readily understood that the customs and ceremonies to which I have alluded belong only to the gross superstitions with which ignorance has overlaid that pure Buddhism of which Professor Max Müller has pointed out the very real beauties.

gate, points out the stone bearing the inscription, the "Tomb of the Hiyoku " (fabulous birds, which, living one within the other—a mysterious duality contained in one body—are the emblem of connubial love and fidelity). By this stone stands another, graven with a longer legend, which runs as follows :—

"In the old days of Genroku, she pined for the beauty of her lover, who was as fair to look upon as the flowers ; and now beneath the moss of this old tombstone all has perished of her save her name. Amid the changes of a fitful world, this tomb is decaying under the dew and rain ; gradually crumbling beneath its own dust, its outline alone remains. Stranger ! bestow an alms to preserve this stone ; and we, sparing neither pain nor labour, will second you with all our hearts. Erecting it again, let us preserve it from decay for future generations, and let us write the following verse upon it :—' These two birds, beautiful as the cherry-blossoms, perished before their time, like flowers broken down by the wind before they have borne seed.' "

Under the first stone is the dust of Gompachi, robber and murderer, mixed with that of his true love Komurasaki, who lies buried with him. Her sorrows and constancy have hallowed the place, and pious people still come to burn incense and lay flowers before the grave. How she loved him even in death may be seen from the following old-world story.

About two hundred and thirty years ago there lived in the service of a daimio of the province of Inaba, a young man, called Shirai Gompachi, who, when he was but sixteen years of age, had already won a name for his personal beauty and valour, and for his skill in the use of arms. Now it happened that one day a dog belonging to him fought with another dog belonging to a fellow-clansman, and the two masters, being both passionate youths, disputing as to whose dog had had the best of the fight, quarrelled and came to blows, and Gompachi slew his adversary ; and in consequence of this, he was obliged to flee from his country, and make his escape to Yedo.

比翠墓

THE TOMB OF THE HIYOKU

And so Gompachi set out on his travels.

One night, weary and footsore, he entered what appeared to him to be a roadside inn, ordered some refreshment, and went to bed, little thinking of the danger that menaced him: for as luck would have it, this inn turned out to be the trysting-place of a gang of robbers, into whose clutches he had thus unwittingly fallen. To be sure, Gompachi's purse was but scantily furnished, but his sword and dirk were worth some three hundred ounces of silver, and upon these the robbers (of whom there were ten) had cast envious eyes, and had determined to kill the owner for their sake; but he, all unsuspicious, slept on in fancied security.

In the middle of the night he was startled from his deep slumbers by some one stealthily opening the sliding door which led into his room, and rousing himself with an effort, he beheld a beautiful young girl, fifteen years of age, who, making signs to him not to stir, came up to his bedside, and said to him in a whisper:—

"Sir, the master of this house is the chief of a gang of robbers, who have been plotting to murder you this night for the sake of your clothes and your sword. As for me, I am the daughter of a rich merchant in Mikawa: last year the robbers came to our house, and carried off my father's treasure and myself. I pray you, sir, take me with you, and let us fly from this dreadful place."

She wept as she spoke, and Gompachi was at first too much startled to answer; but being a youth of high courage and a cunning fencer to boot, he soon recovered his presence of mind, and determined to kill the robbers, and to deliver the girl out of their hands. So he replied:—

"Since you say so, I will kill these thieves, and rescue you this very night; only do you, when I begin the fight, run outside the house, that you may be out of harm's way, and remain in hiding until I join you."

Upon this understanding the maiden left him, and went her way. But he lay awake, holding his breath and watching; and when the thieves crept noiselessly into the room,

GOMPACHI AWAKENED BY THE MAIDEN IN THE ROBBERS' DEN

where they supposed him to be fast asleep, he cut down the first man that entered, and stretched him dead at his feet. The other nine, seeing this, laid about them with their drawn swords, but Gompachi, fighting with desperation, mastered them at last, and slew them. After thus ridding himself of his enemies, he went outside the house, and called to the girl, who came running to his side, and joyfully travelled on with him to Mikawa, where her father dwelt; and when they reached Mikawa, he took the maiden to the old man's house, and told him how, when he had fallen among thieves, his daughter had come to him in his hour of peril, and saved him out of her great pity; and how he, in return, rescuing her from her servitude, had brought her back to her home. When the old folks saw their daughter whom they had lost restored to them, they were beside themselves with joy, and shed tears for very happiness; and, in their gratitude, they pressed Gompachi to remain with them, and they prepared feasts for him, and entertained him hospitably: but their daughter, who had fallen in love with him for his beauty and knightly valour, spent her days in thinking of him, and of him alone. The young man, however, in spite of the kindness of the old merchant, who wished to adopt him as his son, and tried hard to persuade him to consent to this, was fretting to go to Yedo and take service as an officer in the household of some noble lord; so he resisted the entreaties of the father and the soft speeches of the daughter, and made ready to start on his journey; and the old merchant, seeing that he would not be turned from his purpose, gave him a parting gift of two hundred ounces of silver, and sorrowfully bade him farewell.

But alas for the grief of the maiden, who sat sobbing her heart out and mourning over her lover's departure! He, all the while thinking more of ambition than of love, went to her and comforted her, and said: "Dry your eyes, sweetheart, and weep no more, for I shall soon come back to you. Do you, in the meanwhile, be faithful and true to me, and tend your parents with filial piety."

So she wiped away her tears and smiled again, when she heard him promise that he would soon return to her. And Gompachi went his way, and in due time came near to Yedo.

But his dangers were not yet over; for late one night, arriving at a place called Suzugamori, in the neighbourhood of Yedo, he fell in with six highwaymen, who attacked him, thinking to make short work of killing and robbing him. Nothing daunted, he drew his sword, and despatched two out of the six; but, being weary and worn out with his long journey, he was sorely pressed, and the struggle was going hard with him, when a wardsman,[1] who happened to pass that way riding in a chair, seeing the affray, jumped down from his chair and drawing his dirk came to the rescue, and between them they put the robbers to flight.

Now it turned out that this kind tradesman, who had so happily come to the assistance of Gompachi, was no other than Chôbei of Bandzuin, the chief of the *Otokodaté*, or Friendly Society of the wardsmen of Yedo—a man famous in the annals of the city, whose life, exploits, and adventures are recited to this day, and form the subject of another tale.

When the highwaymen had disappeared, Gompachi, turning to his deliverer, said—

"I know not who you may be, sir, but I have to thank you for rescuing me from a great danger."

And as he proceeded to express his gratitude, Chôbei replied—

"I am but a poor wardsman, a humble man in my way, sir; and if the robbers ran away, it was more by good luck than owing to any merit of mine. But I am filled with admiration at the way you fought; you displayed a courage and a skill that were beyond your years, sir."

---

[1] Japanese cities are divided into wards, and every tradesman and artisan is under the authority of the chief of the ward in which he resides. The word *chônin*, or wardsman, is generally used in contradistinction to the word *samurai*, which has already been explained as denoting a man belonging to the military class.

" Indeed," said the young man, smiling with pleasure at hearing himself praised; " I am still young and inexperienced, and am quite ashamed of my bungling style of fencing."

" And now may I ask you, sir, whither you are bound ?"

"That is almost more than I know myself, for I am a *rônin*, and have no fixed purpose in view."

" That is a bad job," said Chôbei, who felt pity for the lad. " However, if you will excuse my boldness in making such an offer, being but a wardsman, until you shall have taken service I would fain place my poor house at your disposal."

Gompachi accepted the offer of his new but trusty friend with thanks; so Chôbei led him to his house, where he lodged him and hospitably entertained him for some months. And now Gompachi, being idle and having nothing to care for, fell into bad ways, and began to lead a dissolute life, thinking of nothing but gratifying his whims and passions; he took to frequenting the Yoshiwara, the quarter of the town which is set aside for tea-houses and other haunts of wild young men, where his handsome face and figure attracted attention, and soon made him a great favourite with all the beauties of the neighbourhood.

About this time men began to speak loud in praise of the charms of Komurasaki, or " Little Purple," a young girl who had recently come to the Yoshiwara, and who in beauty and accomplishments outshone all her rivals. Gompachi, like the rest of the world, heard so much of her fame that he determined to go to the house where she dwelt, at the sign of "The Three Sea-coasts," and judge for himself whether she deserved all that men said of her. Accordingly he set out one day, and having arrived at "The Three Sea-coasts," asked to see Komurasaki; and being shown into the room where she was sitting, advanced towards her; but when their eyes met, they both started back with a cry of astonishment, for this Komurasaki, the famous beauty of the Yoshiwara, proved to be the very girl whom several months before Gompachi had rescued from the robbers' den, and restored to her parents in Mikawa. He had left her in prosperity and affluence, the darling child of a rich father, when they had exchanged vows of love and fidelity; and now they met in a common stew in Yedo. What a change! what a contrast! How had the riches turned to rust, the vows to lies!

"What is this?" cried Gompachi, when he had recovered from his surprise. "How is it that I find you here pursuing this vile calling, in the Yoshiwara? Pray explain this to me, for there is some mystery beneath all this which I do not understand."

But Komurasaki—who, having thus unexpectedly fallen in with her lover that she had yearned for, was divided between joy and shame—answered, weeping:

"Alas! my tale is a sad one, and would be long to tell. After you left us last year, calamity and reverses fell upon our house; and when my parents became poverty-stricken, I was at my wits' end to know how to support them: so I sold this wretched body of mine to the master of this house, and sent the money to my father and mother; but, in spite of this, troubles and misfortunes multiplied upon them, and now, at last, they have died of misery and grief. And, oh! lives there in this wide world so unhappy a wretch as I! But now that I have met you again—you who are so strong—help me who am weak. You saved me once—do not, I implore you, desert me now!" and as she told her piteous tale the tears streamed from her eyes.

"This is, indeed, a sad story," replied Gompachi, much affected by the recital. "There must have been a wonderful run of bad luck to bring such misfortune upon your house, which but a little while ago I recollect so prosperous. However, mourn no more, for I will not forsake you. It is true that I am too poor to redeem you from your servitude, but at any rate I will contrive so that you shall be tormented no more. Love me, therefore, and put your trust in me." When she heard him speak so kindly she was comforted, and wept no more, but poured out her whole heart to him, and forgot her past sorrows in the great joy of meeting him again.

When it became time for them to separate, he embraced her tenderly and returned to Chôbei's house; but he could not banish Komurasaki from his mind, and all day long he thought of her alone; and so it came about that he went daily to the Yoshiwara to see her, and if any accident detained him, she, missing the accustomed visit, would become anxious and write to him to inquire the cause of his absence. At last, pursuing this course of life, his stock of money ran short, and as, being a *rônin* and without any fixed employment, he had no means of renewing his supplies, he was ashamed of showing himself penniless at "The Three Sea-coasts." Then it was that a wicked spirit arose within him, and he went out and murdered a man, and having robbed him of his money carried it to the Yoshiwara.

From bad to worse is an easy step, and the tiger that has once tasted blood is dangerous. Blinded and infatuated by his excessive love, Gompachi kept on slaying and robbing, so that, while his outer man was fair to look upon, the heart within him was that of a hideous devil. At last his friend Chôbei could no longer endure the sight of him, and turned him out of his house; and as, sooner or later, virtue and vice meet with their reward, it came to pass that Gompachi's crimes became notorious, and the Government having set spies upon his track, he was caught redhanded and arrested; and his evil deeds having been fully proved against him, he was carried off to the execution ground at Suzugamori, the "Bell Grove," and beheaded as a common malefactor.

Now when Gompachi was dead, Chôbei's old affection for the young man returned, and, being a kind and pious man, he went and claimed his body and head, and buried him at Meguro, in the grounds of the Temple called Boronji.

When Komurasaki heard the people at Yoshiwara gossiping about her lover's end, her grief knew no bounds, so she fled secretly from "The Three Sea-coasts," and came to Meguro and threw herself upon the newly-made grave. Long she prayed and bitterly she wept over the tomb of him whom, with all his faults, she had loved so well, and then, drawing a dagger from her girdle, she plunged it in her breast and died. The priests of the temple, when they saw what had happened, wondered greatly and were astonished at the loving faithfulness of this beautiful girl, and taking compassion on her, they laid her side by side with Gompachi in one grave, and over the grave they placed a stone which remains to this day, bearing the inscription "The Tomb of the Shiyoku." And still the people of Yedo visit the place, and still they praise the beauty of Gompachi and the filial piety and fidelity of Komurasaki.

Let us linger for a moment longer in the old graveyard. The word which I have translated a few lines above as "loving faithfulness" means literally "chastity." When Komurasaki sold herself to supply the wants of her ruined parents, she was not, according to her lights, forfeiting her claim to virtue. On the contrary, she could perform no greater act of filial piety, and, so far from incurring reproach among her people, her self-sacrifice would be worthy of all praise in their eyes. This idea has led to grave misunderstanding abroad, and indeed no phase of Japanese life has been so misrepresented as this. I have heard it stated, and seen it printed, that it is no disgrace for a respectable Japanese to sell his daughter, that men of position and family often choose their wives from such places as "The Three Sea-coasts," and that up to the time of her marriage the conduct of a young girl is a matter of no importance whatever. Nothing could be more unjust or more untrue. It is only the neediest people that sell their children to be waitresses, singers, or prostitutes. It does occasionally happen that the daughter of a *Samurai*, or gentleman, is found in a house of ill-fame, but such a case could only occur at the death or utter ruin of the parents, and an official investigation of the matter has proved it to be so exceptional, that the presence of a young lady in such a place is an enormous attraction, her superior education and accomplishments shedding a lustre over the house. As for gentlemen marrying women of bad character, are not such things known in Europe? Do ladies of the *demi-monde* never make good marriages? *Mésalliances* are far rarer in Japan than with us. Certainly among the lowest class of the population such marriages may occasionally occur, for it often happens that a woman can lay by a tempting dowry out of her wretched earnings; but amongst the gentry of the country they are unknown.

And yet a girl is not disgraced if for her parents' sake she sells herself to a life of misery so great, that, when a Japanese enters a house of ill-fame, he is forced to leave his sword and dirk at the door for two reasons—first, to prevent brawling; secondly, because it is known that some of the women inside so loathe their existence that they would put an end to it, could they get hold of a weapon.

It is a curious fact that in all the Daimio's castle-towns, with the exception of some which are also seaports, open prostitution is strictly forbidden, although, if report speaks truly, public morality rather suffers than gains by the prohibition.

The misapprehension which exists upon the subject of prostitution in Japan may be accounted for by the fact that foreign writers, basing their judgment upon the vice of the open ports, have not hesitated to pronounce the Japanese women unchaste. As fairly might a Japanese, writing about England, argue from the street-walkers of Portsmouth or Plymouth to the wives, sisters, and daughters of these very authors. In some respects the gulf fixed between virtue and vice in Japan is even greater than in England. The Eastern courtesan is confined to a certain quarter of the town, and distinguished by a peculiarly gaudy costume, and by a head-dress which consists of a forest of light tortoiseshell hair-pins, stuck round her head like a saint's glory—a glory of shame which a modest woman would sooner die than wear. Vice jostling virtue in the public places; virtue imitating the fashions set by vice, and buying trinkets or furniture at the sale of vice's effects—these are social phenomena which the East knows not.

The custom prevalent among the lower orders of bathing in public bath-houses without distinction of the sexes, is another circumstance which has tended to spread abroad very false notions upon the subject of the chastity of the Japanese women. Every traveller is shocked by it, and every writer finds in it matter for a page of pungent description. Yet it is only those who are so poor (and they must be poor indeed) that they cannot afford a bath at home, who, at the end of their day's work, go to the public bath-house to refresh themselves before sitting down to their evening meal: having been used to the scene from their childhood, they see no indelicacy in it; it is a matter of course, and *honi soit qui mal y pense:* certainly there is far less indecency and immorality resulting from this public bathing, than from the promiscuous herding together of all sexes and ages which disgraces our own lodging-houses in the great cities, and the hideous hovels in which some of our labourers have to pass their lives; nor can it be said that there is more confusion of sexes amongst the lowest orders in Japan than in Europe. Speaking upon the subject once with a Japanese gentleman, I observed that we considered it an act of indecency for men and women to wash together. He shrugged his shoulders as he answered, "But then Westerns have such prurient minds." Some time ago, at the open port of Yokohama, the Government, out of deference to the prejudices of foreigners, forbade the men and women to bathe together, and no doubt this was the first step towards putting down the practice altogether: as for women tubbing in the open streets of Yedo, I have read of such things in books written by foreigners; but during a residence of three years and a half, in which time I crossed and recrossed every part of the great city at all hours of the day, I never once saw such a sight. I believe myself that it can only be seen at certain hot mineral springs in remote country districts.

The best answer to the general charge of immorality which has been brought against the Japanese women during their period of unmarried life, lies in the fact that every man who can afford to do so keeps the maidens of his family closely guarded in the strictest seclusion. The daughter of poverty, indeed, must work and go abroad, but not a man is allowed to approach the daughter of a gentleman; and she is taught that if by accident any insult should be offered to her, the knife which she carries at her girdle is meant for use, and not merely as a badge of her rank. Not long ago a tragedy took place in the house of one of the chief nobles in Yedo. One of My Lady's tire-women, herself a damsel of gentle blood, and gifted with rare beauty, had attracted the attention of a retainer in the palace, who fell desperately in love with her. For a long time the strict rules of decorum by which she was hedged in prevented him from declaring his passion; but at last he contrived to gain access to her presence, and so far forgot himself, that she, drawing her poniard, stabbed him in the eye, so that he was carried off fainting, and presently died. The girl's declaration, that the dead man had attempted to insult her, was held to be sufficient justification of her deed, and, instead of being blamed, she was praised and extolled for her valour and chastity. As the affair had taken place within the four walls of a powerful noble, there was no official investigation into the matter, with which the authorities of the palace were competent to deal. The truth of this story was vouched for by two or three persons whose word I have no reason to doubt, and who had themselves been mixed up in it; I can bear witness that it is in complete harmony with Japanese ideas; and certainly it seems more just that Lucretia should kill Tarquin than herself.

The better the Japanese people come to be known and understood, the more, I am certain, will it be felt that a great injustice has been done them in the sweeping attacks which have been made upon their women. Writers are agreed, I believe, that their matrons are, as a rule, without reproach. If their maidens are chaste, as I contend that from very force of circumstances they cannot help being, what becomes of all these charges of vice and immodesty? Do they not rather recoil upon the accusers, who would appear to have studied the Japanese woman only in the harlot of Yokohama?

Having said so much, I will now try to give some account of the famous Yoshiwara[1] of Yedo, to which frequent allusion will have to be made in the course of these tales.

At the end of the sixteenth century the courtesans of Yedo lived in three special places: these were the street called Kôjimachi, in which dwelt the women who came from Kiôto; the Kamakura Street, and a spot opposite the great bridge, in which last two places lived women brought from Suruga. Besides these there afterwards came women from Fushimi and from Nara, who lodged scattered here and there throughout the town. This appears to have scandalised a certain reformer, named Shôji Jinyémon, who, in the year 1612, addressed a memorial to the Government, petitioning that the women who lived in different parts of the town should be collected in one " Flower Quarter." His petition was granted in the year 1617, and he fixed upon a place called Fukiyacho, which, on account of the quantities of rushes which grew there, was named *Yoshi-Wara*, or the rush-moor, a name which now-a-days, by a play upon the word *yoshi*, is written with two Chinese characters, signifying the "good" or "lucky moor." The place was divided into four streets, called the Yedo Street, the Second Yedo Street, the Kiôto Street, and the Second Kiôto Street.

In the eighth month of the year 1655, when Yedo was beginning to increase in size and importance, the Yoshiwara, preserving its name, was transplanted bodily to the spot which it now occupies at the northern end of the town. And the streets in it were named after the places from which the greater number of their inhabitants originally came, as the "Sakai Street," the " Fushimi Street," &c.

The official Guide to the Yoshiwara for 1869 gives a return of 153 brothels, containing 3,289 courtesans of all classes,

1 The name Yoshiwara, which is becoming generic for "Flower Districts," —*Anglicè*, quarters occupied by brothels,—is sometimes derived from the town Yoshiwara, in Sunshine, because it was said that the women of that place furnished a large proportion of the beauties of the Yedo Yoshiwara. The correct derivation is probably that given below.

from the *Oiran*, or proud beauty, who, dressed up in gorgeous brocade of gold and silver, with painted face and gilded lips, and with her teeth fashionably blacked, has all the young bloods of Yedo at her feet, down to the humble *Shinzo*, or white-toothed woman, who rots away her life in the common stews. These figures do not, however, represent the whole of the prostitution of Yedo; the Yoshiwara is the chief, but not the only, abiding-place of the public women. At Fukagawa there is another Flower District, built upon the same principle as the Yoshiwara; while at Shinagawa, Shinjiku, Itabashi, Senji, and Kadzukappara, the hotels contain women who, nominally only waitresses, are in reality prostitutes. There are also women called *Jigoku-Onna*, or hell-women, who, without being borne on the books of any brothel, live in their own houses, and ply their trade in secret. On the whole, I believe the amount of prostitution in Yedo to be wonderfully small, considering the vast size of the city.

There are 394 tea-houses in the Yoshiwara, which are largely used as places of assignation, and which on those occasions are paid, not by the visitors frequenting them, but by the keepers of the brothels. It is also the fashion to give dinners and drinking-parties at these houses, for which the services of *Taikomochi*, or jesters, among whom there are thirty-nine chief celebrities, and of singing and dancing girls, are retained. The Guide to the Yoshiwara gives a list of fifty-five famous singing-girls, besides a host of minor stars. These women are not to be confounded with the courtesans. Their conduct is very closely watched by their masters, and they always go out to parties in couples or in bands, so that they may be a check upon one another. Doubtless, however, in spite of all precautions, the shower of gold does from time to time find its way to Danaë's lap; and to be the favoured lover of a fashionable singer or dancer is rather a feather in the cap of a fast young Japanese gentleman. The fee paid to singing-girls for performing during a space of two hours is one shilling and fourpence each; for six hours the fee is quadrupled, and it is customary to give the girls a *hana*, or present, for themselves, besides their regular pay, which goes to the master of the troupe to which they belong.

Courtesans, singing women, and dancers are bought by contractors, either as children, when they are educated for their calling, or at a more advanced age, when their accomplishments and charms render them desirable investments. The engagement is never made life long, for once past the flower of their youth the poor creatures would be mere burthens upon their masters; a courtesan is usually bought until she shall have reached the age of twenty-seven, after which she becomes her own property. Singers remain longer in harness, but even they rarely work after the age of thirty, for Japanese women, like Italians, age quickly, and have none of that intermediate stage between youth and old age, which seems to be confined to countries where there is a twilight.

Children destined to be trained as singers are usually bought when they are five or six years old, a likely child fetching from about thirty-five to fifty shillings; the purchaser undertakes the education of his charge, and brings the little thing up as his own child. The parents sign a paper absolving him from all responsibility in case of sickness or accident; but they know that their child will be well treated and cared for, the interests of the buyer being their material guarantee. Girls of fifteen or upwards who are sufficiently accomplished to join a company of singers fetch ten times the price paid for children; for in their case there is no risk and no expense of education.

Little children who are bought for purposes of prostitution at the age of five or six years fetch about the same price as those that are bought to be singers. During their novitiate they are employed to wait upon the *Oiran*, or fashionable courtesans, in the capacity of little female pages (*Kamuro*). They are mostly the children of distressed persons, or orphans, whom their relatives cruelly sell rather than be at the expense and trouble of bringing them up. Of the girls who enter the profession later in life, some are orphans, who have no other means of earning a livelihood; others sell their bodies out of filial piety, that they may succour their sick or needy parents; others are married women, who enter the Yoshiwara to supply the wants of their husbands; and a very small proportion is recruited from girls who have been seduced and abandoned, perhaps sold, by faithless lovers.

The time to see the Yoshiwara to the best advantage is just after nightfall, when the lamps are lighted. Then it is that the women—who for the last two hours have been engaged in gilding their lips and painting their eyebrows black, and their throats and bosoms a snowy white, carefully leaving three brown Vandyke-collar points where the back of the head joins the neck, in accordance with one of the strictest rules of Japanese cosmetic science—leave the back rooms, and take their places, side by side, in a kind of long narrow cage, the wooden bars of which open on to the public thoroughfare. Here they sit for hours, gorgeous in dresses of silk and gold and silver embroidery, speechless and motionless as wax figures, until they shall have attracted the attention of some of the passers-by, who begin to throng the place. At Yokohama indeed, and at the other open ports, the women of the Yoshiwara are loud in their invitations to visitors, frequently relieving the monotony of their own language by some blasphemous term of endearment picked up from British and American seamen; but in the Flower District at Yedo, and wherever Japanese customs are untainted, the utmost decorum prevails. Although the shape which vice takes is ugly enough, still it has this merit, that it is unobtrusive. Never need the pure be contaminated by contact with the impure; he who goes to the Yoshiwara, goes there knowing full well what he will find, but the virtuous man may live through his life without having this kind of vice forced upon his sight. Here again do the open ports contrast unfavourably with other places: Yokohama at night is as leprous a place as the London Haymarket.[1]

[1] Those who are interested in this branch of social science, will find much curious information upon the subject of prostitution in Japan in a pamphlet published at Yokohama, by Dr. Newton, R.N., a philanthropist who has

A public woman or singer on entering her profession assumes a *nom de guerre*, by which she is known until her engagement is at an end. Some of these names are so pretty and quaint that I will take a few specimens from the *Yoshiwara Saiken*, the guide-book upon which this notice is based. 'Little Pine,' 'Little Butterfly,' 'Brightness of the Flowers,' 'The Jewel River,' 'Gold Mountain,' 'Pearl Harp,' 'The Stork that lives a Thousand Years,' 'Village of Flowers,' 'Sea Beach,' 'The Little Dragon,' 'Little Purple,' 'Silver,' 'Chrysanthemum,' 'Waterfall,' 'White Brightness,' 'Forest of Cherries,'—these and a host of other quaint conceits are the one prettiness of a very foul place.

been engaged for the last two years in establishing a Lock Hospital at that place. In spite of much opposition, from prejudice and ignorance, his labours have been crowned by great success.

KAZUMA'S REVENGE

It is a law that he who lives by the sword shall die by the sword. In Japan, where there exists a large armed class over whom there is practically little or no control, party and clan broils, and single quarrels ending in bloodshed and death, are matters of daily occurrence; and it has been observed that Edinburgh in the olden time, when the clansmen, roistering through the streets at night, would pass from high words to deadly blows, is perhaps the best European parallel of modern Yedo or Kiôto.

It follows that of all his possessions the Samurai sets most store by his sword, his constant companion, his ally, defensive and offensive. The price of a sword by a famous maker reaches a high sum: a Japanese noble will sometimes be found girding on a sword, the blade of which unmounted is worth from six hundred to a thousand riyos, say from £200 to £300, and the mounting, rich in cunning metal work, will be of proportionate value. These swords are handed down as heirlooms from father to son, and become almost a part of the wearer's own self. Iyéyasu, the founder of the last dynasty of Shoguns, wrote in his Legacy,[1] a code of rules drawn up for the guidance of his successors and their advisers in the government, "The girded sword is the living soul of the Samurai. In the case of a Samurai forgetting his sword, act as is appointed: it may not be overlooked."

The occupation of a swordsmith is an honourable profes-

[1] The Legacy of Iyéyasu, translated by F. Lowder. Yokohama, 1868. (Printed for private circulation.)

sion, the members of which are men of gentle blood. In a country where trade is looked down upon as degrading, it is strange to find this single exception to the general rule. The traditions of the craft are many and curious. During the most critical moment of the forging of the sword, when the steel edge is being welded into the body of the iron blade, it is a custom which still obtains among old-fashioned armourers to put on the cap and robes worn by the Kugé, or nobles of the Mikado's court, and, closing the doors of the workshop, to labour in secrecy and freedom from interruption, the half gloom adding to the mystery of the operation. Sometimes the occasion is even invested with a certain sanctity, a tasselled cord of straw, such as is hung before the shrines of the Kami, or native gods of Japan, being suspended between two bamboo poles in the forge, which for the nonce is converted into a holy altar.

At Osaka, I lived opposite to one Kusano Yoshiaki, a swordsmith, a most intelligent and amiable gentleman, who was famous throughout his neighbourhood for his good and charitable deeds. His idea was that, having been bred up to a calling which trades in life and death, he was bound, so far as in him lay, to atone for this by seeking to alleviate the suffering which is in the world; and he carried out his principle to the extent of impoverishing himself. No neighbour ever appealed to him in vain for help in tending the sick or burying the dead. No beggar or lazar was ever turned from his door without receiving some mark of his bounty, whether in money or in kind. Nor was his scrupulous honesty less remarkable than his charity. While other smiths are in the habit of earning large sums of money by counterfeiting the marks of the famous makers of old, he was able to boast that he had never turned out a weapon which bore any other mark than his own. From his father and his forefathers he inherited his trade, which, in his turn, he will hand over to his son—a hard-working, honest, and sturdy man, the clank of whose hammer and anvil may be heard from daybreak to sundown.

The trenchant edge of the Japanese sword is notorious. It is said that the best blades will in the hands of an expert swordsman cut through the dead bodies of three men, laid one upon the other, at a blow. The swords of the Shogun used to be tried upon the corpses of executed criminals; the public headsman was entrusted with the duty, and for a "nose medicine," or bribe of two bus (about three shillings), would substitute the weapon of a private individual for that of his Lord. Dogs and beggars, lying helpless by the roadside, not unfrequently serve to test a ruffian's sword; but the executioner earns many a fee from those who wish to see how their blades will cut off a head.

The statesman who shall enact a law forbidding the carrying of this deadly weapon will indeed have deserved well of his country; but it will be a difficult task to undertake, and a dangerous one. I would not give much for that man's life. The hand of every swashbuckler in the empire would be against him. One day as we were talking over this and other kindred subjects, a friend of mine, a man of advanced and liberal views, wrote down his opinion, *more Japonico*, in a verse of poetry which ran as follows:—"I would that all the swords and dirks in the country might be collected in one place and molten down, and that, from the metal so produced, one huge sword might be forged, which, being the only blade left, should be the girded sword of Great Japan."

The following history is in more senses than one a "Tale of a Sword."

About two hundred and fifty years ago Ikéda Kunaishôyu was Lord of the Province of Inaba. Among his retainers were two gentlemen, named Watanabé Yukiyé and Kawai Matazayémon, who were bound together by strong ties of friendship, and were in the habit of frequently visiting at one another's houses. One day Yukiyé was sitting conversing with Matazayémon in the house of the latter, when, on a sudden, a sword that was lying in the raised part of the room caught his eye. As he saw it, he started and said—

"Pray tell me, how came you by that sword?"

FORGING THE SWORD

"Well, as you know, when my Lord Ikéda followed my Lord Tokugawa Iyéyasu to fight at Nagakudé, my father went in his train; and it was at the battle of Nagakudé that he picked up this sword."

"My father went too, and was killed in the fight, and this sword, which was an heirloom in our family for many generations, was lost at that time. As it is of great value in my eyes, I do wish that, if you set no special store by it, you would have the great kindness to return it to me."

"That is a very easy matter, and no more than what one friend should do by another. Pray take it."

Upon this Yukiyé gratefully took the sword, and having carried it home put it carefully away.

At the beginning of the ensuing year Matazayémon fell sick and died, and Yukiyé, mourning bitterly for the loss of his good friend, and anxious to requite the favour which he had received in the matter of his father's sword, did many acts of kindness to the dead man's son—a young man twenty-two years of age, named Matagorô.

Now this Matagorô was a base-hearted cur, who had begrudged the sword that his father had given to Yukiyé, and complained publicly and often that Yukiyé had never made any present in return; and in this way Yukiyé got a bad name in my Lord's palace as a stingy and illiberal man.

But Yukiyé had a son, called Kazuma, a youth sixteen years of age, who served as one of the Prince's pages of honour. One evening, as he and one of his brother pages were talking together, the latter said—

"Matagorô is telling everybody that your father accepted a handsome sword from him and never made him any present in return, and people are beginning to gossip about it."

"Indeed," replied the other, "my father received that sword from Matagorô's father as a mark of friendship and goodwill, and, considering that it would be an insult to send a present of money in return, thought to return the favour by acts of kindness towards Matagorô. I suppose it is money he wants."

When Kazuma's service was over, he returned home, and went to his father's room to tell him the report that was being spread in the palace, and begged him to send an ample present of money to Matagorô. Yukiyé reflected for a while, and said—

"You are too young to understand the right line of conduct in such matters. Matagorô's father and myself were very close friends; so, seeing that he had ungrudgingly given me back the sword of my ancestors, I, thinking to requite his kindness at his death, rendered important services to Matagorô. It would be easy to finish the matter by sending a present of money; but I had rather take the sword and return it than be under an obligation to this mean churl, who knows not the laws which regulate the intercourse and dealings of men of gentle blood."

So Yukiyé, in his anger, took the sword to Matagorô's house, and said to him—

"I have come to your house this night for no other purpose than to restore to you the sword which your father gave me;" and with this he placed the sword before Matagorô.

"Indeed," replied the other, "I trust that you will not pain me by returning a present which my father made you."

"Amongst men of gentle birth," said Yukiyé, laughing scornfully, "it is the custom to requite presents, in the first place by kindness, and afterwards by a suitable gift offered with a free heart. But it is no use talking to such as you, who are ignorant of the first principles of good breeding; so I have the honour to give you back the sword."

As Yukiyé went on bitterly to reprove Matagorô, the latter waxed very wroth, and, being a ruffian, would have killed Yukiyé on the spot; but he, old man as he was, was a skilful swordsman, so Matagorô, craven-like, determined to wait until he could attack him unawares. Little suspecting any treachery, Yukiyé started to return home, and Matagorô, under the pretence of attending him to the door, came behind him with his sword drawn and cut him in the shoulder. The older man, turning round, drew and defended himself;

but having received a severe wound in the first instance, he fainted away from loss of blood, and Matagorô slew him.

The mother of Matagorô, startled by the noise, came out; and when she saw what had been done, she was afraid, and said—

"Passionate man! what have you done? You are a murderer; and now your life will be forfeit. What terrible deed is this!"

"I have killed him now, and there's nothing to be done. Come, mother, before the matter becomes known, let us fly together from this house."

"I will follow you; do you go and seek out my Lord Abé Shirogorô, a chief among the Hatamotos,[1] who was my foster-child. You had better fly to him for protection, and remain in hiding."

So the old woman persuaded her son to make his escape, and sent him to the palace of Shirogorô.

Now it happened that at this time the Hatamotos had formed themselves into a league against the powerful Daimios; and Abé Shirogorô, with two other noblemen, named Kondô Noborinosuké and Midzuno Jiurozayémon, was at the head of the league. It followed, as a matter of course, that his forces were frequently recruited by vicious men, who had no means of gaining their living, and whom he received and entreated kindly without asking any questions as to their antecedents; how much the more then, on being applied to for an asylum by the son of his own foster-mother, did he willingly extend his patronage to him, and guarantee him against all danger. So he called a meeting of the principal Hatamotos, and introduced Matagorô to them, saying—

"This man is a retainer of Ikéda Kunaishôyu, who, having cause of hatred against a man named Watanabé Yukiyé, has slain him, and has fled to me for protection; this man's

---

[1] *Hatamotos.* The Hatamotos were the feudatory nobles of the Shogun or Tycoon. The office of Taikun having been abolished, the Hatamotos no longer exist. For further information respecting them, see the note at the end of this story.

MATAGORŌ KILLS YUKIYÉ

mother suckled me when I was an infant, and, right or wrong, I will befriend him. If, therefore, Ikéda Kunaishôyu should send to require me to deliver him up, I trust that you will one and all put forth your strength and help me to defend him."

"Ay! that will we, with pleasure!" replied Kondô Noborinosuké. "We have for some time had cause to complain of the scorn with which the Daimios have treated us. Let Ikéda Kunaishôyu send to claim this man, and we will show him the power of the Hatamotos."

All the other Hatamotos, with one accord, applauded this determination, and made ready their force for an armed resistance, should my Lord Kunaishôyu send to demand the surrender of Matagorô. But the latter remained as a welcome guest in the house of Abé Shirogorô.

Now when Watanabé Kazuma saw that, as the night advanced, his father Yukiyé did not return home, he became anxious, and went to the house of Matagorô to seek for him, and finding to his horror that he was murdered, fell upon the corpse and embraced it, weeping. On a sudden, it flashed across him that this must assuredly be the handiwork of Matagorô; so he rushed furiously into the house, determined to kill his father's murderer upon the spot. But Matagorô had already fled, and he found only the mother, who was making her preparations for following her son to the house of Abé Shirogorô: so he bound the old woman, and searched all over the house for her son; but, seeing that his search was fruitless, he carried off the mother, and handed her over to one of the elders of the clan, at the same time laying information against Matagorô as his father's murderer. When the affair was reported to the Prince, he was very angry, and ordered that the old woman should remain bound and be cast into prison until the whereabouts of her son should be discovered. Then Kazuma buried his father's corpse with great pomp, and the widow and the orphan mourned over their loss.

It soon became known amongst the people of Abé Shirogorô that the mother of Matagorô had been imprisoned for her son's crime, and they immediately set about planning her rescue ; so they sent to the palace of my Lord Kunaishôyu a messenger, who, when he was introduced to the councillor of the Prince, said—

"We have heard that, in consequence of the murder of Yukiyé, my lord has been pleased to imprison the mother of Matagorô. Our master Shirogorô has arrested the criminal, and will deliver him up to you. But the mother has committed no crime, so we pray that she may be released from a cruel imprisonment : she was the foster-mother of our master, and he would fain intercede to save her life. Should you consent to this, we, on our side, will give up the murderer, and hand him over to you in front of our master's gate to-morrow."

The councillor repeated this message to the Prince, who, in his pleasure at being able to give Kazuma his revenge on the morrow, immediately agreed to the proposal, and the messenger returned triumphant at the success of the scheme. On the following day, the Prince ordered the mother of Matagorô to be placed in a litter and carried to the Hatamoto's dwelling, in charge of a retainer named Sasawo Danyémon, who, when he arrived at the door of Abé Shirogorô's house, said—

"I am charged to hand over to you the mother of Matagorô, and, in exchange, I am authorized to receive her son at your hands."

"We will immediately give him up to you ; but, as the mother and son are now about to bid an eternal farewell to one another, we beg you to be so kind as to tarry a little."

With this the retainers of Shirogorô led the old woman inside their master's house, and Sasawo Danyémon remained waiting outside, until at last he grew impatient, and ventured to hurry on the people within.

"We return you many thanks," replied they, "for your kindness in bringing us the mother ; but, as the son cannot go with you at present, you had better return home as quickly as possible. We are afraid we have put you to much trouble." And so they mocked him.

When Danyémon saw that he had not only been cheated into giving up the old woman, but was being made a laughing-stock of into the bargain, he flew into a great rage, and thought to break into the house and seize Matagorô and his mother by force; but, peeping into the courtyard, he saw that it was filled with Hatamotos, carrying guns and naked swords. Not caring then to die fighting a hopeless battle, and at the same time feeling that, after having been so cheated, he would be put to shame before his lord, Sasawo Danyémon went to the burial-place of his ancestors, and disembowelled himself in front of their graves.

When the Prince heard how his messenger had been treated, he was indignant, and summoning his councillors resolved, although he was suffering from sickness, to collect his retainers and attack Abé Shirogorô; and the other chief Daimios, when the matter became publicly known, took up the cause, and determined that the Hatamotos must be chastised for their insolence. On their side, the Hatamotos put forth all their efforts to resist the Daimios. So Yedo became disturbed, and the riotous state of the city caused great anxiety to the Government, who took counsel together how they might restore peace. As the Hatamotos were directly under the orders of the Shogun, it was no difficult matter to put them down: the hard question to solve was how to put a restraint upon the great Daimios. However, one of the Gorôjiu,[1] named Matsudaira Idzu no Kami, a man of great intelligence, hit upon a plan by which he might secure this end.

There was at this time in the service of the Shogun a physician, named Nakarai Tsusen, who was in the habit of frequenting the palace of my Lord Kunaishôyu, and who for some time past had been treating him for the disease from

[1] The first Council of the Shogun's ministers; literally, "assembly of imperial elders."

THE DEATH OF DANYÉMON

which he was suffering. Idzu no Kami sent secretly for this physician, and, summoning him to his private room, engaged him in conversation, in the midst of which he suddenly dropped his voice and said to him in a whisper—

"Listen, Tsusen. You have received great favours at the hands of the Shogun. The Government is now sorely straitened: are you willing to carry your loyalty so far as to lay down your life on its behalf?"

"Ay, my lord; for generations my forefathers have held their property by the grace of the Shogun. I am willing this night to lay down my life for my Prince, as a faithful vassal should."

"Well, then, I will tell you. The great Daimios and the Hatamotos have fallen out about this affair of Matagorô, and lately it has seemed as if they meant to come to blows. The country will be agitated, and the farmers and townsfolk suffer great misery, if we cannot quell the tumult. The Hatamotos will be easily kept under, but it will be no light task to pacify the great Daimios. If you are willing to lay down your life in carrying out a stratagem of mine, peace will be restored to the country; but your loyalty will be your death."

"I am ready to sacrifice my life in this service."

"This is my plan. You have been attending my Lord Kunaishôyu in his sickness; to-morrow you must go to see him, and put poison in his physic. If we can kill him, the agitation will cease. This is the service which I ask of you."

Tsusen agreed to undertake the deed; and on the following day, when he went to see Kunaishôyu, he carried with him poisoned drugs. Half the draught he drank himself,[1] and thus put the Prince off his guard, so that he swallowed the remainder fearlessly. Tsusen, seeing this, hurried away, and as he was carried home in his litter the death-agony seized him, and he died, vomiting blood.

[1] A physician attending a personage of exalted rank has always to drink half the potion he prescribes as a test of his good faith.

My Lord Kunaishôyu died in the same way in great torture, and in the confusion attending upon his death and funeral ceremonies the struggle which was impending with the Hatamotos was delayed.

In the meanwhile the Gorôjiu Idzu no Kami summoned the three leaders of the Hatamotos and addressed them as follows:—

" The secret plottings and treasonable, turbulent conduct of you three men, so unbecoming your position as Hatamotos, have enraged my lord the Shogun to such a degree, that he has been pleased to order that you be imprisoned in a temple, and that your patrimony be given over to your next heirs."

Accordingly the three Hatamotos, after having been severely admonished, were confined in a temple called Kanyeiji; and the remaining Hatamotos, scared by this example, dispersed in peace. As for the great Daimios, inasmuch as after the death of my Lord Kunaishôyu the Hatamotos were all dispersed, there was no enemy left for them to fight with; so the tumult was quelled, and peace was restored.

Thus it happened that Matagorô lost his patron; so, taking his mother with him, he went and placed himself under the protection of an old man named Sakurai Jiuzayémon. This old man was a famous teacher of lance exercise, and enjoyed both wealth and honour; so he took in Matagorô, and having engaged as a guard thirty Rônins, all resolute fellows and well skilled in the arts of war, they all fled together to a distant place called Sagara.

All this time Watanabé Kazuma had been brooding over his father's death, and thinking how he should be revenged upon the murderer; so when my Lord Kunaishôyu suddenly died, he went to the young Prince who succeeded him and obtained leave of absence to go and seek out his father's enemy. Now Kazuma's elder sister was married to a man named Araki Matayémon, who at that time was famous as the first swordsman in Japan. As Kazuma was but sixteen years of age, this Matayémon, taking into consideration his near relationship as son-in-law to the murdered man, determined to go forth with the lad, as his guardian, and help him to seek out Matagorô; and two of Matayémon's retainers, named Ishidomé Busuké and Ikezoyé Magohachi, made up their minds, at all hazards, to follow their master. The latter, when he heard their intention, thanked them, but refused the offer, saying that as he was now about to engage in a vendetta in which his life would be continually in jeopardy, and as it would be a lasting grief to him should either of them receive a wound in such a service, he must beg them to renounce their intention ; but they answered—

"Master, this is a cruel speech of yours. All these years have we received nought but kindness and favours at your hands ; and now that you are engaged in the pursuit of this murderer, we desire to follow you, and, if needs must, to lay down our lives in your service. Furthermore, we have heard that the friends of this Matagorô are no fewer than thirty-six men ; so, however bravely you may fight, you will be in peril from the superior numbers of your enemy. However, if you are pleased to persist in your refusal to take us, we have made up our minds that there is no resource for us but to disembowel ourselves on the spot."

When Matayémon and Kazuma heard these words, they wondered at these faithful and brave men, and were moved to tears. Then Matayémon said—

"The kindness of you two brave fellows is without precedent. Well, then, I will accept your services gratefully."

Then the two men, having obtained their wish, cheerfully followed their master; and the four set out together upon their journey to seek out Matagorô, of whose whereabouts they were completely ignorant.

Matagorô in the meanwhile had made his way, with the old man Sakurai Jiuzayémon and his thirty Rônins, to Osaka. But, strong as they were in numbers, they travelled in great secrecy. The reason for this was, that the old man's younger brother, Sakurai Jinsuké, a fencing-master by profession, had once had a fencing-match with Matayémon, Kazuma's brother-in-law, and had been shamefully beaten; so that the party were greatly afraid of Matayémon, and felt that, since he was taking up Kazuma's cause and acting as his guardian, they might be worsted in spite of their numbers: so they went on their way with great caution, and, having reached Osaka, put up at an inn in a quarter called Ikutama, and hid from Kazuma and Matayémon.

The latter also in good time reached Osaka, and spared no pains to seek out Matagorô. One evening towards dusk, as Matayémon was walking in the quarter where the enemy were staying, he saw a man, dressed as a gentleman's servant, enter a cook-shop and order some buckwheat porridge for thirty-six men, and, looking attentively at the man, he recognized him as the servant of Sakurai Jiuzayémon; so he hid himself in a dark place and watched, and heard the fellow say—

"My master, Sakurai Jiuzayémon, is about to start for Sagara to-morrow morning, to return thanks to the gods for his recovery from a sickness from which he has been suffering; so I am in a great hurry."

With these words the servant hastened away; and Matayémon, entering the shop, called for some porridge, and as he ate it, made some inquiries as to the man who had just given so large an order for buckwheat porridge. The master of the shop answered that he was the attendant of a party of thirty-six gentlemen who were staying at such and such an inn. Then Matayémon, having found out all that he wanted to know, went home and told Kazuma, who was delighted at the prospect of carrying his revenge into execution on the morrow. That same evening Matayémon sent one of his two faithful retainers as a spy to the inn, to find out at what hour Matagorô was to set out on the following morning; and he ascertained from the servants of the inn, that the party was to start at daybreak for Sagara, stopping at Isé to worship at the shrine of Tershô Daijin.[1]

Matayémon made his preparations accordingly, and, with

[1] Goddess of the sun, and ancestress of the Mikados.

Kazuma and his two retainers, started before dawn. Beyond Uyéno, in the province of Iga, the castle town of the Daimio Tôdô Idzumi no Kami, there is a wide and lonely moor; and this was the place upon which they fixed for the attack upon the enemy. When they had arrived at the spot, Matayémon went into a tea-house by the roadside, and wrote a petition to the governor of the Daimio's castle town for permission to carry out the vendetta within its precincts;[1] then he addressed Kazuma, and said—

"When we fall in with Matagorô and begin the fight, do you engage and slay your father's murderer; attack him and him only, and I will keep off his guard of Rônins;" then turning to his two retainers, "As for you, keep close to Kazuma; and should the Rônins attempt to rescue Matagorô, it will be your duty to prevent them, and succour Kazuma." And having further laid down each man's duties with great minuteness, they lay in wait for the arrival of the enemy. Whilst they were resting in the tea-house, the governor of the castle town arrived, and, asking for Matayémon, said—

"I have the honour to be the governor of the castle town of Tôdô Idzumi no Kami. My lord, having learnt your intention of slaying your enemy within the precincts of his citadel, gives his consent; and as a proof of his admiration of your fidelity and valour, he has further sent you a detachment of infantry, one hundred strong, to guard the place; so that should any of the thirty-six men attempt to escape, you may set your mind at ease, for flight will be impossible."

When Matayémon and Kazuma had expressed their thanks

[1] " In respect to revenging injury done to master or father, it is granted by the wise and virtuous (Confucius) that you and the injurer cannot live together under the canopy of heaven.

"A person harbouring such vengeance shall notify the same in writing to the Criminal Court; and although no check or hindrance may be offered to his carrying out his desire within the period allowed for that purpose, it is forbidden that the chastisement of an enemy be attended with riot.

"Fellows who neglect to give notice of their intended revenge are like wolves of pretext, and their punishment or pardon should depend upon the circumstances of the case."—*Legacy of Iyéyasu*, ut suprà.

for his lordship's gracious kindness, the governor took his leave and returned home. At last the enemy's train was seen in the distance. First came Sakurai Jiuzayémon and his younger brother Jinsuké; and next to them followed Kawai Matagorô and Takénouchi Gentan. These four men, who were the bravest and the foremost of the band of Rônins, were riding on pack-horses, and the remainder were marching on foot, keeping close together.

As they drew near, Kazuma, who was impatient to avenge his father, stepped boldly forward and shouted in a loud voice—

"Here stand I, Kazuma, the son of Yukiyé, whom you, Matagorô, treacherously slew, determined to avenge my father's death. Come forth, then, and do battle with me, and let us see which of us twain is the better man."

And before the Rônins had recovered from their astonishment, Matayémon said—

"I, Araké Matayémon, the son-in-law of Yukiyé, have come to second Kazuma in his deed of vengeance. Win or lose, you must give us battle."

When the thirty-six men heard the name of Matayémon, they were greatly afraid; but Sakurai Jiuzayémon urged them to be upon their guard, and leaped from his horse; and Matayémon, springing forward with his drawn sword, cleft him from the shoulder to the nipple of his breast, so that he fell dead. Sakurai Jinsuké, seeing his brother killed before his eyes, grew furious, and shot an arrow at Matayémon, who deftly cut the shaft in two with his dirk as it flew; and Jinsuké, amazed at this feat, threw away his bow and attacked Matayémon, who, with his sword in his right hand and his dirk in his left, fought with desperation. The other Rônins attempted to rescue Jinsuké, and, in the struggle, Kazuma, who had engaged Matagorô, became separated from Matayémon, whose two retainers, Busuké and Magohachi, bearing in mind their master's orders, killed five Rônins who had attacked Kazuma, but were themselves badly wounded. In the meantime, Matayémon, who had killed seven of the

Rônins, and who the harder he was pressed the more bravely he fought, soon cut down three more, and the remainder dared not approach him. At this moment there came up one Kanô Tozayémon, a retainer of the lord of the castle town, and an old friend of Matayémon, who, when he heard that Matayémon was this day about to avenge his father-in-law, had seized his spear and set out, for the sake of the old goodwill between them, to help him, and act as his second, and said—

"Sir Matayémon, hearing of the perilous adventure in which you have engaged, I have come out to offer myself as your second."

Matayémon, hearing this, was rejoiced, and fought with renewed vigour. Then one of the Rônins, named Takénouchi Gentan, a very brave man, leaving his companions to do battle with Matayémon, came to the rescue of Matagorô, who was being hotly pressed by Kazuma, and, in attempting to prevent this, Busuké fell covered with wounds. His companion Magohachi, seeing him fall, was in great anxiety; for should any harm happen to Kazuma, what excuse could he make to Matayémon? So, wounded as he was, he too engaged Takénouchi Gentan, and, being crippled by the gashes he had received, was in deadly peril. Then the man who had come up from the castle town to act as Matayémon's second cried out—

"See there, Sir Matayémon, your follower who is fighting with Gentan is in great danger. Do you go to his rescue, and second Sir Kazuma: I will give an account of the others!"

"Great thanks to you, sir. I will go and second Kazuma."

So Matayémon went to help Kazuma, whilst his second and the infantry soldiers kept back the surviving Rônins, who, already wearied by their fight with Matayémon, were unfit for any further exertion. Kazuma meanwhile was still fighting with Matagorô, and the issue of the conflict was doubtful; and Takénouchi Gentan, in his attempt to rescue Matagorô, was being kept at bay by Magohachi, who, weakened by his wounds, and blinded by the blood which was streaming into his eyes from a cut in the forehead, had given himself up for lost when Matayémon came and cried—

"Be of good cheer, Magohachi; it is I, Matayémon, who have come to the rescue. You are badly hurt; get out of harm's way, and rest yourself."

Then Magohachi, who until then had been kept up by his anxiety for Kazuma's safety, gave in, and fell fainting from loss of blood; and Matayémon worsted and slew Gentan; and even then, although he had received two wounds, he was not exhausted, but drew near to Kazuma and said—

"Courage, Kazuma! The Rônins are all killed, and there now remains only Matagorô, your father's murderer. Fight and win!"

The youth, thus encouraged, redoubled his efforts; but Matagorô, losing heart, quailed and fell. So Kazuma's vengeance was fulfilled, and the desire of his heart was accomplished.

The two faithful retainers, who had died in their loyalty, were buried with great ceremony, and Kazuma carried the head of Matagorô and piously laid it upon his father's tomb.

So ends the tale of Kazuma's revenge.

———

I fear that stories of which killing and bloodshed form the principal features can hardly enlist much sympathy in these peaceful days. Still, when such tales are based upon history, they are interesting to students of social phenomena. The story of Kazuma's revenge is mixed up with events which at the present time are peculiarly significant: I mean the feud between the great Daimios and the Hatamotos. Those who have followed the modern history of Japan will see that the recent struggle, which has ended in the ruin of the Tycoon's power and the abolition of his office, was the outburst of a hidden fire which had been smouldering for centuries. But the repressive might had been gradually weakened, and contact with Western powers had rendered still more odious a feudality which men felt to be out of date. The revolution which has ended in the triumph of the Daimios over the Tycoon, is also the triumph of the vassal over his feudal lord, and is the harbinger of political life to the people at large. In the time of Iyéyasu the burden might be hateful, but it had to be borne; and so it would have been to this day, had not circumstances from without broken the spell. The Japanese Daimio, in advocating the isolation of his country, was hugging the very yoke which he hated. Strange to say, however, there are still men who, while they embrace the new political creed, yet praise the past, and look back with regret upon the day when Japan stood alone, without part or share in the great family of nations.

NOTE.—*Hatamoto*. This word means "*under the flag.*" The Hatamotos were men who, as their name implied, rallied round the standard of the Shogun, or Tycoon, in war-time. They were eighty thousand in number. When Iyéyasu left the Province of Mikawa and became Shogun, the retainers whom he ennobled, and who received from him grants of land yielding revenue to the amount of ten thousand kokus of rice a year, and from that down to one hundred kokus, were called *Hatamoto*. In return for these grants of land, the Hatamotos had in war-time to furnish a contingent of soldiers in proportion to their revenue. For every thousand kokus of rice five men were required. Those Hatamotos whose revenue fell short of a thousand kokus substituted a quota of money. In time of peace most of the minor offices of the Tycoon's government were filled by Hatamotos, the more important places being held by the Fudai, or vassal Daimios of the Shogun. Seven years ago, in imitation of the customs of foreign nations, a standing army was founded; and then the Hatamotos had to contribute their quota of men or of money, whether the country were at peace or at war. When the Shogun was reduced in 1868 to the rank of a simple Daimio, his revenue of eight million kokus reverted to the Government, with the exception of seven hundred thousand kokus. The title of Hatamoto exists no more, and those who until a few months ago held the rank are for the most part ruined or dispersed. From having been perhaps the proudest and most overbearing class in Japan, they are driven to the utmost straits of poverty. Some have gone into trade, with the heirlooms of their families as their stock; others are wandering through the country as Rônins; while a small minority have been allowed to follow the fallen fortunes of their master's family, the present chief of which is known as the Prince of Tokugawa. Thus are the eighty thousand dispersed.

The koku of rice, in which all revenue is calculated, is of varying value. At the cheapest it is worth rather more than a pound sterling, and sometimes almost three times as much. The salaries of officials being paid in rice, it follows that there is a large and influential class throughout the country who are interested in keeping up the price of the staple article of food. Hence the opposition with which a free trade in rice has met, even in famine times. Hence also the frequent so-called " Rice Riots."

The amounts at which the lands formerly held by the chief Daimios, but now patriotically given up by them to the Mikado, were assessed, sound fabulous. The Prince of Kaga alone had an income of more than one million two hundred thousand kokus. Yet these great proprietors were, latterly at least, embarrassed men. They had many thousand mouths to feed, and were mulcted of their dues right and left; while their mania for buying foreign ships and munitions of war, often at exorbitant prices, had plunged them heavily in debt.

A STORY OF THE OTOKODATÉ OF YEDO;

BEING THE SUPPLEMENT OF

THE STORY OF GOMPACHI AND KOMURASAKI

THE word Otokodaté occurs several times in these Tales; and as I cannot convey its full meaning by a simple translation, I must preserve it in the text, explaining it by the following note, taken from the Japanese of a native scholar.

The Otokodaté were friendly associations of brave men bound together by an obligation to stand by one another in weal or in woe, regardless of their own lives, and without inquiring into one another's antecedents. A bad man, however, having joined the Otokodaté must forsake his evil ways; for their principle was to treat the oppressor as an enemy, and to help the feeble as a father does his child. If they had money, they gave it to those that had none, and their charitable deeds won for them the respect of all men. The head of the society was called its "Father;" if any of the others, who were his apprentices, were homeless, they lived with the Father and served him, paying him at the same time a small fee, in consideration of which, if they fell sick or into misfortune, he took charge of them and assisted them.

The Father of the Otokodaté pursued the calling of farming out coolies to the Daimios and great personages for their journeys to and from Yedo, and in return for this received from them rations in rice. He had more influence with the lower classes even than the officials; and if the coolies had struck work or refused to accompany a Daimio on his journey, a word from the Father would produce as many men as might be required. When Prince Tokugawa Iyémochi, the last but one of the Shoguns, left Yedo for Kiyôto, one Shimmon Tatsugorô, chief of the Otokodaté, undertook the management of his journey, and some three or four years ago was raised to the dignity of Hatamoto for many faithful services. After the battle of Fushimi, and the abolition of the Shogunate, he accompanied the last of the Shoguns in his retirement.

In old days there were also Otokodaté among the Hatamotos; this was after the civil wars of the time of Iyéyasu, when, though the country was at peace, the minds of men were still in a state of high excitement, and could not be reconciled to the dulness of a state of rest; it followed that broils and faction fights were continually taking place among the young men of the Samurai class, and that those who distinguished themselves by their personal strength and valour were looked up to as captains. Leagues after the manner of those existing among the German students were formed in different quarters of the city, under various names, and used to fight for the honour of victory. When the country became more thoroughly tranquil, the custom of forming these leagues amongst gentlemen fell into disuse.

The past tense is used in speaking even of the Otokodaté of the lower classes; for although they nominally exist, they have no longer the power and importance which they enjoyed at the time to which these stories belong. They then, like the 'prentices of Old London, played a considerable part in the society of the great cities, and that man was lucky, were he gentle Samurai or simple wardsman, who could claim the Father of the Otokodaté for his friend.

The word, taken by itself, means a manly or plucky fellow.

Chôbei of Bandzuin was the chief of the Otokodaté of Yedo. He was originally called Itarô, and was the son of a certain Rônin who lived in the country. One day, when he was only ten years of age, he went out with a playfellow to bathe in the river ; and as the two were playing they quarrelled over their game, and Itarô, seizing the other boy, threw him into the river and drowned him.

Then he went home, and said to his father—

"I went to play by the river to-day, with a friend ; and as he was rude to me, I threw him into the water and killed him."

When his father heard him speak thus, quite calmly, as if nothing had happened, he was thunderstruck, and said—

"This is indeed a fearful thing. Child as you are, you will have to pay the penalty of your deed ; so to-night you must fly to Yedo in secret, and take service with some noble Samurai, and perhaps in time you may become a soldier yourself."

With these words he gave him twenty ounces of silver and a fine sword, made by the famous swordsmith Rai Kunitoshi, and sent him out of the province with all despatch. The following morning the parents of the murdered child came to claim that Itarô should be given up to their vengeance ; but it was too late, and all they could do was to bury their child and mourn for his loss.

Itarô made his way to Yedo in hot haste, and there found employment as a shop-boy ; but soon tiring of that sort of life, and burning to become a soldier, he found means at last to enter the service of a certain Hatamoto called Sakurai Shôzayémon, and changed his name to Tsunéhei. Now this Sakurai Shôzayémon had a son, called Shônosuké, a young man in his seventeenth year, who grew so fond of Tsunéhei that he took him with him wherever he went, and treated him in all ways as an equal.

When Shônosuké went to the fencing-school Tsunéhei would accompany him, and thus, as he was by nature strong and active, soon became a good swordsman.

One day, when Shôzayémon had gone out, his son Shônosuké said to Tsunéhei—

"You know how fond my father is of playing at football :

it must be great sport. As he has gone out to-day, suppose you and I have a game?"

"That will be rare sport," answered Tsunéhei. "Let us make haste and play, before my lord comes home."

So the two boys went out into the garden, and began trying to kick the football; but, lacking skill, do what they would, they could not lift it from the ground At last Shônosuké, with a vigorous kick, raised the football; but, having missed his aim, it went tumbling over the wall into the next garden, which belonged to one Hikosaka Zempachi, a teacher of lance exercise, who was known to be a surly, ill-tempered fellow.

"Oh, dear! what shall we do?" said Shônosuké. "We have lost my father's football in his absence; and if we go and ask for it back from that churlish neighbour of ours, we shall only be scolded and sworn at for our pains."

"Oh, never mind," answered Tsunéhei; "I will go and apologize for our carelessness, and get the football back."

"Well, but then you will be chidden, and I don't want that."

"Never mind me. Little care I for his cross words." So Tsunéhei went to the next-door house to reclaim the ball.

Now it so happened that Zempachi, the surly neighbour, had been walking in his garden whilst the two youths were playing; and as he was admiring the beauty of his favourite chrysanthemums, the football came flying over the wall and struck him full in the face. Zempachi, not used to anything but flattery and coaxing, flew into a violent rage at this; and while he was thinking how he would revenge himself upon any one who might be sent to ask for the lost ball, Tsunéhei came in, and said to one of Zempachi's servants—

"I am sorry to say that in my lord's absence I took his football, and, in trying to play with it, clumsily kicked it over your wall. I beg you to excuse my carelessness, and to be so good as to give me back the ball."

The servant went in and repeated this to Zempachi, who

worked himself up into a great rage, and ordered Tsunéhei to be brought before him, and said—

"Here, fellow, is your name Tsunéhei?"

"Yes, sir, at your service. I am almost afraid to ask pardon for my carelessness; but please forgive me, and let me have the ball."

"I thought your master, Shôzayémon, was to blame for this; but it seems that it was you who kicked the football."

"Yes, sir. I am sure I am very sorry for what I have done. Please, may I ask for the ball?" said Tsunehei, bowing humbly.

For a while Zempachi made no answer, but at length he said—

"Do you know, villain, that your dirty football struck me in the face? I ought, by rights, to kill you on the spot for this; but I will spare your life this time, so take your football and be off." And with that he went up to Tsunéhei and beat him, and kicked him in the head, and spat in his face.

Then Tsunéhei, who up to that time had demeaned himself very humbly, in his eagerness to get back the football, jumped up in a fury, and said—

"I made ample apologies to you for my carelessness, and now you have insulted and struck me. Ill-mannered ruffian! take back the ball,—I'll none of it;" and he drew his dirk, and cutting the football in two, threw it at Zempachi, and returned home.

But Zempachi, growing more and more angry, called one of his servants, and said to him—

"That fellow, Tsunéhei, has been most insolent: go next door and find out Shôzayémon, and tell him that I have ordered you to bring back Tsunéhei, that I may kill him."

So the servant went to deliver the message.

In the meantime Tsunéhei went back to his master's house; and when Shônosuké saw him, he said—

"Well, of course you have been ill treated; but did you get back the football?"

"When I went in, I made many apologies; but I was beaten, and kicked in the head, and treated with the greatest indignity. I would have killed that wretch, Zempachi, at once, but that I knew that, if I did so while I was yet a member of your household, I should bring trouble upon your family. For your sake I bore this ill-treatment patiently; but now I pray you let me take leave of you and become a Rônin, that I may be revenged upon this man."

"Think well what you are doing," answered Shônosuké. "After all, we have only lost a football; and my father will not care, nor upbraid us."

But Tsunéhei would not listen to him, and was bent upon wiping out the affront that he had received. As they were talking, the messenger arrived from Zempachi, demanding the surrender of Tsunéhei, on the ground that he had insulted him : to this Shônosuké replied that his father was away from home, and that in his absence he could do nothing.

At last Shôzayémon came home; and when he heard what had happened he was much grieved, and at a loss what to do, when a second messenger arrived from Zempachi, demanding that Tsunéhei should be given up without delay. Then Shôzayémon, seeing that the matter was serious, called the youth to him, and said—

"This Zempachi is heartless and cruel, and if you go to his house will assuredly kill you ; take, therefore, these fifty riyos, and fly to Osaka or Kiyôto, where you may safely set up in business."

"Sir," answered Tsunéhei, with tears of gratitude for his lord's kindness, "from my heart I thank you for your great goodness ; but I have been insulted and trampled upon, and, if I lay down my life in the attempt, I will repay Zempachi for what he has this day done."

"Well, then, since you needs must be revenged, go and fight, and may success attend you ! Still, as much depends upon the blade you carry, and I fear yours is likely to be but a sorry weapon, I will give you a sword ;" and with this he offered Tsunéhei his own.

"Nay, my lord," replied Tsunéhei; "I have a famous sword, by Rai Kunitoshi, which my father gave me. I have never shown it to your lordship, but I have it safely stowed away in my room."

When Shôzayémon saw and examined the sword, he admired it greatly, and said, "This is indeed a beautiful blade, and one on which you may rely. Take it, then, and bear yourself nobly in the fight; only remember that Zempachi is a cunning spearsman, and be sure to be very cautious."

So Tsunéhei, after thanking his lord for his manifold kindnesses, took an affectionate leave, and went to Zempachi's house, and said to the servant—

"It seems that your master wants to speak to me. Be so good as to take me to see him."

So the servant led him into the garden, where Zampachi, spear in hand, was waiting to kill him. When Zampachi saw him, he cried out—

"Ha! so you have come back; and now for your insolence, this day I mean to kill you with my own hand."

"Insolent yourself!" replied Tsunéhei. "Beast, and no Samurai! Come, let us see which of us is the better man."

Furiously incensed, Zempachi thrust with his spear at Tsunéhei; but he, trusting to his good sword, attacked Zempachi, who, cunning warrior as he was, could gain no advantage. At last Zempachi, losing his temper, began fighting less carefully, so that Tsunéhei found an opportunity of cutting the shaft of his spear. Zempachi then drew his sword, and two of his retainers came up to assist him; but Tsunéhei killed one of them, and wounded Zempachi in the forehead. The second retainer fled affrighted at the youth's valour, and Zempachi was blinded by the blood which flowed from the wound on his forehead. Then Tsunéhei said—

"To kill one who is as a blind man were unworthy a soldier. Wipe the blood from your eyes, Sir Zempachi, and let us fight it out fairly."

So Zempachi, wiping away his blood, bound a kerchief round his head, and fought again desperately. But at last the pain of his wound and the loss of blood overcame him, and Tsunéhei cut him down with a wound in the shoulder and easily despatched him.

Then Tsunéhei went and reported the whole matter to the Governor of Yedo, and was put in prison until an inquiry could be made. But the Chief Priest of Bandzuin, who had heard of the affair, went and told the governor all the bad deeds of Zempachi, and having procured Tsunéhei's pardon, took him home and employed him as porter in the temple. So Tsunéhei changed his name to Chôbei, and earned much respect in the neighbourhood, both for his talents and for his many good works. If any man were in distress, he would help him, heedless of his own advantage or danger, until men came to look up to him as to a father, and many youths joined him and became his apprentices. So he built a house at Hanakawado, in Asakusa, and lived there with his apprentices, whom he farmed out as spearsmen and footmen to the Daimios and Hatamotos, taking for himself the tithe of their earnings. But if any of them were sick or in trouble, Chôbei would nurse and support them, and provide physicians and medicine. And the fame of his goodness went abroad until his apprentices were more than two thousand men, and were employed in every part of the city. But as for Chôbei, the more he prospered, the more he gave in charity, and all men praised his good and generous heart.

This was the time when the Hatamotos had formed themselves into bands of Otokodaté,[1] of which Midzuno Jiurozayémon, Kondô Noborinosuké, and Abé Shirogorô were the chiefs. And the leagues of the nobles despised the leagues of the wardsmen, and treated them with scorn, and tried to put to shame Chôbei and his brave men ; but the nobles' weapons recoiled upon themselves, and, whenever they tried to bring contempt upon Chôbei, they themselves were brought to ridicule. So there was great hatred on both sides.

[1] See the story of Kazuma's Revenge.

One day, that Chôbei went to divert himself in a tea-house in the Yoshiwara, he saw a felt carpet spread in an upper room, which had been adorned as for some special occasion ; and he asked the master of the house what guest of distinction was expected. The landlord replied that my Lord Jiurozayémon, the chief of the Otokodaté of the Hatamotos, was due there that afternoon. On hearing this, Chôbei replied that as he much wished to meet my Lord Jiurozayémon, he would lie down and await his coming. The landlord was put out at this, and knew not what to say ; but yet he dare not thwart Chôbei, the powerful chief of the Otokodaté. So Chôbei took off his clothes and laid himself down upon the carpet. After a while my Lord Jiurozayémon arrived, and going upstairs found a man of large stature lying naked upon the carpet which had been spread for him.

"What low ruffian is this?" shouted he angrily to the landlord.

"My lord, it is Chôbei, the chief of the Otokodaté," answered the man, trembling.

Jiurozayémon at once suspected that Chôbei was doing this to insult him ; so he sat down by the side of the sleeping man, and lighting his pipe began to smoke. When he had finished his pipe, he emptied the burning ashes into Chôbei's navel ; but Chôbei, patiently bearing the pain, still feigned sleep. Ten times did Jiurozayémon fill his pipe,[1] and ten times he shook out the burning ashes on to Chôbei's navel ; but he neither stirred nor spoke. Then Jiurozayémon, astonished at his fortitude, shook him, and roused him, saying—

"Chôbei! Chôbei! wake up, man."

"What is the matter?" said Chôbei, rubbing his eyes as though he were awaking from a deep sleep ; then seeing Jiurozayémon, he pretended to be startled, and said, "Oh, my lord, I know not who you are ; but I have been very rude to

---

[1] The tiny Japanese pipe contains but two or three whiffs ; and as the tobacco is rolled up tightly in the fingers before it is inserted, the ash, when shaken out, is a little fire-ball from which a second pipe is lighted.

your lordship. I was overcome with wine, and fell asleep : I pray your lordship to forgive me."

"Is your name Chôbei?"

"Yes, my lord, at your service. A poor wardsman, and ignorant of good manners, I have been very rude; but I pray your lordship to excuse my ill-breeding."

"Nay, nay; we have all heard the fame of Chôbei, of Bandzuin, and I hold myself lucky to have met you this day. Let us be friends."

"It is a great honour for a humble wardsman to meet a nobleman face to face."

As they were speaking, the waitresses brought in fish and wine, and Jiurozayémon pressed Chôbei to feast with him; and thinking to annoy Chôbei, offered him a large wine-cup,[1] which, however, he drank without shrinking, and then returned to his entertainer, who was by no means so well able to bear the fumes of the wine. Then Jiurozayémon hit upon another device for annoying Chôbei, and, hoping to frighten him, said—

"Here, Chôbei, let me offer you some fish;" and with those words he drew his sword, and, picking up a cake of baked fish upon the point of it, thrust it towards the wardsman's mouth. Any ordinary man would have been afraid to accept the morsel so roughly offered ; but Chôbei simply opened his mouth, and taking the cake off the sword's point ate it without wincing. Whilst Jiurozayémon was wondering in his heart what manner of man this was, that nothing could daunt, Chôbei said to him—

"This meeting with your lordship has been an auspicious occasion to me, and I would fain ask leave to offer some humble gift to your lordship in memory of it.[2] Is there anything which your lordship would specially fancy?"

[1] It is an act of rudeness to offer a large wine-cup. As, however, the same cup is returned to the person who has offered it, the ill carries with it its own remedy. At a Japanese feast the same cup is passed from hand to hand, each person rinsing it in a bowl of water after using it, and before offering it to another.

[2] The giving of presents from inferiors to superiors is a common custom.

"I am very fond of cold maccaroni."

"Then I shall have the honour of ordering some for your lordship;" and with this Chôbei went downstairs, and calling one of his apprentices, named Tôken Gombei,[1] who was waiting for him, gave him a hundred riyos (about £28), and bade him collect all the cold maccaroni to be found in the neighbouring cook-shops and pile it up in front of the tea-house. So Gombei went home, and, collecting Chôbei's apprentices, sent them out in all directions to buy the maccaroni. Jiurozayémon all this while was thinking of the pleasure he would have in laughing at Chôbei for offering him a mean and paltry present; but when, by degrees, the maccaroni began to be piled mountain-high around the tea-house, he saw that he could not make a fool of Chôbei, and went home discomfited.

It has already been told how Shirai Gompachi was befriended and helped by Chôbei.[2] His name will occur again in this story.

At this time there lived in the province of Yamato a certain Daimio, called Honda Dainaiki, who one day, when surrounded by several of his retainers, produced a sword, and bade them look at it and say from what smith's workshop the blade had come.

"I think this must be a Masamuné blade," said one Fuwa Banzayémon.

"No," said Nagoya Sanza, after examining the weapon attentively, "this certainly is a Muramasa."[3]

---

[1] *Tôken*, a nickname given to Gombei, after a savage dog that he killed. As a Chônin, or wardsman, he had no surname.

[2] See the story of Gompachi and Komurasaki.

[3] The swords of Muramasa, although so finely tempered that they are said to cut hard iron as though it were a melon, have the reputation of being unlucky: they are supposed by the superstitious to hunger after taking men's lives, and to be unable to repose in their scabbard. The principal duty of a sword is to preserve tranquillity in the world, by punishing the wicked and protecting the good. But the bloodthirsty swords of Muramasa rather have the effect of maddening their owners, so that they either kill others indiscriminately or commit suicide. At the end of the sixteenth century Prince Tokugawa Iyéyasu was in the habit of carrying a spear made by Muramasa

A third Samurai, named Takagi Umanojô, pronounced it to be the work of Shidzu Kanenji; and as they could not agree, but each maintained his opinion, their lord sent for a famous connoisseur to decide the point; and the sword proved, as Sanza had said, to be a genuine Muramasa. Sanza was delighted at the verdict; but the other two went home rather crestfallen. Umanojô, although he had been worsted in the argument, bore no malice nor ill-will in his heart; but Banzayémon, who was a vain-glorious personage, puffed up with the idea of his own importance, conceived a spite against Sanza, and watched for an opportunity to put him to shame. At last, one day Banzayémon, eager to be revenged upon Sanza, went to the Prince, and said, "Your lordship ought to see Sanza fence; his swordsmanship is beyond all praise. I know that I am no match for him; still, if it will please your lordship, I will try a bout with him;" and the Prince, who was a mere stripling, and thought it would be rare sport, immediately sent for Sanza and desired he would fence with Banzayémon. So the two went out into the garden, and stood up facing each other, armed with wooden swords.

with which he often scratched or cut himself by mistake. Hence the Tokugawa family avoid girding on Muramasa blades, which are supposed to be specially unlucky to their race. The murders of Gompachi, who wore a sword by this maker, also contributed to give his weapons a bad name.

The swords of one Tôshirô Yoshimitsu, on the other hand, are specially auspicious to the Tokugawa family, for the following reason. After Iyéyasu had been defeated by Takéta Katsuyori, at the battle of the river Tenrin, he took refuge in the house of a village doctor, intending to put an end to his existence by *hara-kiri*, and drawing his dirk, which was made by Yoshimitsu, tried to plunge it into his belly, when, to his surprise, the blade turned. Thinking that the dirk must be a bad one, he took up an iron mortar for grinding medicines and tried it upon that, and the point entered and transfixed the mortar. He was about to stab himself a second time, when his followers, who had missed him, and had been searching for him everywhere, came up, and seeing their master about to kill himself, stayed his hand, and took away the dirk by force. Then they set him upon his horse, and compelled him to fly to his own province of Mikawa, whilst they kept his pursuers at bay. After this, when, by the favour of Heaven, Iyéyasu became Shogun, it was considered that of a surety there must have been a good spirit in the blade that refused to drink his blood; and ever since that time the blades of Yoshimitsu have been considered lucky in his family.

Now Banzayémon was proud of his skill, and thought he had no equal in fencing; so he expected to gain an easy victory over Sanza, and promised himself the luxury of giving his adversary a beating that should fully make up for the mortification which he had felt in the matter of the dispute about the sword. It happened, however, that he had undervalued the skill of Sanza, who, when he saw that his adversary was attacking him savagely and in good earnest, by a rapid blow struck Banzayémon so sharply on the wrist that he dropped the sword, and, before he could pick it up again, delivered a second cut on the shoulder, which sent him rolling over in the dust. All the officers present, seeing this, praised Sanza's skill, and Banzayémon, utterly stricken with shame, ran away home and hid himself.

After this affair Sanza rose high in the favour of his lord; and Banzayémon, who was more than ever jealous of him, feigned sickness, and stayed at home devising schemes for Sanza's ruin.

Now it happened that the Prince, wishing to have the Muramasa blade mounted, sent for Sanza and entrusted it to his care, ordering him to employ the most cunning workmen in the manufacture of the scabbard-hilt and ornaments; and Sanza, having received the blade, took it home, and put it carefully away. When Banzayémon heard of this, he was overjoyed; for he saw that his opportunity for revenge had come. He determined, if possible, to kill Sanza, but at any rate to steal the sword which had been committed to his care by the Prince, knowing full well that if Sanza lost the sword he and his family would be ruined. Being a single man, without wife or child, he sold his furniture, and, turning all his available property into money, made ready to fly the country. When his preparations were concluded, he went in the middle of the night to Sanza's house and tried to get in by stealth; but the doors and shutters were all carefully bolted from the inside, and there was no hole by which he could effect an entrance. All was still, however, and the people of the house were evidently fast asleep; so he climbed up to the second story, and, having contrived to unfasten a window, made his way in. With soft, cat-like footsteps he crept downstairs, and, looking into one of the rooms, saw Sanza and his wife sleeping on the mats, with their little son Kosanza, a boy of thirteen, curled up in his quilt between them. The light in the night-lamp was at its last flicker, but, peering through the gloom, he could just see the Prince's famous Muramasa sword lying on a sword-rack in the raised part of the room; so he crawled stealthily along until he could reach it, and stuck it in his girdle. Then, drawing near to Sanza, he bestrode his sleeping body, and, brandishing the sword, made a thrust at his throat; but in his excitement his hand shook, so that he missed his aim, and only scratched Sanza, who, waking with a start and trying to jump up, felt himself held down by a man standing over him. Stretching out his hands, he would have wrestled with his enemy; when Banzayémon, leaping back, kicked over the night-lamp, and throwing open the shutters, dashed into the garden. Snatching up his sword, Sanza rushed out after him; and his wife, having lit a lantern and armed herself with a halberd,[1] went out, with her son Kosanza, who carried a drawn dirk, to help her husband. Then Banzayémon, who was hiding in the shadow of a large pine-tree, seeing the lantern and dreading detection, seized a stone and hurled it at the light, and, chancing to strike it, put it out, and then scrambling over the fence unseen, fled into the darkness. When Sanza had searched all over the garden in vain, he returned to his room and examined his wound, which proving very slight, he began to look about to see whether the thief had carried off anything; but when his eye fell upon the place where the Muramasa sword had lain, he saw that it was gone. He hunted everywhere, but it was not to be found. The precious blade with which his Prince had entrusted him had

[1] The halberd is the special arm of the Japanese woman of gentle blood. That which was used by Kasa Gozen, one of the ladies of Yoshitsuné, the hero of the twelfth century, is still preserved at Asakusa. In old-fashioned families young ladies are regularly instructed in fencing with the halberds.

been stolen, and the blame would fall heavily upon him. Filled with grief and shame at the loss, Sanza and his wife and child remained in great anxiety until the morning broke, when he reported the matter to one of the Prince's councillors, and waited in seclusion until he should receive his lord's commands.

It soon became known that Banzayémon, who had fled the province, was the thief; and the councillors made their report accordingly to the Prince, who, although he expressed his detestation of the mean action of Banzayémon, could not absolve Sanza from blame, in that he had not taken better precautions to insure the safety of the sword that had been committed to his trust. It was decided, therefore, that Sanza should be dismissed from his service, and that his goods should be confiscated; with the proviso that should he be able to find Banzayémon, and recover the lost Muramasa blade, he should be restored to his former position. Sanza, who from the first had made up his mind that his punishment would be severe, accepted the decree without a murmur; and, having committed his wife and son to the care of his relations, prepared to leave the country as a Rônin and search for Banzayémon.

Before starting, however, he thought that he would go to his brother-officer, Takagi Umanojô, and consult with him as to what course he should pursue to gain his end. But this Umanojô, who was by nature a churlish fellow, answered him unkindly, and said—

"It is true that Banzayémon is a mean thief; but still it was through your carelessness that the sword was lost. It is of no avail your coming to me for help: you must get it back as best you may."

"Ah!" replied Sanza, "I see that you too bear me a grudge because I defeated you in the matter of the judgment of the sword. You are no better than Banzayémon yourself."

And his heart was bitter against his fellow-men, and he left the house determined to kill Umanojô first and afterwards to track out Banzayémon; so, pretending to start on his journey, he hid in an inn, and waited for an opportunity to attack Umanojô.

One day Umanojô, who was very fond of fishing, had taken his son Umanosuké, a lad of sixteen, down to the sea-shore with him; and as the two were enjoying themselves, all of a sudden they perceived a Samurai running towards them, and when he drew near they saw that it was Sanza. Umanojô, thinking that Sanza had come back in order to talk over some important matter, left his angling and went to meet him. Then Sanza cried out—

"Now, Sir Umanojô, draw and defend yourself. What! were you in league with Banzayémon to vent your spite upon me? Draw, sir, draw! You have spirited away your accomplice; but, at any rate, you are here yourself, and shall answer for your deed. It is no use playing the innocent; your astonished face shall not save you. Defend yourself, coward and traitor!" and with these words Sanza flourished his naked sword.

"Nay, Sir Sanza," replied the other, anxious by a soft answer to turn away his wrath; "I am innocent of this deed. Waste not your valour on so poor a cause."

"Lying knave!" said Sanza; "think not that you can impose upon me. I know your treacherous heart;" and, rushing upon Umanojô, he cut him on the forehead so that he fell in agony upon the sand.

Umanosuké in the meanwhile, who had been fishing at some distance from his father, rushed up when he saw him in this perilous situation and threw a stone at Sanza, hoping to distract his attention; but, before he could reach the spot, Sanza had delivered the death-blow, and Umanojô lay a corpse upon the beach.

"Stop, Sir Sanza—murderer of my father!" cried Umanosuké, drawing his sword, "stop and do battle with me, that I may avenge his death."

"That you should wish to slay your father's enemy," replied Sanza, "is but right and proper; and although I had just cause of quarrel with your father, and killed him, as a

Samurai should, yet would I gladly forfeit my life to you here; but my life is precious to me for one purpose—that I may punish Banzayémon and get back the stolen sword. When I shall have restored that sword to my lord, then will I give you your revenge, and you may kill me. A soldier's word is truth; but, as a pledge that I will fulfil my promise, I will give to you, as hostages, my wife and boy. Stay your avenging hand, I pray you, until my desire shall have been attained."

Umanosuké, who was a brave and honest youth, as famous in the clan for the goodness of his heart as for his skill in the use of arms, when he heard Sanza's humble petition, relented, and said—

"I agree to wait, and will take your wife and boy as hostages for your return."

"I humbly thank you," said Sanza. "When I shall have chastised Banzayémon, I will return, and you shall claim your revenge."

So Sanza went his way to Yedo to seek for Banzayémon, and Umanosuké mourned over his father's grave.

Now Banzayémon, when he arrived in Yedo, found himself friendless and without the means of earning his living, when by accident he heard of the fame of Chôbei of Bandzuin, the chief of the Otokodaté, to whom he applied for assistance; and having entered the fraternity, supported himself by giving fencing-lessons. He had been plying this trade for some time, and had earned some little reputation, when Sanza reached the city and began his search for him. But the days and months passed away, and, after a year's fruitless seeking, Sanza, who had spent all his money without obtaining a clue to the whereabouts of his enemy, was sorely perplexed, and was driven to live by his wits as a fortune-teller. Work as he would, it was a hard matter for him to gain the price of his daily food, and, in spite of all his pains, his revenge seemed as far off as ever, when he bethought him that the Yoshiwara was one of the most bustling places in the city, and that if he kept watch there, sooner or later he would be sure to fall in with Banzayémon. So he bought a hat of plaited bamboo, that completely covered his face, and lay in wait at the Yoshiwara.

One day Banzayémon and two of Chôbei's apprentices Tôken Gombei and Shirobei, who, from his wild and indocile nature, was surnamed "the Colt," were amusing themselves and drinking in an upper story of a tea-house in the Yoshiwara, when Tôken Gombei, happening to look down upon the street below, saw a Samurai pass by, poorly clad in worn-out old clothes, but whose poverty-stricken appearance contrasted with his proud and haughty bearing.

"Look there!" said Gombei, calling the attention of the others; "look at that Samurai. Dirty and ragged as his coat is, how easy it is to see that he is of noble birth! Let us wardsmen dress ourselves up in never so fine clothes, we could not look as he does."

"Ay," said Shirobei, "I wish we could make friends with him, and ask him up here to drink a cup of wine with us. However, it would not be seemly for us wardsmen to go and invite a person of his condition."

"We can easily get over that difficulty," said Banzayémon. "As I am a Samurai myself, there will be no impropriety in my going and saying a few civil words to him, and bringing him in."

The other two having joyfully accepted the offer, Banzayémon ran downstairs, and went up to the strange Samurai and saluted him, saying—

"I pray you to wait a moment, Sir Samurai. My name is Fuwa Banzayémon at your service. I am a Rônin, as I judge from your appearance that you are yourself. I hope you will not think me rude if I venture to ask you to honour me with your friendship, and to come into this tea-house to drink a cup of wine with me and two of my friends."

The strange Samurai, who was no other than Sanza, looking at the speaker through the interstices of his deep bamboo hat, and recognizing his enemy Banzayémon, gave a start of surprise, and, uncovering his head, said sternly—

"Have you forgotten my face, Banzayémon?"

For a moment Banzayémon was taken aback, but quickly recovering himself, he replied, "Ah! Sir Sanza, you may well be angry with me; but since I stole the Muramasa sword and fled to Yedo I have known no peace: I have been haunted by remorse for my crime. I shall not resist your vengeance: do with me as it shall seem best to you; or rather take my life, and let there be an end of this quarrel."

"Nay," answered Sanza, "to kill a man who repents him of his sins is a base and ignoble action. When you stole from me the Muramasa blade which had been confided to my care by my lord, I became a disgraced and ruined man. Give me back that sword, that I may lay it before my lord, and I will spare your life. I seek to slay no man needlessly."

"Sir Sanza, I thank you for your mercy. At this moment I have not the sword by me, but if you will go into yonder tea-house and wait awhile, I will fetch it and deliver it into your hands."

Sanza having consented to this, the two men entered the tea-house, where Banzayémon's two companions were waiting for them. But Banzayémon, ashamed of his own evil deed, still pretended that Sanza was a stranger, and introduced him as such, saying—

"Come, Sir Samurai, since we have the honour of your company, let me offer you a wine-cup."

Banzayémon and the two men pressed the wine-cup upon Sanza so often that the fumes gradually got into his head and he fell asleep; the two wardsmen, seeing this, went out for a walk, and Banzayémon, left alone with the sleeping man, began to revolve fresh plots against him in his mind. On a sudden, a thought struck him. Noiselessly seizing Sanza's sword, which he had laid aside on entering the room, he stole softly downstairs with it, and, carrying it into the back yard, pounded and blunted its edge with a stone, and having made it useless as a weapon, he replaced it in its scabbard, and running upstairs again laid it in its place without disturbing Sanza, who, little suspecting treachery, lay sleeping off the effects of the wine. At last, however, he awoke, and, ashamed at having been overcome by drink, he said to Banzayémon—

"Come, Banzayémon, we have dallied too long; give me the Muramasa sword, and let me go."

"Of course," replied the other, sneeringly, "I am longing to give it back to you; but unfortunately, in my poverty, I have been obliged to pawn it for fifty ounces of silver. If you have so much money about you, give it to me and I will return the sword to you."

"Wretch!" cried Sanza, seeing that Banzayémon was trying to fool him, "have I not had enough of your vile tricks? At any rate, if I cannot get back the sword, your head shall be laid before my lord in its place. Come," added he, stamping his foot impatiently, "defend yourself."

"With all my heart. But not here in this tea-house. Let us go to the Mound, and fight it out."

"Agreed! There is no need for us to bring trouble on the landlord. Come to the Mound of the Yoshiwara."

So they went to the Mound, and drawing their swords, began to fight furiously. As the news soon spread abroad through the Yoshiwara that a duel was being fought upon the Mound, the people flocked out to see the sight; and among them came Tôken Gombei and Shirobei, Banzayémon's companions, who, when they saw that the combatants were their own friend and the strange Samurai, tried to interfere and stop the fight, but, being hindered by the thickness of the crowd, remained as spectators. The two men fought desperately, each driven by fierce rage against the other; but Sanza, who was by far the better fencer of the two, once, twice, and again dealt blows which should have cut Banzayémon down, and yet no blood came forth. Sanza, astonished at this, put forth all his strength, and fought so skilfully, that all the bystanders applauded him, and Banzayémon, though he knew his adversary's sword to be blunted, was so terrified that he stumbled and fell. Sanza, brave soldier that he was, scorned to strike a fallen foe, and bade him rise and fight again. So they engaged again, and Sanza, who from the beginning had had the advantage, slipped and fell in his turn; Banzayémon, forgetting the mercy which had been shown to him, rushed up, with bloodthirsty joy glaring in his eyes, and stabbed Sanza in the side as he lay on the ground. Faint as he was, he could not lift his hand to save himself; and his craven foe was about to strike him again, when the bystanders all cried shame upon his baseness. Then Gombei and Shirobei lifted up their voices and said—

"Hold, coward! Have you forgotten how your own life was spared but a moment since? Beast of a Samurai, we have been your friends hitherto, but now behold in us the avengers of this brave man."

With these words the two men drew their dirks, and the spectators fell back as they rushed in upon Banzayémon, who, terror-stricken by their fierce looks and words, fled without having dealt the deathblow to Sanza. They tried to pursue him, but he made good his escape, so the two men returned to help the wounded man. When he came to himself by dint of their kind treatment, they spoke to him and comforted him, and asked him what province he came from, that they might write to his friends and tell them what had befallen him. Sanza, in a voice faint from pain and loss of blood, told them his name and the story of the stolen sword, and of his enmity against Banzayémon. "But," said he, "just now, when I was fighting, I struck Banzayémon more than once, and without effect. How could that have been?" Then they looked at his sword, which had fallen by his side, and saw that the edge was all broken away. More than ever they felt indignant at the baseness of Banzayémon's heart, and redoubled their kindness to Sanza; but, in spite of all their efforts, he grew weaker and weaker, until at last his breathing ceased altogether. So they buried the corpse honourably in an adjoining temple, and wrote to Sanza's wife and son, describing to them the manner of his death.

Now when Sanza's wife, who had long been anxiously expecting her husband's return, opened the letter and learned the cruel circumstances of his death, she and her son Kosanza mourned bitterly over his loss. Then Kosanza, who was now fourteen years old, said to his mother—

"Take comfort, mother; for I will go to Yedo and seek out this Banzayémon, my father's murderer, and I will surely avenge his death. Now, therefore, make ready all that I need for this journey."

And as they were consulting over the manner of their revenge, Umanosuké, the son of Umanojô, whom Sanza had slain, having heard of the death of his father's enemy, came to the house. But he came with no hostile intent. True, Sanza had killed his father, but the widow and the orphan were guiltless, and he bore them no ill-will; on the contrary, he felt that Banzayémon was their common enemy. It was he who by his evil deeds had been the cause of all the mischief that had arisen, and now again, by murdering Sanza, he had robbed Umanosuké of his revenge. In this spirit he said to Kosanza—

"Sir Kosanza, I hear that your father has been cruelly murdered by Banzayémon at Yedo. I know that you will avenge the death of your father, as the son of a soldier should: if, therefore, you will accept my poor services, I will be your second, and will help you to the best of my ability. Banzayémon shall be my enemy, as he is yours."

"Nay, Sir Umanosuké, although I thank you from my heart, I cannot accept this favour at your hands. My father Sanza slew your noble father: that you should requite this misfortune thus is more than kind, but I cannot think of suffering you to risk your life on my behalf."

"Listen to me," replied Umanosuké, smiling, "and you will think it less strange that I should offer to help you. Last year, when my father lay a bleeding corpse on the sea-shore, your father made a covenant with me that he would return to give me my revenge, so soon as he should have regained the stolen sword. Banzayémon, by murdering him on the Mound of the Yoshiwara, has thwarted me in this; and now upon whom can I avenge my father's death but upon him whose baseness was indeed its cause? Now, therefore, I am determined to go with you to Yedo, and not before the murders of our two fathers shall have been fully atoned for will we return to our own country."

When Kosanza heard this generous speech, he could not conceal his admiration; and the widow, prostrating herself at Umanosuké's feet, shed tears of gratitude.

The two youths, having agreed to stand by one another, made all ready for their journey, and obtained leave from their prince to go in search of the traitor Banzayémon. They reached Yedo without meeting with any adventures, and, taking up their abode at a cheap inn, began to make their inquiries; but, although they sought far and wide, they could learn no tidings of their enemy. When three months had passed thus, Kosanza began to grow faint-hearted at their repeated failures; but Umanosuké supported and comforted him, urging him to fresh efforts. But soon a great misfortune befell them : Kosanza fell sick with ophthalmia, and neither the tender nursing of his friend, nor the drugs and doctors upon whom Umanosuké spent all their money, had any effect on the suffering boy, who soon became stone blind. Friendless and penniless, the one deprived of his eyesight and only a clog upon the other, the two youths were thrown upon their own resources. Then Umanosuké, reduced to the last extremity of distress, was forced to lead out Kosanza to Asakusa to beg sitting by the roadside, whilst he himself, wandering hither and thither, picked up what he could from the charity of those who saw his wretched plight. But all this while he never lost sight of his revenge, and almost thanked the chance which had made him a beggar, for the opportunity which it gave him of hunting out strange and hidden haunts of vagabond life into which in his more prosperous condition he could not have penetrated. So he walked to and fro through the city, leaning on a stout staff, in which he had hidden his sword, waiting patiently for fortune to bring him face to face with Banzayémon.

Now Banzayémon, after he had killed Sanza on the Mound of the Yoshiwara, did not dare to show his face again in the house of Chôbei, the Father of the Otokodaté; for he knew that the two men, Tôken Gombei and Shirobei "the loose Colt," would not only bear an evil report of him, but would even kill him if he fell into their hands, so great had been their indignation at his cowardly conduct; so he entered a company of mountebanks, and earned his living by showing tricks of swordsmanship, and selling tooth-powder at the Okuyama, at Asakusa.[1] One day, as he was going towards Asakusa to ply his trade, he caught sight of a blind beggar, in whom, in spite of his poverty-stricken and altered appearance, he recognized the son of his enemy. Rightly he judged that, in spite of the boy's apparently helpless condition, the discovery boded no weal for him; so mounting to the upper story of a tea-house hard by, he watched to see who should come to Kosanza's assistance. Nor had he to wait long, for presently he saw a second beggar come up and speak words of encouragement and kindness to the blind youth; and looking attentively, he saw that the new-comer was Umanosuké. Having thus discovered who was on his track, he went home and sought means of killing the two beggars; so he lay in wait and traced them to the poor hut where they dwelt, and one night, when he knew Umanosuké to be absent, he crept in. Kosanza, being blind, thought that the footsteps were those of Umanosuké, and jumped up to welcome him; but he, in his heartless cruelty, which not even the boy's piteous state could move, slew Kosanza as he helplessly stretched out his hands to feel for his friend. The deed was yet unfinished when Umanosuké returned, and, hearing a scuffle inside the hut, drew the sword which was hidden in his staff and rushed in; but Banzayémon, profiting by the darkness, eluded him and fled from the hut. Umanosuké followed swiftly after him; but just as he was on the point of catching him, Banzayémon, making a sweep backwards with his drawn sword, wounded Umanosuké in the thigh, so that he stumbled and fell, and the murderer, swift of foot, made good his escape. The wounded youth tried to pursue him again, but being compelled by the

[1] See Note at end of story.

TRICKS OF SWORDSMANSHIP AT ASAKUSA

pain of his wound to desist, returned home and found his blind companion lying dead, weltering in his own blood. Cursing his unhappy fate, he called in the beggars of the fraternity to which he belonged, and between them they buried Kosanza, and he himself being too poor to procure a surgeon's aid, or to buy healing medicaments for his wound, became a cripple.

It was at this time that Shirai Gompachi, who was living under the protection of Chôbei, the Father of the Otokodaté, was in love with Komurasaki, the beautiful courtesan who lived at the sign of the Three Sea-shores, in the Yoshiwara. He had long exhausted the scanty supplies which he possessed, and was now in the habit of feeding his purse by murder and robbery, that he might have means to pursue his wild and extravagant life. One night, when he was out on his cut-throat business, his fellows, who had long suspected that he was after no good, sent one of their number, named Seibei, to watch him. Gompachi, little dreaming that any one was following him, swaggered along the street until he fell in with a wardsman, whom he cut down and robbed; but the booty proving small, he waited for a second chance, and, seeing a light moving in the distance, hid himself in the shadow of a large tub for catching rain-water till the bearer of the lantern should come up. When the man drew near, Gompachi saw that he was dressed as a traveller, and wore a long dirk; so he sprung out from his lurking-place and made to kill him; but the traveller nimbly jumped on one side, and proved no mean adversary, for he drew his dirk and fought stoutly for his life. However, he was no match for so skilful a swordsman as Gompachi, who, after a sharp struggle, despatched him, and carried off his purse, which contained two hundred riyos. Overjoyed at having found so rich a prize, Gompachi was making off for the Yoshiwara, when Seibei, who, horror-stricken, had seen both murders, came up and began to upbraid him for his wickedness. But Gompachi was so smooth-spoken and so well liked by his comrades, that he easily persuaded Seibei to hush the matter up, and accompany him to the Yoshiwara for a little diversion. As they were talking by the way, Seibei said to Gompachi—

"I bought a new dirk the other day, but I have not had an opportunity to try it yet. You have had so much experience in swords that you ought to be a good judge. Pray look at this dirk, and tell me whether you think it good for anything."

"We'll soon see what sort of metal it is made of," answered Gompachi. "We'll just try it on the first beggar we come across."

At first Seibei was horrified by this cruel proposal, but by degrees he yielded to his companion's persuasions; and so they went on their way until Seibei spied out a crippled beggar lying asleep on the bank outside the Yoshiwara. The sound of their footsteps aroused the beggar, who seeing a Samurai and a wardsman pointing at him, and evidently speaking about him, thought that their consultation could bode him no good. So he pretended to be still asleep, watching them carefully all the while; and when Seibei went up to him, brandishing his dirk, the beggar, avoiding the blow, seized Seibei's arm, and twisting it round, flung him into the ditch below. Gompachi, seeing his companion's discomfiture, attacked the beggar, who, drawing a sword from his staff, made such lightning-swift passes that, crippled though he was, and unable to move his legs freely, Gompachi could not overpower him; and although Seibei crawled out of the ditch and came to his assistance, the beggar, nothing daunted, dealt his blows about him to such good purpose that he wounded Seibei in the temple and arm. Then Gompachi, reflecting that after all he had no quarrel with the beggar, and that he had better attend to Seibei's wounds than go on fighting to no purpose, drew Seibei away, leaving the beggar, who was too lame to follow them, in peace. When he examined Seibei's wounds, he found that they were so severe that they must give up their night's frolic and go home. So they went back to the house of Chôbei, the Father of the Otokodaté.

and Seibei, afraid to show himself with his sword-cuts, feigned sickness, and went to bed. On the following morning Chôbei, happening to need his apprentice Seibei's services, sent for him, and was told that he was sick; so he went to the room, where he lay abed, and, to his astonishment, saw the cut upon his temple. At first the wounded man refused to answer any questions as to how he had been hurt; but at last, on being pressed by Chôbei, he told the whole story of what had taken place the night before. When Chôbei heard the tale, he guessed that the valiant beggar must be some noble Samurai in disguise, who, having a wrong to avenge, was biding his time to meet with his enemy; and wishing to help so brave a man, he went in the evening, with his two faithful apprentices, Tôken Gombei and Shirobei "the loose Colt," to the bank outside the Yoshiwara to seek out the beggar. The latter, not one whit frightened by the adventure of the previous night, had taken his place as usual, and was lying on the bank, when Chôbei came up to him, and said—

"Sir, I am Chôbei, the chief of the Otokodaté, at your service. I have learnt with deep regret that two of my men insulted and attacked you last night. However, happily, even Gompachi, famous swordsman though he be, was no match for you, and had to beat a retreat before you. I know, therefore, that you must be a noble Samurai, who by some ill chance have become a cripple and a beggar. Now, therefore, I pray you tell me all your story; for, humble wardsman as I am, I may be able to assist you, if you will condescend to allow me."

The cripple at first tried to shun Chôbei's questions; but at last, touched by the honesty and kindness of his speech, he replied—

"Sir, my name is Takagi Umanosuké, and I am a native of Yamato;" and then he went on to narrate all the misfortunes which the wickedness of Banzayémon had brought about.

"This is indeed a strange story," said Chôbei, who had

listened with indignation. "This Banzayémon, before I knew the blackness of his heart, was once under my protection. But after he murdered Sanza, hard by here, he was pursued by these two apprentices of mine, and since that day he has been no more to my house."

When he had introduced the two apprentices to Umanosuké, Chôbei pulled forth a suit of silk clothes befitting a gentleman, and having made the crippled youth lay aside his beggar's raiment, led him to a bath, and had his hair dressed. Then he bade Tôken Gombei lodge him and take charge of him, and, having sent for a famous physician, caused Umanosuké to undergo careful treatment for the wound in his thigh. In the course of two months the pain had almost disappeared, so that he could stand easily; and when, after another month, he could walk about a little, Chôbei removed him to his own house, pretending to his wife and apprentices that he was one of his own relations who had come on a visit to him.

After a while, when Umanosuké had become quite cured, he went one day to worship at a famous temple, and on his way home after dark he was overtaken by a shower of rain, and took shelter under the eaves of a house, in a part of the city called Yanagiwara, waiting for the sky to clear. Now it happened that this same night Gompachi had gone out on one of his bloody expeditions, to which his poverty and his love for Komurasaki drove him in spite of himself, and, seeing a Samurai standing in the gloom, he sprang upon him before he had recognized Umanosuké, whom he knew as a friend of his patron Chôbei. Umanosuké drew and defended himself, and soon contrived to slash Gompachi on the forehead; so that the latter, seeing himself overmatched, fled under the cover of the night. Umanosuké, fearing to hurt his recently healed wound, did not give chase, and went quietly back to Chôbei's house. When Gompachi returned home, he hatched a story to deceive Chôbei as to the cause of the wound on his forehead. Chôbei, however, having overheard Umanosuké reproving Gompachi for his wickedness, soon became aware of the truth; and not caring to keep a robber and murderer near him, gave Gompachi a present of money, and bade him return to his house no more.

And now Chôbei, seeing that Umanosuké had recovered his strength, divided his apprentices into bands, to hunt out Banzayémon, in order that the vendetta might be accomplished. It soon was reported to him that Banzayémon was earning his living among the mountebanks of Asakusa; so Chôbei communicated this intelligence to Umanosuké, who made his preparations accordingly; and on the following morning the two went to Asakusa, where Banzayémon was astonishing a crowd of country boors by exhibiting tricks with his sword.

Then Umanosuké, striding through the gaping rabble, shouted out—

"False, murderous coward, your day has come! I, Umanosuké, the son of Umanojô, have come to demand vengeance for the death of three innocent men who have perished by your treachery. If you are a man, defend yourself. This day shall your soul see hell!"

With these words he rushed furiously upon Banzayémon, who, seeing escape to be impossible, stood upon his guard. But his coward's heart quailed before the avenger, and he soon lay bleeding at his enemy's feet.

But who shall say how Umanosuké thanked Chôbei for his assistance; or how, when he had returned to his own country, he treasured up his gratitude in his heart, looking upon Chôbei as more than a second father?

Thus did Chôbei use his power to punish the wicked, and to reward the good—giving of his abundance to the poor, and succouring the unfortunate, so that his name was honoured far and near. It remains only to record the tragical manner of his death.

We have already told how my lord Midzuno Jiurozayémon, the chief of the associated nobles, had been foiled in his attempts to bring shame upon Chôbei, the Father of the Otokodaté; and how, on the contrary, the latter, by his ready wit, never failed to make the proud noble's weapons recoil upon him. The failure of these attempts rankled in the breast of Jiurozayémon, who hated Chôbei with an intense hatred, and sought to be revenged upon him. One day he sent a retainer to Chôbei's house with a message to the effect that on the following day my lord Jiurozayémon would be glad to see Chôbei at his house, and to offer him a cup of wine, in return for the cold maccaroni with which his lordship had been feasted some time since. Chôbei immediately suspected that in sending this friendly summons the cunning noble was hiding a dagger in a smile; however, he knew that if he stayed away out of fear he would be branded as a coward, and made a laughing-stock for fools to jeer .at. Not caring that Jiurozayémon should succeed in his desire to put him to shame, he sent for his favourite apprentice, Tôken Gombei, and said to him—

"I have been invited to a drinking-bout by Midzuno Jiurozayémon. I know full well that this is but a stratagem to requite me for having fooled him, and maybe his hatred will go the length of killing me. However, I shall go and take my chance; and if I detect any sign of foul play, I'll try to serve the world by ridding it of a tyrant, who passes his life in oppressing the helpless farmers and wardsmen. Now as, even if I succeed in killing him in his own house, my life must pay forfeit for the deed, do you come to-morrow night with a burying-tub,[1] and fetch my corpse from this Jiurozayémon's house."

Tôken Gombei, when he heard the "Father" speak thus, was horrified, and tried to dissuade him from obeying the

[1] The lowest classes in Japan are buried in a squatting position, in a sort of barrel. One would have expected a person of Chôbei's condition and means to have ordered a square box. It is a mistake to suppose the burning of the dead to be universal in Japan: only about thirty per cent. of the lower classes, chiefly belonging to the Montô sect of Buddhism, are burnt. The rich and noble are buried in several square coffins, one inside the other, in a sitting position; and their bodies are partially preserved from decay by filling the nose, ears, and mouth with vermilion. In the case of the very wealthy, the coffin is completely filled in with vermilion. The family of the Princes of Mito, and some other nobles, bury their dead in a recumbent position.

invitation. But Chôbei's mind was fixed, and, without heeding Gombei's remonstrances, he proceeded to give instructions as to the disposal of his property after his death, and to settle all his earthly affairs.

On the following day, towards noon, he made ready to go to Jiurozayémon's house, bidding one of his apprentices precede him with a complimentary present.[1] Jiurozayémon, who was waiting with impatience for Chôbei to come, so soon as he heard of his arrival ordered his retainers to usher him into his presence; and Chôbei, having bade his apprentices without fail to come and fetch him that night, went into the house.

No sooner had he reached the room next to that in which Jiurozayémon was sitting than he saw that his suspicions of treachery were well founded; for two men with drawn swords rushed upon him, and tried to cut him down. Deftly avoiding their blows, however, he tripped up the one, and kicking the other in the ribs, sent him reeling and breathless against the wall; then, as calmly as if nothing had happened, he presented himself before Jiurozayémon, who, peeping through a chink in the sliding-doors, had watched his retainers' failure.

"Welcome, welcome, Master Chôbei," said he. " I always had heard that you were a man of mettle, and I wanted to see what stuff you were made of; so I bade my retainers put your courage to the test. That was a masterly throw of yours. Well, you must excuse this churlish reception : come and sit down by me."

"Pray do not mention it, my lord," said Chôbei, smiling rather scornfully. " I know that my poor skill is not to be measured with that of a noble Samurai; and if these two good gentlemen had the worst of it just now, it was mere luck—that's all."

So, after the usual compliments had been exchanged, Chôbei sat down by Jiurozayémon, and the attendants

[1] It is customary, on the occasion of a first visit to a house to carry a present to the owner, who gives something of equal value on returning the visit.

brought in wine and condiments. Before they began to drink, however, Jiurozayémon said—

"You must be tired and exhausted with your walk this hot day, Master Chôbei. I thought that perhaps a bath might refresh you, so I ordered my men to get it ready for you. Would you not like to bathe and make yourself comfortable ?"

Chôbei suspected that this was a trick to strip him, and take him unawares when he should have laid aside his dirk. However, he answered cheerfully—

"Your lordship is very good. I shall be glad to avail myself of your kind offer. Pray excuse me for a few moments."

So he went to the bath-room, and, leaving his clothes outside, he got into the bath, with the full conviction that it would be the place of his death. Yet he never trembled nor quailed, determined that, if he needs must die, no man should say he had been a coward. Then Jiurozayémon, calling to his attendants, said—

"Quick ! lock the door of the bath-room ! We hold him fast now. If he gets out, more than one life will pay the price of his. He's a match for any six of you in fair fight. Lock the door, I say, and light up the fire under the bath ;[1] and we'll boil him to death, and be rid of him. Quick, men, quick !"

So they locked the door, and fed the fire until the water hissed and bubbled within ; and Chôbei, in his agony, tried to burst open the door, but Jiurozayémon ordered his men to thrust their spears through the partition wall and despatch him. Two of the spears Chôbei clutched and broke short off ; but at last he was struck by a mortal blow under the ribs, and died a brave man by the hands of cowards.

That evening Tôken Gombei, who, to the astonishment of

[1] This sort of bath, in which the water is heated by the fire of a furnace, which is lighted from outside, is called Goyémon-buro, or *Goyémon's bath,* after a notorious robber named Goyémon, who attempted the life of Taiko Sama, the famous general and ruler of the sixteenth century, and suffered for his crimes by being boiled to death in oil—a form of execution which is now obsolete.

THE DEATH OF CHÔBEI OF BANDZUIN

Chôbei's wife, had bought a burying-tub, came, with seven other apprentices, to fetch the Father of the Otokodaté from Jiurozayémon's house; and when the retainers saw them, they mocked at them, and said—

"What, have you come to fetch your drunken master home in a litter?"

"Nay," answered Gombei, "but we have brought a coffin for his dead body, as he bade us."

When the retainers heard this, they marvelled at the courage of Chôbei, who had thus wittingly come to meet his fate. So Chôbei's corpse was placed in the burying-tub, and handed over to his apprentices, who swore to avenge his death. Far and wide, the poor and friendless mourned for this good man. His son Chômatsu inherited his property; and his wife remained a faithful widow until her dying day, praying that she might sit with him in paradise upon the cup of the same lotus-flower.

Many a time did the apprentices of Chôbei meet together to avenge him; but Jiurozayémon eluded all their efforts, until, having been imprisoned by the Government in the temple called Kanyeiji, at Uyéno, as is related in the story of "Kazuma's Revenge," he was placed beyond the reach of their hatred.

So lived and so died Chôbei of Bandzuin, the Father of the Otokodaté of Yedo.

NOTE ON ASAKUSA

Translated from a native book called the "Yedo Hanjôki," or Guide to the prosperous City of Yedo, and other sources.

ASAKUSA is the most bustling place in all Yedo. It is famous for the Temple Sensôji, on the hill of Kinriu, or the Golden Dragon, which from morning till night is thronged with visitors, rich and poor, old and young, flocking in sleeve to sleeve. The origin of the temple was as follows:—In the days of the Emperor Suiko, who reigned in the thirteenth century A.D., a certain noble, named Hashi no Nakatomo, fell into disgrace and left the Court; and having become a Rônin, or masterless man, he took up his abode on the Golden Dragon Hill, with two retainers, being brothers, named Hinokuma Hamanari and Hinokuma Takénari. These three men being reduced to great straits, and without means of earning their living, became fishermen. Now it happened that on the 6th day of the 3rd month of the 36th year of the reign of the Emperor Suiko (A.D. 1241), they went down in the morning to the Asakusa River to ply their trade; and having cast their nets took no fish, but at every throw they pulled up a figure of the Buddhist god Kwannon, which they threw into the river again. They sculled their boat away to another spot, but the same luck followed them, and nothing came to their nets save the figure of Kwannon. Struck by the miracle, they carried home the image, and, after fervent prayer, built a temple on the Golden Dragon Hill, in which they enshrined it. The temple thus founded was enriched by the benefactions of wealthy and pious persons, whose care raised its buildings to the dignity of the first temple in Yedo. Tradition says that the figure of Kwannon which was fished up in the net was one inch and eight-tenths in height.

The main hall of the temple is sixty feet square, and is adorned with much curious workmanship of gilding and of silvering, so that no place can be more excellently beautiful. There are two gates in front of it. The first is called the Gate of the Spirits of the Wind and of the Thunder, and is adorned with figures of those two gods. The Wind-god, whose likeness is that of a devil, carries the wind-bag; and the Thunder-god, who is also shaped like a devil, carries a drum and a drumstick.[1] The second gate is called the Gate of the gods Niô, or the Two Princes, whose colossal statues, painted red, and hideous to look upon, stand on either side of it. Between the gates is an approach four hundred yards in length, which is occupied by the stalls of hucksters, who sell toys and trifles for women and children, and by foul and loathsome beggars. Passing through the gate of the gods Niô, the main hall of the temple strikes the eye. Countless niches and shrines of the gods stand outside it, and an old woman earns her livelihood at a tank filled with water, to which the votaries of the gods come and wash themselves that they may pray with clean hands. Inside are the

---

[1] This gate was destroyed by fire a few years since.

images of the gods, lanterns, incense-burners, candlesticks, a huge money-box, into which the offerings of the pious are thrown, and votive tablets [1] representing the famous gods and goddesses, heroes and heroines, of old. Behind the chief building is a broad space called the *okuyama*, where young and pretty waitresses, well dressed and painted, invite the weary pilgrims and holiday-makers to refresh themselves with tea and sweetmeats. Here, too, are all sorts of sights to be seen, such as wild beasts, performing monkeys, automata, conjurers, wooden and paper figures, which take the place of the waxworks of the West, acrobats, and jesters for the amusement of women and children. Altogether it is a lively and a joyous scene ; there is not its equal in the city.

At Asakusa, as indeed all over Yedo, are to be found fortune-tellers, who prey upon the folly of the superstitious. With a treatise on physiognomy laid on a desk before them, they call out to this man that he has an ill-omened forehead, and to that man that the space between his nose and his lips is unlucky. Their tongues wag like flowing water until the passers-by are attracted to their stalls. If the seer finds a customer, he closes his eyes, and, lifting the divining-sticks reverently to his forehead, mutters incantations between his teeth. Then, suddenly parting the sticks in two bundles, he prophesies good or evil, according to the number in each. With a magnifying-glass he examines his dupe's face and the palms of his hands. By the fashion of his clothes and his general manner the prophet sees whether he is a countryman or from the city. "I am afraid, sir," says he, "you have not been altogether fortunate in life, but I foresee that great luck awaits you in two or three months ;" or, like a clumsy doctor who makes his diagnosis according to his patient's fancies, if he sees his customer frowning and anxious, he adds, "Alas ! in seven or eight months you must beware of great misfortune. But I cannot tell you all about it for a

[1] Sir Rutherford Alcock, in his book upon Japan, states that the portraits of the most famous courtesans of Yedo are yearly hung up in the temple at Asakusa. No such pictures are to be seen now, and no Japanese of whom I have made inquiries have heard of such a custom. The priests of the temple deny that their fane was ever so polluted, and it is probable that the statement is but one of the many strange mistakes into which an imperfect knowledge of the language led the earlier travellers in Japan. In spite of all that has been said by persons who have had no opportunity of associating and exchanging ideas with the educated men of Japan, I maintain that in no country is the public harlot more abhorred and looked down upon.

slight fee : " with a long sigh he lays down the divining-sticks on the desk, and the frightened boor pays a further fee to hear the sum of the misfortune which threatens him, until, with three feet of bamboo slips and three inches of tongue, the clever rascal has made the poor fool turn his purse inside out.

The class of diviners called *Ichiko* profess to give tidings of the dead, or of those who have gone to distant countries. The Ichiko exactly corresponds to the spirit medium of the West. The trade is followed by women, of from fifteen or sixteen to some fifty years of age, who walk about the streets, carrying on their backs a divining-box about a foot square ; they have no shop or stall, but wander about, and are invited into their customers' houses. The ceremony of divination is very simple. A porcelain bowl filled with water is placed upon a tray, and the customer, having written the name of the person with whom he wishes to hold communion on a long slip of paper, rolls it into a spill, which he dips into the water, and thrice sprinkles the Ichiko, or medium. She, resting her elbow upon her divining-box, and leaning her head upon her hand, mutters prayers and incantations until she has summoned the soul of the dead or absent person, which takes possession of her, and answers questions through her mouth. The prophecies which the Ichiko utters during her trance are held in high esteem by the superstitious and vulgar.

Hard by Asakusa is the theatre street. The theatres are called *Shiba-i*,[1] "turf places," from the fact that the first theatrical performances were held on a turf plot. The origin of the drama in Japan, as elsewhere, was religious. In the reign of the Emperor Heijô (A.D. 805), there was a sudden volcanic depression of the earth close by a pond called Sarusawa, or the Monkey's Marsh, at Nara, in the province of Yamato, and a poisonous smoke issuing from the cavity struck down with sickness all those who came within its baneful influence; so the people brought quantities of firewood, which they burnt in order that the poisonous vapour might be dispelled. The fire, being the male influence, would assimilate with and act as an antidote upon the mephitic smoke, which was a

[1] In Dr. Hepburn's Dictionary of the Japanese language, the Chinese characters given for the word *Shiba-i* are *chi chang* (*keih chang*, Morrison's Dictionary), "theatrical arena." The characters which are usually written, and which are etymologically correct, are *chih chü* (*che keu*, Morrison), "the place of plants or turf-plot."

female influence.[1] Besides this, as a further charm to exorcise the portent, the dance called Sambasô, which is still performed as a prelude to theatrical exhibitions by an actor dressed up as a venerable old man, emblematic of long life and felicity, was danced on a plot of turf in front of the Temple Kofukuji. By these means the smoke was dispelled, and the drama was originated. The story is to be found in the *Zoku Nihon Ki*, or supplementary history of Japan.

Three centuries later, during the reign of the Emperor Toba (A.D. 1108), there lived a woman called Iso no Zenji, who is looked upon as the mother of the Japanese drama. Her performances, however, seem only to have consisted in dancing or posturing dressed up in the costume of the nobles of the Court, from which fact her dance was called Otoko-mai, or the man's dance. Her name is only worth mentioning on account of the respect in which her memory is held by actors.

It was not until the year 1624 A.D. that a man named Saruwaka Kanzaburô, at the command of the Shogun, opened the first theatre in Yedo in the Nakabashi, or Middle Bridge Street, where it remained until eight years later, when it was removed to the Ningiyô, or Doll Street. The company of this theatre was formed by two families named Miako and Ichimura, who did not long enjoy their monopoly, for in the year 1644 we find a third family, that of Yamamura, setting up a rival theatre in the Kobiki, or Sawyer Street.

In the year 1651, the Asiatic prejudice in favour of keeping persons of one calling in one place exhibited itself by the removal of the play-houses to their present site, and the street was called the Saruwaka Street, after Saruwaka Kanzaburo, the founder of the drama in Yedo.

Theatrical performances go on from six in the morning until six in the evening. Just as the day is about to dawn in the east, the sound of the drum is heard, and the dance Sambasô is danced as a prelude, and after this follow the dances of the famous actors of old ; these are called the extra performances (*waki kiyôgen*).

The dance of Nakamura represents the demon Shudendôji, an ogre who was destroyed by the hero Yorimitsu according to the

[1] This refers to the Chinese doctrine of the Yang and Yin, the male and female influences pervading all creation.

following legend :—At the beginning of the eleventh century, when Ichijô the Second was Emperor, lived the hero Yorimitsu. Now it came to pass that in those days the people of Kiyôto were sorely troubled by an evil spirit, which took up its abode near the Rashô gate. One night, as Yorimitsu was making merry with his retainers, he said, "Who dares go and defy the demon of the Rashô gate, and set up a token that he has been there ?" "That dare I," answered Tsuna, who, having donned his coat of mail, mounted his horse, and rode out through the dark bleak night to the Rashô gate. Having written his name upon the gate, he was about to turn homewards when his horse began to shiver with fear, and a huge hand coming forth from the gate seized the back of the knight's helmet. Tsuna, nothing daunted, struggled to get free, but in vain, so drawing his sword he cut off the demon's arm, and the spirit with a howl fled into the night. But Tsuna carried home the arm in triumph, and locked it up in a box. One night the demon, having taken the shape of Tsuna's aunt, came to him and said, "I pray thee show me the arm of the fiend." Tsuna answered, "I have shown it to no man, and yet to thee I will show it." So he brought forth the box and opened it, when suddenly a black cloud shrouded the figure of the supposed aunt, and the demon, having regained its arm, disappeared. From that time forth the people were more than ever troubled by the demon, who carried off to the hills all the fairest virgins of Kiyôto, whom he ravished and ate, so that there was scarce a beautiful damsel left in the city. Then was the Emperor very sorrowful, and he commanded Yorimitsu to destroy the monster ; and the hero, having made ready, went forth with four trusty knights and another great captain to search among the hidden places of the mountains. One day as they were journeying far from the haunts of men, they fell in with an old man, who, having bidden them to enter his dwelling, treated them kindly, and set before them wine to drink ; and when they went away, and took their leave of him, he gave them a present of more wine to take away with them. Now this old man was a mountain god. As they went on their way they met a beautiful lady, who was washing blood-stained clothes in the waters of the valley, weeping bitterly the while. When they asked her why she shed tears, she answered, "Sirs, I am a woman from Kiyôto, whom the demon has carried off ; he makes me wash his clothes, and when he is weary of me, he will kill and eat me. I pray your lordships to save me." Then the six heroes bade the woman lead them to the ogre's cave, where a hundred devils were mounting guard and waiting upon him. The woman, having gone in first, told the fiend of their coming ; and he, thinking to slay and eat them, called them to him ; so they entered the cave, which reeked with the smell of the flesh and blood of men, and they saw Shudendôji, a huge monster with the face of a little child. The six men offered him the wine which they had received from the mountain god, and he, laughing in his heart, drank and made merry, so that little by little the fumes of the wine got into his head, and he fell asleep. The heroes, themselves feigning sleep, watched for a moment when the devils were all off their guard to put on their armour and steal one by one into the demon's chamber. Then Yorimitsu, seeing that all was still, drew his sword, and cut off Shudendôji's head, which sprung up and bit at his head ; luckily, however, Yorimitsu had put on two helmets, the one over the other, so he was not hurt. When all the devils had been slain, the heroes and the woman returned to Kiyôto carrying with them the head of Shudendôji, which was laid before the Emperor ; and the fame of their action was spread abroad under heaven.

This Shudendôji is the ogre represented in the Nakamura dance. The Ichimura dance represents the seven gods of wealth ; and the Morita dance represents a large ape, and is emblematical of drinking wine.

As soon as the sun begins to rise in the heaven, sign-boards all glistening with paintings and gold are displayed, and the play-goers flock in crowds to the theatre. The farmers and country-folk hurry over their breakfast, and the women and children, who have got up in the middle of the night to paint and adorn themselves, come from all the points of the compass to throng the gallery, which is hung with curtains as bright as the rainbow in the departing clouds. The place soon becomes so crowded that the heads of the spectators are like the scales on a dragon's back. When the play begins, if the subject be tragic the spectators are so affected that they weep till they have to wring their sleeves dry. If the piece be comic they laugh till their chins are out of joint. The tricks and stratagems of the drama baffle description, and the actors are as graceful as the flight of the swallow. The triumph of persecuted virtue and the punishment of wickedness invariably crown the story.

When a favourite actor makes his appearance, his entry is hailed with cheers. Fun and diversion are the order of the day, and rich and poor alike forget the cares which they have left behind them at home; and yet it is not all idle amusement, for there is a moral taught, and a practical sermon preached in every play.

The subjects of the pieces are chiefly historical, feigned names being substituted for those of the real heroes. Indeed, it is in the popular tragedies that we must seek for an account of many of the events of the last two hundred and fifty years; for only one very bald history[1] of those times has been published, of which but a limited number of copies were struck off from copper plates, and its circulation was strictly forbidden by the Shogun's Government. The stories are rendered with great minuteness and detail, so much so, that it sometimes takes a series of representations to act out one piece in its entirety. The Japanese are far in advance of the Chinese in their scenery and properties and their pieces are sometimes capitally got up: a revolving stage enables them to shift from one scene to another with great rapidity. First-rate actors receive as much as a thousand riyos (about £300) as their yearly salary. This, however, is a high rate of pay, and many a man has to strut before the public for little more than his daily rice; to a clever young actor it is almost enough reward to be allowed to enter a company in which there is a famous star. The salary of the actor, however, may depend upon the success of the theatre; for dramatic exhibitions are often undertaken as speculations by wealthy persons, who pay their company in proportion to their own profit. Beside his regular pay, a popular Japanese actor has a small mine of wealth in his patrons, who open their purses freely for the privilege of frequenting the green-room. The women's parts are all taken by men, as they used to be with us in ancient days. Touching the popularity of plays, it is related that in the year 1833, when two actors called Bandô Shûka and Segawa Rokô, both famous players of women's parts, died at the same time, the people of Yedo mourned to heaven and to earth; and if a million riyos could have brought back their lives, the money would have been forthcoming. Thousands flocked to their funeral,

[1] I allude to the *Tai Hei Nem-piyô*, or Annals of the Great Peace, a very rare work, only two or three copies of which have found their way into the libraries of foreigners.

and the richness of their coffins and of the clothes laid upon them was admired by all.

" When I heard this," says Terakado Seiken, the author of the *Yedo Hanjôki,* " I lifted my eyes to heaven and heaved a great sigh. When my friend Saitô Shimei, a learned and good man, died, there was barely enough money to bury him; his needy pupils and friends subscribed to give him a humble coffin. Alas! alas! here was a teacher who from his youth up had honoured his parents, and whose heart knew no guile : if his friends were in need, he ministered to their wants; he grudged no pains to teach his fellow-men; his goodwill and charity were beyond praise; under the blue sky and bright day he never did a shameful deed. His merits were as those of the sages of old; but because he lacked the cunning of a fox or badger he received no patronage from the wealthy, and, remaining poor to the day of his death, never had an opportunity of making his worth known. Alas! alas!"

The drama is exclusively the amusement of the middle and lower classes. Etiquette, sternest of tyrants, forbids the Japanese of high rank to be seen at any public exhibition, wrestling-matches alone excepted. Actors are, however, occasionally engaged to play in private for the edification of my lord and his ladies; and there is a kind of classical opera, called Nô, which is performed on stages specially built for the purpose in the palaces of the principal nobles. These Nô represent the entertainments by which the Sun Goddess was lured out of the cave in which she had hidden, a fable said to be based upon an eclipse. In the reign of the Emperor Yômei (A.D. 586—593), Hada Kawakatsu, a man born in Japan, but of Chinese extraction, was commanded by the Emperor to arrange an entertainment for the propitiation of the gods and the prosperity of the country. Kawakatsu wrote thirty-three plays, introducing fragments of Japanese poetry with accompaniments of musical instruments. Two performers, named Takéta and Hattori, having especially distinguished themselves in these entertainments, were ordered to prepare other similar plays, and their productions remain to the present day. The pious intention of the Nô being to pray for the prosperity of the country, they are held in the highest esteem by the nobles of the Court, the Daimios, and the military class : in old days they alone performed in these plays, but now ordinary actors take part in them.

The Nô are played in sets. The first of the set is specially dedicated to the propitiation of the gods ; the second is performed in full armour, and is designed to terrify evil spirits, and to insure the punishment of malefactors ; the third is of a gentler intention, and its special object is the representation of all that is beautiful and fragrant and delightful. The performers wear hideous wigs and masks, not unlike those of ancient Greece, and gorgeous brocade dresses. The masks, which belong to what was the private company of the Shogun, are many centuries old, and have been carefully preserved as heirlooms from generation to generation ; being made of very thin wood lacquered over, and kept each in a silken bag, they have been uninjured by the lapse of time.

During the Duke of Edinburgh's stay in Yedo, this company was engaged to give a performance in the Yashiki of the Prince of Kishiu, which has the reputation of being the handsomest palace in all Yedo. So far as I know, such an exhibition had never before been witnessed by foreigners, and it may be interesting to give an account of it. Opposite the principal reception-room, where his Royal Highness sat, and separated from it by a narrow courtyard, was a covered stage, approached from the green-room by a long gallery at an angle of forty-five degrees. Half a dozen musicians, clothed in dresses of ceremony, marched slowly down the gallery, and, having squatted down on the stage, bowed gravely. The performances then began. There was no scenery, nor stage appliances ; the descriptions of the chorus or of the actors took their place. The dialogue and choruses are given in a nasal recitative, accompanied by the mouth-organ, flute, drum, and other classical instruments, and are utterly unintelligible. The ancient poetry is full of puns and plays upon words, and it was with no little difficulty that, with the assistance of a man of letters, I prepared beforehand the arguments of the different pieces.

The first play was entitled *Hachiman of the Bow*. Hachiman is the name under which the Emperor Ojin (270—312 A.D.) was deified as the God of War. He is specially worshipped on account of his miraculous birth ; his mother, the Empress Jingo, having, by the virtue of a magic stone which she wore at her girdle, borne him in her womb for three years, during which she made war upon and conquered the Coreans. The time of the plot is laid in the reign of the Emperor Uda the Second (1275—1289 A.D.). In the second month of the year pilgrims are flocking to the temple of Hachiman at Mount Otoko, between Osaka and Kiyôto. All this is explained by the chorus. A worshipper steps forth, sent by the Emperor, and delivers a congratulatory oration upon the peace and prosperity of the land. The chorus follows in the same strain : they sing the praises of Hachiman and of the reigning Emperor. An old man enters, bearing something which appears to be a bow in a brocade bag. On being asked who he is, the old man answers that he is an aged servant of the shrine, and that he wishes to present his mulberry-wood bow to the Emperor ; being too humble to draw near to his Majesty he has waited for this festival, hoping that an opportunity might present itself. He explains that with this bow, and with certain arrows made of the Artemisia, the heavenly gods pacified the world. On being asked to show his bow, he refuses ; it is a mystic protector of the country, which in old days was overshadowed by the mulberry-tree. The peace which prevails in the land is likened to a calm at sea. The Emperor is the ship, and his subjects the water. The old man dwells upon the ancient worship of Hachiman, and relates how his mother, the Empress Jingo, sacrificed to the gods before invading Corea, and how the present prosperity of the country is to be attributed to the acceptance of those sacrifices. After having revealed himself as the god Hachiman in disguise, the old man disappears. The worshipper, awe-struck, declares that he must return to Kiyôto and tell the Emperor what he has seen. The chorus announces that sweet music and fragrant perfumes issue from the mountain, and the piece ends with felicitations upon the visible favour of the gods, and especially of Hachiman.

The second piece was *Tsunémasa.* Tsunémasa was a hero of the twelfth century, who died in the civil wars ; he was famous for his skill in playing on the *biwa*, a sort of four-stringed lute.

A priest enters, and announces that his name is Giyôkei, and that before he retired from the world he held high rank at court. He relates how Tsunémasa, in his childhood the favourite of the Emperor, died in the wars by the western seas. During his lifetime the Emperor gave him a lute, called Sei-zan, "the Azure Mountain ;" this lute at his death was placed in a shrine erected to his honour, and at his funeral music and plays were performed during seven days within the palace, by the special grace of the Emperor. The scene is laid at the shrine. The lonely and awesome appearance of the spot is described. Although the sky is clear, the wind rustles through the trees like the sound of falling rain ; and although it is now summer-time, the moonlight on the sand looks like hoar-frost. All nature is sad and downcast. The ghost appears, and sings that it is the spirit of Tsunémasa, and has come to thank those who have piously celebrated his obsequies. No one answers him, and the spirit vanishes, its voice becoming fainter and fainter, an unreal and illusory vision haunting the scenes amid which its life was spent. The priest muses on the portent. Is it a dream or a reality ? Marvellous ! The ghost, returning, speaks of former days, when it lived as a child in the palace, and received the Azure Mountain lute from the Emperor— that lute with the four strings of which its hand was once so familiar, and the attraction of which now draws it from the grave. The chorus recites the virtues of Tsunémasa—his benevolence, justice, humanity, talents, and truth; his love of poetry and music; the trees, the flowers, the birds, the breezes, the moon— all had a charm for him. The ghost begins to play upon the Azure Mountain lute, and the sounds produced from the magical instrument are so delicate, that all think it is a shower falling from heaven. The priest declares that it is not rain, but the sound of the enchanted lute. The sound of the first and second strings is as the sound of gentle rain, or of the wind stirring the pine-trees ; and the sound of the third and fourth strings is as the song of birds and pheasants calling to their young. A rhapsody in praise of music follows. Would that such strains could last for ever ! The ghost bewails its fate that it cannot remain to play on, but must return whence it came. The priest addresses the ghost, and asks whether the vision is indeed the spirit of Tsunémasa. Upon this the ghost calls out in an agony of sorrow and terror at having been seen by mortal eyes, and bids that the lamps be put out: on its return to the abode of the dead it will suffer for having shown itself : it describes the fiery torments which will be its lot. Poor fool ! it has been lured to its destruction, like the insect of summer that flies into the flame. Summoning the winds to its aid, it puts out the lights, and disappears.

The Suit of Feathers is the title of a very pretty conceit which followed. A fisherman enters, and in a long recitative describes the scenery at the sea-shore of Miwo, in the province of Suruga.

at the foot of Fujiyama, the Peerless Mountain. The waves are still, and there is a great calm ; the fishermen are all out plying their trade. The speaker's name is Hakuriyô, a fisherman living in the pine-grove of Miwo. The rains are now over, and the sky is serene ; the sun rises bright and red over the pine-trees and rippling sea ; while last night's moon is yet seen faintly in the heaven. Even he, humble fisher though he be, is softened by the beauty of the nature which surrounds him. A breeze springs up, the weather will change ; clouds and waves will succeed sunshine and calm ; the fishermen must get them home again. No ; it is but the gentle breath of spring, after all ; it scarcely stirs the stout fir-trees, and the waves are hardly heard to break upon the shore. The men may go forth in safety. The fisherman then relates how, while he was wondering at the view, flowers began to rain from the sky, and sweet music filled the air, which was perfumed by a mystic fragrance. Looking up, he saw hanging on a pine-tree a fairy's suit of feathers, which he took home, and showed to a friend, intending to keep it as a relic in his house. A heavenly fairy makes her appearance, and claims the suit of feathers ; but the fisherman holds to his treasure trove. She urges the impiety of his act—a mortal has no right to take that which belongs to the fairies. He declares that he will hand down the feather suit to posterity as one of the treasures of the country. The fairy bewails her lot ; without her wings how can she return to heaven? She recalls the familiar joys of heaven, now closed to her ; she sees the wild geese and the gulls flying to the skies, and longs for their power of flight ; the tide has its ebb and its flow, and the sea-breezes blow whither they list ; for her alone there is no power of motion, she must remain on earth. At last, touched by her plaint, the fisherman consents to return the feather suit, on condition that the fairy shall dance and play heavenly music for him. She consents, but must first obtain the feather suit, without which she cannot dance. The fisherman refuses to give it up, lest she should fly away to heaven without redeeming her pledge. The fairy reproaches him for his want of faith : how should a heavenly being be capable of falsehood? He is ashamed, and gives her the feather suit, which she dons, and begins to dance, singing of the delights of heaven, where she is one of the fifteen attendants who minister to the moon. The fisherman is so transported with joy, that he fancies himself in heaven, and wishes to detain the fairy to dwell with him for ever.

A song follows in praise of the scenery and of the Peerless Mountain capped with the snows of spring. When her dance is concluded, the fairy, wafted away by the sea-breeze, floats past the pine-grove to Ukishima and Mount Ashidaka, over Mount Fuji, till she is seen dimly like a cloud in the distant sky, and vanishes into thin air.

The last of the Nô was *The Little Smith*, the scene of which is laid in the reign of the Emperor Ichijô (987—1011 A.D.). A noble of the court enters, and proclaims himself to be Tachibana Michinari. He has been commanded by the Emperor, who has seen a dream of good omen on the previous night, to order a sword of the smith Munéchika of Sanjô. He calls Munéchika, who comes out, and, after receiving the order, expresses the difficulty he is in, having at that time no fitting mate to help him ; he cannot forge a blade alone. The excuse is not admitted ; the smith pleads hard to be saved from the shame of a failure. Driven to a compliance, there is nothing left for it but to appeal to the gods for aid. He prays to the patron god of his family, Inari Sama.[1] A man suddenly appears, and calls the smith ; this man is the god Inari Sama in disguise. The smith asks who is his visitor, and how does he know him by name. The stranger answers, " Thou hast been ordered to make a blade for the Emperor." " This is passing strange," says the smith. "I received the order but a moment since ; how comest thou to know of it ? " " Heaven has a voice which is heard upon the earth. Walls have ears, and stones tell tales.[2] There are no secrets in the world. The flash of the blade ordered by him who is above the clouds (the Emperor) is quickly seen. By the grace of the Emperor the sword shall be quickly made." Here follows the praise of certain famous blades, and an account of the part they played in history, with special reference to the sword which forms one of the regalia. The sword which the Emperor has sent for shall be inferior to none of these ; the smith may set his heart at rest. The smith, awestruck, expresses his wonder, and asks again who is addressing him. He is bidden to go and deck out his anvil, and a supernatural power will help him. The visitor disappears in a cloud. The smith prepares his anvil, at the four corners of which he places images of

[1] The note at the end of the Story of the Grateful Foxes contains an account of Inari Sama, and explains how the foxes minister to him.

[2] This is a literal translation of a Japanese proverb.

the gods, while above it he stretches the straw rope and paper pendants hung up in temples to shut out foul or ill-omened influences. He prays for strength to make the blade, not for his own glory, but for the honour of the Emperor. A young man, a fox in disguise, appears, and helps Munéchika to forge the steel. The noise of the anvil resounds to heaven and over the earth. The chorus announces that the blade is finished ; on one side is the mark of Munéchika, on the other is graven "The Little Fox" in clear characters.

The subjects of the Nô are all taken from old legends of the country; a shrine at Miwo, by the sea-shore, marks the spot where the suit of feathers was found, and the miraculously forged sword is supposed to be in the armoury of the Emperor to this day. The beauty of the poetry—and it is very beautiful—is marred by the want of scenery and by the grotesque dresses and make-up. In the *Suit of Feathers*, for instance, the fairy wears a hideous mask and a wig of scarlet elf locks : the suit of feathers itself is left entirely to the imagination ; and the heavenly dance is a series of whirls, stamps, and jumps, accompanied by unearthly yells and shrieks ; while the vanishing into thin air is represented by pirouettes something like the motion of a dancing dervish. The intoning of the recitative is unnatural and unintelligible, so much so that not even a highly educated Japanese could understand what is going on unless he were previously acquainted with the piece. This, however, is supposing that which is not, for the Nô are as familiarly known as the master-pieces of our own dramatists.

The classical severity of the Nô is relieved by the introduction between the pieces of light farces called Kiyôgen. The whole entertainment having a religious intention, the Kiyôgen stand to the Nô in the same relation as the small shrines to the main temple ; they, too, are played for the propitiation of the gods, and for the softening of men's hearts. The farces are acted without wigs or masks ; the dialogue is in the common spoken language, and there being no musical accompaniment it is quite easy to follow. The plots of the two farces which were played before the Duke of Edinburgh are as follows :—

In the *Ink Smearing* the hero is a man from a distant part of the country, who, having a petition to prefer, comes to the capital, where he is detained for a long while. His suit being at last successful, he communicates the joyful news to his servant, Tarô-kaja (the conventional name of the Leporello of these farces). The two congratulate one another. To while away his idle hours during his sojourn at the capital the master has entered into a flirtation with a certain young lady : master and servant now hold a consultation as to whether the former should not go and take leave of her. Tarôkaja is of opinion that as she is of a very jealous nature, his master ought to go. Accordingly the two set out to visit her, the servant leading the way. Arrived at her house, the gentleman goes straight in without the knowledge of the lady, who, coming out and meeting Tarôkaja, asks after his master. He replies that his master is inside the house. She refuses to believe him, and complains that, for some time past, his visits have been few and far between. Why should he come now? Surely Tarô-kaja is hoaxing her. The servant protests that he is telling the truth, and that his master really has entered the house. She, only half persuaded, goes in, and finds that my lord is indeed there. She welcomes him, and in the same breath upbraids him. Some other lady has surely found favour in his eyes. What fair wind has wafted him back to her? He replies that business alone has kept him from her ; he hopes that all is well with her. With her, indeed, all is well, and there is no change ; but she fears that his heart is changed. Surely, surely he has found mountains upon mountains of joy elsewhere ; even now, perhaps, he is only calling on his way homeward from some haunt of pleasure. What pleasure can there be away from her? answers he. Indeed, his time has not been his own, else he would have come sooner. Why, then, did he not send his servant to explain? Tarôkaja here puts in his oar, and protests that, between running on errands and dancing attendance upon his lord, he has not had a moment to himself. "At any rate," says the master, "I must ask for your congratulations ; for my suit, which was so important, has prospered." The lady expresses her happiness, and the gentleman then bids his servant tell her the object of their visit. Tarôkaja objects to this ; his lord had better tell his own story. While the two are disputing as to who shall speak, the lady's curiosity is aroused. "What terrible tale is this that neither of you dare tell? Pray let one or other of you speak" At last the master explains that he has come to take leave of her, as he must forthwith return to his own province. The girl begins to weep, and the gentleman following suit, the two shed tears in concert. She uses all her art to cajole him, and secretly produces from her sleeve a cup of water, with which she smears her eyes to imitate tears. He, deceived by the trick, tries to console her, and swears that as soon as he reaches his own country he will send a messenger to fetch her ; but she pretends to weep all the more, and goes on rubbing her face with water. Tarôkaja, in the meanwhile, detects the trick, and, calling his master on one side, tells him what she is doing. The gentleman, however, refuses to believe him, and scolds him right roundly for telling lies. The lady calls my lord to her, and weeping more bitterly than ever, tries to coax him to remain. Tarôkaja slily fills another cup with ink and water, and substitutes it for the cup of clear water. She, all unconcerned, goes on smearing her face. At last she lifts her face, and her lover, seeing it all black and sooty, gives a start. What can be the matter with the girl's face? Tarôkaja, in an aside, explains what he has done. They determine to put her to shame. The lover, producing from his bosom a box containing a mirror, gives it to the girl, who, thinking that it is a parting gift, at first declines to receive it. It is pressed upon her ; she opens the box and sees the reflection of her dirty face. Master and man burst out laughing. Furious, she smears Tarôkaja's face with the ink ; he protests that he is not the author of the trick, and the girl flies at her lover and rubs his face too. Both master and servant run off, pursued by the girl.

The second farce was shorter than the first, and was called *The Theft of the Sword*. A certain gentleman calls his servant Tarôkaja, and tells him that he is going out for a little diversion. Bidding Tarôkaja follow him, he sets out. On their way they meet another gentleman, carrying a handsome sword in his hand, and going to worship at the Kitano shrine at Kiyôto. Tarôkaja points out the beauty of the sword to his master, and says what a fine thing it would be if they could manage to obtain possession of it. Tarôkaja borrows his master's sword, and goes up to the stranger, whose attention is taken up by looking at the wares set out for sale in a shop. Tarôkaja lays his hand on the guard of the stranger's sword ; and the latter, drawing it, turns round, and tries to cut the thief down. Tarôkaja takes to his heels, praying hard that his life may be spared. The stranger takes away the sword which Tarôkaja has borrowed from his master, and goes on his way to the shrine, carrying the two swords. Tarôkaja draws a long breath of relief when he sees that his life is not forfeited ; but what account is he to give of his master's sword which he has lost. There is no help for it, he must go back and make a clean breast of it. His master is very angry ; and the two, after consulting together, await the stranger's return from the shrine. The latter makes his appearance, and announces that he is going home. Tarôkaja's master falls upon the stranger from behind, and pinions him, ordering Tarôkaja to fetch a rope and bind him. The knave brings the cord ; but, while he is getting it ready, the stranger knocks him over with his sword. His master calls out to him to get up quickly and bind the gentleman from behind, and not from before. Tarôkaja runs behind the struggling pair, but is so clumsy that he slips the noose over his master's head by mistake, and drags him down. The stranger, seeing this, runs away laughing with the two swords. Tarôkaja, frightened at his blunder, runs off too, his master pursuing him off the stage. A general run off, be it observed, something like the "spill-and-pelt" scene in an English pantomime, is the legitimate and invariable termination of the Kiyôgen.

NOTE ON THE GAME OF FOOTBALL

THE game of football is in great favour at the Japanese Court. The days on which it takes place are carefully noted in the "Daijôkwan Nishi," or Government Gazette. On the 25th of February, 1869, for instance, we find two entries : "The Emperor wrote characters of good omen," and "The game of football was played at the palace." The game was first introduced from China in the year of the Empress Kôkiyoku, in the middle of the seventh century. The Emperor Mommu, who reigned at the end of the same century, was the first emperor who took part in the sport. His Majesty Toba the Second became very expert at it, as also did the noble Asukai Chiujo, and from that time a sort of football club was formed at the palace. During the days of the extreme poverty of the Mikado and his Court, the Asukai family, notwithstanding their high rank, were wont to eke out their scanty income by giving lessons in the art of playing football.

THE WONDERFUL ADVENTURES OF
FUNAKOSHI JIUYÉMON

THE doughty deeds and marvellous experiences of Funa-
koshi Jiuyémon are perhaps, like those of Robin Hood and
his Merry Men, rather traditional than historical; but even
if all or part of the deeds which popular belief ascribes to
him be false, his story conveys a true picture of manners and
customs.   Above all, the manner of the vengeance which he
wreaked upon the wife who had dishonoured him, and upon
her lover, shows the high importance which the Japanese
attach to the sanctity of the marriage tie.

The 50th and 51st chapters of the "Legacy of Iyéyasu,"
already quoted, say: "If a married woman of the agricul-
tural, artisan, or commercial class shall secretly have inter-
course with another man, it is not necessary for the husband
to enter a complaint against the persons thus confusing
the great relation of mankind, but he may put them both
to death.   Nevertheless, should he slay one of them and
spare the other, his guilt is the same as that of the unright-
eous persons.

" In the event, however, of advice being sought, the parties
not having been slain, accede to the wishes of the complain-
ant with regard to putting them to death or not.

" Mankind, in whose bodies the male and female elements
induce a natural desire towards the same object, do not look
upon such practices with aversion ; and the adjudication of
such cases is a matter of special deliberation and consultation.

" Men and women of the military class are expected to
know better than to occasion disturbance by violating exist-

142

ing regulations; and such an one breaking the regulations by lewd, trifling, or illicit intercourse shall at once be punished, without deliberation or consultation. It is not the same in this case as in that of agriculturists, artisans, and traders."

As a criminal offence, adultery was, according to the ancient laws of Japan, punished by crucifixion. In more modern times it has been punished by decapitation and the disgraceful exposure of the head after death; but if the murder of the injured husband accompany the crime of adultery, then the guilty parties are crucified to this day. At the present time the husband is no longer allowed to take the law into his own hands: he must report the matter to the Government, and trust to the State to avenge his honour.

Sacred as the marriage tie is so long as it lasts, the law which cuts it is curiously facile, or rather there is no law: a man may turn his wife out of doors, as it may suit his fancy. An example of this practice was shown in the story of "The Forty-seven Rônins." A husband has but to report the matter to his lord, and the ceremony of divorce is completed. Thus, in the days of the Shogun's power, a Hatamoto who had divorced his wife reported the matter to the Shogun. A Daimio's retainer reports the matter to his Prince.

The facility of divorce, however, seems to be but rarely taken advantage of: this is probably owing to the practice of keeping concubines. It has often been asked, Are the Japanese polygamists? The answer is, Yes and no. They marry but one wife; but a man may, according to his station and means, have one or more concubines in addition. The Emperor has twelve concubines, called Kisaki; and Iyéyasu, alluding forcibly to excess in this respect as *teterrima belli causa*, laid down that the princes might have eight, high officers five, and ordinary Samurai two handmaids. "In the olden times," he writes, "the downfall of castles and the overthrow of kingdoms all proceeded from this alone. Why is not the indulgence of passions guarded against?"

The difference between the position of the wife and that of the concubine is marked. The legitimate wife is to the handmaid as a lord is to his vassal. Concubinage being a legitimate institution, the son of a handmaid is no bastard, nor is he in any way the child of shame; and yet, as a general rule, the son of the bondwoman is not heir with the son of the free, for the son of the wife inherits before the son of a concubine, even where the latter be the elder; and it frequently happens that a noble, having children by his concubines but none by his wife, selects a younger brother of his own, or even adopts the son of some relative, to succeed him in the family honours. The family line is considered to be thus more purely preserved. The law of succession is, however, extremely lax. Excellent personal merits will sometimes secure to the left-handed son the inheritance of his ancestors; and it often occurs that the son of a concubine, who is debarred from succeeding to his own father, is adopted as the heir of a relation or friend of even higher rank. When the wife of a noble has a daughter but no son, the practice is to adopt a youth of suitable family and age, who marries the girl and inherits as a son.

The principle of adoption is universal among all classes, from the Emperor down to his meanest subject; nor is the family line considered to have been broken because an adopted son has succeeded to the estates. Indeed, should a noble die without heir male, either begotten or adopted, his lands are forfeited to the State. It is a matter of care that the person adopted should be himself sprung from a stock of rank suited to that of the family into which he is to be received.

Sixteen and upwards being considered the marriageable age for a man, it is not usual for persons below that age to adopt an heir; yet an infant at the point of death may adopt a person older than himself, that the family line may not become extinct.

An account of the marriage ceremony will be found in the Appendix upon the subject.

In the olden time, in the island of Shikoku [1] there lived one Funakoshi Jiuyémon, a brave Samurai and accomplished man, who was in great favour with the prince, his master. One day, at a drinking-bout, a quarrel sprung up between him and a brother-officer, which resulted in a duel upon the spot, in which Jiuyémon killed his adversary. When Jiuyémon awoke to a sense of what he had done, he was struck with remorse, and he thought to disembowel himself; but, receiving a private summons from his lord, he went to the castle, and the prince said to him—

"So it seems that you have been getting drunk and quarrelling, and that you have killed one of your friends; and now I suppose you will have determined to perform *hara kiri*. It is a great pity, and in the face of the laws I can do nothing for you openly. Still, if you will escape and fly from this part of the country for a while, in two years' time the affair will have blown over, and I will allow you to return."

And with these words the prince presented him with a fine sword, made by Sukésada, [2] and a hundred ounces of silver, and, having bade him farewell, entered his private apartments ; and Jiuyémon, prostrating himself, wept tears of gratitude; then, taking the sword and the money, he went home and prepared to fly from the province, and secretly took leave of his relations, each of whom made him some parting present. These gifts, together with his own money, and what he had received from the prince, made up a sum of two hundred and fifty ounces of silver, with which and his Sukésada sword he escaped under cover of darkness, and went to a sea-port called Marugamé, in the province of

[1] *Shikoku*, one of the southern islands separated from the chief island of Japan by the beautiful "Inland Sea;" it is called *Shikoku*, or the "Four Provinces," because it is divided into the four provinces, *Awa, Sanuki, Iyo,* and *Tosa*.

[2] *Sukésada*, a famous family of swordsmiths, belonging to the Bizen clan. The Bizen men are notoriously good armourers, and their blades fetch high prices. The sword of Jiuyémon is said to have been made by one of the Sukésada who lived about 290 years ago.

Sanuki, where he proposed to wait for an opportunity of setting sail for Osaka. As ill luck would have it, the wind being contrary, he had to remain three days idle; but at last the wind changed; so he went down to the beach, thinking that he should certainly find a junk about to sail; and as he was looking about him, a sailor came up, and said—

"If your honour is minded to take a trip to Osaka, my ship is bound thither, and I should be glad to take you with me as passenger."

"That's exactly what I wanted. I will gladly take a passage," replied Jiuyémon, who was delighted at the chance.

"Well then we must set sail at once, so please come on board without delay."

So Jiuyémon went with him and embarked; and as they left the harbour and struck into the open sea, the moon was just rising above the eastern hills, illumining the dark night like a noonday sun; and Jiuyémon, taking his place in the bows of the ship, stood wrapt in contemplation of the beauty of the scene.

Now it happened that the captain of the ship, whose name was Akagôshi Kuroyémon, was a fierce pirate, who, attracted by Jiuyémon's well-to-do appearance, had determined to decoy him on board, that he might murder and rob him; and while Jiuyémon was looking at the moon, the pirate and his companions were collected in the stern of the ship, taking counsel together in whispers as to how they might slay him. He, on the other hand, having for some time past fancied their conduct somewhat strange, bethought him that it was not prudent to lay aside his sword, so he went towards the place where he had been sitting, and had left his weapon lying, to fetch it, when he was stopped by three of the pirates, who blocked up the gangway, saying—

"Stop, Sir Samurai! Unluckily for you, this ship in which you have taken a passage belongs to the pirate Akagôshi Kuroyémon. Come, sir! whatever money you may chance to have about you is our prize."

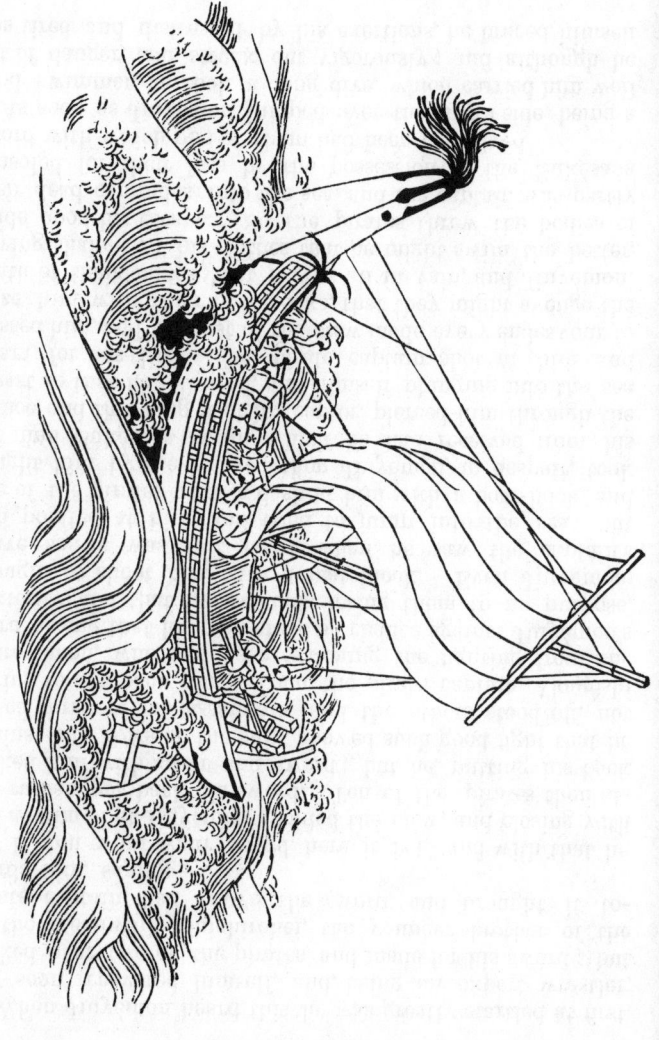

JIUYÉMON ON BOARD THE PIRATE SHIP

When Jiuyémon heard this he was greatly startled at first, but soon recovered himself, and, being an expert wrestler, kicked over two of the pirates, and made for his sword; but in the meanwhile Shichirohei, the younger brother of the pirate captain, had drawn the sword, and brought it towards him, saying—

"If you want your sword, here it is!" and with that he cut at him; but Jiuyémon avoided the blow, and closing with the ruffian, got back his sword. Ten of the pirates then attacked him with spear and sword; but he, putting his back against the bows of the ship, showed such good fight that he killed three of his assailants, and the others stood off, not daring to approach him. Then the pirate captain, Akagôshi Kuroyémon, who had been watching the fighting from the stern, seeing that his men stood no chance against Jiuyémon's dexterity, and that he was only losing them to no purpose, thought to shoot him with a matchlock. Even Jiuyémon, brave as he was, lost heart when he saw the captain's gun pointed at him, and tried to jump into the sea; but one of the pirates made a dash at him with a boat-hook, and caught him by the sleeve; then Jiuyémon, in despair, took the fine Sukésada sword which he had received from his prince, and throwing it at his captor, pierced him through the breast so that he fell dead, and himself plunging into the sea swam for his life. The pirate captain shot at him and missed him, and the rest of the crew made every endeavour to seize him with their boat-hooks, that they might avenge the death of their mates; but it was all in vain, and Jiuyémon, having shaken off his clothes that he might swim the better, made good his escape. So the pirates threw the bodies of their dead comrades into the sea, and the captain was partly consoled for their loss by the possession of the Sukésada sword with which one of them had been transfixed.

As soon as Jiuyémon jumped over the ship's side, being a good swimmer, he took a long dive, which carried him well out of danger, and struck out vigorously; and although he was tired and distressed by his exertions, he braced himself up to greater energy, and faced the waves boldly. At last, in the far distance, to his great joy, he spied a light, for which he made, and found that it was a ship carrying lanterns marked with the badge of the governor of Osaka; so he hailed her, saying—

"I have fallen into great trouble among pirates: pray rescue me."

"Who and what are you?" shouted an officer, some forty years of age.

"My name is Funakoshi Jiuyémon, and I have unwittingly fallen in with pirates this night. I have escaped so far: I pray you save me, lest I die."

"Hold on to this, and come up," replied the other, holding out the butt end of a spear to him, which he caught hold of and clambered up the ship's side. When the officer saw before him a handsome gentleman, naked all but his loin-cloth, and with his hair all in disorder, he called to his servants to bring some of his own clothes, and, having dressed him in them, said—

"What clan do you belong to, sir?"

"Sir, I am a Rônin, and was on my way to Osaka; but the sailors of the ship on which I had embarked were pirates;" and so he told the whole story of the fight and of his escape.

"Well done, sir!" replied the other, astonished at his prowess. "My name is Kajiki Tozayémon, at your service. I am an officer attached to the governor of Osaka. Pray, have you any friends in that city?"

"No, sir, I have no friends there; but as in two years I shall be able to return to my own country, and re-enter my lord's service, I thought during that time to engage in trade and live as a common wardsman."

"Indeed, that's a poor prospect! However, if you will allow me, I will do all that is in my power to assist you. Pray excuse the liberty I am taking in making such a proposal."

Jiuyémon warmly thanked Kajiki Tozayémon for his kindness; and so they reached Osaka without further adventures.

Jiuyémon, who had secreted in his girdle the two hundred and fifty ounces which he had brought with him from home, bought a small house, and started in trade as a vendor of perfumes, tooth-powder, combs, and other toilet articles ; and Kajiki Tozayémon, who treated him with great kindness, and rendered him many services, prompted him, as he was a single man, to take to himself a wife. Acting upon this advice, he married a singing-girl, called O Hiyaku.[1]

Now this O Hiyaku, although at first she seemed very affectionately disposed towards Jiuyémon, had been, during the time that she was a singer, a woman of bad and profligate character; and at this time there was in Osaka a certain wrestler, named Takaségawa Kurobei, a very handsome man, with whom O Hiyaku fell desperately in love; so that at last, being by nature a passionate woman, she became unfaithful to Jiuyémon. The latter, little suspecting that anything was amiss, was in the habit of spending his evenings at the house of his patron Kajiki Tozayémon, whose son, a youth of eighteen, named Tônoshin, conceived a great friendship for Jiuyémon, and used constantly to invite him to play a game at checkers; and it was on these occasions that O Hiyaku, profiting by her husband's absence, used to arrange her meetings with the wrestler Takaségawa.

One evening, when Jiuyémon, as was his wont, had gone out to play at checkers with Kajiki Tônoshin, O Hiyaku took advantage of the occasion to go and fetch the wrestler, and invite him to a little feast ; and as they were enjoying themselves over their wine, O Hiyaku said to him—

" Ah! Master Takaségawa, how wonderfully chance favours us ! and how pleasant these stolen interviews are ! How much nicer still it would be if we could only be married. But, as long as Jiuyémon is in the way, it is impossible; and that is my one cause of distress."

" It's no use being in such a hurry. If you only have a

---

[1] The O before women's names signifies "*Imperial*," and is simply an honorific.

patience, we shall be able to marry, sure enough. What you have got to look out for now is, that Jiuyémon does not find out what we are about. I suppose there is no chance of his coming home to-night, is there?"

"Oh dear, no! You need not be afraid. He is gone to Kajiki's house to play checkers; so he is sure to spend the night there."

And so the guilty couple went on gossiping, with their minds at ease, until at last they dropped off asleep.

In the meanwhile Jiuyémon, in the middle of his game at checkers, was seized with a sudden pain in his stomach, and said to Kajiki Tônoshin, "Young sir, I feel an unaccountable pain in my stomach. I think I had better go home, before it gets worse."

"That is a bad job. Wait a little, and I will give you some physic; but, at any rate, you had better spend the night here."

"Many thanks for your kindness," replied Jiuyémon; "but I had rather go home."

So he took his leave, and went off to his own house, bearing the pain as best he might. When he arrived in front of his own door, he tried to open it; but the lock was fastened, and he could not get in, so he rapped violently at the shutters to try and awaken his wife. When O Hiyaku heard the noise, she woke with a start, and roused the wrestler, saying to him in a whisper—

"Get up! get up! Jiuyémon has come back. You must hide as fast as possible."

"Oh dear! oh dear!" said the wrestler, in a great fright; "here's a pretty mess! Where on earth shall I hide myself?" and he stumbled about in every direction looking for a hiding-place, but found none.

Jiuyémon, seeing that his wife did not come to open the door, got impatient at last, and forced it open by unfixing the sliding shutter, and, entering the house, found himself face to face with his wife and her lover, who were both in such confusion that they did not know what to do. Jiuyémon, however, took no notice of them, but lit his pipe and sat smoking and watching them in silence. At last the wrestler, Takaségawa, broke the silence by saying—

"I thought, sir, that I should be sure to have the pleasure of finding you at home this evening, so I came out to call upon you. When I got here, the Lady O Hiyaku was so kind as to offer me some wine; and I drank a little more than was good for me, so that it got into my head, and I fell asleep. I must really apologize for having taken such a liberty in your absence; but, indeed, although appearances are against us, there has been nothing wrong."

"Certainly," said O Hiyaku, coming to her lover's support, "Master Takaségawa is not at all to blame. It was I who invited him to drink wine; so I hope you will excuse him."

Jiuyémon sat pondering the matter over in his mind for a moment, and then said to the wrestler, "You say that you are innocent; but, of course, that is a lie. It's no use trying to conceal your fault. However, next year I shall, in all probability, return to my own country, and then you may take O Hiyaku and do what you will with her: far be it from me to care what becomes of a woman with such a stinking heart."

When the wrestler and O Hiyaku heard Jiuyémon say this quite quietly, they could not speak, but held their peace for very shame.

"Here, you Takaségawa," pursued he; "you may stop here to-night, if you like it, and go home to-morrow."

"Thank you, sir," replied the wrestler, "I am much obliged to you; but the fact is, that I have some pressing business in another part of the town, so, with your permission, I will take my leave;" and so he went out, covered with confusion.

As for the faithless wife, O Hiyaku, she was in great agitation, expecting to be severely reprimanded at least; but Jiuyémon took no notice of her, and showed no anger; only from that day forth, although she remained in his house as his wife, he separated himself from her entirely.

Matters went on in this way for some time, until at last, one fine day, O Hiyaku, looking out of doors, saw the wrestler Takaségawa passing in the street, so she called out to him—

"Dear me, Master Takaségawa, can that be you! What a long time it is since we have met! Pray come in, and have a chat."

"Thank you, I am much obliged to you; but as I do not like the sort of scene we had the other day, I think I had rather not accept your invitation."

"Pray do not talk in such a cowardly manner. Next year, when Jiuyémon goes back to his own country, he is sure to give me this house, and then you and I can marry and live as happily as possible."

"I don't like being in too great a hurry to accept fair offers."[1]

"Nonsense! There's no need for showing such delicacy about accepting what is given you."

And as she spoke, she caught the wrestler by the hand and led him into the house. After they had talked together for some time, she said—

"Listen to me, Master Takaségawa. I have been thinking over all this for some time, and I see no help for it but to kill Jiuyémon and make an end of him."

"What do you want to do that for?"

"As long as he is alive, we cannot be married. What I propose is that you should buy some poison, and I will put it secretly into his food. When he is dead, we can be happy to our hearts' content."

At first Takaségawa was startled and bewildered by the audacity of their scheme; but forgetting the gratitude which he owed to Jiuyémon for sparing his life on the previous occasion, he replied—

"Well, I think it can be managed. I have a friend who is a physician, so I will get him to compound some poison for

[1] The original is a proverbial expression like "Timeo Danaos et dona ferentes."

me, and will send it to you. You must look out for a moment
when your husband is not on his guard, and get him to
take it."

Having agreed upon this, Takaségawa went away, and,
having employed a physician to make up the poison, sent
it to O Hiyaku in a letter, suggesting that the poison
should be mixed up with a sort of macaroni, of which
Jiuyémon was very fond. Having read the letter, she put
it carefully away in a drawer of her cupboard, and waited
until Jiuyémon should express a wish to eat some macaroni.

One day, towards the time of the New Year, when O Hiyaku
had gone out to a party with a few of her friends, it hap-
pened that Jiuyémon, being alone in the house, was in want of
some little thing, and, failing to find it anywhere, at last be-
thought himself to look for it in O Hiyaku's cupboard ; and
as he was searching amongst the odds and ends which it con-
tained, he came upon the fatal letter. When he read the
scheme for putting poison in his macaroni, he was taken
aback, and said to himself, " When I caught those two
beasts in their wickedness I spared them, because their
blood would have defiled my sword ; and now they are not
even grateful for my mercy. Their crime is beyond all power
of language to express, and I will kill them together."

So he put back the letter in its place, and waited for
his wife to come home. So soon as she made her appear-
ance he said—

" You have come home early, O Hiyaku. I feel very dull
and lonely this evening ; let us have a little wine."

And as he spoke without any semblance of anger, it never
entered O Hiyaku's mind that he had seen the letter ; so
she went about her household duties with a quiet mind.

The following evening, as Jiuyémon was sitting in his
shop casting up his accounts, with his counting-board[1] in his

---

[1] The *abacus*, or counting-board, is the means of calculation in use through-
out the Continent from St. Petersburg to Peking, in Corea, Japan, and the
Liukiu Islands.

hand, Takaségawa passed by, and Jiuyémon called out to him, saying—

" Well met, Takaségawa ! I was just thinking of drinking a cup of wine to-night; but I have no one to keep me company, and it is dull work drinking alone. Pray come in, and drink a bout with me."

" Thank you, sir, I shall have much pleasure," replied the wrestler, who little expected what the other was aiming at; and so he went in, and they began to drink and feast.

" It's very cold to-night," said Jiuyémon, after a while; " suppose we warm up a little macaroni, and eat it nice and hot. Perhaps, however, you do not like it ?"

" Indeed, I am very fond of it, on the contrary."

" That is well. O Hiyaku, please go and buy a little for us."

" Directly," replied his wife, who hurried off to buy the paste, delighted at the opportunity for carrying out her murderous design upon her husband. As soon she had prepared it, she poured it into bowls and set it before the two men ; but into her husband's bowl only she put poison. Jiuyémon, who well knew what she had done, did not eat the mess at once, but remained talking about this, that, and the other; and the wrestler, out of politeness, was obliged to wait also. All of a sudden, Jiuyémon cried out—

" Dear me ! whilst we have been gossiping, the macaroni has been getting cold. Let us put it all together and warm it up again. As no one has put his lips to his bowl yet, it will all be clean ; so none need be wasted." And with these words he took the macaroni that was in the three bowls, and, pouring it altogether into an iron pot, boiled it up again. This time Jiuyémon served out the food himself, and, setting it before his wife and the wrestler, said—

" There ! make haste and eat it up before it gets cold."

Jiuyémon, of course, did not eat any of the mess ; and the would-be murderers, knowing that sufficient poison had been originally put into Jiuyémon's bowl to kill them all three, and that now the macaroni, having been well mixed up, would all be poisoned, were quite taken aback, and did not know what to do.

"Come! make haste, or it will be quite cold. You said you liked it, so I sent to buy it on purpose. O Hiyaku! come and make a hearty meal. I will eat some presently."

At this the pair looked very foolish, and knew not what to answer; at last the wrestler got up and said—

"I do not feel quite well. I must beg to take my leave; and, if you will allow me, I will come and accept your hospitality to-morrow instead."

"Dear me! I am sorry to hear you are not well. However, O Hiyaku, there will be all the more macaroni for you."

As for O Hiyaku, she put a bold face upon the matter, and replied that she had supped already, and had no appetite for any more.

Then Jiuyémon, looking at them both with a scornful smile, said—

"It seems that you, neither of you, care to eat this macaroni; however, as you, Takaségawa, are unwell, I will give you some excellent medicine;" and going to the cupboard, he drew out the letter, and laid it before the wrestler. When O Hiyaku and the wrestler saw that their wicked schemes had been brought to light, they were struck dumb with shame.

Takaségawa, seeing that denial was useless, drew his dirk and cut at Jiuyémon; but he, being nimble and quick, dived under the wrestler's arm, and seizing his right hand from behind, tightened his grasp upon it until it became numbed, and the dirk fell to the ground; for, powerful man as the wrestler was, he was no match for Jiuyémon, who held him in so fast a grip that he could not move. Then Jiuyémon took the dirk which had fallen to the ground, and said—

"Oh! I thought that you, being a wrestler, would at least be a strong man, and that there would be some pleasure in fighting you; but I see that you are but a poor feckless creature, after all. It would have defiled my sword to have killed such an ungrateful hound with it; but luckily here is your own dirk, and I will slay you with that."

JIUYÉMON PUNISHES HIS WIFE AND THE WRESTLER

Takaségawa struggled to escape, but in vain; and O Hiyaku, seizing a large kitchen knife, attacked Jiuyémon; but he, furious, kicked her in the loins so violently that she fell powerless, then brandishing the dirk, he cleft the wrestler from the shoulder down to the nipple of his breast, and the big man fell in his agony. O Hiyaku, seeing this, tried to fly; but Jiuyémon, seizing her by the hair of the head, stabbed her in the bosom, and, placing her by her lover's side, gave her the death-blow.

On the following day, he sent in a report of what he had done to the governor of Osaka, and buried the corpses; and from that time forth he remained a single man, and pursued his trade as a seller of perfumery and such-like wares; and his leisure hours he continued to spend as before, at the house of his patron, Kajiki Tozayémon.

One day, when Jiuyémon went to call upon Kajiki Tozayémon, he was told by the servant-maid, who met him at the door, that her master was out, but that her young master, Tônoshin, was at home; so, saying that he would go in and pay his respects to the young gentleman, he entered the house; and as he suddenly pushed open the sliding-door of the room in which Tônoshin was sitting, the latter gave a great start, and his face turned pale and ghastly.

"How now, young sir!" said Jiuyémon, laughing at him, "surely you are not such a coward as to be afraid because the sliding-doors are opened? That is not the way in which a brave Samurai should behave."

"Really I am quite ashamed of myself," replied the other, blushing at the reproof; "but the fact is that I had some reason for being startled. Listen to me, Sir Jiuyémon, and I will tell you all about it. To-day, when I went to the academy to study, there were a great number of my fellow-students gathered together, and one of them said that a ruinous old shrine, about two miles and a half to the east of this place, was the nightly resort of all sorts of hobgoblins, who have been playing pranks and bewitching the people for some time past; and he proposed that we should all draw lots, and that the one upon whom the lot fell should go to-night and exorcise those evil beings ; and further that, as a proof of his having gone, he should write his name upon a pillar in the shrine. All the rest agreed that this would be very good sport ; so I, not liking to appear a coward, consented to take my chance with the rest ; and, as ill luck would have it, the lot fell upon me. I was thinking over this as you came in, and so it was that, when you suddenly opened the door, I could not help giving a start."

"If you only think for a moment," said Jiuyémon, "you will see that there is nothing to fear. How can beasts[1] and hobgoblins exercise any power over men ? However, do not let the matter trouble you. I will go in your place to-night, and see if I cannot get the better of these goblins, if any there be, having done which, I will write your name upon the pillar, so that everybody may think that you have been there."

"Oh ! thank you : that will indeed be a service. You can dress yourself up in my clothes, and nobody will be the wiser. I shall be truly grateful to you."

So Jiuyémon having gladly undertaken the job, as soon as the night set in made his preparations, and went to the place indicated—an uncanny-looking, tumble-down, lonely old shrine, all overgrown with moss and rank vegetation. However, Jiuyémon, who was afraid of nothing, cared little for the appearance of the place, and having made himself as comfortable as he could in so dreary a spot, sat down on the floor, lit his pipe, and kept a sharp look-out for the goblins. He had not been waiting long before he saw a movement among the bushes; and presently he was surrounded by a host of elfish-looking creatures, of all shapes and kinds, who came and made hideous faces at him. Jiuyémon quietly knocked the ashes out of his pipe, and then, jumping up, kicked over first one and then another of the elves, until several of them lay sprawling in the grass ; and the rest made off, greatly astonished at at this unexpected reception. When Jiuyémon took his lan-

---

[1] Foxes, badgers, and cats. See the stories respecting their tricks.

FUNAKOSHI JIUYÉMON AND THE GOBLINS

tern and examined the fallen goblins attentively, he saw that they were all Tônoshin's fellow-students, who had painted their faces, and made themselves hideous, to frighten their companion, whom they knew to be a coward : all they got for their pains, however, was a good kicking from Jiuyémon, who left them groaning over their sore bones, and went home chuckling to himself at the result of the adventure.

The fame of this exploit soon became noised about Osaka, so that all men praised Jiuyémon's courage ; and shortly after this he was elected chief of the Otokodaté,[1] or friendly society of the wardsmen, and busied himself no longer with his trade, but lived on the contributions of his numerous apprentices.

Now Kajiki Tônoshin was in love with a singing-girl named Kashiku, upon whom he was in the habit of spending a great deal of money. She, however, cared nothing for him, for she had a sweetheart named Hichirobei, whom she used to contrive to meet secretly, although, in order to support her parents, she was forced- to become the mistress of Tônoshin. One evening, when the latter was on guard at the office of his chief, the Governor of Osaka, Kashiku sent word privately to Hichirobei, summoning him to go to her house, as the coast would be clear.

While the two were making merry over a little feast, Tônoshin, who had persuaded a friend to take his duty for him on the plea of urgent business, knocked at the door, and Kashiku, in a great fright, hid her lover in a long clothes-box, and went to let in Tônoshin, who, on entering the room and seeing the litter of the supper lying about, looked more closely, and perceived a man's sandals, on which, by the light of a candle, he saw the figure seven.[2] Tônoshin had heard some ugly reports of Kashiku's proceedings with this man Hichirobei, and when he saw this proof before his eyes he grew very angry ; but he suppressed his feelings, and, pointing to the wine-cups and bowls, said—

[1] See the Introduction to the Story of Chobei of Bandzuin.
[2] *Hichi*, the first half of *Hichirobei*, signifies seven.

"Whom have you been feasting with to-night?"

"Oh!" replied Kashiku, who, notwithstanding her distress, was obliged to invent an answer, "I felt so dull all alone here, that I asked an old woman from next door to come in and drink a cup of wine with me, and have a chat."

All this while Tônoshin was looking for the hidden lover; but, as he could not see him, he made up his mind that Kashiku must have let him out by the back door; so he secreted one of the sandals in his sleeve as evidence, and, without seeming to suspect anything, said—

"Well, I shall be very busy this evening, so I must go home."

"Oh! won't you stay a little while? It is very dull here, when I am all alone without you. Pray stop and keep me company."

But Tônoshin made no reply, and went home. Then Kashiku saw that one of the sandals was missing, and felt certain that he must have carried it off as proof; so she went in great trouble to open the lid of the box, and let out Hichirobei. When the two lovers talked over the matter, they agreed that, as they both were really in love, let Tônoshin kill them if he would, they would gladly die together: they would enjoy the present; let the future take care of itself.

The following morning Kashiku sent a messenger to Tônoshin to implore his pardon; and he, being infatuated by the girl's charms, forgave her, and sent a present of thirty ounces of silver to her lover, Hichirobei, on the condition that he was never to see her again; but, in spite of this, Kashiku and Hichirobei still continued their secret meetings.

It happened that Hichirobei, who was a gambler by profession, had an elder brother called Chôbei, who kept a wine-shop in the Ajikawa-street, at Osaka; so Tônoshin thought that he could not do better than depute Jiuyémon to go and seek out this man Chôbei, and urge him to persuade his younger brother to give up his relations with Kashiku; acting upon this resolution, he went to call upon Jiuyémon, and said to him—

" Sir Jiuyémon, I have a favour to ask of you in connection with that girl Kashiku, whom you know all about. You are aware that I paid thirty ounces of silver to her lover Hichirobei to induce him to give up going to her house; but, in spite of this, I cannot help suspecting that they still meet one another. It seems that this Hichirobei has an elder brother—one Chôbei; now, if you would go to this man and tell him to reprove his brother for his conduct, you would be doing me a great service. You have so often stood my friend, that I venture to pray you to oblige me in this matter, although I feel that I am putting you to great inconvenience."

Jiuyémon, out of gratitude for the kindness which he had received at the hands of Kajiki Tozayémon, was always willing to serve Tônoshin; so he went at once to find out Chôbei, and said to him—

" My name, sir, is Jiuyémon, at your service; and I have come to beg your assistance in a matter of some delicacy."

" What can I do to oblige you, sir?" replied Chôbei, who felt bound to be more than usually civil, as his visitor was the chief of the Otokodaté.

"It is a small matter, sir," said Jiuyémon. " Your younger brother Hichirobei is intimate with a woman named Kashiku, whom he meets in secret. Now, this Kashiku is the mistress of the son of a gentleman to whom I am under great obligation: he bought her of her parents for a large sum of money, and, besides this, he paid your brother thirty ounces of silver some time since, on condition of his separating himself from the girl; in spite of this, it appears that your brother continues to see her, and I have come to beg that you will remonstrate with your brother on his conduct, and make him give her up."

" That I certainly will. Pray do not be uneasy; I will soon find means to put a stop to my brother's bad behaviour."

And so they went on talking of one thing and another, until Jiuyémon, whose eyes had been wandering about the room, spied out a very long dirk lying on a cupboard, and all at once it occurred to him that this was the very sword which had been a parting gift to him from his lord: the hilt, the mountings, and the tip of the scabbard were all the same, only the blade had been shortened and made into a long dirk. Then he looked more attentively at Chôbei's features, and saw that he was no other than Akagôshi Kuroyémon, the pirate chief. Two years had passed by, but he could not forget that face.

Jiuyémon would have liked to have arrested him at once; but thinking that it would be a pity to give so vile a robber a chance of escape, he constrained himself, and, taking his leave, went straightway and reported the matter to the Governor of Osaka. When the officers of justice heard of the prey that awaited them, they made their preparations forthwith. Three men of the secret police went to Chôbei's wine-shop, and, having called for wine, pretended to get up a drunken brawl; and as Chôbei went up to them and tried to pacify them, one of the policemen seized hold of him, and another tried to pinion him. It at once flashed across Chôbei's mind that his old misdeeds had come to light at last, so with a desperate effort he shook off the two policemen and knocked them down, and, rushing into the inner room, seized the famous Sukésada sword and sprang upstairs. The three policemen, never thinking that he could escape, mounted the stairs close after him; but Chôbei with a terrible cut cleft the front man's head in sunder, and the other two fell back appalled at their comrade's fate. Then Chôbei climbed on to the roof, and, looking out, perceived that the house was surrounded on all sides by armed men. Seeing this, he made up his mind that his last moment was come, but, at any rate, he determined to sell his life dearly, and to die fighting; so he stood up bravely, when one of the officers, coming up from the roof of a neighbouring house, attacked him with a spear; and at the same time several other soldiers clambered up. Chôbei, seeing that he was overmatched, jumped down, and before the soldiers below had recovered from their surprise he had dashed through their ranks, laying about him right and left, and cutting down three men. At top speed, he fled, with his pursuers close behind him; and, seeing the broad river ahead of him, jumped into a small boat that lay moored there, of which the boatmen, frightened at the sight of his bloody sword, left him in undisputed possession. Chôbei pushed off, and sculled vigorously into the middle of the river; and the officers—there being no other boat near— were for a moment baffled. One of them, however, rushing down the river bank, hid himself on a bridge, armed with a spear, and lay in wait for Chôbei to pass in his boat; but when the little boat came up, he missed his aim, and only scratched Chôbei's elbow; and he, seizing the spear, dragged down his adversary into the river, and killed him as he was struggling in the water; then, sculling for his life, he gradually drew near to the sea. The other officers in the mean time had secured ten boats, and, having come up with Chôbei, surrounded him; but he, having formerly been a pirate, was far better skilled in the management of a boat than his pursuers, and had no great difficulty in eluding them; so at last he pushed out to sea, to the great annoyance of the officers, who followed him closely.

Then Jiuyémon, who had come up, said to one of the officers on the shore—

"Have you caught him yet?"

"No; the fellow is so brave and so cunning that our men can do nothing with him."

"He's a determined ruffian, certainly. However, as the fellow has got my sword, I mean to get it back by fair means or foul: will you allow me to undertake the job of seizing him?"

"Well, you may try; and you will have officers to assist you, if you are in peril."

Jiuyémon, having received this permission, stripped off his clothes and jumped into the sea, carrying with him a policeman's mace, to the great astonishment of all the bystanders When he got near Chôbei's boat, he dived and came up alongside, without the pirate perceiving him until he had clambered into the boat. Chôbei had the good Sukésada sword, and Jiuyémon was armed with nothing but a mace; but Chôbei, on the other hand, was exhausted with his previous exertions, and was taken by surprise at a moment when he was thinking of nothing but how he should scull away from the pursuing boats; so it was not long before Jiuyémon mastered and secured him.

For this feat, besides recovering his Sukésada sword, Jiuyémon received many rewards and great praise from the Governor of Osaka. But the pirate Chôbei was cast into prison.

Hichirobei, when he heard of his brother's capture, was away from home; but seeing that he too would be sought for, he determined to escape to Yedo at once, and travelled along the Tôkaidô, the great highroad, as far as Kuana. But the secret police had got wind of his movements, and one of them was at his heels disguised as a beggar, and waiting for an opportunity to seize him.

Hichirobei in the meanwhile was congratulating himself on his escape; and, little suspecting that he would be in danger so far away from Osaka, he went to a house of pleasure, intending to divert himself at his ease. The policeman, seeing this, went to the master of the house and said—

"The guest who has just come in is a notorious thief, and I am on his track, waiting to arrest him. Do you watch for the moment when he falls asleep, and let me know. Should he escape, the blame will fall upon you."

The master of the house, who was greatly taken aback, consented of course; so he told the woman of the house to hide Hichirobei's dirk, and as soon as the latter, wearied with his journey, had fallen asleep, he reported it to the policeman, who went upstairs, and having bound Hichirobei as he lay wrapped up in his quilt, led him back to Osaka to be imprisoned with his brother.

When Kashiku became aware of her lover's arrest, she felt certain that it was the handiwork of Jiuyémon; so she determined to kill him, were it only that she might die with

"GOKUMON"

Hichirobei. So hiding a kitchen knife in the bosom of her dress, she went at midnight to Jiuyémon's house, and looked all round to see if there were no hole or cranny by which she might slip in unobserved; but every door was carefully closed, so she was obliged to knock at the door and feign an excuse.

"Let me in! let me in! I am a servant-maid in the house of Kajiki Tozayémon, and am charged with a letter on most pressing business to Sir Jiuyémon."

Hearing this, one of Jiuyémon's servants, thinking her tale was true, rose and opened the door; and Kashiku, stabbing him in the face, ran past him into the house. Inside she met another apprentice, who had got up, aroused by the noise; him too she stabbed in the belly, but as he fell he cried out to Jiuyémon, saying—

"Father, father![1] take care! Some murderous villain has broken into the house."

And Kashiku, desperate, stopped his further utterance by cutting his throat. Jiuyémon, hearing his apprentice cry out, jumped up, and, lighting his night-lamp, looked about him in the half-gloom, and saw Kashiku with the bloody knife, hunting for him that she might kill him. Springing upon her before she saw him, he clutched her right hand, and, having secured her, bound her with cords so that she could not move. As soon as he had recovered from his surprise, he looked about him, and searched the house, when, to his horror, he found one of his apprentices dead, and the other lying bleeding from a frightful gash across the face. With the first dawn of day, he reported the affair to the proper authorities, and gave Kashiku in custody. So, after due examination, the two pirate brothers and the girl Kashiku were executed, and their heads were exposed together.[2]

Now the fame of all the valiant deeds of Jiuyémon having

---

[1] The apprentice addresses his patron as "father."

[2] The exposure of the head, called *Gokumon*, is a disgraceful addition to the punishment of beheading. A document, placed on the execution-ground, sets forth the crime which has called forth the punishment.

reached his own country, his lord ordered that he should be pardoned for his former offence, and return to his allegiance; so, after thanking Kajiki Tozayémon for the manifold favours which he had received at his hands, he went home, and became a Samurai as before.

The fat wrestlers of Japan, whose heavy paunches and unwieldy, puffy limbs, however much they may be admired by their own country-people, form a striking contrast to our Western notions of training, have attracted some attention from travellers; and those who are interested in athletic sports may care to learn something about them.

The first historical record of wrestling occurs in the sixth year of the Emperor Suinin (B.C. 24), when one Taima no Kéhaya, a noble of great stature and strength, boasting that there was not his match under heaven, begged the Emperor that his strength might be put to the test. The Emperor accordingly caused the challenge to be proclaimed; and one Nomi no Shikuné answered it, and having wrestled with Kéhaya, kicked him in the ribs and broke his bones, so that he died. After this Shikuné was promoted to high office, and became further famous in Japanese history as having substituted earthen images for the living men who, before his time, used to be buried with the coffin of the Mikado.

In the year 858 A.D. the throne of Japan was wrestled for. The Emperor Buntoku had two sons, called Koréshito and Korétaka, both of whom aspired to the throne. Their claims were decided in a wrestling-match, in which one Yoshirô was the champion of Koréshito, and Natora the champion of Korétaka. Natora having been defeated, Koreshito ascended his father's throne under the style of Seiwa.

In the eighth century, when Nara was the capital of Japan, the Emperor Shômu instituted wrestling as part of the ceremonies of the autumn festival of the Five Grains, or Harvest Home; and as the year proved a fruitful one, the custom was continued as auspicious. The strong men of the various pro-

A WRESTLING MATCH

vinces were collected, and one Kiyobayashi was proclaimed the champion of Japan. Many a brave and stout man tried a throw with him, but none could master him. Rules of the ring were now drawn up; and in order to prevent disputes, Kiyobayashi was appointed by the Emperor to be the judge of wrestling-matches, and was presented, as a badge of his office, with a fan, upon which were inscribed the words the "Prince of Lions." The wrestlers were divided into wrestlers of the eastern and of the western provinces, Omi being taken as the centre province. The eastern wrestlers wore in their hair the badge of the hollyhock; the western wrestlers took for their sign the gourd-flower. Hence the passage leading up to the wrestling-stage was called the "Flower Path." Forty-eight various falls were fixed upon as fair—twelve throws, twelve lifts, twelve twists, and twelve throws over the back. All other throws not included in these were foul, and it was the duty of the umpire to see that no unlawful tricks were resorted to. It was decided that the covered stage should be composed of sixteen rice-bales, in the shape of one huge bale, supported by four pillars at the four points of the compass, each pillar being painted a different colour, thus, together with certain paper pendants, making up five colours, to symbolize the Five Grains.

The civil wars by which the country was disturbed for a while put a stop to the practice of wrestling; but when peace was restored it was proposed to re-establish the athletic games, and the umpire Kiyobayashi, the "Prince of Lions," was sought for; but he had died or disappeared, and could not be found, and there was no umpire forthcoming. The various provinces were searched for a man who might fill his place, and one Yoshida Iyétsugu, a Rônin of the province of Echizen, being reported to be well versed in the noble science, was sent for to the capital, and proved to be a pupil of Kiyobayashi. The Emperor, having approved him, ordered that the fan of the "Prince of Lions" should be made over to him, and gave him the title of Bungo no Kami, and commanded that his name in the ring should be Oi-Kazé, the

"Driving Wind." Further, as a sign that there should not be two styles of wrestling, a second fan was given to him bearing the inscription, "A single flavour is a beautiful custom." The right of acting as umpire in wrestling-matches was vested in his family, that the "Driving Wind" might for future generations preside over athletic sports. In ancient days, the prizes for the three champion wrestlers were a bow, a bowstring, and an arrow: these are still brought into the ring, and, at the end of the bout, the successful competitors go through a variety of antics with them.

To the champion wrestlers—to two or three men only in a generation—the family of the "Driving Wind" awards the privilege of wearing a rope-girdle. In the time of the Shogunate these champions used to wrestle before the Shogun.

At the beginning of the 17th century (A.D. 1606) wrestling-matches, as forming a regular part of a religious ceremony, were discontinued. They are still held, however, at the shrines of Kamo, at Kiyôto, and of Kasuga, in Yamato. They are also held at Kamakura every year, and at the shrines of the patron saints of the various provinces, in imitation of the ancient customs.

In the year 1623 one Akashi Shiganosuké obtained leave from the Government to hold public wrestling-matches in the streets of Yedo. In the year 1644 was held the first wrestling-match for the purpose of raising a collection for building a temple. This was done by the priests of Kofukuji, in Yamashiro. In the year 1660 the same expedient was resorted to in Yedo, and the custom of getting up wrestling-matches for the benefit of temple funds holds good to this day.

The following graphic description of a Japanese wrestling-match is translated from the "Yedo Hanjôki": —

"From daybreak till eight in the morning a drum is beaten to announce that there will be wrestling. The spectators rise early for the sight. The adversaries having been settled, the wrestlers enter the ring from the east and from the west. Tall stalwart men are they, with sinews and

CHAMPION WRESTLER

bones of iron. Like the Gods Niô,[1] they stand with their arms akimbo, and, facing one another, they crouch in their strength. The umpire watches until the two men draw their breath at the same time, and with his fan gives the signal. They jump up and close with one another, like tigers springing on their prey, or dragons playing with a ball. Each is bent on throwing the other by twisting or by lifting him. It is no mere trial of brute strength; it is a tussle of skill against skill. Each of the forty-eight throws is tried in turn. From left to right, and from right to left, the umpire hovers about, watching for the victory to declare itself. Some of the spectators back the east, others back the west The patrons of the ring are so excited that they feel the strength tingling within them; they clench their fists, and watch their men, without so much as blinking their eyes. At last one man, east or west, gains the advantage, and the umpire lifts his fan in token of victory. The plaudits of the bystanders shake the neighbourhood, and they throw their clothes or valuables into the ring, to be redeemed afterwards in money; nay, in his excitement, a man will even tear off his neighbour's jacket and throw it in."

Before beginning their tussle, the wrestlers work up their strength by stamping their feet and slapping their huge thighs. This custom is derived from the following tale of the heroic or mythological age :—

After the seven ages of the heavenly gods came the reign of Tensho Daijin, the Sun Goddess, and first Empress of Japan. Her younger brother, Sosanöô no Mikoto, was a mighty and a brave hero, but turbulent, and delighted in hunting the deer and the boar. After killing these beasts, he would throw their dead bodies into the sacred hall of his sister, and otherwise defile her dwelling. When he had done this several times, his sister was angry, and hid in the cave called the Rock Gate of Heaven; and when her face was not seen, there was no difference between the night and the day. The heroes who served her, mourning over this, went to seek

---

[1] The Japanese Gog and Magog.

her ; but she placed a huge stone in front of the cave, and would not come forth. The heroes, seeing this, consulted together, and danced and played antics before the cave to lure her out. Tempted by curiosity to see the sight, she opened the gate a little and peeped out. Then the hero Tajikaraô, or "Great Strength," clapping his hands and stamping his feet, with a great effort grasped and threw down the stone door, and. the heroes fetched back the Sun Goddess.[1] As Tajikaraô is the patron god of Strength, wrestlers, on entering the ring, still commemorate his deed by clapping their hands and stamping their feet as a preparation for putting forth their strength.

The great Daimios are in the habit of attaching wrestlers to their persons, and assigning to them a yearly portion of rice. It is usual for these athletes to take part in funeral or wedding processions, and to escort the princes on journeys. The rich wardsmen or merchants give money to their favourite wrestlers, and invite them to their houses to drink wine and feast. Though low, vulgar fellows, they are allowed something of the same familiarity which is accorded to prize-fighters, jockeys, and the like, by their patrons in our own country.

The Japanese wrestlers appear to have no regular system of training; they harden their naturally powerful limbs by much beating, and by butting at wooden posts with their shoulders. Their diet is stronger than that of the ordinary Japanese, who rarely touch meat.

[1] The author of the history called "Kokushi Riyaku" explains this fable as being an account of the first eclipse.

THE ETA MAIDEN AND THE HATAMOTO

It will be long before those who were present at the newly opened port of Kôbé on the 4th of February, 1868, will forget that day. The civil war was raging, and the foreign Legations, warned by the flames of burning villages, no less than by the flight of the Shogun and his ministers, had left Osaka, to take shelter at Kôbé, where they were not, as at the former place, separated from their ships by more than twenty miles of road, occupied by armed troops in a high state of excitement, with the alternative of crossing in tempestuous weather a dangerous bar, which had already taken much valuable life. It was a fine winter's day, and the place was full of bustle, and of the going and coming of men busy with the care of housing themselves and their goods and chattels. All of a sudden, a procession of armed men, belonging to the Bizen clan, was seen to leave the town, and to advance along the high road leading to Osaka; and without apparent reason—it was said afterwards that two Frenchmen had crossed the line of march—there was a halt, a stir, and a word of command given. Then the little clouds of white smoke puffed up, and the sharp "ping" of the rifle bullets came whizzing over the open space, destined for a foreign settlement, as fast as the repeating breech-loaders could be discharged. Happily, the practice was very bad; for had the men of Bizen been good shots, almost all the principal foreign officials in the country, besides many merchants and private gentlemen, must have been killed: as it was, only two or three men were wounded. If they were bad marksmen, however, they were mighty

runners; for they soon found that they had attacked a
hornets' nest. In an incredibly short space of time, the
guards of the different Legations and the sailors and ma-
rines from the ships of war were in hot chase after the
enemy, who were scampering away over the hills as fast as
their legs could carry them, leaving their baggage ingloriously
scattered over the road, as many a cheap lacquered hat and
flimsy paper cartridge-box, preserved by our Blue Jackets as
trophies, will testify. So good was the stampede, that the
enemy's loss amounted only to one aged coolie, who, being too
decrepit to run, was taken prisoner, after having had seven-
teen revolver shots fired at him without effect; and the only
injury that our men inflicted was upon a solitary old woman,
who was accidently shot through the leg.

If it had not been for the serious nature of the offence
given, which was an attack upon the flags of all the treaty
Powers, and for the terrible retribution which was of necessity
exacted, the whole affair would have been recollected chiefly
for the ludicrous events which it gave rise to. The mounted
escort of the British Legation executed a brilliant charge of
cavalry down an empty road; a very pretty line of skirmishers
along the fields fired away a great deal of ammunition with
no result; earthworks were raised, and Kôbé was held in
military occupation for three days, during which there were
alarms, cutting-out expeditions with armed boats, steamers
seized, and all kinds of martial effervescence. In fact, it
was like fox-hunting: it had "all the excitement of war,
with only ten per cent. of the danger."

The first thought of the kind-hearted doctor of the British
Legation was for the poor old woman who had been wounded,
and was bemoaning herself piteously. When she was carried
in, a great difficulty arose, which, I need hardly say, was
overcome; for the poor old creature belonged to the Etas, the
Pariah race, whose presence pollutes the house even of the
poorest and humblest Japanese; and the native servants
strongly objected to her being treated as a human being,
saying that the Legation would be for ever defiled if she

were admitted within its sacred precincts. No account of Japanese society would be complete without a notice of the Etas; and the following story shows well, I think the position which they hold.

Their occupation is to slay beasts, work leather, attend upon criminals, and do other degrading work. Several accounts are given of their origin; the most probable of which is, that when Buddhism, the tenets of which forbid the taking of life, was introduced, those who lived by the infliction of death became accursed in the land, their trade being made hereditary, as was the office of executioner in some European countries. Another story is, that they are the descendants of the Tartar invaders left behind by Kublai Khan. Some further facts connected with the Etas are given in a note at the end of the tale.

Once upon a time, some two hundred years ago, there lived at a place called Honjô, in Yedo, a Hatamoto named Takoji Genzaburô; his age was about twenty-four or twenty-five, and he was of extraordinary personal beauty. His official duties made it incumbent on him to go to the Castle by way of the Adzuma Bridge, and here it was that a strange adventure befel him. There was a certain Eta, who used to earn his living by going out every day to the Adzuma Bridge, and mending the sandals of the passers-by. Whenever Genzaburô crossed the bridge, the Eta used always to bow to him. This struck him as rather strange; but one day when Genzaburô was out alone, without any retainers following him, and was passing the Adzuma Bridge, the thong of his sandal suddenly broke: this annoyed him very much; however, he recollected the Eta cobbler who always used to bow to him so regularly, so he went to the place where he usually sat, and ordered him to mend his sandal, saying to him, "Tell me why it is that

GENZABURŌ'S MEETING WITH THE ETA MAIDEN

every time that I pass by this bridge, you salute me so respectfully."

When the Eta heard this, he was put out of countenance, and for a while he remained silent; but at last taking courage, he said to Genzaburô, " Sir, having been honoured with your commands, I am quite put to shame. I was originally a gardener, and used to go to your honour's house and lend a hand in trimming up the garden. In those days your honour was very young, and I myself little better than a child ; and so I used to play with your honour, and received many kindnesses at your hands. My name, sir, is Chokichi. Since those days I have fallen by degrees into dissolute habits, and little by little have sunk to be the vile thing that you now see me."

When Genzaburô heard this he was very much surprised, and, recollecting his old friendship for his playmate, was filled with pity, and said, " Surely, surely, you have fallen very low. Now all you have to do is to persevere and use your utmost endeavours to find a means of escape from the class into which you have fallen, and become a wardsman again. Take this sum: small as it is, let it be a foundation for more to you." And with these words he took ten riyos out of his pouch and handed them to Chokichi, who at first refused to accept the present, but, when it was pressed upon him, received it with thanks. Genzaburô was leaving him to go home, when two wandering singing-girls came up and spoke to Chokichi; so Genzaburô looked to see what the two women were like. One was a woman of some twenty years of age, and the other was a peerlessly beautiful girl of sixteen ; she was neither too fat nor too thin, neither too tall nor too short ; her face was oval, like a melon-seed, and her complexion fair and white ; her eyes were narrow and bright, her teeth small and even ; her nose was aquiline, and her mouth delicately formed, with lovely red lips ; her eyebrows were long and fine ; she had a profusion of long black hair ; she spoke modestly, with a soft sweet voice ; and when she smiled, two lovely dimples appeared in her cheeks; in all her movements she was gentle and refined. Genzaburô fell in love with her at first sight; and she, seeing what a handsome man he was, equally fell in love with him; so that the woman that was with her, perceiving that they were struck with one another, led her away as fast as possible.

Genzaburô remained as one stupefied, and, turning to Chokichi, said, "Are you acquainted with those two women who came up just now?"

"Sir," replied Chokichi, "those are two women of our people. The elder woman is called O Kuma, and the girl, who is only sixteen years old, is named O Koyo. She is the daughter of one Kihachi, a chief of the Etas. She is a very gentle girl, besides being so exceedingly pretty; and all our people are loud in her praise."

When he heard this, Genzaburô remained lost in thought for a while, and then said to Chokichi, "I want you to do something for me. Are you prepared to serve me in whatever respect I may require you?"

Chokichi answered that he was prepared to do anything in his power to oblige his honour. Upon this, Genzaburô smiled and said, "Well, then, I am willing to employ you in a certain matter; but as there are a great number of passers-by here, I will go and wait for you in a tea-house at Hanakawado; and when you have finished your business here, you can join me, and I will speak to you." With these words Genzaburô left him, and went off to the tea-house.

When Chokichi had finished his work, he changed his clothes, and, hurrying to the tea-house, inquired for Genzaburô, who was waiting for him upstairs. Chokichi went up to him, and began to thank him for the money which he had bestowed upon him. Genzaburô smiled, and handed him a wine-cup, inviting him to drink, and said—

"I will tell you the service upon which I wish to employ you. I have set my heart upon that girl O Koyo, whom I met to-day upon the Adzuma Bridge, and you must arrange a meeting between us."

When Chokichi heard these words, he was amazed and frightened, and for awhile he made no answer. At last he said—

" Sir, there is nothing that I would not do for you after the favours that I have received from you. If this girl were the daughter of any ordinary man, I would move heaven and earth to comply with your wishes; but for your honour, a handsome and noble Hatamoto, to take for his concubine the daughter of an Eta is a great mistake. By giving a little money you can get the handsomest woman in the town. Pray, sir, abandon the idea."

Upon this Genzaburô was offended, and said—

" This is no matter for you to give advice in. I have told you to get me the girl, and you must obey."

Chokichi, seeing that all that he could say would be of no avail, thought over in his mind how to bring about a meeting between Genzaburô and O Koyo, and replied—

" Sir, I am afraid when I think of the liberty that I have taken. I will go to Kihachi's house, and will use my best endeavours with him that I may bring the girl to you. But for to-day, it is getting late, and night is coming on ; so I will go and speak to her father to-morrow."

Genzaburô was delighted to find Chokichi willing to serve him.

" Well," said he, " the day after to-morrow I will await you at the tea-house at Oji, and you can bring O Koyo there. Take this present, small as it is, and do your best for me."

With this he pulled out three riyos from his pocket and handed them to Chokichi, who declined the money with thanks, saying that he had already received too much, and could accept no more ; but Genzaburô pressed him, adding, that if the wish of his heart were accomplished he would do still more for him. So Chokichi, in great glee at the good luck which had befallen him, began to revolve all sorts of schemes in his mind; and the two parted.

But O Koyo, who had fallen in love at first sight with Genzaburô on the Adzuma Bridge, went home and could think of nothing but him. Sad and melancholy she sat, and her friend O Kuma tried to comfort her in various ways; but O Koyo yearned, with all her heart, for Genzaburô; and the more she thought over the matter, the better she perceived that she, as the daughter of an Eta, was no match for a noble Hatamoto. And yet, in spite of this, she pined for him, and bewailed her own vile condition.

Now it happened that her friend O Kuma was in love with Chokichi, and only cared for thinking and speaking of him; one day, when Chokichi went to pay a visit at the house of Kihachi the Eta chief, O Kuma, seeing him come, was highly delighted, and received him very politely; and Chokichi, interrupting her, said—

"O Kuma, I want you to answer me a question: where has O Koyo gone to amuse herself to-day?"

"Oh, you know the gentleman who was talking with you the other day, at the Adzuma Bridge? Well, O Koyo has fallen desperately in love with him, and she says that she is too low-spirited and out of sorts to get up yet."

Chokichi was greatly pleased to hear this, and said to O Kuma—

"How delightful! Why, O Koyo has fallen in love with the very gentleman who is burning with passion for her, and who has employed me to help him in the matter. However, as he is a noble Hatamoto, and his whole family would be ruined if the affair became known to the world, we must endeavour to keep it as secret as possible."

"Dear me!" replied O Kuma; "when O Koyo hears this, how happy she will be, to be sure! I must go and tell her at once."

"Stop!" said Chokichi, detaining her; "if her father, Master Kihachi, is willing, we will tell O Koyo directly. You had better wait here a little until I have consulted him;" and with this he went into an inner chamber to see Kihachi; and, after talking over the news of the day, told him how Genzaburô had fallen passionately in love with O Koyo, and had employed him as a go-between. Then he described how he had received kindness at the hands of Genzaburô when he was in better circumstances, dwelt on the wonderful personal beauty of his lordship, and upon the lucky chance by which he and O Koyo had come to meet each other.

When Kihachi heard this story, he was greatly flattered, and said—

"I am sure I am very much obliged to you. For one of our daughters, whom even the common people despise and shun as a pollution, to be chosen as the concubine of a noble Hatamoto — what could be a greater matter for congratulation!"

So he prepared a feast for Chokichi, and went off at once to tell O Koyo the news. As for the maiden, who had fallen over head and ears in love, there was no difficulty in obtaining her consent to all that was asked of her.

Accordingly Chokichi, having arranged to bring the lovers together on the following day at Oji, was preparing to go and report the glad tidings to Genzaburô; but O Koyo, who knew that her friend O Kuma was in love with Chokichi, and thought that if she could throw them into one another's arms, they, on their side, would tell no tales about herself and Genzaburô, worked to such good purpose that she gained her point. At last Chokichi, tearing himself from the embraces of O Kuma, returned to Genzaburô, and told him how he had laid his plans so as, without fail, to bring O Koyo to him, the following day, at Oji; and Genzaburô, beside himself with impatience, waited for the morrow.

The next day Genzaburô, having made his preparations, and taking Chokichi with him, went to the teahouse at Oji, and sat drinking wine, waiting for his sweetheart to come.

As for O Koyo, who was half in ecstasies, and half shy at the idea of meeting on this day the man of her heart's desire, she put on her holiday clothes, and went with O Kuma to Oji; and as they went out together, her natural beauty being enhanced by her smart dress, all the people turned round to look at her, and praise her pretty face. And so, after a while, they arrived at Oji, and went into the tea-house that had been agreed upon; and Chokichi, going out to meet them, exclaimed—

"Dear me, Miss O Koyo, his lordship has been all impatience waiting for you: pray make haste and come in."

But, in spite of what he said, O Koyo, on account of her virgin modesty, would not go in. O Kuma, however, who was not quite so particular, cried out—

"Why, what is the meaning of this? As you've come here, O Koyo, it's a little late for you to be making a fuss about being shy. Don't be a little fool, but come in with me at once." And with these words she caught fast hold of O Koyo's hand, and, pulling her by force into the room, made her sit down by Genzaburô.

When Genzaburô saw how modest she was, he reassured her, saying—

"Come, what is there to be so shy about? Come a little nearer to me, pray."

"Thank you, sir. How could I, who am such a vile thing, pollute your nobility by sitting by your side?" And, as she spoke, the blushes mantled over her face; and the more Genzaburô looked at her, the more beautiful she appeared in his eyes, and the more deeply he became enamoured of her charms. In the meanwhile he called for wine and fish, and all four together made a feast of it. When Chokichi and O Kuma saw how the land lay, they retired discreetly into another chamber, and Genzaburô and O Koyo were left alone together, looking at one another.

"Come," said Genzaburô, smiling, "hadn't you better sit a little closer to me?"

"Thank you, sir; really I'm afraid."

But Genzaburô, laughing at her for her idle fears, said—

"Don't behave as if you hated me."

"Oh, dear! I'm sure I don't hate you, sir. That would be very rude; and, indeed, it's not the case. I loved you when I first saw you at the Adzuma Bridge, and longed for you with all my heart; but I knew what a despised race I belonged to, and that I was no fitting match for you, and so I tried to be resigned. But I am very young and inexperienced, and so I could not help thinking of you, and you alone; and then Chokichi came, and when I heard what you had said about me, I thought, in the joy of my heart, that it must be a dream of happiness."

And as she spoke these words, blushing timidly, Genzaburô was dazzled with her beauty, and said—

"Well, you're a clever child. I'm sure, now, you must have some handsome young lover of your own, and that is why you don't care to come and drink wine and sit by me. Am I not right, eh?"

"Ah, sir, a nobleman like you is sure to have a beautiful wife at home; and then you are so handsome that, of course, all the pretty young ladies are in love with you."

"Nonsense! Why, how clever you are at flattering and paying compliments! A pretty little creature like you was just made to turn all the men's heads—a little witch."

"Ah! those are hard things to say of a poor girl! Who could think of falling in love with such a wretch as I am? Now, pray tell me all about your own sweetheart: I do so long to hear about her."

"Silly child! I'm not the sort of man to put thoughts into the heads of fair ladies. However, it is quite true that there is some one whom I want to marry."

At this O Koyo began to feel jealous.

"Ah!" said she, "how happy that some one must be! Do, pray, tell me the whole story." And a feeling of jealous spite came over her, and made her quite unhappy.

Genzaburô laughed as he answered—

"Well, that some one is yourself, and nobody else. There!" and as he spoke, he gently tapped the dimple on her cheek with his finger; and O Koyo's heart beat so, for very joy, that, for a little while, she remained speechless. At last she turned her face towards Genzaburô, and said—

"Alas! your lordship is only trifling with me, when you know that what you have just been pleased to propose is the darling wish of my heart. Would that I could only go into your house as a maid-servant, in any capacity, however mean, that I might daily feast my eyes on your handsome face!"

"Ah! I see that you think yourself very clever at hoaxing men, and so you must needs tease me a little;" and, as he spoke, he took her hand, and drew her close up to him, and she, blushing again, cried—

"Oh! pray wait a moment, while I shut the sliding-doors."

"Listen to me, O Koyo! I am not going to forget the promise which I made you just now; nor need you be afraid of my harming you; but take care that you do not deceive me."

"Indeed, sir, the fear is rather that you should set your heart on others; but, although I am no fashionable lady, take pity on me, and love me well and long."

"Of course! I shall never care for another woman but you."

"Pray, pray, never forget those words that you have just spoken."

"And now," replied Genzaburô, "the night is advancing, and, for to-day, we must part; but we will arrange matters, so as to meet again in this tea-house. But, as people would make remarks if we left the tea-house together, I will go out first."

And so, much against their will, they tore themselves from one another, Genzaburô returning to his house, and O Koyo going home, her heart filled with joy at having found the man for whom she had pined; and from that day forth they used constantly to meet in secret at the tea-house; and Genzaburô, in his infatuation, never thought that the matter must surely become notorious after a while, and that he himself would be banished, and his family ruined: he only took care for the pleasure of the moment.

Now Chokichi, who had brought about the meeting between Genzaburô and his love, used to go every day to the tea-house at Oji, taking with him O Koyo; and Genzaburô neglected all his duties for the pleasure of these secret meetings. Chokichi saw this with great regret, and thought to himself that if Genzaburô gave himself up entirely to pleasure, and laid aside his duties, the secret would certainly be made public, and Genzaburô would bring ruin on himself and his family; so he began to devise some plan by which he might separate them, and plotted as eagerly to estrange them as he had formerly done to introduce them to one another.

At last he hit upon a device which satisfied him. Accordingly one day he went to O Koyo's house, and, meeting her father Kihachi, said to him—

"I've got a sad piece of news to tell you. The family of my lord Genzaburô have been complaining bitterly of his conduct in carrying on his relationship with your daughter, and of the ruin which exposure would bring upon the whole house; so they have been using their influence to persuade him to hear reason, and give up the connection. Now his lordship feels deeply for the damsel, and yet he cannot sacrifice his family for her sake. For the first time, he has become alive to the folly of which he has been guilty, and, full of remorse, he has commissioned me to devise some stratagem to break off the affair. Of course, this has taken me by surprise; but as there is no gainsaying the right of the case, I have had no option but to promise obedience: this promise I have come to redeem; and now, pray, advise your daughter to think no more of his lordship."

When Kihachi heard this he was surprised and distressed, and told O Koyo immediately; and she, grieving over the sad news, took no thought either of eating or drinking, but remained gloomy and desolate.

In the meanwhile, Chokichi went off to Genzaburô's house, and told him that O Koyo had been taken suddenly ill, and could not go to meet him, and begged him to wait patiently until she should send to tell him of her recovery. Genzaburô, never suspecting the story to be false, waited for thirty days, and still Chokichi brought him no tidings of O Koyo. At last he met Chokichi, and besought him to arrange a meeting for him with O Koyo.

"Sir," replied Chokichi, "she is not yet recovered; so it would be difficult to bring her to see your honour. But I have been thinking much about this affair, sir. If it becomes public, your honour's family will be plunged in ruin. I pray you, sir, to forget all about O Koyo."

"It's all very well for you to give me advice," answered Genzaburô, surprised; "but, having once bound myself to O Koyo, it would be a pitiful thing to desert her; I therefore implore you once more to arrange that I may meet her."

However, he would not consent upon any account; so Genzaburô returned home, and, from that time forth, daily entreated Chokichi to bring O Koyo to him, and, receiving nothing but advice from him in return, was very sad and lonely.

One day Genzaburô, intent on ridding himself of the grief he felt at his separation from O Koyo, went to the Yoshiwara, and, going into a house of entertainment, ordered a feast to be prepared; but, in the midst of gaiety, his heart yearned all the while for his lost love, and his merriment was but mourning in disguise. At last the night wore on; and as he was retiring along the corridor, he saw a man of about forty years of age, with long hair, coming towards him, who, when he saw Genzaburô, cried out, "Dear me! why this must be my young lord Genzaburô who has come out to enjoy himself."

Genzaburô thought this rather strange; but, looking at the man attentively, recognised him as a retainer whom he had had in his employ the year before, and said—

"This is a curious meeting: pray what have you been about since you left my service? At any rate, I may congratulate you on being well and strong. Where are you living now?"

"Well, sir, since I parted from you I have been earning a living as a fortune-teller at Kanda, and have changed my name to Kaji Sazen. I am living in a poor and humble house; but if your lordship, at your leisure, would honour me with a visit——"

" Well, it's a lucky chance that has brought us together, and I certainly will go and see you; besides, I want you to do something for me. Shall you be at home the day after to-morrow ? "

" Certainly, sir, I shall make a point of being at home."

" Very well, then, the day after to-morrow I will go to your house."

" I shall be at your service, sir. And now, as it is getting late, I will take my leave for to-night."

" Good night, then. We shall meet the day after to-morrow." And so the two parted, and went their several ways to rest.

On the appointed day Genzaburô made his preparations, and went in disguise, without any retainers, to call upon Sazen, who met him at the porch of his house, and said, " This is a great honour ! My lord Genzaburô is indeed welcome. My house is very mean, but let me invite your lordship to come into an inner chamber."

" Pray," replied Genzaburô, " don't make any ceremony for me. Don't put yourself to any trouble on my account."

And so he passed in, and Sazen called to his wife to prepare wine and condiments; and they began to feast. At last Genzaburô, looking Sazen in the face, said, " There is a service which I want you to render me—a very secret service; but as, if you were to refuse me, I should be put to shame, before I tell you what that service is, I must know whether you are willing to assist me in anything that I may require of you."

" Yes; if it is anything that is within my power, I am at your disposal."

" Well, then," said Genzaburô, greatly pleased, and drawing ten riyos from his bosom, " this is but a small present to make to you on my first visit, but pray accept it."

" No, indeed ! I don't know what your lordship wishes of me; but, at any rate, I cannot receive this money. I really must beg you lordship to take it back again."

But Genzaburô pressed it upon him by force, and at last he was obliged to accept the money. Then Genzaburô told him the whole story of his loves with O Koyo—how he had first met her and fallen in love with her at the Adzuma Bridge how Chokichi had introduced her to him at the tea-house at Oji, and then when she fell ill, and he wanted to see her again, instead of bringing her to him, had only given him good advice ; and so Genzaburô drew a lamentable picture of his state of despair.

Sazen listened patiently to his story, and, after reflecting for a while, replied, "Well, sir, it's not a difficult matter to set right ; and yet it will require some little management. However, if your lordship will do me the honour of coming to see me again the day after to-morrow, I will cast about me in the meanwhile, and will let you know then the result of my deliberations."

When Genzaburô heard this he felt greatly relieved, and, recommending Sazen to do his best in the matter, took his leave and returned home. That very night Sazen, after thinking over all that Genzaburô had told him, laid his plans accordingly, and went off to the house of Kihachi, the Eta chief, and told him the commission with which he had been entrusted.

Kihachi was of course greatly astonished, and said, "Some time ago, sir, Chokichi came here and said that my lord Genzaburô, having been rebuked by his family for his profligate behaviour, had determined to break off his connection with my daughter. Of course I knew that the daughter of an Eta was no fitting match for a nobleman ; so when Chokichi came and told me the errand upon which he had been sent, I had no alternative but to announce to my daughter that she must give up all thought of his lordship. Since that time she has been fretting and pining and starving for love. But when I tell her what you have just said, how glad and happy she will be ! Let me go and talk to her at once." And with these words, he went to O Koyo's room ; and when he looked upon her thin wasted face, and saw how sad she was, he felt more and more pity for her, and said, "Well, O Koyo, are you in better spirits to-day ? Would you like something to eat ?"

" Thank you, I have no appetite."

" Well, at any rate, I have some news for you that will make you happy. A messenger has come from my lord Genzaburô, for whom your heart yearns."

At this O Koyo, who had been crouching down like a drooping flower, gave a great start, and cried out, " Is that really true ? Pray tell me all about it as quickly as possible."

" The story which Chokichi came and told us, that his lordship wished to break off the connection, was all an invention. He has all along been wishing to meet you, and constantly urged Chokichi to bring you a message from him. It is Chokichi who has been throwing obstacles in the way. At last his lordship has secretly sent a man, called Kaji Sazen, a fortune-teller, to arrange an interview between you. So now, my child, you may cheer up, and go to meet your lover as soon as you please."

When O Koyo heard this, she was so happy that she thought it must all be a dream, and doubted her own senses.

Kihachi in the meanwhile rejoined Sazen in the other room, and, after telling him of the joy with which his daughter had heard the news, put before him wine and other delicacies. " I think," said Sazen, " that the best way would be for O Koyo to live secretly in my lord Genzaburô's house ; but as it will never do for all the world to know of it, it must be managed very quietly ; and further, when I get home, I must think out some plan to lull the suspicions of that fellow Chokichi, and let you know my idea by letter. Meanwhile O Koyo had better come home with me to-night : although she is so terribly out of spirits now, she shall meet Genzaburô the day after to-morrow."

Kihachi reported this to O Koyo ; and as her pining for Genzaburô was the only cause of her sickness, she recovered her spirits at once, and, saying that she would go with Sazen immediately, joyfully made her preparations. Then Sazen, having once more warned Kihachi to keep the matter secret from Chokichi, and to act upon the letter which he should send him, returned home, taking with him O Koyo ; and after

O Koyo had bathed and dressed her hair, and painted herself and put on beautiful clothes, she came out looking so lovely that no princess in the land could vie with her; and Sazen, when he saw her, said to himself that it was no wonder that Genzaburô had fallen in love with her; then, as it was getting late, he advised her to go to rest, and, after showing her to her apartments, went to his own room and wrote his letter to Kihachi, containing the scheme which he had devised. When Kihachi received his instructions, he was filled with admiration at Sazen's ingenuity, and, putting on an appearance of great alarm and agitation, went off immediately to call on Chokichi, and said to him—

"Oh, Master Chokichi, such a terrible thing has happened! Pray, let me tell you all about it."

"Indeed! what can it be?"

"Oh! sir," answered Kihachi, pretending to wipe away his tears, "my daughter O Koyo, mourning over her separation from my lord Genzaburô, at first refused all sustenance, and remained nursing her sorrows until, last night, her woman's heart failing to bear up against her great grief, she drowned herself in the river, leaving behind her a paper on which she had written her intention."

When Chokichi heard this, he was thunderstruck, and exclaimed, "Can this really be true! And when I think that it was I who first introduced her to my lord, I am ashamed to look you in the face."

"Oh, say not so: misfortunes are the punishment due for our misdeeds in a former state of existence. I bear you no ill-will. This money which I hold in my hand was my daughter's; and in her last instructions she wrote to beg that it might be given, after her death, to you, through whose intervention she became allied with a nobleman: so please accept it as my daughter's legacy to you;" and as he spoke, he offered him three riyos.

"You amaze me!" replied the other. "How could I, above all men, who have so much to reproach myself with in my conduct towards you, accept this money?"

"Nay; it was my dead daughter's wish. But since you reproach yourself in the matter when you think of her, I will beg you to put up a prayer and to cause masses to be said for her."

At last, Chokichi, after much persuasion, and greatly to his own distress, was obliged to accept the money; and when Kihachi had carried out all Sazen's instructions, he returned home, laughing in his sleeve.

Chokichi was sorely grieved to hear of O Koyo's death, and remained thinking over the sad news; when all of a sudden looking about him, he saw something like a letter lying on the spot where Kihachi had been sitting, so he picked it up and read it; and, as luck would have it, it was the very letter which contained Sazen's instructions to Kihachi, and in which the whole story which had just affected him so much was made up. When he perceived the trick that had been played upon him, he was very angry, and exclaimed, "To think that I should have been so hoaxed by that hateful old dotard, and such a fellow as Sazen! And Genzaburô, too!—out of gratitude for the favours which I had received from him in old days, I faithfully gave him good advice, and all in vain. Well, they've gulled me once; but I'll be even with them yet, and hinder their game before it is played out!" And so he worked himself up into a fury, and went off secretly to prowl about Sazen's house to watch for O Koyo, determined to pay off Genzaburô and Sazen for their conduct to him.

In the meanwhile Sazen, who did not for a moment suspect what had happened, when the day which had been fixed upon by him and Genzaburô arrived, made O Koyo put on her best clothes, smartened up his house, and got ready a feast against Genzaburô's arrival. The latter came punctually to his time, and, going in at once, said to the fortune-teller, "Well, have you succeeded in the commission with which I entrusted you?"

At first Sazen pretended to be vexed at the question, and said, "Well, sir, I've done my best; but it's not a matter which can be settled in a hurry. However, there's a young lady of high birth and wonderful beauty upstairs, who has come here secretly to have her fortune told; and if your lordship would like to come with me and see her, you can do so."

But Genzaburô, when he heard that he was not to meet O Koyo, lost heart entirely, and made up his mind to go home again. Sazen, however, pressed him so eagerly, that at last he went upstairs to see this vaunted beauty; and Sazen, drawing aside a screen, showed him O Koyo, who was sitting there. Genzaburô gave a great start, and, turning to Sazen, said, "Well, you certainly are a first-rate hand at keeping up a hoax. However, I cannot sufficiently praise the way in which you have carried out my instructions."

"Pray, don't mention it, sir. But as it is a long time since you have met the young lady, you must have a great deal to say to one another; so I will go downstairs, and, if you want anything, pray call me." And so he went downstairs and left them.

Then Genzaburô, addressing O Koyo, said, "Ah! it is indeed a long time since we met. How happy it makes me to see you again! Why, your face has grown quite thin. Poor thing! have you been unhappy?" And O Koyo, with the tears starting from her eyes for joy, hid her face; and her heart was so full that she could not speak. But Genzaburô, passing his hand gently over her head and back, and comforting her, said, "Come, sweetheart, there is no need to sob so. Talk to me a little, and let me hear your voice."

At last O Koyo raised her head and said, "Ah! when I was separated from you by the tricks of Chokichi, and thought that I should never meet you again, how tenderly I thought of you! I thought I should have died, and waited for my hour to come, pining all the while for you. And when at last, as I lay between life and death, Sazen came with a message from you, I thought it was all a dream." And as she spoke, she bent her head and sobbed again; and in Genzaburô's eyes she seemed more beautiful than ever, with her pale, delicate face; and he loved her better than before. Then she said, "If I were to tell you all I have suffered until to-day, I should never stop."

"Yes," replied Genzaburô, "I too have suffered much;" and so they told one another their mutual griefs, and from that day forth they constantly met at Sazen's house.

One day, as they were feasting and enjoying themselves in an upper story in Sazen's house, Chokichi came to the house and said, "I beg pardon; but does one Master Sazen live here?"

"Certainly, sir: I am Sazen, at your service. Pray where are you from?"

"Well, sir, I have a little business to transact with you. May I make so bold as to go in?" And with these words, he entered the house.

"But who and what are you?" said Sazen.

"Sir, I am an Eta; and my name is Chokichi. I beg to bespeak your goodwill for myself: I hope we may be friends."

Sazen was not a little taken aback at this; however, he put on an innocent face, as though he had never heard of Chokichi before, and said, "I never heard of such a thing! Why, I thought you were some respectable person; and you have the impudence to tell me that your name is Chokichi, and that you're one of those accursed Etas. To think of such a shameless villain coming and asking to be friends with me, forsooth! Get you gone!—the quicker, the better: your presence pollutes the house."

Chokichi smiled contemptuously, as he answered, "So you deem the presence of an Eta in your house a pollution—eh? Why, I thought you must be one of us."

"Insolent knave! Begone as fast as possible."

"Well, since you say that I defile your house, you had better get rid of O Koyo as well. I suppose she must equally be a pollution to it."

This put Sazen rather in a dilemma; however, he made up his mind not to show any hesitation, and said, "What are you talking about? There is no O Koyo here; and I never saw such a person in my life."

Chokichi quietly drew out of the bosom of his dress the letter from Sazen to Kihachi, which he had picked up a few days before, and, showing it to Sazen, replied, "If you wish to dispute the genuineness of this paper, I will report the whole matter to the Governor of Yedo; and Genzaburô's family will be ruined, and the rest of you who are parties in this affair will come in for your share of trouble. Just wait a little."

And as he pretended to leave the house, Sazen, at his wits' end, cried out, "Stop! stop! I want to speak to you. Pray, stop and listen quietly. It is quite true, as you said, that O Koyo is in my house; and really your indignation is perfectly just. Come! let us talk over matters a little. Now you yourself were originally a respectable man; and although you have fallen in life, there is no reason why your disgrace should last for ever. All that you want in order to enable you to escape out of this fraternity of Etas is a little money. Why should you not get this from Genzaburô, who is very anxious to keep his intrigue with O Koyo secret?"

Chokichi laughed disdainfully. "I am ready to talk with you; but I don't want any money. All I want is to report the affair to the authorities, in order that I may be revenged for the fraud that was put upon me."

"Wont you accept twenty-five riyos?"

"Twenty-five riyos! No, indeed! I will not take a fraction less than a hundred; and if I cannot get them I will report the whole matter at once."

Sazen, after a moment's consideration, hit upon a scheme, and answered, smiling, "Well, Master Chokichi, you're a fine fellow, and I admire your spirit. You shall have the hundred riyos you ask for; but, as I have not so much money by me at present, I will go to Genzaburô's house and fetch it. It's getting dark now, but it's not very late; so I'll trouble you to come with me, and then I can give you the money to-night."

Chokichi consenting to this, the pair left the house together.

Now Sazen, who as a Rônin wore a long dirk in his girdle, kept looking out for a moment when Chokichi should be off his guard, in order to kill him; but Chokichi kept his eyes open, and did not give Sazen a chance. At last Chokichi, as ill-luck would have it, stumbled against a stone and fell; and Sazen, profiting by the chance, drew his dirk and stabbed him in the side; and as Chokichi, taken by surprise, tried to get up, he cut him severely over the head, until at last he fell dead. Sazen then looking around him, and seeing, to his great delight, that there was no one near, returned home. The following day, Chokichi's body was found by the police; and when they examined it, they found nothing upon it save a paper, which they read, and which proved to be the very letter which Sazen had sent to Kihachi, and which Chokichi had picked up. The matter was immediately reported to the governor, and, Sazen having been summoned, an investigation was held. Sazen, cunning and bold murderer as he was, lost his self-possession when he saw what a fool he had been not to get back from Chokichi the letter which he had written, and, when he was put to a rigid examination under torture, confessed that he had hidden O Koyo at Genzaburô's instigation, and then killed Chokichi, who had found out the secret. Upon this the governor, after consulting about Genzaburô's case, decided that, as he had disgraced his position as a Hatamoto by contracting an alliance with the daughter of an Eta, his property should be confiscated, his family blotted out, and himself banished. As for Kihachi, the Eta chief, and his daughter O Koyo, they were handed over for punishment to the chief of the Etas, and by him they too were banished; while Sazen, against whom the murder of Chokichi had been fully proved, was executed according to law.

NOTE

At Asakusa, in Yedo, there lives a man called Danzayémon, the chief of the Etas. This man traces his pedigree back to Minamoto no Yoritomo, who founded the Shogunate in the year 1192 A.D. The whole of the Etas in Japan are under his jurisdiction: his subordinates are called Koyagashira, or "chiefs of the huts;" and he and they constitute the government of the Etas. In the "Legacy of Iyéyasu," already quoted, the 36th Law provides as follows:— "All wandering mendicants, such as male sorcerers, female diviners, hermits, blind people, beggars, and tanners (Etas), have had from of old their respective rulers. Be not disinclined, however, to punish any such who give rise to disputes, or who overstep the boundaries of their own classes and are disobedient to existing laws."

The occupation of the Etas is to kill and flay horses, oxen, and other beasts, to stretch drums and make shoes; and if they are very poor, they wander from house to house, working as cobblers, mending old shoes and leather, and so earn a scanty livelihood. Besides this, their daughters and young married women gain a trifle as wandering minstrels, called Torioi, playing on the *shamisen*, a sort of banjo, and singing ballads. They never marry out of their own fraternity, but remain apart, a despised and shunned race.

At executions by crucifixion it is the duty of the Etas to transfix the victims with spears; and, besides this, they have to perform all sorts of degrading offices about criminals, such as carrying sick prisoners from their cells to the hall of justice, and burying the bodies of those that have been executed. Thus their race is polluted and accursed, and they are hated accordingly.

Now this is how the Etas come to be under the jurisdiction of Danzayémon:—

When Minamoto no Yoritomo was yet a child, his father, Minamoto no Yoshitomo, fought with Taira no Kiyomori, and was killed by treachery: so his family was ruined, and Yoshitomo's concubine, whose name was Tokiwa, took her children and fled from the house, to save her own and their lives. But Kiyomori, desiring to destroy the family of Yoshitomo root and branch, ordered his retainers to divide themselves into bands, and seek out the children. At last they were found; but Tokiwa was so exceedingly beautiful that Kiyomori was inflamed with love for her, and desired her to become his own concubine. Then Tokiwa told Kiyomori that if he would spare her little ones she would share his couch; but that if he killed her children she would destroy herself rather than yield to his desire. When he heard this,

Kiyomori, bewildered by the beauty of Tokiwa, spared the lives of her children, but banished them from the capital.

So Yoritomo was sent to Hirugakojima, in the province of Idzu; and when he grew up and became a man, he married the daughter of a peasant. After a while Yoritomo left the province, and went to the wars, leaving his wife pregnant; and in due time she was delivered of a male child, to the delight of her parents, who rejoiced that their daughter should bear seed to a nobleman; but she soon fell sick and died, and the old people took charge of the babe. And when they also died, the care of the child fell to his mother's kinsmen, and he grew up to be a peasant.

Now Kiyomori, the enemy of Yoritomo, had been gathered to his fathers; and Yoritomo had avenged the death of his father by slaying Munémori, the son of Kiyomori; and there was peace throughout the land. And Yoritomo became the chief of all the noble houses in Japan, and first established the government of the country. When Yoritomo had thus raised himself to power, if the son that his peasant wife had born to him had proclaimed himself the son of the mighty prince, he would have been made lord over a province; but he took no thought of this, and remained a tiller of the earth, forfeiting a glorious inheritance; and his descendants after him lived as peasants in the same village, increasing in prosperity and in good repute among their neighbours.

But the princely line of Yoritomo came to an end in three generations, and the house of Hôjô was all-powerful in the land.

Now it happened that the head of the house of Hôjô heard that a descendant of Yoritomo was living as a peasant in the land, so he summoned him and said—

"It is a hard thing to see the son of an illustrious house live and die a peasant. I will promote you to the rank of Samurai."

Then the peasant answered, "My lord, if I become a Samurai, and the retainer of some noble, I shall not be so happy as when I was my own master. If I may not remain a husbandman, let me be a chief over men, however humble they may be."

But my lord Hôjô was angry at this, and, thinking to punish the peasant for his insolence, said—

"Since you wish to become a chief over men, no matter how humble, there is no means of gratifying your strange wish but by making you chief over the Etas of the whole country. So now see that you rule them well."

When he heard this, the peasant was afraid; but because he had said that he wished to become a chief over men, however humble, he could not choose but become chief of the Etas, he and his children after him for ever; and Danzayémon, who rules the Etas at the present time, and lives at Asakusa, is his lineal descendant.

FAIRY TALES

FAIRY TALES

I THINK that their quaintness is a sufficient apology for the following little children's stories. With the exception of that of the "Elves and the Envious Neighbour," which comes out of a curious book on etymology and proverbial lore, called the Kotowazagusa, these stories are found printed in little separate pamphlets, with illustrations, the stereotype blocks of which have become so worn that the print is hardly legible. These are the first tales which are put into a Japanese child's hands; and it is with these, and such as these, that the Japanese mother hushes her little ones to sleep. Knowing the interest which many children of a larger growth take in such Baby Stories, I was anxious to have collected more of them. I was disappointed, however, for those which I give here are the only ones which I could find in print; and if I asked the Japanese to tell me others, they only thought I was laughing at them, and changed the subject. The stories of the Tongue-cut Sparrow, and the Old Couple and their Dog, have been paraphrased in other works upon Japan; but I am not aware of their having been literally translated before.

THE TONGUE-CUT SPARROW

Once upon a time there lived an old man and an old woman. The old man, who had a kind heart, kept a young sparrow, which he tenderly nurtured. But the dame was a cross-grained old thing; and one day, when the sparrow had pecked at some paste with which she was going to starch her linen, she flew into a great rage, and cut the sparrow's tongue and let it loose. When the old man came home from the hills and found that the bird had flown, he asked what had become of it; so the old woman answered that she had cut its tongue and let it go, because it had stolen her starching-paste. Now the old man, hearing this cruel tale, was sorely grieved, and thought to himself, "Alas! where can my bird be gone? Poor thing! Poor little tongue-cut sparrow! where is your home now?" and he wandered far and wide, seeking for his pet, and crying, "Mr. Sparrow! Mr. Sparrow! where are you living?"

One day, at the foot of a certain mountain, the old man fell in with the lost bird; and when they had congratulated one another on their mutual safety, the sparrow led the old man to his home, and, having introduced him to his wife and chicks, set before him all sorts of dainties, and entertained him hospitably.

"Please partake of our humble fare," said the sparrow "poor as it is, you are very welcome."

"What a polite sparrow!" answered the old man, who remained for a long time as the sparrow's guest, and was daily feasted right royally. At last the old man said that he must take his leave and return home; and the bird, offering

THE TONGUE-CUT SPARROW

him two wicker baskets, begged him to carry them with him as a parting present. One of the baskets was heavy, and the other was light; so the old man, saying that as he was feeble and stricken in years he would only accept the light one, shouldered it, and trudged off home, leaving the sparrow-family disconsolate at parting from him.

When the old man got home, the dame grew very angry, and began to scold him, saying, "Well, and pray where have you been this many a day? A pretty thing, indeed, to be gadding about at your time of life!"

"Oh!" replied he, "I have been on a visit to the sparrows; and when I came away, they gave me this wicker basket as a parting gift." Then they opened the basket to see what was inside, and, lo and behold! it was full of gold and silver and precious things. When the old woman, who was as greedy as she was cross, saw all the riches displayed before her, she changed her scolding strain, and could not contain herself for joy.

"I'll go and call upon the sparrows, too," said she, "and get a pretty present." So she asked the old man the way to the sparrows' house, and set forth on her journey. Following his directions, she at last met the tongue-cut sparrow, and exclaimed—

"Well met! well met! Mr. Sparrow. I have been looking forward to the pleasure of seeing you." So she tried to flatter and cajole the sparrow by soft speeches.

The bird could not but invite the dame to its home; but it took no pains to feast her, and said nothing about a parting gift. She, however, was not to be put off; so she asked for something to carry away with her in remembrance of her visit. The sparrow accordingly produced two baskets, as before, and the greedy old woman, choosing the heavier of the two, carried it off with her. But when she opened the basket to see what was inside, all sorts of hobgoblins and elves sprang out of it, and began to torment her.

But the old man adopted a son, and his family grew rich and prosperous. What a happy old man!

THE ACCOMPLISHED AND LUCKY TEA-KETTLE

A LONG time ago, at a temple called Morinji, in the province of Jôshiu, there was an old tea-kettle. One day, when the priest of the temple was about to hang it over the hearth to boil the water for his tea, to his amazement, the kettle all of a sudden put forth the head and tail of a badger. What a wonderful kettle, to come out all over fur! The priest, thunderstruck, called in the novices of the temple to see the sight; and whilst they were stupidly staring, one suggesting one thing and another another, the kettle, jumping up into the air, began flying about the room. More astonished than ever, the priest and his pupils tried to pursue it; but no thief or cat was ever half so sharp as this wonderful badger-kettle. At last, however, they managed to knock it down and secure it; and, holding it in with their united efforts, they forced it into a box, intending to carry it off and throw it away in some distant place, so that they might be no more plagued by the goblin. For this day their troubles were over; but, as luck would have it, the tinker who was in the habit of working for the temple called in, and the priest suddenly bethought him that it was a pity to throw the kettle away for nothing, and that he might as well get a trifle for it, no matter how small. So he brought out the kettle, which had resumed its former shape and had got rid of its head and tail, and showed it to the tinker. When the tinker saw the kettle, he offered twenty copper coins for it, and the priest was only too glad to close the bargain and be rid of his troublesome piece of furniture. But the tinker trudged off home with his pack and his new purchase. That

THE ACCOMPLISHED AND LUCKY TEA-KETTLE

night, as he lay asleep, he heard a strange noise near his pillow; so he peeped out from under the bedclothes, and there he saw the kettle that he had bought in the temple covered with fur, and walking about on four legs. The tinker started up in a fright to see what it could all mean, when all of a sudden the kettle resumed its former shape. This happened over and over again, until at last the tinker showed the tea-kettle to a friend of his, who said, "This is certainly an accomplished and lucky tea-kettle. You should take it about as a show, with songs and accompaniments of musical instruments, and make it dance and walk on the tight rope."

The tinker, thinking this good advice, made arrangements with a showman, and set up an exhibition. The noise of the kettle's performances soon spread abroad, until even the princes of the land sent to order the tinker to come to them; and he grew rich beyond all his expectations. Even the princesses, too, and the great ladies of the court, took great delight in the dancing kettle, so that no sooner had it shown its tricks in one place than it was time for them to keep some other engagement. At last the tinker grew so rich that he took the kettle back to the temple, where it was laid up as a precious treasure, and worshipped as a saint.

THE CRACKLING MOUNTAIN

ONCE upon a time there lived an old man and an old woman, who kept a pet white hare, by which they set great store. One day, a badger, that lived hard by, came and ate up the food which had been put out for the hare; so the old man, flying into a great rage, seized the badger, and, tying the beast up to a tree, went off to the mountain to cut wood, while the old woman stopped at home and ground the wheat for the evening porridge. Then the badger, with tears in his eyes, said to the old woman—

"Please, dame, please untie this rope!"

The dame, thinking that it was a cruel thing to see a poor beast in pain, undid the rope; but the ungrateful brute was no sooner loose, than he cried out—

"I'll be revenged for this," and was off in a trice.

When the hare heard this, he went off to the mountain to warn the old man; and whilst the hare was away on this errand, the badger came back, and killed the dame. Then the beast, having assumed the old woman's form, made her dead body into broth, and waited for the old man to come home from the mountain. When he returned, tired and hungry, the pretended old woman said—

"Come, come; I've made such a nice broth of the badger you hung up. Sit down, and make a good supper of it."

With these words she set out the broth, and the old man made a hearty meal, licking his lips over it, and praising the savoury mess. But as soon as he had finished eating, the badger, reassuming its natural shape, cried out—

"Nasty old man! you've eaten your own wife. Look at her bones, lying in the kitchen sink!" and, laughing contemptuously, the badger ran away, and disappeared.

Then the old man, horrified at what he had done, set up a great lamentation; and whilst he was bewailing his fate, the hare came home, and, seeing how matters stood, determined to avenge the death of his mistress. So he went back to the mountain, and, falling in with the badger, who was carrying a faggot of sticks on his back, he struck a light and set fire to the sticks, without letting the badger see him. When the badger heard the crackling noise of the faggot burning on his back, he called out—

"Holloa! what is that noise?"

"Oh!" answered the hare, "this is called the Crackling Mountain. There's always this noise here."

And as the fire gathered strength, and went pop! pop! pop! the badger said again—

"Oh dear! what can this noise be?"

"This is called the 'Pop! Pop! Mountain,'" answered the hare.

All at once the fire began to singe the badger's back, so that he fled, howling with pain, and jumped into a river hard by. But, although the water put out the fire, his back was burnt as black as a cinder. The hare, seeing an opportunity for torturing the badger to his heart's content. made a poultice of cayenne pepper, which he carried to the badger's house, and, pretending to condole with him, and to have a sovereign remedy for burns, he applied his hot plaister to his enemy's sore back. Oh! how it smarted and pained! and how the badger yelled and cried!

When, at last, the badger got well again, he went to the hare's house, thinking to reproach him for having caused him so much pain. When he got there, he found that the hare had built himself a boat.

"What have you built that boat for, Mr. Hare?" said the badger.

"I'm going to the capital of the moon,"[1] answered the hare; "won't you come with me?"

"I had enough of your company on the Crackling Mountain, where you played me such tricks. I'd rather make a boat for myself," replied the badger, who immediately began building himself a boat of clay.

The hare, seeing this, laughed in his sleeve; and so the two launched their boats upon the river. The waves came plashing against the two boats; but the hare's boat was built of wood, while that of the badger was made of clay, and, as they rowed down the river, the clay boat began to crumble away; then the hare, seizing his paddle, and brandishing it in the air, struck savagely at the badger's boat, until he had smashed it to pieces, and killed his enemy.

When the old man heard that his wife's death had been avenged, he was glad in his heart, and more than ever petted and loved the hare, whose brave deeds had caused him to welcome the returning spring.

---

[1] The mountains in the moon are supposed to resemble a hare in shape. Hence there is a fanciful connection between the hare and the moon.

THE STORY OF THE OLD MAN WHO MADE
WITHERED TREES TO BLOSSOM

In the old, old days, there lived an honest man with his wife, who had a favourite dog, which they used to feed with fish and titbits from their own kitchen. One day, as the old folks went out to work in their garden, the dog went with them, and began playing about. All of a sudden, the dog stopped short, and began to bark, "Bow, wow, wow!" wagging his tail violently. The old people thought that there must be something nice to eat under the ground, so they brought a spade and began digging, when, lo and behold! the place was full of gold pieces and silver, and all sorts of precious things, which had been buried there. So they gathered the treasure together, and, after giving alms to the poor, bought themselves rice-fields and corn-fields, and became wealthy people.

Now, in the next house there dwelt a covetous and stingy old man and woman, who, when they heard what had happened, came and borrowed the dog, and, having taken him home, prepared a great feast for him, and said—

"If you please, Mr. Dog, we should be much obliged to you if you would show us a place with plenty of money in it."

The dog, however, who up to that time had received nothing but cuffs and kicks from his hosts, would not eat any of the dainties which they set before him; so the old people began to get cross, and, putting a rope round the dog's neck, led him out into the garden. But it was all in vain; let them lead him where they might, not a sound would the dog utter : he had no "bow-wow" for them. At last, however, the dog stopped at a certain spot, and began to sniff; so, thinking

THE OLD MAN WHO CAUSED WITHERED TREES TO FLOWER

that this must surely be the lucky place, they dug, and found nothing but a quantity of dirt and nasty offal, over which they had to hold their noses. Furious at being disappointed, the wicked old couple seized the dog, and killed him.

When the good old man saw that the dog, whom he had lent, did not come home, he went next door to ask what had become of him; and the wicked old man answered that he had killed the dog, and buried him at the root of a pine-tree; so the good old fellow, with a heavy heart, went to the spot, and, having set out a tray with delicate food, burnt incense, and adorned the grave with flowers, as he shed tears over his lost pet.

But there was more good luck in store yet for the old people—the reward of their honesty and virtue. How do you think that happened, my children? It is very wrong to be cruel to dogs and cats.

That night, when the good old man was fast asleep in bed, the dog appeared to him, and, after thanking him for all his kindness, said—

"Cause the pine-tree, under which I am buried, to be cut down and made into a mortar, and use it, thinking of it as if it were myself."

The old man did as the dog had told him to do, and made a mortar out of the wood of the pine-tree; but when he ground his rice in it, each grain of rice was turned into some rich treasure. When the wicked old couple saw this, they came to borrow the mortar; but no sooner did they try to use it, than all their rice was turned into filth; so, in a fit of rage, they broke up the mortar and burnt it. But the good old man, little suspecting that his precious mortar had been broken and burnt, wondered why his neighbours did not bring it back to him.

One night the dog appeared to him again in a dream, and told him what had happened, adding that if he would take the ashes of the burnt mortar and sprinkle them on withered trees, the trees would revive, and suddenly put out flowers. After saying this the dream vanished, and the old man, who heard for the first time of the loss of his mortar, ran off weeping to the neighbours' house, and begged them, at any rate, to give him back the ashes of his treasure. Having obtained these, he returned home, and made a trial of their virtues upon a withered cherry-tree, which, upon being touched by the ashes, immediately began to sprout and blossom. When he saw this wonderful effect, he put the ashes into a basket, and went about the country, announcing himself as an old man who had the power of bringing dead trees to life again.

A certain prince, hearing of this, and thinking it a mighty strange thing, sent for the old fellow, who showed his power by causing all the withered plum and cherry-trees to shoot out and put forth flowers. So the prince gave him a rich reward of pieces of silk and cloth and other presents, and sent him home rejoicing.

So soon as the neighbours heard of this they collected all the ashes that remained, and, having put them in a basket, the wicked old man went out into the castle town, and gave out that he was the old man who had the power of reviving dead trees, and causing them to flower. He had not to wait long before he was called into the prince's palace, and ordered to exhibit his power. But when he climbed up into a withered tree, and began to scatter the ashes, not a bud nor a flower appeared; but the ashes all flew into the prince's eyes and mouth, blinding and choking him. When the prince's retainers saw this, they seized the old man, and beat him almost to death, so that he crawled off home in a very sorry plight. When he and his wife found out what a trap they had fallen into, they stormed and scolded, and put themselves into a passion; but that did no good at all.

The good old man and woman, so soon as they heard of their neighbours' distress, sent for them, and, after reproving them for their greed and cruelty, gave them a share of their own riches, which, by repeated strokes of luck, had now increased to a goodly sum. So the wicked old people mended their ways, and led good and virtuous lives ever after.

THE BATTLE OF THE APE AND THE CRAB

IF a man thinks only of his own profit, and tries to benefit himself at the expense of others, he will incur the hatred of Heaven. Men should lay up in their hearts the story of the Battle of the Ape and Crab, and teach it, as a profitable lesson, to their children.

Once upon a time there was a crab who lived in a marsh in a certain part of the country. It fell out one day that, the crab having picked up a rice cake, an ape, who had got a nasty hard persimmon-seed, came up, and begged the crab to make an exchange with him. The crab, who was a simple-minded creature, agreed to this proposal; and they each went their way, the ape chuckling to himself at the good bargain which he had made.

When the crab got home, he planted the persimmon-seed in his garden, and, as time slipped by, it sprouted, and by degrees grew to be a big tree. The crab watched the growth of his tree with great delight; but when the fruit ripened, and he was going to pluck it, the ape came in, and offered to gather it for him. The crab consenting, the ape climbed up into the tree, and began eating all the ripe fruit himself, while he only threw down the sour persimmons to the crab, inviting him, at the same time, to eat heartily. The crab, however, was not pleased at this arrangement, and thought that it was his turn to play a trick upon the ape; so he called out to him to come down head foremost. The ape did as he was bid; and as he crawled down, head foremost, the ripe fruit all came tumbling out of his pockets, and the crab, having picked up the persimmons, ran off and hid himself in a hole. The ape,

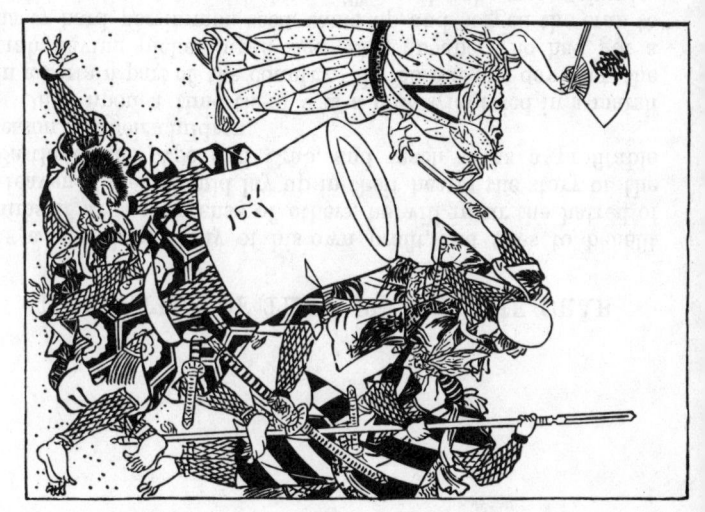

THE APE AND THE CRAB

seeing this, lay in ambush, and as soon as the crab crept out of his hiding-place gave him a sound drubbing, and went home. Just at this time a friendly egg and a bee, who were the apprentices of a certain rice-mortar, happened to pass that way, and, seeing the crab's piteous condition, tied up his wounds, and, having escorted him home, began to lay plans to be revenged upon the cruel ape.

Having agreed upon a scheme, they all went to the ape's house, in his absence; and each one having undertaken to play a certain part, they waited in secret for their enemy to come home. The ape, little dreaming of the mischief that was brewing, returned home, and, having a fancy to drink a cup of tea, began lighting the fire in the hearth, when, all of a sudden, the egg, which was hidden in the ashes, burst with the heat, and bespattered the frightened ape's face, so that he fled, howling with pain, and crying, "Oh! what an unlucky beast I am!" Maddened with the heat of the burst egg, he tried to go to the back of the house, when the bee darted out of a cupboard, and a piece of seaweed, who had joined the party, coming up at the same time, the ape was surrounded by enemies. In despair, he seized the clothes-rack, and fought valiantly for awhile; but he was no match for so many, and was obliged to run away, with the others in hot pursuit after him. Just as he was making his escape by a back door, however, the piece of seaweed tripped him up, and the rice-mortar, closing with him from behind, made an end of him.

So the crab, having punished his enemy, went home in triumph, and lived ever after on terms of brotherly love with the seaweed and the mortar. Was there ever such a fine piece of fun!

THE ADVENTURES OF LITTLE PEACHLING

MANY hundred years ago there lived an honest old wood-cutter and his wife. One fine morning the old man went off to the hills with his billhook, to gather a faggot of sticks, while his wife went down to the river to wash the dirty clothes. When she came to the river, she saw a peach floating down the stream; so she picked it up, and carried it home with her, thinking to give it to her husband to eat when he should come in. The old man soon came down from the hills, and the good wife set the peach before him, when, just as she was inviting him to eat it, the fruit split in two, and a little puling baby was born into the world. So the old couple took the babe, and brought it up as their own; and, because it had been born in a peach, they called it *Momotarô*,[1] or Little Peachling.

By degrees Little Peachling grew up to be strong and brave, and at last one day he said to his old foster-parents—

"I am going to the ogres' island to carry off the riches that they have stored up there. Pray, then, make me some millet dumplings for my journey."

So the old folks ground the millet, and made the dumplings for him; and Little Peachling, after taking an affectionate leave of them, cheerfully set out on his travels.

As he was journeying on, he fell in with an ape, who gibbered at him, and said, "Kia! kia! kia! where are you off to, Little Peachling?"

---

[1] *Momo* means a peach, and *Tarô* is the termination of the names of eldest sons, as *Hikotarô, Tokutarô,* &c. In modern times, however, the termination has been applied indifferently to any male child.

"I'm going to the ogres' island, to carry off their treasure," answered Little Peachling.

"What are you carrying at your girdle?"

"I'm carrying the very best millet dumplings in all Japan.

"If you'll give me one, I will go with you," said the ape.

So Little Peachling gave one of his dumplings to the ape, who received it and followed him. When he had gone a little further, he heard a pheasant calling—

"Ken! ken! ken!¹ where are you off to, Master Peachling?"

Little Peachling answered as before; and the pheasant, having begged and obtained a millet dumpling, entered his service, and followed him. A little while after this, they met a dog, who cried—

"Bow! wow! wow! whither away, Master Peachling?"

"I'm going off to the ogres' island, to carry off their treasure."

"If you will give me one of those nice millet dumplings of yours, I will go with you," said the dog.

"With all my heart," said Little Peachling. So he went on his way, with the ape, the pheasant, and the dog following after him.

When they got to the ogres' island, the pheasant flew over the castle gate, and the ape clambered over the castle wall, while Little Peachling, leading the dog, forced in the gate, and got into the castle. Then they did battle with the ogres, and put them to flight, and took their king prisoner. So all the ogres did homage to Little Peachling, and brought out the treasures which they had laid up. There were caps and coats that made their wearers invisible, jewels which governed the ebb and flow of the tide, coral, musk, emeralds, amber, and tortoiseshell, besides gold and silver. All these were laid before Little Peachling by the conquered ogres.

So Little Peachling went home laden with riches, and maintained his foster-parents in peace and plenty for the remainder of their lives.

¹ The country folk in Japan pretend that the pheasant's call is a sign of an approaching earthquake.

THE FOXES' WEDDING

ONCE upon a time there was a young white fox, whose name was Fukuyémon. When he had reached the fitting age, he shaved off his forelock [1] and began to think of taking to himself a beautiful bride. The old fox, his father, resolved to give up his inheritance to his son, [2] and retired into private life; so the young fox, in gratitude for this, laboured hard and earnestly to increase his patrimony. Now it happened that in a famous old family of foxes there was a beautiful young lady-fox, with such lovely fur that the fame of her jewel-like charms was spread far and wide. The young white fox, who had heard of this, was bent on making her his wife, and a meeting was arranged between them. There was not a fault to be found on either side; so the preliminaries were settled, and the wedding presents sent from the bridegroom to the bride's house, with congratulatory speeches from the messenger, which were duly acknowledged by the person deputed to receive the gifts; the bearers, of course, received the customary fee in copper cash.

When the ceremonies had been concluded, an auspicious day was chosen for the bride to go to her husband's house, and she was carried off in solemn procession during a shower of rain, the sun shining all the while. [3] After the ceremonies of drinking wine had been gone through, the

[1] See the Appendix on "Ceremonies."

[2] See the note on the word Inkiyo, in the story of the "Prince and the Badger."

[3] A shower during sunshine, which we call "the devil beating his wife," is called in Japan "the fox's bride going to her husband's house."

THE FOXES' WEDDING

bride changed her dress, and the wedding was concluded, without let or hindrance, amid singing and dancing and merry making.

The bride and bridegroom lived lovingly together, and a litter of little foxes were born to them, to the great joy of the old grandsire, who treated the little cubs as tenderly as if they had been butterflies or flowers. "They're the very image of their old grandfather," said he, as proud as possible. "As for medicine, bless them, they're so healthy that they'll never need a copper coin's worth !"

As soon as they were old enough, they were carried off to the temple of Inari Sama, the patron saint of foxes, and the old grandparents prayed that they might be delivered from dogs and all the other ills to which fox flesh is heir.

In this way the white fox by degrees waxed old and prosperous, and his children, year by year, became more and more numerous around him; so that, happy in his family and his business, every recurring spring brought him fresh cause for joy.

THE HISTORY OF SAKATA KINTOKI

A LONG time ago there was an officer of the Emperor's body-guard, called Sakata Kurando, a young man who, although he excelled in valour and in the arts of war, was of a gentle and loving disposition. This young officer was deeply ena-moured of a fair young lady, called Yaégiri, who lived at Gojôzaka, at Kiyôto. Now it came to pass that, having incurred the jealousy of certain other persons, Kurando fell into disgrace with the Court, and became a Rônin, so he was no longer able to keep up any communication with his love Yaégiri ; indeed, he became so poor that it was a hard matter for him to live. So he left the place and fled, no one knew whither. As for Yaégiri, lovesick and lorn, and pining for her lost darling, she escaped from the house where she lived, and wandered hither and thither through the country, seeking everywhere for Kurando.

Now Kurando, when he left the palace, turned tobacco merchant, and, as he was travelling about hawking his goods, it chanced that he fell in with Yaégiri ; so, having communicated to her his last wishes, he took leave of her and put an end to his life.

Poor Yaégiri, having buried her lover, went to the Ashigara Mountain, a distant and lonely spot, where she gave birth to a little boy, who, as soon as he was born, was of such wonderful strength that he walked about and ran playing all over the mountain. A woodcutter, who chanced to see the marvel, was greatly frightened at first, and thought the thing altogether uncanny ; but after a while he got used to the child, and became quite fond of him, and called him

"Little Wonder," and gave his mother the name of the "Old Woman of the Mountain."

One day, as "Little Wonder" was playing about, he saw that on the top of a high cedar-tree there was a tengu's nest; [1] so he began shaking the tree with all his might, until at last the tengu's nest came tumbling down.

As luck would have it, the famous hero, Minamoto no Yorimitsu, with his retainers, Watanabé Isuna, Usui Sadamitsu, and several others, had come to the mountain to hunt, and seeing the feat which "Little Wonder" had performed, came to the conclusion that he could be no ordinary child. Minamoto no Yorimitsu ordered Watanabé Isuna to find out the child's name and parentage. The Old Woman of the Mountain, on being asked about him, answered that she was the wife of Kurando, and that "Little Wonder" was the child of their marriage. And she proceeded to relate all the adventures which had befallen her.

When Yorimitsu heard her story, he said, "Certainly this child does not belie his lineage. Give the brat to me, and I will make him my retainer." The Old Woman of the Mountain gladly consented, and gave "Little Wonder" to Yorimitsu; but she herself remained in her mountain home. So "Little Wonder" went off with the hero Yorimitsu, who named him Sakata Kintoki; and in aftertimes he became famous and illustrious as a warrior, and his deeds are recited to this day. He is the favourite hero of little children, who carry his portrait in their bosom, and wish that they could emulate his bravery and strength.

---

[1] *Tengu*, or the Heavenly Dog, a hobgoblin who infests desert places, and is invoked to frighten naughty little children.

THE ELVES AND THE ENVIOUS NEIGHBOUR

ONCE upon a time there was a certain man, who, being over-taken by darkness among the mountains, was driven to seek shelter in the trunk of a hollow tree. In the middle of the night, a large company of elves assembled at the place ; and the man, peeping out from his hiding-place, was frightened out of his wits. After a while, however, the elves began to feast and drink wine, and to amuse themselves by singing and dancing, until at last the man, caught by the infection of the fun, forgot all about his fright, and crept out of his hollow tree to join in the revels. When the day was about to dawn, the elves said to the man, "You're a very jolly companion, and must come out and have a dance with us again. You must make us a promise, and keep it." So the elves, thinking to bind the man over to return, took a large wen that grew on his forehead and kept it in pawn ; upon this they all left the place, and went home. The man walked off to his own house in high glee at having passed a jovial night, and got rid of his wen into the bargain. So he told the story to all his friends, who congratulated him warmly on being cured of his wen. But there was a neighbour of his who was also troubled with a wen of long standing, and, when he heard of his friend's luck, he was smitten with envy, and went off to hunt for the hollow tree, in which, when he had found it, he passed the night.

Towards midnight the elves came, as he had expected, and began feasting and drinking, with songs and dances as before. As soon as he saw this, he came out of his hollow tree, and began dancing and singing as his neighbour had done. The elves, mistaking him for their former boon-companion, were delighted to see him, and said—

"You're a good fellow to recollect your promise, and we'll give you back your pledge;" so one of the elves, pulling the pawned wen out of his pocket, stuck it on to the man's forehead, on the top of the other wen which he already had. So the envious neighbour went home weeping, with two wens instead of one. This is a good lesson to people who cannot see the good luck of others, without coveting it for themselves.

THE GHOST OF SAKURA

THE misfortunes and death of the farmer Sôgorô, which, although the preternatural appearances by which they are said to have been followed may raise a smile, are matters of historic notoriety with which every Japanese is familiar, furnish a forcible illustration of the relations which exist between the tenant and the lord of the soil, and of the boundless power for good or for evil exercised by the latter. It is rather remarkable that in a country where the peasant—placed as he is next to the soldier, and before the artisan and merchant, in the four classes into which the people are divided—enjoys no small consideration, and where agriculture is protected by law from the inroads of wild vegetation, even to the lopping of overshadowing branches and the cutting down of hedgerow timber, the lord of the manor should be left practically without control in his dealings with his people.

The land-tax, or rather the yearly rent paid by the tenant, is usually assessed at forty per cent. of the produce; but there is no principle clearly defining it, and frequently the land-owner and the cultivator divide the proceeds of the harvest in equal shares. Rice land is divided into three classes; and, according to these classes, it is computed that one *tan* (1,800 square feet) of the best land should yield to the owner a revenue of five bags of rice per annum; each of these bags holds four tô (a tô is rather less than half an imperial bushel), and is worth at present (1868) three riyos, or about sixteen shillings; land of the middle class should yield a revenue of three or four bags. The rent is paid either in rice or in money, according to the actual price of the grain, which varies considerably. It is due in the eleventh month of the year, when the crops have all been gathered, and their market value fixed.

The rent of land bearing crops other than rice, such as cotton, beans, roots, and so forth, is payable in money during the twelfth month. The choice of the nature of the crops to be grown appears to be left to the tenant.

The Japanese landlord, when pressed by poverty, does not confine himself to the raising of his legitimate rents : he can always enforce from his needy tenantry the advancement of a year's rent, or the loan of so much money as may be required to meet his immediate necessities. Should the lord be just, the peasant is repaid by instalments, with interest, extending over ten or twenty years. But it too often happens that unjust and merciless lords do not repay such loans, but, on the contrary, press for further advances. Then it is that the farmers, dressed in their grass rain-coats, and carrying sickles and bamboo poles in their hands, assemble before the gate of their lord's palace at the capital, and represent their grievances, imploring the intercession of the retainers, and even of the womankind who may chance to go forth. Sometimes they pay for their temerity by their lives ; but, at any rate, they have the satisfaction of bringing shame upon their persecutor, in the eyes of his neighbours and of the populace.

The official reports of recent travels in the interior of Japan have fully proved the hard lot with which the peasantry had to put up during the government of the Tycoons, and especially under the Hatamotos, the created nobility of the dynasty. In one province, where the village mayors appear to have seconded the extortions of their lord, they have had to flee before an exasperated population, who, taking advantage of the revolution, laid waste and pillaged their houses, loudly praying for a new and just assessment of the land; while, throughout the country, the farmers have hailed with acclamations the resumption of the sovereign power by the Mikado, and the abolition of the petty nobility

THE DEPUTATION OF PEASANTS AT THEIR LORD'S GATE

who exalted themselves upon the misery of their dependants. Warming themselves in the sunshine of the court at Yedo, the Hatamotos waxed fat and held high revel, and little cared they who groaned or who starved. Money must be found, and it was found.

It is necessary here to add a word respecting the position of the village mayors, who play so important a part in the tale.

The peasants of Japan are ruled by three classes of officials: the Nanushi, or mayor; the Kumigashira, or chiefs of companies; and the Hiyakushôdai, or farmers' representatives. The village, which is governed by the Nanushi, or mayor, is divided into companies, which, consisting of five families each, are directed by a Kumigashira; these companies, again, are subdivided into groups of five men each, who choose one of their number to represent them in case of their having any petition to present, or any affairs to settle with their superiors. This functionary is the Hiyakushôdai. The mayor, the chief of the company, and the representative keep registers of the families and people under their control, and are responsible for their good and orderly behaviour. They pay taxes like the other farmers, but receive a salary, the amount of which depends upon the size and wealth of the village. Five per cent. of the yearly land tax forms the salary of the mayor, and the other officials each receive five per cent. of the tax paid by the little bodies over which they respectively rule.

The average amount of land for one family to cultivate is about one chô, or 9,000 square yards; but there are farmers who have inherited as much as five or even six chô from their ancestors. There is also a class of farmers called, from their poverty, "water-drinking farmers," who have no land of their own, but hire that of those who have more than they can keep in their own hands. The rent so paid varies; but good rice land will bring in as high a rent as from £1 18s. to £2 6s. per tan (1,800 square feet).

Farm labourers are paid from six or seven riyos a year to as much as thirty riyos (the riyo being worth about 5s. 4d.);

besides this, they are clothed and fed, not daintily indeed, but amply. The rice which they cultivate is to them an almost unknown luxury : millet is their staple food, and on high days and holidays they receive messes of barley or buckwheat. Where the mulberry-tree is grown, and the silkworm is "educated," there the labourer receives the highest wage.

The rice crop on good land should yield twelve and a half fold, and on ordinary land from six to seven fold only. Ordinary arable land is only half as valuable as rice land, which cannot be purchased for less than forty riyos per tan of 1,800 square feet. Common hill or wood land is cheaper, again, than arable land ; but orchards and groves of the Pawlonia are worth from fifty to sixty riyos per tan.

With regard to the punishment of crucifixion, by which Sôgorô was put to death, it is inflicted for the following offences : — parricide (including the murder or striking of parents, uncles, aunts, elder brothers, masters, or teachers) coining counterfeit money, and passing the barriers of the Tycoon's territory without a permit.[1] The criminal is attached to an upright post with two cross bars, to which his arms and feet are fastened by ropes. He is then transfixed with spears by men belonging to the Eta or Pariah class. I once passed the execution-ground near Yedo, when a body was attached to the cross. The dead man had murdered his employer, and, having been condemned to death by crucifixion, had died in prison before the sentence could be carried out. He was accordingly packed, in a squatting position, in a huge red earthenware jar, which, having been tightly filled up with salt, was hermetically sealed. On the anniversary of the commission of the crime, the jar was carried down to the execution-ground and broken, and the body was taken out and tied to the cross, the joints of the knees and arms having been cut, to allow of the extension of the stiffened and shrunken limbs ; it was then transfixed with spears, and allowed to remain exposed for three days. An open grave, the upturned soil of which seemed almost entirely composed

---

[1] This last crime is, of course, now obsolete.

of dead men's remains, waited to receive the dishonoured corpse, over which three or four Etas, squalid and degraded beings, were mounting guard, smoking their pipes by a scanty charcoal fire, and bandying obscene jests. It was a hideous and ghastly warning, had any cared to read the lesson; but the passers-by on the high road took little or no notice of the sight, and a group of chubby and happy children were playing not ten yards from the dead body, as if no strange or uncanny thing were near them.

THE GHOST OF SAKURA [1]

How true is the principle laid down by Confucius, that the benevolence of princes is reflected in their country, while their wickedness causes sedition and confusion!

In the province of Shimôsa, and the district of Sôma, Hotta Kaga no Kami was lord of the castle of Sakura, and chief of a family which had for generations produced famous warriors. When Kaga no Kami, who had served in the Gorôjiu, the cabinet of the Shogun, died at the castle of Sakura, his eldest son Kôtsuké no Suké Masanobu inherited his estates and honours, and was appointed to a seat in the Gorôjiu; but he was a different man from the lords who had preceded him. He treated the farmers and peasants unjustly, imposing additional and grievous taxes, so that the tenants on his estates were driven to the last extremity of poverty; and although year after year, and month after month, they prayed for mercy, and remonstrated against this injustice, no heed was paid to them, and the people throughout the villages were reduced to the utmost distress. Accordingly, the chiefs of the one hundred and thirty-six villages, producing a total revenue of 40,000 kokus of rice, assembled together in council and determined

[1] The story, which also forms the subject of a play, is published, but with altered names, in order that offence may not be given to the Hotta family. The real names are preserved here. The events related took place during the rule of the Shogun Iyémitsu, in the first half of the seventeenth century.

unanimously to present a petition to the Government, sealed with their seals, stating that their repeated remonstrances had been taken no notice of by their local authorities. Then they assembled in numbers before the house of one of the councillors of their lord, named Ikéura Kazuyé, in order to show the petition to him first, but even then no notice was taken of them; so they returned home, and resolved, after consulting together, to proceed to their lord's yashiki, or palace, at Yedo, on the seventh day of the tenth month. It was determined, with one accord, that one hundred and forty-three village chiefs should go to Yedo; and the chief of the village of Iwahashi, one Sôgorô, a man forty-eight years of age, distinguished for his ability and judgment, ruling a district which produced a thousand kokus, stepped forward, and said—

"This is by no means an easy matter, my masters. It certainly is of great importance that we should forward our complaint to our lord's palace at Yedo; but what are your plans? Have you any fixed intentions?"

"It is, indeed, a most important matter," rejoined the others; but they had nothing further to say. Then Sôgorô went on to say—

"We have appealed to the public office of our province, but without avail; we have petitioned the Prince's councillors, also in vain. I know that all that remains for us is to lay our case before our lord's palace at Yedo; and if we go there, it is equally certain that we shall not be listened to—on the contrary, we shall be cast into prison. If we are not attended to here, in our own province, how much less will the officials at Yedo care for us. We might hand our petition into the litter of one of the Gorôjiu, in the public streets; but, even in that case, as our lord is a member of the Gorôjiu, none of his peers would care to examine into the rights and wrongs of our complaint, for fear of offending him, and the man who presented the petition in so desperate a manner would lose his life on a bootless errand. If you have made up your minds to this, and are determined, at all hazards, to start, then go to Yedo by all means, and bid a long farewell to parents, children, wives, and relations. This is my opinion."

The others all agreeing with what Sôgorô said, they determined that, come what might, they would go to Yedo; and they settled to assemble at the village of Funabashi on the thirteenth day of the eleventh month.

On the appointed day all the village officers met at the place agreed upon,—Sôgorô, the chief of the village of Iwahashi, alone being missing; and as on the following day Sôgorô had not yet arrived, they deputed one of their number, named Rokurobei, to inquire the reason. Rokurobei arrived at Sôgorô's house towards four in the afternoon, and found him warming himself quietly over his charcoal brazier, as if nothing were the matter. The messenger, seeing this, said rather testily—

"The chiefs of the villages are all assembled at Funabashi according to covenant, and as you, Master Sôgorô, have not arrived, I have come to inquire whether it is sickness or some other cause that prevents you."

"Indeed," replied Sôgorô, "I am sorry that you should have had so much trouble. My intention was to have set out yesterday; but I was taken with a cholic, with which I am often troubled, and, as you may see, I am taking care of myself; so for a day or two I shall not be able to start. Pray be so good as to let the others know this."

Rokurobei, seeing that there was no help for it, went back to the village of Funabashi and communicated to the others what had occurred. They were all indignant at what they looked upon as the cowardly defection of a man who had spoken so fairly, but resolved that the conduct of one man should not influence the rest, and talked themselves into the belief that the affair which they had in hand would be easily put through; so they agreed with one accord to start and present the petition, and, having arrived at Yedo, put up in the street called Bakurochô. But although they tried to forward their complaint to the various officers of their lord, no one would listen to them; the doors were all shut in their faces, and they had to go back to their inn, crestfallen and without success.

On the following day, being the 18th of the month, they all met together at a tea-house in an avenue, in front of a shrine of Kwannon Sama;[1] and having held a consultation, they determined that, as they could hit upon no good expedient, they would again send for Sôgorô to see whether he could devise no plan. Accordingly, on the 19th, Rokurobei and one Jiuyémon started for the village of Iwahashi at noon, and arrived the same evening.

Now the village chief Sôgorô, who had made up his mind that the presentation of this memorial was not a matter to be lightly treated, summoned his wife and children and his relations, and said to them—

"I am about to undertake a journey to Yedo, for the following reasons:—Our present lord of the soil has increased the land-tax, in rice and the other imposts, more than tenfold, so that pen and paper would fail to convey an idea of the poverty to which the people are reduced, and the peasants are undergoing the tortures of hell upon earth. Seeing this, the chiefs of the various villages have presented petitions, but with what result is doubtful. My earnest desire, therefore, is to devise some means of escape from this cruel persecution. If my ambitious scheme does not succeed, then shall I return home no more; and even should I gain my end, it is hard to say how I may be treated by those in power. Let us drink a cup of wine together, for it may be that you shall see my face no more. I give my life to allay the misery of the people of this estate. If I die, mourn not over my fate; weep not for me."

Having spoken thus, he addressed his wife and his four children, instructing them carefully as to what he desired to be done after his death, and minutely stating every wish of his heart. Then, having drunk a parting cup with them, he cheerfully took leave of all present, and went to a tea-house

[1] A Buddhist deity.

in the neighbouring village of Funabashi, where the two messengers, Rokurobei and Jiuyémon, were anxiously awaiting his arrival, in order that they might recount to him all that had taken place at Yedo.

" In short," said they, " it appears to us that we have failed completely; and we have come to meet you in order to hear what you propose. If you have any plan to suggest, we would fain be made acquainted with it."

"We have tried the officers of the district," replied Sôgorô, "and we have tried my lord's palace at Yedo. However often we might assemble before my lord's gate, no heed would be given to us. There is nothing left for us but to appeal to the Shogun."

So they sat talking over their plans until the night was far advanced, and then they went to rest. The winter night was long; but when the cawing of the crows was about to announce the morning, the three friends started on their journey for the tea-house at Asakusa, at which, upon their arrival, they found the other village elders already assembled.

" Welcome, Master Sôgorô," said they. " How is it that you have come so late? We have petitioned all the officers to no purpose, and we have broken our bones in vain. We are at our wits' end, and can think of no other scheme. If there is any plan which seems good to you, we pray you to act upon it."

" Sirs," replied Sôgorô, speaking very quietly, " although we have met with no better success here than in our own place, there is no use in grieving. In a day or two the Gorôjiu will be going to the castle; we must wait for this opportunity, and following one of the litters, thrust in our memorial. This is my opinion: what think you of it, my masters?"

One and all, the assembled elders were agreed as to the excellence of this advice; and having decided to act upon it, they returned to their inn.

Then Sôgorô held a secret consultation with Jiuyémon, Hanzô, Rokurobei, Chinzô, and Kiushirô, five of the elders, and, with their assistance, drew up the memorial; and having heard that on the 26th of the month, when the Gorôjiu should go to the castle, Kuzé Yamato no Kami would proceed to a palace under the western enclosure of the castle, they kept watch in a place hard by. As soon as they saw the litter of the Gorôjiu approach, they drew near to it, and, having humbly stated their grievances, handed in the petition; and as it was accepted, the six elders were greatly elated, and doubted not that their hearts' desire would be attained; so they went off to a tea-house at Riyôgoku, and Jiuyémon said—

"We may congratulate ourselves on our success. We have handed in our petition to the Gorôjiu, and now we may set our minds at rest; before many days have passed, we shall hear good news from the rulers. To Master Sôgorô is due great praise for his exertions."

Sôgorô, stepping forward, answered, "Although we have presented our memorial to the Gorôjiu, the matter will not be so quickly decided; it is therefore useless that so many of us should remain here: let eleven men stay with me, and let the rest return home to their several villages. If we who remain are accused of conspiracy and beheaded, let the others agree to reclaim and bury our corpses. As for the expenses which we shall incur until our suit is concluded, let that be according to our original covenant. For the sake of the hundred and thirty-six villages we will lay down our lives, if needs must, and submit to the disgrace of having our heads exposed as those of common malefactors."

Then they had a parting feast together, and, after a sad leave-taking, the main body of the elders went home to their own country; while the others, wending their way to their quarters, waited patiently to be summoned to the Supreme Court. On the 2d day of the 12th month, Sôgorô, having received a summons from the residence of the Gorôjiu Kuzé Yamato no Kami, proceeded to obey it, and was ushered to the porch of the house, where two councillors, named Aijima Gidaiyu and Yamaji Yôri, met him, and said—

"Some days since you had the audacity to thrust a

memorial into the litter of our lord Yamato no Kami. By an extraordinary exercise of clemency, he is willing to pardon this heinous offence; but should you ever again endeavour to force your petitions upon him, you will be held guilty of riotous conduct;" and with this they gave back the memorial.

"I humbly admit the justice of his lordship's censure. But oh! my lords, this is no hasty nor ill-considered action. Year after year, affliction upon affliction has been heaped upon us, until at last the people are without even the necessaries of life; and we, seeing no end to the evil, have humbly presented this petition. I pray your lordships of your great mercy to consider our case, and deign to receive our memorial. Vouchsafe to take some measures that the people may live, and our gratitude for your great kindness will know no bounds."

"Your request is a just one," replied the two councillors, after hearing what he said; "but your memorial cannot be received: so you must even take it back."

With this they gave back the document, and wrote down the names of Sôgorô and six of the elders who had accompanied him. There was no help for it: they must take back their petition, and return to their inn. The seven men, dispirited and sorrowful, sat with folded arms considering what was best to be done, what plan should be devised, until at last, when they were at their wits' end, Sôgorô said, in a whisper—

"So our petition, which we gave in after so much pains, has been returned after all! With what face can we return to our villages after such a disgrace? I, for one, do not propose to waste my labour for nothing; accordingly, I shall bide my time until some day, when the Shogun shall go forth from the castle, and, lying in wait by the roadside, I shall make known our grievances to him, who is lord over our lord. This is our last chance."

The others all applauded this speech, and, having with one accord hardened their hearts, waited for their opportunity.

Now it so happened that, on the 20th day of the 12th

SÔGORÔ THRUSTING THE PETITION INTO THE SHOGUN'S LITTER

month, the then Shogun, Prince Iyémitsu, was pleased to worship at the tombs of his ancestors at Uyéno ;[1] and Sôgorô and the other elders, hearing this, looked upon it as a special favour from the gods, and felt certain that this time they would not fail. So they drew up a fresh memorial, and at the appointed time Sôgorô hid himself under the Sammayé Bridge, in front of the black gate at Uyéno. When Prince Iyémitsu passed in his litter, Sôgorô clambered up from under the bridge, to the great surprise of the Shogun's attendants, who called out, "Push the fellow on one side;" but, profiting by the confusion, Sôgorô, raising his voice and crying, "I wish to humbly present a petition to his Highness in person," thrust forward his memorial, which he had tied on to the end of a bamboo stick six feet long, and tried to put it into the litter; and although there were cries to arrest him, and he was buffeted by the escort, he crawled up to the side of the litter, and the Shogun accepted the document. But Sôgorô was arrested by the escort, and thrown into prison. As for the memorial, his Highness ordered that it should be handed in to the Gorôjiu Hotta Kôtsuké no Suké, the lord of the petitioners.

When Hotta Kôtsuké no Suké had returned home and read the memorial, he summoned his councillor, Kojima Shikibu, and said—

"The officials of my estate are mere bunglers. When the peasants assembled and presented a petition, they refused to receive it, and have thus brought this trouble upon me. Their folly has been beyond belief; however, it cannot be helped. We must remit all the new taxes, and you must inquire how much was paid to the former lord of the castle. As for this Sôgorô, he is not the only one who is at the bottom of the conspiracy; however, as this heinous offence of his in going out to lie in wait for the Shogun's procession is unpardonable, we must manage to get him given up to us by the Government, and, as an example for

---

[1] Destroyed during the revolution, in the summer of 1868, by the troops of the Mikado. See note on the tombs of the Shoguns, at the end of the story.

the rest of my people, he shall be crucified—he and his wife and his children; and, after his death, all that he possesses shall be confiscated. The other six men shall be banished; and that will suffice."

"My lord," replied Shikibu, prostrating himself, "your lordship's intentions are just. Sôgorô, indeed, deserves any punishment for his outrageous crime. But I humbly venture to submit that his wife and children cannot be said to be guilty in the same degree: I implore your lordship mercifully to be pleased to absolve them from so severe a punishment."

"Where the sin of the father is great, the wife and children cannot be spared," replied Kôtsuké no Suké; and his councillor, seeing that his heart was hardened, was forced to obey his orders without further remonstrance.

So Kôtsuké no Suké, having obtained that Sôgorô should be given up to him by the Government, caused him to be brought to his estate of Sakura as a criminal, in a litter covered with nets, and confined him in prison. When his case had been inquired into, a decree was issued by the Lord Kôtsuké no Suké that he should be punished for a heinous crime; and on the 9th day of the 2nd month of the second year of the period styled Shôhô (1644 A.D.) he was condemned to be crucified. Accordingly Sôgorô, his wife and children, and the elders of the hundred and thirty-six villages were brought before the Court-house of Sakura, in which were assembled forty-five chief officers. The elders were then told that, yielding to their petition, their lord was graciously pleased to order that the oppressive taxes should be remitted, and that the dues levied should not exceed those of the olden time. As for Sôgorô and his wife, the following sentence was passed upon them :—

"Whereas you have set yourself up as the head of the villagers; whereas, secondly, you have dared to make light of the Government by petitioning his Highness the Shogun directly, thereby offering an insult to your lord; and whereas, thirdly, you have presented a memorial to the Gorôjiu; and, whereas, fourthly, you were privy to a conspiracy: for these four heinous crimes you are sentenced to death by crucifixion. Your wife is sentenced to die in like manner; and your children will be decapitated.

"This sentence is passed upon the following persons :—

"Sôgorô, chief of the village of Iwahashi, aged 48.

"His wife, Man, aged 38.

"His son, Gennosuké, aged 13.

"His son, Sôhei, aged 10.

"His son, Kihachi, aged 7."

The eldest daughter of Sôgorô, named Hatsu, nineteen years of age, was married to a man named Jiuyémon, in the village of Hakamura, in Shitachi, beyond the river, in the territory of Matsudaira Mutsu no Kami [the Prince of Sendai]. His second daughter, whose name was Saki, sixteen years of age, was married to one Tôjiurô, chief of a village on the property of my lord Naitô Geki. No punishment was decreed against these two women.

The six elders who had accompanied Sôgorô were told that although by good rights they had merited death, yet by the special clemency of their lord their lives would be spared, but that they were condemned to banishment. Their wives and children would not be attainted, and their property would be spared. The six men were banished to Oshima, in the province of Idzu.

Sôgorô heard his sentence with pure courage.

The six men were banished; but three of them lived to be pardoned on the occasion of the death of the Shogun, Prince Genyuin,[1] and returned to their country.

According to the above decision, the taxes were remitted; and men and women, young and old, rejoiced over the advantage that been gained for them by Sôgorô and by the six elders, and there was not one that did not mourn for their fate.

When the officers of the several villages left the Courthouse, one Zembei, the chief of the village of Sakato, told the others that he had some important subjects to speak to

[1] The name assigned after death to Iyétsuna, the fourth of the dynasty of Tokugawa, who died on the 8th day of the 5th month of the year 1680 A.D.

them upon, and begged them to meet him in the temple called Fukushôin. Every man having consented, and the hundred and thirty-six men having assembled at the temple, Zembei addressed them as follows—

"The success of our petition, in obtaining the reduction of our taxes to the same amount as was levied by our former lord, is owing to Master Sôgorô, who has thus thrown away his life for us. He and his wife and children are now to suffer as criminals for the sake of the one hundred and thirty-six villages. That such a thing should take place before our very eyes seems to me not to be borne. What say you, my masters ?"

"Ay! ay! what you say is just from top to bottom," replied the others. Then Hanzayémon, the elder of the village of Katsuta, stepped forward and said—

"As Master Zembei has just said, Sôgorô is condemned to die for a matter in which all the village elders are concerned to a man. We cannot look on unconcerned. Full well I know that it is useless our pleading for Sôgorô; but we may, at least, petition that the lives of his wife and children may be spared."

The assembled elders having all applauded this speech, they determined to draw up a memorial; and they resolved, should their petition not be accepted by the local authorities, to present it at their lord's palace in Yedo, and, should that fail, to appeal to the Government. Accordingly, before noon on the following day, they all affixed their seals to the memorial, which four of them, including Zembei and Hanzayémon, composed, as follows :—

"With deep fear we humbly venture to present the following petition, which the elders of the one hundred and thirty-six villages of this estate have sealed with their seals. In consequence of the humble petition which we lately offered up, the taxes have graciously been reduced to the rates levied by the former lord of the estate, and new laws have been vouchsafed to us. With reverence and joy the peasants, great and small, have gratefully acknowledged these favours. With regard to Sôgorô, the elder of the village of Iwahashi, who ventured to petition his Highness the Shogun in person, thus being guilty of a heinous crime, he has been sentenced to death in the castle town. With fear and trembling we recognize the justice of his sentence. But in the matter of his wife and children, she is but a woman, and they are so young and innocent that they cannot distinguish the east from the west: we pray that in your great clemency you will remit their sin, and give them up to the representatives of the one hundred and thirty-six villages, for which we shall be ever grateful. We, the elders of the villages, know not to what extent we may be transgressing in presenting this memorial. We were all guilty of affixing our seals to the former petition; but Sôgorô, who was chief of a large district, producing a thousand kokus of revenue, and was therefore a man of experience, acted for the others; and we grieve that he alone should suffer for all. Yet in his case we reverently admit that there can be no reprieve. For his wife and children, however, we humbly implore your gracious mercy and consideration.

"Signed by the elders of the villages of the estate, the 2d year of Shôhô, and the 2d month."

Having drawn up this memorial, the hundred and thirty-six elders, with Zembei at their head, proceeded to the Court-house to present the petition, and found the various officers seated in solemn conclave. Then the clerk took the petition, and, having opened it, read it aloud; and the councillor, Ikéura Kazuyé, said—

"The petition which you have addressed to us is worthy of all praise. But you must know that this is a matter which is no longer within our control. The affair has been reported to the Government; and although the priests of my lord's ancestral temple have interceded for Sôgorô, my lord is so angry that he will not listen even to them, saying that, had he not been one of the Gorôjiu, he would have been in danger of being ruined by this man: his high station alone saved him. My lord spoke so severely that the priests themselves dare not recur to the subject. You see, therefore, that it will be no use your attempting to take any steps in the matter, for most certainly your petition will not be received. You had better, then, think no more about it." And with these words he gave back the memorial.

Zembei and the elders, seeing, to their infinite sorrow, that their mission was fruitless, left the Court-house, and most sorrowfully took counsel together, grinding their teeth in their disappointment when they thought over what the councillor had said as to the futility of their attempt. Out of grief for this,·Zembei, with Hanzayémon and Heijiurô, on the 11th day of the 2d month (the day on which Sôgorô and his wife and children suffered), left Ewaradai, the place of execution, and went to the temple Zenkôji, in the province of Shinshiu, and from thence they ascended Mount Kôya in Kishiu, and, on the 1st day of the 8th month, shaved their heads and became priests; Zembei changed his name to Kakushin, and Hanzayémon changed his to Zenshô: as for Heijiurô, he fell sick at the end of the 7th month, and on the 11th day of the 8th month died, being forty-seven years old that year. These three men, who had loved Sôgorô as the fishes love water, were true to him to the last. Heijiurô was buried on Mount Kôya. Kakushin wandered through the country as a priest, praying for the entry of Sôgorô and his children into the perfection of paradise; and, after visiting all the shrines and temples, came back at last to his own province of Shimôsa, and took up his abode at the temple Riukakuji, in the village of Kano, and in the district of Imban, praying and making offerings on behalf of the souls of Sôgorô, his wife and children. Hanzayémon, now known as the priest Zenshô, remained at Shinagawa, a suburb of Yedo, and, by the charity of good people, collected enough money to erect six bronze Buddhas, which remain standing to this day. He fell sick and died, at the age of seventy, on the 10th day of the 2d month of the 13th year of the period styled Kambun. Zembei, who, as a priest, had changed his name to Kakushin, died, at the age of seventy-six, on the 17th day of the 10th month of the 2d year of the period styled Empô. Thus did these men, for the sake of Sôgorô and his family, give themselves up to works of devotion; and the other villagers also brought food to soothe the spirits of the dead, and prayed for their entry into paradise; and as litanies were repeated without intermission, there can be no doubt that Sôgorô attained salvation.

"In paradise, where the blessings of God are distributed without favour, the soul learns its faults by the measure of the rewards given. The lusts of the flesh are abandoned; and the soul, purified, attains to the glory of Buddha."[1]

On the 11th day of the 2d month of the 2d year of Shôhô, Sôgorô having been convicted of a heinous crime, a scaffold was erected at Ewaradai, and the councillor who resided at Yedo and the councillor who resided on the estate, with the other officers, proceeded to the place in all solemnity. Then the priests of Tôkôji, in the village of Sakénaga, followed by coffin-bearers, took their places in front of the councillors, and said—

"We humbly beg leave to present a petition."

"What have your reverences to say?"

"We are men who have forsaken the world and entered the priesthood," answered the monks, respectfully; "and we would fain, if it be possible, receive the bodies of those who are to die, that we may bury them decently. It will be a great joy to us if our humble petition be graciously heard and granted."

"Your request shall be granted; but as the crime of Sôgorô was great, his body must be exposed for three days and three nights, after which the corpse shall be given to you."

At the hour of the snake (10 A.M.), the hour appointed for the execution, the people from the neighbouring villages and the castle town, old and young, men and women, flocked to see the sight: numbers there were, too, who came to bid a last farewell to Sôgorô, his wife and children, and to put up a

[1] Buddhist text.

prayer for them. When the hour had arrived, the condemned were dragged forth bound, and made to sit upon coarse mats. Sôgorô and his wife closed their eyes, for the sight was more than they could bear; and the spectators, with heaving breasts and streaming eyes, cried "Cruel!" and "Pitiless!" and taking sweetmeats and cakes from the bosoms of their dresses threw them to the children. At noon precisely Sôgorô and his wife were bound to the crosses, which were then set upright and fixed in the ground. When this had been done, their eldest son Gennosuké was led forward to the scaffold, in front of the two parents. Then Sôgorô cried out—

"Oh! cruel, cruel! what crime has this poor child committed that he is treated thus? As for me, it matters not what becomes of me." And the tears trickled down his face.

The spectators prayed aloud, and shut their eyes; and the executioner himself, standing behind the boy, and saying that it was a pitiless thing that the child should suffer for the father's fault, prayed silently. Then Gennosuké, who had remained with his eyes closed, said to his parents—

"Oh! my father and mother, I am going before you to paradise, that happy country, to wait for you. My little brothers and I will be on the banks of the river Sandzu,[1] and stretch out our hands and help you across. Farewell, all you who have come to see us die; and now please cut off my head at once."

With this he stretched out his neck, murmuring a last prayer; and not only Sôgorô and his wife, but even the executioner and the spectators could not repress their tears; but the headsman, unnerved as he was, and touched to the very heart, was forced, on account of his office, to cut off the child's head, and a piteous wail arose from the parents and the spectators.

Then the younger child Sôhei said to the headsman, "Sir,

---

[1] The Buddhist Styx, which separates paradise from hell, across which the dead are ferried by an old woman, for whom a small piece of money is buried with them.

I have a sore on my right shoulder : please, cut my head off from the left shoulder, lest you should hurt me. Alas ! I know not how to die, nor what I should do."

When the headsman and the officers present heard the child's artless speech, they wept again for very pity ; but there was no help for it, and the head fell off more swiftly than water is drunk up by sand. Then little Kihachi, the third son, who, on account of his tender years, should have been spared, was butchered as he was in his simplicity eating the sweetmeats which had been thrown to him by the spectators.

When the execution of the children was over, the priests of Tôkôji took their corpses, and, having placed them in their coffins, carried them away, amidst the lamentations of the bystanders, and buried them with great solemnity.

Then Shigayémon, one of the servants of Danzayémon, the chief of the Etas, who had been engaged for the purpose, was just about to thrust his spear, when O Man, Sôgorô's wife, raising her voice, said—

"Remember, my husband, that from the first you had made up your mind to this fate. What though our bodies be disgracefully exposed on these crosses ?—we have the promises of the gods before us ; therefore, mourn not. Let us fix our minds upon death : we are drawing near to paradise, and shall soon be with the saints. Be calm, my husband. Let us cheerfully lay down our single lives for the good of many. Man lives but for one generation ; his name, for many. A good name is more to be prized than life."

So she spoke ; and Sôgorô on the cross, laughing gaily, answered—

"Well said, wife ! What though we are punished for the many ? Our petition was successful, and there is nothmg left to wish for. Now I am happy, for I have attained my heart's desire. The changes and chances of life are manifold. But if I had five hundred lives, and could five hundred times assume this shape of mine, I would die five hundred times to avenge this iniquity. For myself I care not ; but that my wife and children should be punished also is too much.

Pitiless and cruel! Let my lord fence himself in with iron walls, yet shall my spirit burst through them and crush his bones, as a return for this deed."

And as he spoke, his eyes became vermilion red, and flashed like the sun or the moon, and he looked like the demon Razetsu.[1]

"Come," shouted he, "make haste and pierce me with the spear."

"Your wishes shall be obeyed," said the Eta, Shigayémon, and thrust in a spear at his right side until it came out at his left shoulder, and the blood streamed out like a fountain. Then he pierced the wife from the left side; and she, opening her eyes, said in a dying voice—

"Farewell, all you who are present. May harm keep far from you. Farewell! farewell!" and as her voice waxed faint, the second spear was thrust in from her right side, and she breathed out her spirit. Sôgorô, the colour of his face not even changing, showed no sign of fear, but opening his eyes wide, said—

"Listen, my masters! all you who have come to see this sight. Recollect that I shall pay my thanks to my lord Kôtsuké no Suké for this day's work. You shall see it for yourselves, so that it shall be talked of for generations to come. As a sign, when I am dead, my head shall turn and face towards the castle. When you see this, doubt not that my words shall come true."

When he had spoken thus, the officer directing the execution gave a sign to the Eta, Shigayémon, and ordered him to finish the execution, so that Sôgorô should speak no more. So Shigayémon pierced him twelve or thirteen times, until he died. And when he was dead, his head turned and faced the castle. When the two councillors beheld this miracle, they came down from their raised platform, and knelt down before Sôgorô's dead body and said—

"Although you were but a peasant on this estate, you conceived a noble plan to succour the other farmers in their

[1] A Buddhist fiend.

distress. You bruised your bones, and crushed your heart, for their sakes. Still, in that you appealed to the Shogun in person, you committed a grievous crime, and made light of your superiors; and for this it was impossible not to punish you. Still we admit that to include your wife and children in your crime, and kill them before your eyes, was a cruel deed What is done, is done, and regret is of no avail. However, honours shall be paid to your spirit: you shall be canonized as the Saint Daimiyô, and you shall be placed among the tutelar deities of my lord's family."

With these words the two councillors made repeated reverences before the corpse; and in this they showed their faithfulness to their lord. But he, when the matter was reported to him, only laughed scornfully at the idea that the hatred of a peasant could affect his feudal lord; and said that a vassal who had dared to hatch a plot which, had it not been for his high office, would have been sufficient to ruin him, had only met with his deserts. As for causing him to be canonized, let him be as he was. Seeing their lord's anger, his councillors could only obey. But it was not long before he had cause to know that, though Sôgorô was dead, his vengeance was yet alive.

The relations of Sôgorô and the elders of the villages having been summoned to the Court-house, the following document was issued :—

" Although the property of Sôgorô, the elder of the village of Iwahashi, is confiscated, his household furniture shall be made over to his two married daughters; and the village officials will look to it that these few poor things be not stolen by lawless and unprincipled men.

" His rice-fields and corn-fields, his mountain land and forest land, will be sold by auction. His house and grounds will be given over to the elder of the village. The price fetched by his property will be paid over to the lord of the estate.

"The above decree will be published, in full, to the peasants of the village; and it is strictly forbidden to find fault with this decision.

"The 12th day of the 2d month, of the 2d year of the period Shôhô."

The peasants, having heard this degree with all humility, left the Court-house. Then the following punishments were awarded to the officers of the castle, who, by rejecting the petition of the peasants in the first instance, had brought trouble upon their lord :—

"Dismissed from their office, the resident councillors at Yedo and at the castle town.

"Banished from the province, four district governors, and three bailiffs, and nineteen petty officers.

"Dismissed from office, three metsukés, or censors, and seven magistrates.

"Condemned to hara-kiri, one district governor and one Yedo bailiff.

"The severity of this sentence is owing to the injustice of the officials in raising new and unprecedented taxes, and bringing affliction upon the people, and in refusing to receive the petitions of the peasants, without consulting their lord, thus driving them to appeal to the Shogun in person. In their avarice they looked not to the future, but laid too heavy a burden on the peasants, so that they made an appeal to a higher power, endangering the honour of their lord's house. For this bad government the various officials are to be punished as above."

In this wise was justice carried out at the palace at Yedo and at the Court-house at home. But in the history of the world, from the dark ages down to the present time, there are few instances of one man laying down his life for the many, as Sôgorô did : noble and peasant praise him alike.

As month after month passed away, towards the fourth year of the period Shôhô, the wife of my lord Kôtsuké no Suké, being with child, was seized with violent pains ; and retainers were sent to all the different temples and shrines to pray by proxy, but all to no purpose : she continued to suffer as before. Towards the end of the seventh month of the year, there appeared. every night, a preternatural light above the lady's chamber; this was accompanied by hideous sounds as of many people laughing fiendishly, and sometimes by piteous wailings, as though myriads of persons were lamenting. The profound distress caused by this added to her sufferings; so her own privy councillor, an old man, took his place in the adjoining chamber, and kept watch. All of a sudden, he heard a noise as if a number of people were walking on the boards of the roof of my lady's room; then there was a sound of men and women weeping; and when, thunderstruck, the councillor was wondering what it could all be, there came a wild burst of laughter, and all was silent. Early the following morning, the old women who had charge of my lady's household presented themselves before my lord Kôtsuké no Suké, and said—

"Since the middle of last month, the waiting-women have been complaining to us of the ghostly noises by which my lady is nightly disturbed, and they say that they cannot continue to serve her. We have tried to soothe them, by saying that the devils should be exorcised at once, and that there was nothing to be afraid of. Still we feel that their fears are not without reason, and that they really cannot do their work; so we beg that your lordship will take the matter into your consideration."

"This is a passing strange story of yours; however, I will go myself to-night to my lady's apartments and keep watch. You can come with me."

Accordingly, that night my lord Kôtsuké no Suké sat up in person. At the hour of the rat (midnight) a fearful noise of voices was heard, and Sôgorô and his wife, bound to the fatal crosses, suddenly appeared; and the ghosts, seizing the lady by the hand, said—

"We have come to meet you. The pains you are suffering are terrible, but they are nothing in comparison with those of the hell to which we are about to lead you."

At these words, Kôtsuké no Suké, seizing his sword, tried to sweep the ghosts away with a terrific cut; but a loud peal of laughter was heard, and the visions faded away.

Kôtsuké no Suké, terrified, sent his retainers to the temples and shrines to pray that the demons might be cast out; but the noises were heard nightly, as before. When the eleventh month of the year came round, the apparitions of human forms in my lady's apartments became more and more frequent and terrible, all the spirits railing at her, and howling out that they had come to fetch her. The women would all scream and faint; and then the ghosts would disappear amid yells of laughter. Night after night this happened, and even in the daytime the visions would manifest themselves; and my lady's sickness grew worse daily, until in the last month of the year she died, of grief and terror. Then the ghost of Sôgorô and his wife crucified would appear day and night in the chamber of Kôtsuké no Suké, floating round the room, and glaring at him with red and flaming eyes. The hair of the attendants would stand on end with terror; and if they tried to cut at the spirits, their limbs would be cramped, and their feet and hands would not obey their bidding. Kôtsuké no Suké would draw the sword that lay by his bedside; but, as often as he did so, the ghosts faded away, only to appear again in a more hideous shape than before, until at last, having exhausted his strength and spirits, even he became terror-stricken. The whole household was thrown into confusion, and day after day mystic rites and incantations were performed by the priests over braziers of charcoal, while prayers were recited without ceasing; but the visions only became more frequent, and there was no sign of their ceasing. After the 5th year of Shôhô, the style of the years was changed to Keian; and during the 1st year of Keian the spirits continued to haunt the palace; and now they appeared in the chamber of Kôtsuké no Suké's eldest son, surrounding themselves with even more terrors than before; and when Kôtsuké no Suké was about to go to the Shogun's castle, they were seen howling out their cries of vengeance in the porch of the house. At last the relations of the family and the members of the household took counsel together, and told Kôtsuké no Suké that without doubt no ordinary means world suffice to lay the ghosts; a shrine must be erected to Sôgorô, and divine honours paid to him, after which the apparitions would assuredly cease. Kôtsuké no Suké having carefully considered the matter and given his consent, Sôgorô was canonized under the name of Sôgo Daimiyô, and a shrine was erected in his honour. After divine honours had been paid to him, the awful visions were no more seen, and the ghost of Sôgorô was laid for ever.

In the 2d year of the period Keian, on the 11th day of the 10th month, on the occasion of the festival of first lighting the fire on the hearth, the various Daimios and Hatamotos of distinction went to the castle of the Shogun, at Yedo, to offer their congratulations on this occasion. During the ceremonies, my lord Hotta Kôtsuké no Suké and Sakai Iwami no Kami, lord of the castle of Matsumoto, in the province of Shinshiu, had a quarrel, the origin of which was not made public; and Sakai Iwami no Kami, although he came of a brave and noble family, received so severe a wound that he died on the following day, at the age of forty-three; and in consequence of this, his family was ruined and disgraced.[1] My lord Kôtsuké no Suké, by great good fortune, contrived to escape from the castle, and took refuge in his own house, whence, mounting a famous horse called Hira-Abumi,[2] he fled to his castle of Sakura, in Shimôsa, accomplishing the distance, which is about sixty miles, in six hours. When he arrived in front of the castle, he called out in a loud voice to the guard within to open the gate, answering, in reply to their challenge, that he was Kôtsuké no Suké, the lord of the castle. The guard, not believing their ears, sent word to the councillor in charge of the castle, who rushed out to see if the person demanding

---

[1] In the old days, if a noble was murdered, and died outside his own house, he was disgraced, and his estates were forfeited. When the Regent of the Shogun was murdered, some years since, outside the castle of Yedo, by a legal fiction it was given out that he had died in his own palace, in order that his son might succeed to his estates. [2] Level stirrups.

admittance were really their lord. When he saw Kôtsuké no Suké, he caused the gates to be opened, and, thinking it more than strange, said—

"Is this indeed you, my lord? What strange chance brings your lordship hither thus late at night, on horseback and alone, without a single follower?"

With these words he ushered in Kôtsuké no Suké, who, in reply to the anxious inquiries of his people as to the cause of his sudden appearance, said—

"You may well be astonished. I had a quarrel to-day in the castle at Yedo, with Sakai Iwami no Kami, the lord of the castle of Matsumoto, and I cut him down. I shall soon ·be pursued; so we must strengthen the fortress, and prepare for an attack."

The household, hearing this, were greatly alarmed, and the whole castle was thrown into confusion. In the meanwhile the people of Kôtsuké no Suké's palace at Yedo, not knowing whither their lord had fled, were in the greatest anxiety until a messenger came from Sakura, and reported his arrival there.

When the quarrel inside the castle of Yedo and Kôtsuké no Suké's flight had been taken cognizance of, he was attainted of treason, and soldiers were sent to seize him, dead or alive. Midzuno Setsu no Kami and Gotô Yamato no Kami were charged with the execution of the order, and sallied forth, on the 13th day of the 10th month, to carry it out. When they arrived at the town of Sasai, they sent a herald with the following message :—

"Whereas Kôtsuké no Suké killed Sakai Iwami no Kami inside the castle of Yedo, and has fled to his own castle without leave, he is attainted of treason ; and we, being connected with him by ties of blood and of friendship, have been charged to seize him."

The herald delivered this message to the councillor of Kôtsuké no Suké, who, pleading as an excuse that his lord was mad, begged the two nobles to intercede for him. Gotô Yamato no Kami upon this called the councillor to him, and

spoke privately to him, after which the latter took his leave
and returned to the castle of Sakura.

In the meanwhile, after consultation at Yedo, it was decided
that, as Gotô Yamato no Kami and Midzuno Setsu no Kami
were related to Kôtsuke no Suké, and might meet with diffi-
culties for that very reason, two other nobles, Ogasawara Iki
no Kami and Nagai Hida no Kami, should be sent to assist
them, with orders that should any trouble arise they should
send a report immediately to Yedo. In consequence of this
order, the two nobles, with five thousand men, were about to
march for Sakura, on the 15th of the month, when a messenger
arrived from that place bearing the following despatch for
the Gorôjiu, from the two nobles who had preceded them :— .

"In obedience to the orders of His Highness the Shogun,
we proceeded, on the 13th day of this month, to the castle
of Sakura, and conducted a thorough investigation of the
affair. It is true that Kôtsuké no Suké has been guilty of
treason, but he is out of his mind ; his retainers have called
in physicians, and he is undergoing treatment by which his
senses are being gradually restored, and his mind is being
awakened from its sleep. At the time when he slew Sakai
Iwami no Kami he was not accountable for his actions, and
will be sincerely penitent when he is aware of his crime.
We have taken him prisoner, and have the honour to await
your instructions ; in the meanwhile, we beg by these present
to let you know what we have done.

(Signed)   GOTÔ YAMATO NO KAMI.
       "   MIDZUNO SETSU NO KAMI.
"To the Gorôjiu, 2d year of Keian, 2d month, 14th day."

This despatch reached Yedo on the 16th of the month,
and was read by the Gorôjiu after they had left the castle ;
and in consequence of the report of Kôtsuké no Suké's
madness, the second expedition was put a stop to, and the
following instructions were sent to Gotô Yamato no Kami
and Midzuno Setsu no Kami :—

"With reference to the affair of Hotta Kôtsuké no Suké,

lord of the castle of Sakura, in Shimôsa, whose quarrel with Sakai Iwami no Kami within the castle of Yedo ended in bloodshed. For this heinous crime and disregard of the sanctity of the castle, it is ordered that Kôtsuké no Suké be brought as a prisoner to Yedo, in a litter covered with nets, that his case may be judged.

"2d year of Kei-an, 2d month.

(Signed by the Gorojiu) INABA MINO NO KAMI.

INOUYE KAWACHI NO KAMI.

KATÔ ECCHIU NO KAMI."

Upon the receipt of this despatch, Hotta Kôtsuké no Suké was immediately placed in a litter covered with a net of green silk, and conveyed to Yedo, strictly guarded by the retainers of the two nobles; and, having arrived at the capital, was handed over to the charge of Akimoto Tajima no Kami. All his retainers were quietly dispersed; and his empty castle was ordered to be thrown open, and given in charge to Midzuno Iki no Kami.

At last Kôtsuké no Suké began to feel that the death of his wife and his own present misfortunes were a just retribution for the death of Sôgorô and his wife and children, and he was as one awakened from a dream. Then night and morning, in his repentance, he offered up prayers to the sainted spirit of the dead farmer, and acknowledged and bewailed his crime, vowing that, if his family were spared from ruin and re-established, intercession should be made at the court of the Mikado,[1] at Kiyôto, on behalf of the spirit of Sôgorô, so that, being worshipped with even greater honours than before, his name should be handed down to all generations.

In consequence of this it happened that the spirit of Sôgorô having relaxed in its vindictiveness, and having

[1] In the days of Shogun's power, the Mikado remained the Fountain of Honour, and, as chief of the national religion and the direct descendant of the gods, dispensed divine honours. So recently as last year, a decree of the Mikado appeared in the Government Gazette conferring posthumous divine honours upon an ancestor of the Prince of Choshiu.

ceased to persecute the house of Hotta, in the 1st month of the 4th year of Keian, Kôtsuké no Suké received a summons from the Shogun, and, having been forgiven, was made lord of the castle of Matsuyama, in the province of Déwa, with a revenue of twenty thousand kokus. In the same year, on the 20th day of the 4th month, the Shogun, Prince Iyémitsu, was pleased to depart this life, at the age of forty-eight; and whether by the forgiving spirit of the prince, or by the divine interposition of the sainted Sôgorô, Kôtsuké no Suké was promoted to the castle of Utsu no Miya, in the province of Shimotsuké, with a revenue of eighty thousand kokus; and his name was changed to Hotta Hida no Kami. He also received again his original castle of Sakura, with a revenue of twenty thousand kokus: so that there can be no doubt that the saint was befriending him. In return for these favours, the shrine of Sôgorô was made as beautiful as a gem. It is needless to say how many of the peasants of the estate flocked to the shrine: any good luck that might befall the people was ascribed to it, and night and day the devout worshipped at it.

Here follows a copy of the petition which Sôgorô presented to the Shogun:—

"We, the elders of the hundred and thirty-six villages of the district of Chiba, in the province of Shimôsa, and of the district of Buji, in the province of Kadzusa, most reverently offer up this our humble petition.

"When our former lord, Doi Shosho, was transferred to another castle, in the 9th year of the period Kanyé, Hotta Kaga no Kami became lord of the castle of Sakura; and in the 17th year of the same period, my lord Kôtsuké no Suké succeeded him. Since that time the taxes laid upon us have been raised in the proportion of one tô and two sho to each koku.[1]

"*Item.*—At the present time, taxes are raised on nineteen of

[1] 10 Sho = 1 Tô.
10 Tô = 1 Koku.

our articles of produce; whereas our former lord only required that we should furnish him with pulse and sesamum, for which he paid in rice.

"*Item.*—Not only are we not paid now for our produce, but, if it is not given in to the day, we are driven and goaded by the officials; and if there be any further delay, we are manacled and severely reprimanded; so that if our own crops fail, we have to buy produce from other districts, and are pushed to the utmost extremity of affliction.

"*Item.*—We have over and over again prayed to be relieved from these burthens, but our petitions are not received. The people are reduced to poverty, so that it is hard for them to live under such grievous taxation. Often they have tried to sell the land which they till, but none can be found to buy; so they have sometimes given over their land to the village authorities, and fled with their wives to other provinces, and seven hundred and thirty men or more have been reduced to begging, one hundred and eighty-five houses have fallen into ruins; land producing seven thousand kokus has been given up, and remains untilled, and eleven temples have fallen into decay in consequence of the ruin of those upon whom they depended.

"Besides this, the poverty-stricken farmers and women, having been obliged to take refuge in other provinces, and having no abiding-place, have been driven to evil courses and bring men to speak ill of their lord; and the village officials, being unable to keep order, are blamed and reproved. No attention has been paid to our repeated representations upon this point; so we were driven to petition the Gorôjiu Kuzé Yamato no Kami as he was on his way to the castle, but our petition was returned to us. And now, as a last resource, we tremblingly venture to approach his Highness the Shogun in person.

"The 1st year of the period Shôhô, 12th month, 20th day.

O The seals of the elders of the 136 villages."

The Shogun at that time was Prince Iyémitsu, the grandson of Iyéyasu. He received the name of Dai-yu-In after his death.

The Gorôjiu at that time were Hotta Kôtsuké no Suké, Sakai Iwami no Kami, Inaba Mino no Kami, Katô Ecchiu no Kami, Inouyé Kawachi no Kami.

The Wakadoshiyôri (or 2d council) were Torii Wakasa no Kami, Tsuchiya Dewa no Kami, and Itakura Naizen no Sho.

The belief in ghosts appears to be as universal as that in the immortality of the soul, upon which it depends. Both in China and Japan the departed spirit is invested with the power of revisiting the earth, and, in a visible form, tormenting its enemies and haunting those places where the perishable part of it mourned and suffered. Haunted houses are slow to find tenants, for ghosts almost always come with revengeful intent; indeed, the owners of such houses will almost pay men to live in them, such is the dread which they inspire, and the anxiety to blot out the stigma.

One cold winter's night at Yedo, as I was sitting, with a few Japanese friends, huddled round the imperfect heat of a brazier of charcoal, the conversation turned upon the story of Sôgorô and upon ghostly apparitions in general. Many a weird tale was told that evening, and I noted down the three or four which follow, for the truth of which the narrators vouched with the utmost confidence.

About ten years ago there lived a fishmonger, named Zenroku, in the Mikawa-street, at Kanda, in Yedo. He was a poor man, living with his wife and one little boy. His wife fell sick and died, so he engaged an old woman to look after his boy while he himself went out to sell his fish. It happened, one day, that he and the other hucksters of his guild were gambling; and this coming to the ears of the authorities, they were all thrown into prison. Although their offence was in itself a light one, still they were kept for some time in durance while the matter was being investigated; and Zenroku, owing to the damp and foul air of the prison, fell sick with fever. His little child, in the meantime, had been handed over by the authorities to the charge of the petty officers of the ward to which his father belonged, and was being well cared for; for Zenroku was known to be an honest fellow, and his fate excited much compassion. One night Zenroku, pale and emaciated, entered the house in which his boy was living; and all the people joyfully congratulated him on his escape from jail. "Why, we heard that you were sick in prison. This is, indeed, a joyful return." Then Zenroku thanked those who had taken care of the child, saying that he had returned secretly by the favour of his jailers that night; but that on the following day his offence would be remitted, and he should be able to take possession of his house again publicly. For that night, he must return to the prison. With this he begged those present to continue their good offices to his babe; and, with a sad and reluctant expression of countenance, he left the house. On the following day, the officers of that ward were sent for by the prison authorities. They thought that they were summoned that Zenroku might be handed back to them a free man, as he himself had said to them; but to their surprise, they were told that he had died the night before in prison, and were ordered to carry away his dead body for burial. Then they knew that they had seen Zenroku's ghost; and that when he said that he should be returned to them on the morrow, he had alluded to his corpse. So they buried him decently, and brought up his son, who is alive to this day.

The next story was told by a professor in the college at Yedo, and, although it is not of so modern a date as the last, he stated it to be well authenticated, and one of general notoriety.

About two hundred years ago there was a chief of the police, named Aoyama Shuzen, who lived in the street called Bancho, at Yedo. His duty was to detect thieves and incendiaries. He was a cruel and violent man, without heart or compassion, and thought nothing of killing or torturing a man to gratify spite or revenge. This man Shuzen had in his house a servant-maid, called O Kiku (the Chrysanthemum), who had lived in the family since her childhood, and was well acquainted with her master's temper. One day O Kiku accidentally broke one of a set of ten porcelain plates, upon which he set a high value. She knew that she would suffer for her carelessness; but she thought that if she concealed the matter her punishment would be still more severe; so she went at once to her master's wife, and, in fear and trembling, confessed what she had done. When Shuzen came home, and heard that one of his favourite plates was broken, he flew into a violent rage, and took the girl to a cupboard, where he left her bound with cords, and every day cut off one of her fingers. O Kiku, tightly bound and in agony, could not move; but at last she contrived to bite or cut the ropes asunder, and, escaping into the garden, threw herself into a well, and was drowned. From that time forth, every night a voice was heard coming from the well, counting one, two, three, and so on up to nine—the number of the plates that remained unbroken—and then, when the tenth plate should have been counted, would come a burst of lamentation. The servants of the house, terrified at this, all left their master's service, until Shuzen, not having a single retainer left, was unable to perform his public duties; and when the officers of the government heard of this, he was dismissed from his office. At this time there was a famous priest, called Mikadzuki Shônin, of the temple Denzuin, who, having been told of the affair, came one night to the house, and, when the ghost began to count the plates, reproved the spirit, and by his prayers and admonitions caused it to cease from troubling the living.

The laying of disturbed spirits appears to form one of the regular functions of the Buddhist priests; at least, we find them playing a conspicuous part in almost every ghost-story.

About thirty years ago there stood a house at Mitsumé,

in the Honjô of Yedo, which was said to be nightly visited by ghosts, so that no man dared to live in it, and it remained untenanted on that account. However, a man called Miura Takéshi, a native of the province of Oshiu, who came to Yedo to set up in business as a fencing-master, but was too poor to hire a house, hearing that there was a haunted house, for which no tenant could be found, and that the owner would let any man live in it rent free, said that he feared neither man nor devil, and obtained leave to occupy the house. So he hired a fencing-room, in which he gave his lessons by day, and after midnight returned to the haunted house. One night, his wife, who took charge of the house in his absence, was frightened by a fearful noise proceeding from a pond in the garden, and, thinking that this certainly must be the ghost that she had heard so much about, she covered her head with the bed-clothes and remained breathless with terror. When her husband came home, she told him what had happened; and on the following night he returned earlier than usual, and waited for the ghostly noise. At the same time as before, a little after midnight, the same sound was heard — as though a gun had been fired inside the pond. Opening the shutters, he looked out, and saw something like a black cloud floating on the water, and in the cloud was the form of a bald man. Thinking that there must be some cause for this, he instituted careful inquiries, and learned that the former tenant, some ten years previously, had borrowed money from a blind shampooer,[1] and, being unable to pay the debt, had murdered his creditor, who began to press him for his money and had thrown his head into the pond. The fencing-master accordingly collected his pupils and emptied the pond, and found a skull at the bottom of it; so he called in a priest, and buried the skull in a temple, causing prayers

---

[1] The apparently poor shaven-pated and blind shampooers of Japan drive a thriving trade as money-lenders. They give out small sums at an interest of 20 per cent. per month—240 per cent. per annum—and woe betide the luckless wight who falls into their clutches.

to be offered up for the repose of the murdered man's soul. Thus the ghost was laid, and appeared no more.

The belief in curses hanging over families for generations is as common as that in ghosts and supernatural apparitions. There is a strange story of this nature in the house of Asai, belonging to the Hatamoto class. The ancestor of the present representative, six generations ago, had a certain concubine, who was in love with a man who frequented the house, and wished in her heart to marry him; but, being a virtuous woman, she never thought of doing any evil deed. But the wife of my lord Asai was jealous of the girl, and persuaded her husband that her rival in his affections had gone astray; when he heard this he was very angry, and beat her with a candlestick so that he put out her left eye. The girl, who had indignantly protested her innocence, finding herself so cruelly handled, pronounced a curse against the house; upon which, her master, seizing the candlestick again, dashed out her brains and killed her. Shortly afterwards, my lord Asai lost his left eye, and fell sick and died; and from that time forth to this day, it is said that the representatives of the house have all lost their left eyes after the age of forty, and shortly afterwards they have fallen sick and died at the same age as the cruel lord who killed his concubine.

NOTE

OF the many fair scenes of Yedo, none is better worth visiting than the temple of Zôjôji, one of the two great burial-places of the Shoguns; indeed, if you wish to see the most beautiful spots of any Oriental city, ask for the cemeteries: the homes of the dead are ever the loveliest places. Standing in a park of glorious firs and pines beautifully kept, which contains quite a little town of neat, clean-looking houses, together with thirty-four temples for the use of the priests and attendants of the shrines, the main temple, with its huge red pillars supporting a heavy Chinese roof of grey tiles, is approached through a colossal open hall which leads into a stone courtyard. At one end of this courtyard is a broad flight of steps—the three or four lower ones of stone, and the upper ones of red wood. At these the visitor is warned by a notice to take off his boots, a request which Englishmen, with characteristic disregard of the feelings of others, usually neglect to comply with. The main hall of the temple is of large proportions, and the high altar is decorated with fine bronze candelabra, incense-burners, and other ornaments, and on two days of the year a very curious collection of pictures representing the five hundred gods, whose images are known to all persons who have visited Canton, is hung along the walls. The big bell outside the main hall is rather remarkable on account of the great beauty of the deep bass waves of sound which it rolls through the city than on account of its size, which is as nothing when compared with that of the big bells of Moscow and Peking; still it is not to be despised even in that respect, for it is ten feet high and five feet eight inches in diameter, while its metal is a foot thick: it was hung up in the year 1673. But the chief objects of interest in these beautiful grounds are the chapels attached to the tombs of the Shoguns.

It is said that as Prince Iyéyasu was riding into Yedo to take possession of his new castle, the Abbot of Zôjôji, an ancient temple which then stood at Hibiya, near the castle, went forth and waited before the gate to do homage to the Prince. Iyéyasu, seeing that the Abbot was no ordinary man, stopped and asked his name, and entered the temple to rest himself. The smooth-spoken monk soon found such favour with Iyéyasu, that he chose Zôjôji to be his family temple; and seeing that its grounds were narrow and inconveniently near the castle, he caused it to be removed to its present site. In the year 1610 the temple was raised, by the intercession of Iyéyasu, to the dignity of the Imperial Temples, which, until the last revolution, were presided over by princes of the blood; and to the Abbot was granted the right, on going to the castle, of sitting in his litter as far as the entrance-hall, instead of dismounting at the usual place and proceeding on foot through several gates and courtyards. Nor were the privileges of the temple confined to barren honours, for it was endowed with lands of the value of five thousand kokus of rice yearly.

When Iyéyasu died, the shrine called Antoku In was erected in his honour to the south of the main temple. Here, on the seventeenth day of the fourth month, the anniversary of his death, ceremonies are held in honour of his spirit, deified as Gongen Sama, and the place is thrown open to all who may wish to come and pray. But Iyéyasu is not buried here; his remains lie in a gorgeous shrine among the mountains some eighty miles north of Yedo, at Nikkô, a place so beautiful that the Japanese have a rhyming proverb which says, that he who has not seen Nikkô should never pronounce the word Kekkô (charming, delicious, grand, beautiful).

Hidétada, the son and successor of Iyéyasu, together with Iyénobu, Iyétsugu, Iyéshigé, Iyéyoshi, and Iyémochi, the sixth, seventh, ninth, twelfth, and fourteenth Shoguns of the Tokugawa dynasty, are buried in three shrines attached to the temple ; the remainder, with the exception of Iyémitsu, the third Shogun, who lies with his grandfather at Nikkô, are buried at Uyéno.

The shrines are of exceeding beauty, lying on one side of a splendid avenue of Scotch firs, which border a broad, well-kept gravel walk. Passing through a small gateway of rare design, we come into a large stone courtyard, lined with a long array of colossal stone lanterns, the gift of the vassals of the departed Prince. A second gateway, supported by gilt pillars carved all round with figures of dragons, leads into another court, in which are a bell tower, a great cistern cut out of a single block of stone like a sarcophagus, and a smaller number of lanterns of bronze ; these are given by the Go San Ké, the three princely families in which the succession to the office of Shogun was vested. Inside this is a third court, partly covered like a cloister, the approach to which is a doorway of even greater beauty and richness than the last ; the ceiling is gilt, and painted with arabesques and with heavenly angels playing on musical instruments, and the panels of the walls are sculptured in high relief with admirable representations of birds and flowers, life-size, life-like, all being coloured to imitate nature. Inside this enclosure stands a shrine, before the closed door of which a priest on one side, and a retainer of the house of Tokugawa on the other, sit mounting guard, mute and immoveable as though they themselves were part of the carved ornaments. Passing on one side of the shrine, we come to another court, plainer than the last, and at the back of the little temple inside it is a flight of stone steps, at the top of which, protected by a bronze door, stands a simple monumental urn of bronze on a stone pedestal. Under this is the grave itself ; and it has always struck me that there is no small amount of poetical feeling in this simple ending to so much magnificence; the sermon may have been preached by design, or it may have been by accident, but the lesson is there.

There is little difference between the three shrines, all of which are decorated in the same manner. It is very difficult to do justice to their beauty in words. Writing many thousand miles away from them, I have the memory before me of a place green in winter, pleasant and cool in the hottest summer; of peaceful cloisters, of the fragrance of incense, of the subdued chant of richly robed priests, and the music of bells; of exquisite designs, harmonious colouring, rich gilding. The hum of the vast city outside is unheard here: Iyéyasu himself, in the mountains of Nikkô, has no quieter resting-place than his descendants in the heart of the city over which they ruled.

Besides the graves of the Shoguns, Zôjôji contains other lesser shrines, in which are buried the wives of the second, sixth, and eleventh Shoguns, and the father of Iyénobu, the sixth Shogun, who succeeded to the office by adoption. There is also a holy place called the Satsuma Temple, which has a special interest; in it is a tablet in honour of Tadayoshi, the fifth son of Iyéyasu, whose title was Matsudaira Satsuma no Kami, and who died young. At his death, five of his retainers, with one Ogasasawara Kemmotsu at their head, disembowelled themselves, that they might follow their young master into the next world. They were buried in this place; and I believe that this is the last instance on record of the ancient Japanese custom of *Junshi*, that is to say, "dying with the master."

There are, during the year, several great festivals which are specially celebrated at Zôjôji; the chief of these are the Kaisanki, or founder's day, which is on the eighteenth day of the seventh month; the twenty-fifth day of the first month, the anniversary of the death of the monk Hônen, the founder of the Jôdo sect of Buddhism (that to which the temple belongs); the anniversary of the death of Buddha, on the fifteenth of the second month; the birthday of Buddha, on the eighth day of the fourth month; and from the sixth to the fifteenth of the tenth month.

At Uyéno is the second of the burial-grounds of the Shoguns. The Temple Tô-yei-zan, which stood in the grounds of Uyéno, was built by Iyémitsu, the third of the Shoguns of the house of Tokugawa, in the year 1625, in honour of Yakushi Niôrai, the Buddhist

Æsculapius. It faces the Ki-mon, or Devil's Gate, of the castle, and was erected upon the model of the temple of Hi-yei-zan, one of the most famous of the holy places of Kiôto. Having founded the temple, the next care of Iyémitsu was to pray that Morizumi, the second son of the retired emperor, should come and reside there; and from that time until 1868, the temple was always presided over by a Miya, or member of the Mikado's family, who was specially charged with the care of the tomb of Iyéyasu at Nikkô, and whose position was that of an ecclesiastical chief or primate over the east of Japan.

The temples in Yedo are not to be compared in point of beauty with those in and about Peking; what is marble there is wood here. Still they are very handsome, and in the days of its magnificence the Temple of Uyéno was one of the finest. Alas! the main temple, the hall in honour of the sect to which it belongs, the hall of services, the bell-tower, the entrance-hall, and the residence of the prince of the blood, were all burnt down in the battle of Uyéno, in the summer of 1868, when the Shogun's men made their last stand in Yedo against the troops of the Mikado. The fate of the day was decided by two field-pieces, which the latter contrived to mount on the roof of a neighbouring tea-house; and the Shogun's men, driven out of the place, carried off the Miya in the vain hope of raising his standard in the north as that of a rival Mikado. A few of the lesser temples and tombs, and the beautiful park-like grounds, are but the remnants of the former glory of Uyéno. Among these is a temple in the form of a roofless stage, in honour of the thousand-handed Kwannon. In the middle ages, during the civil wars between the houses of Gen and Hei, one Morihisa, a captain of the house of Hei, after the destruction of his clan, went and prayed for a thousand days at the temple of the thousand-handed Kwannon at Kiyomidzu, in Kiyôto. His retreat having been discovered, he was seized and brought bound to Kamakura, the chief town of the house of Gen. Here he was condemned to die at a place called Yui, by the sea-shore; but every time that the executioner lifted his sword to strike, the blade was broken by the god Kwannon, and at the same time the wife of Yoritomo, the chief of the house of Gen, was warned in a dream to spare Morihisa's life. So Morihisa was reprieved, and rose to power in the state; and all this was by the miraculous intervention of the god Kwannon, who takes such good care of his faithful votaries. To him this temple is dedicated. A colossal bronze Buddha, twenty-two feet high, set up some two hundred years ago, and a stone lantern, twenty feet high, and twelve feet round at the top, are greatly admired by the Japanese. There are only three such lanterns in the empire; the other two being at Nanzenji—a temple in Kiyôto, and Atsura, a shrine in the province of Owari. All three were erected by the piety of one man, Sakuma Daizen no Suké, in the year 1631 A.D.

Iyémitsu, the founder of the temple, was buried with his grandfather, Iyéyasu, at Nikkô; but both of these princes are honoured with shrines here. The Shoguns who are interred at Uyéno are Iyétsuna, Tsunayoshi, Yoshimuné, Iyéharu, Iyénori, and Iyésada, the fourth, fifth, eighth, tenth, eleventh, and thirteenth Princes of the Line. Besides them, are buried five wives of the Shoguns, and the father of the eleventh Shogun.

HOW TAJIMA SHUMÉ WAS TORMENTED BY A DEVIL OF HIS OWN CREATION

ONCE upon a time, a certain Rônin, Tajima Shumé by name, an able and well-read man, being on his travels to see the world, went up to Kiyôto by the Tôkaidô[1] One day, in the neighbourhood of Nagoya, in the province of Owari, he fell in with a wandering priest, with whom he entered into conversation. Finding that they were bound for the same place, they agreed to travel together, beguiling their weary way by pleasant talk on divers matters; and so by degrees, as they became more intimate, they began to speak without restraint about their private affairs; and the priest, trusting thoroughly in the honour of his companion, told him the object of his journey.

"For some time past," said he, "I have nourished a wish that has engrossed all my thoughts; for I am bent on setting up a molten image in honour of Buddha; with this object I have wandered through various provinces collecting alms and (who knows by what weary toil ?) we have succeeded in amassing two hundred ounces of silver—enough, I trust, to erect a handsome bronze figure."

What says the proverb? "He who bears a jewel in his bosom bears poison." Hardly had the Rônin heard these words of the priest than an evil heart arose within him, and

---

[1] The road of the Eastern Sea, the famous high-road leading from Kiyôto to Yedo. The name is also used to indicate the provinces through which it runs.

he thought to himself, " Man's life, from the womb to the grave, is made up of good and of ill luck. Here am I, nearly forty years old, a wanderer, without a calling, or even a hope of advancement in the world. To be sure, it seems a shame; yet if I could steal the money this priest is boasting about, I could live at ease for the rest of my days;" and so he began casting about how best he might compass his purpose. But the priest, far from guessing the drift of his comrade's thoughts, journeyed cheerfully on, till they reached the town of Kuana. Here there is an arm of the sea, which is crossed in ferry-boats, that start as soon as some twenty or thirty passengers are gathered together; and in one of these boats the two travellers embarked. About half-way across, the priest was taken with a sudden necessity to go to the side of the boat; and the Rônin, following him, tripped him up whilst no one was looking, and flung him into the sea. When the boatmen and passengers heard the splash, and saw the priest struggling in the water, they were afraid, and made every effort to save him; but the wind was fair, and the boat running swiftly under the bellying sails, so they were soon a few hundred yards off from the drowning man, who sank before the boat could be turned to rescue him.

When he saw this, the Rônin feigned the utmost grief and dismay, and said to his fellow-passengers, " This priest, whom we have just lost, was my cousin: he was going to Kiyôto, to visit the shrine of his patron; and as I happened to have business there as well, we settled to travel together. Now, alas! by this misfortune, my cousin is dead, and I am left alone."

He spoke so feelingly, and wept so freely, that the passengers believed his story, and pitied and tried to comfort him. Then the Rônin said to the boatmen—

" We ought, by rights, to report this matter to the authorities; but as I am pressed for time, and the business might bring trouble on yourselves as well, perhaps we had better hush it up for the present; and I will at once go on to Kiyôto and tell my cousin's patron, besides writing home about it.

What think you, gentlemen?" added he, turning to the other travellers.

They, of course, were only too glad to avoid any hindrance to their onward journey, and all with one voice agreed to what the Rônin had proposed; and so the matter was settled. When, at length, they reached the shore, they left the boat, and every man went his way; but the Rônin, overjoyed in his heart, took the wandering priest's luggage, and, putting it with his own, pursued his journey to Kiyôto.

On reaching the capital, the Rônin changed his name from Shumé to Tokubei, and, giving up his position as a Samurai, turned merchant, and traded with the dead man's money. Fortune favouring his speculations, he began to amass great wealth, and lived at his ease, denying himself nothing; and in course of time he married a wife, who bore him a child.

Thus the days and months wore on, till one fine summer's night, some three years after the priest's death, Tokubei stepped out on to the verandah of his house to enjoy the cool air and the beauty of the moonlight. Feeling dull and lonely, he began musing over all kinds of things, when on a sudden the deed of murder and theft, done so long ago, vividly recurred to his memory, and he thought to himself, "Here am I, grown rich and fat on the money I wantonly stole. Since then, all has gone well with me; yet, had I not been poor, I had never turned assassin nor thief. Woe betide me! what a pity it was!" and as he was revolving the matter in his mind, a feeling of remorse came over him, in spite of all he could do. While his conscience thus smote him, he suddenly, to his utter amazement, beheld the faint outline of a man standing near a fir-tree in the garden: on looking more attentively, he perceived that the man's whole body was thin and worn and the eyes sunken and dim; and in the poor ghost that was before him he recognized the very priest whom he had thrown into the sea at Kuana. Chilled with horror, he looked again, and saw that the priest was smiling in scorn. He would have fled into the house, but the ghost stretched forth its withered arm, and, clutching the back of his neck, scowled at him with a vindictive glare, and a hideous ghastliness of mien, so unspeakably awful that any ordinary man would have swooned with fear. But Tokubei, tradesman though he was, had once been a soldier, and was not easily matched for daring; so he shook off the ghost, and, leaping into the room for his dirk, laid about him boldly enough; but, strike as he would, the spirit, fading into the air, eluded his blows, and suddenly reappeared only to vanish again: and from that time forth Tokubei knew no rest, and was haunted night and day.

At length, undone by such ceaseless vexation, Tokubei fell ill, and kept muttering, "Oh, misery! misery!—the wandering priest is coming to torture me!" Hearing his moans and the disturbance he made, the people in the house fancied he was mad, and called in a physician, who prescribed for him. But neither pill nor potion could cure Tokubei, whose strange frenzy soon became the talk of the whole neighbourhood.

Now it chanced that the story reached the ears of a certain wandering priest who lodged in the next street. When he heard the particulars, this priest gravely shook his head, as though he knew all about it, and sent a friend to Tokubei's house to say that a wandering priest, dwelling hard by, had heard of his illness, and, were it never so grievous, would undertake to heal it by means of his prayers; and Tokubei's wife, driven half wild by her husband's sickness, lost not a moment in sending for the priest, and taking him into the sick man's room.

But no sooner did Tokubei see the priest than he yelled out, "Help! help! Here is the wandering priest come to torment me again. Forgive! forgive!" and hiding his head under the coverlet, he lay quivering all over. Then the priest turned all present out of the room, put his mouth to the affrighted man's ear, and whispered—

"Three years ago, at the Kuana ferry, you flung me into the water; and well you remember it."

But Tokubei was speechless, and could only quake with fear.

" Happily," continued the priest, " I had learned to swim and to dive as a boy ; so I reached the shore, and, after wandering through many provinces, succeeded in setting up a bronze figure to Buddha, thus fulfilling the wish of my heart. On my journey homewards, I took a lodging in the next street, and there heard of your marvellous ailment. Thinking I could divine its cause, I came to see you, and am glad to find I was not mistaken. You have done a hateful deed ; but am I not a priest ; and have I not forsaken the things of this world ? and would it not ill become me to bear malice ? Repent, therefore, and abandon your evil ways. To see you do so I should esteem the height of happiness. Be of good cheer, now, and look me in the face, and you will see that I am really a living man, and no vengeful goblin come to torment you."

Seeing he had no ghost to deal with, and overwhelmed by the priest's kindness, Tokubei burst into tears, and answered, " Indeed, indeed, I don't know what to say. In a fit of madness I was tempted to kill and rob you. Fortune befriended me ever after ; but the richer I grew, the more keenly I felt how wicked I had been, and the more I foresaw that my victim's vengeance would some day overtake me. Haunted by this thought, I lost my nerve, till one night I beheld your spirit, and from that time forth fell ill. But how you managed to escape, and are still alive, is more than I can understand."

" A guilty man," said the priest, with a smile, " shudders at the rustling of the wind or the chattering of a stork's beak : a murderer's conscience preys upon his mind till he sees what is not. Poverty drives a man to crimes which he repents of in his wealth. How true is the doctrine of Môshi,[1] that the heart of man, pure by nature, is corrupted by circumstances."

Thus he held forth ; and Tokubei, who had long since repented of his crime, implored forgiveness, and gave him a large sum of money, saying, " Half of this is the amount I stole from you three years since ; the other half I entreat you to accept as interest, or as a gift."

[1] Mencius.

The priest at first refused the money; but Tokubei insisted on his accepting it, and did all he could to detain him, but in vain; for the priest went his way, and bestowed the money on the poor and needy.   As for Tokubei himself, he soon shook off his disorder, and thenceforward lived at peace with all men, revered both at home and abroad, and ever intent on good and charitable deeds.

CONCERNING CERTAIN SUPERSTITIONS

CONCERNING CERTAIN SUPERSTITIONS

CATS, foxes, and badgers are regarded with superstitious awe by the Japanese, who attribute to them the power of assuming the human shape in order to bewitch mankind. Like the fairies of our Western tales, however, they work for good as well as for evil ends. To do them a good turn is to secure powerful allies; but woe betide him who injures them!—he and his will assuredly suffer for it. Cats and foxes seem to have been looked upon as uncanny beasts all the world over; but it is new to me that badgers should have a place in fairy-land. The island of Shikoku, the southernmost of the great Japanese islands, appears to be the part of the country in which the badger is regarded with the greatest veneration. Among the many tricks which he plays upon the human race is one, of which I have a clever representation carved in ivory. Lying in wait in lonely places after dusk, the badger watches for benighted wayfarers: should one appear, the beast, drawing a long breath, distends his belly and drums delicately upon it with his clenched fist, producing such entrancing tones, that the traveller cannot resist turning aside to follow the sound, which, Will-o'-the-wisp-like, recedes as he advances, until it lures him on to his destruction. Love is, however, the most powerful engine which the cat, the fox, and the badger alike put forth for the ruin of man. No German poet ever imagined a more captivating water-nymph than the fair virgins by whom the knight of Japanese romance is assailed : the true hero recognizes and slays the beast ; the weaker mortal yields and perishes.

The Japanese story-books abound with tales about the pranks of these creatures, which, like ghosts, even play a part in the histories of ancient and noble families. I have collected a few of these, and now beg a hearing for a distinguished and two-tailed[1] connection of Puss in Boots and the Chatte Blanche.

[1] Cats are found in Japan, as in the Isle of Man, with stumps, where they should have tails. Sometimes this is the result of art, sometimes of a natural shortcoming. The cats of Yedo are of bad repute as mousers, their energies being relaxed by much petting at the hands of ladies. The Cat of Nabé shima, so says tradition, was a monster with two tails.

THE VAMPIRE CAT OF NABÉSHIMA

THERE is a tradition in the Nabéshima[1] family that, many years ago, the Prince of Hizen was bewitched and cursed by a cat that had been kept by one of his retainers. This prince had in his house a lady of rare beauty, called O Toyo: amongst all his ladies she was the favourite, and there was none who could rival her charms and accomplishments. One day the Prince went out into the garden with O Toyo, and remained enjoying the fragrance of the flowers until sunset, when they returned to the palace, never noticing that they were being followed by a large cat. Having parted with her lord, O Toyo retired to her own room and went to bed. At midnight she awoke with a start, and became aware of a huge cat that crouched watching her; and when she cried out, the beast sprang on her, and, fixing its cruel teeth in her delicate throat, throttled her to death. What a piteous end for so fair a dame, the darling of her prince's heart, to die suddenly, bitten to death by a cat! Then the cat, having scratched out a grave under the verandah, buried the corpse of O Toyo, and assuming her form, began to bewitch the Prince.

But my lord the Prince knew nothing of all this, and little thought that the beautiful creature who caressed and fondled him was an impish and foul beast that had slain his mistress and assumed her shape in order to drain out his life's blood. Day by day, as time went on, the Prince's strength dwindled away; the colour of his face was changed, and became pale and livid; and he was as a man suffering from a deadly

[1] The family of the Prince of Hizen, one of the eighteen chief Daimios of Japan.

THE CAT OF NABÉSHIMA

sickness. Seeing this, his councillors and his wife became greatly alarmed; so they summoned the physicians, who prescribed various remedies for him; but the more medicine he took, the more serious did his illness appear, and no treatment was of any avail. But most of all did he suffer in the night-time, when his sleep would be troubled and disturbed by hideous dreams. In consequence of this, his councillors nightly appointed a hundred of his retainers to sit up and watch over him; but, strange to say, towards ten o'clock on the very first night that the watch was set, the guard were seized with a sudden and unaccountable drowsiness, which they could not resist, until one by one every man had fallen asleep. Then the false O Toyo came in and harassed the Prince until morning. The following night the same thing occurred, and the Prince was subjected to the imp's tyranny, while his guards slept helplessly around him. Night after night this was repeated, until at last three of the Prince's councillors determined themselves to sit up on guard, and see whether they could overcome this mysterious drowsiness; but they fared no better than the others, and by ten o'clock were fast asslep. The next day the three councillors held a solemn conclave, and their chief, one Isahaya Buzen, said—

"This is a marvellous thing, that a guard of a hundred men should thus be overcome by sleep. Of a surety, the spell that is upon my lord and upon his guard must be the work of witchcraft. Now, as all our efforts are of no avail, let us seek out Ruiten, the chief priest of the temple called Miyô In, and beseech him to put up prayers for the recovery of my lord."

And the other councillors approving what Isahaya Buzen had said, they went to the priest Ruiten and engaged him to recite litanies that the Prince might be restored to health.

So it came to pass that Ruiten, the chief priest of Miyô In, offered up prayers nightly for the Prince. One night, at the ninth hour (midnight), when he had finished his religious exercises and was preparing to lie down to sleep, he fancied that he heard a noise outside in the garden, as if some one were washing himself at the well. Deeming this passing strange, he looked down from the window; and there in the moonlight he saw a handsome young soldier, some twenty-four years of age, washing himself, who, when he had finished cleaning himself and had put on his clothes, stood before the figure of Buddha and prayed fervently for the recovery of my lord the Prince. Ruiten looked on with admiration; and the young man, when he had made an end of his prayer, was going away; but the priest stopped him, calling out to him—

"Sir, I pray you to tarry a little: I have something to say to you."

"At your reverence's service. What may you please to want?"

"Pray be so good as to step up here, and have a little talk."

"By your reverence's leave;" and with this he went upstairs.

Then Ruiten said—

"Sir, I cannot conceal my admiration that you, being so young a man, should have so loyal a spirit. I am Ruiten, the chief priest of this temple, who am engaged in praying for the recovery of my lord. Pray what is your name?"

"My name, sir, is Itô Sôda, and I am serving in the infantry of Nabéshima. Since my lord has been sick, my one desire has been to assist in nursing him; but, being only a simple soldier, I am not of sufficient rank to come into his presence, so I have no resource but to pray to the gods of the country and to Buddha that my lord may regain his health."

When Ruiten heard this, he shed tears in admiration of the fidelity of Itô Sôda, and said—

"Your purpose is, indeed, a good one; but what a strange sickness this is that my lord is afflicted with! Every night he suffers from horrible dreams; and the retainers who sit up with him are all seized with a mysterious sleep, so that not one can keep awake. It is very wonderful."

"Yes," replied Sôda, after a moment's reflection, "this

certainly must be witchcraft. If I could but obtain leave to sit up one night with the Prince, I would fain see whether I could not resist this drowsiness and detect the goblin."

At last the priest said, "I am in relations of friendship with Isahaya Buzen, the chief councillor of the Prince. I will speak to him of you and of your loyalty, and will intercede with him that you may attain your wish."

"Indeed, sir, I am most thankful. I am not prompted by any vain thought of self-advancement, should I succeed : all I wish for is the recovery of my lord. I commend myself to your kind favour."

"Well, then, to-morrow night I will take you with me to the councillor's house."

"Thank you, sir, and farewell." And so they parted.

On the following evening Itô Sôda returned to the temple Miyô In, and having found Ruiten, accompanied him to the house of Isahaya Buzen : then the priest, leaving Sôda outside, went in to converse with the councillor, and inquire after the Prince's health.

"And pray, sir, how is my lord ? Is he in any better condition since I have been offering up prayers for him ?"

"Indeed, no; his illness is very severe. We are certain that he must be the victim of some foul sorcery; but as there are no means of keeping a guard awake after ten o'clock, we cannot catch a sight of the goblin, so we are in the greatest trouble."

"I feel deeply for you : it must be most distressing. However, I have something to tell you. I think that I have found a man who will detect the goblin; and I have brought him with me."

"Indeed! who is the man ?"

"Well, he is one of my lord's foot-soldiers, named Itô Sôda, a faithful fellow, and I trust that you will grant his request to be permitted to sit up with my lord."

"Certainly, it is wonderful to find so much loyalty and zeal in a common soldier," replied Isahaya Buzen, after a moment's reflection; "still it is impossible to allow a man of such low rank to perform the office of watching over my lord."

"It is true that he is but a common soldier," urged the priest; "but why not raise his rank in consideration of his fidelity, and then let him mount guard?"

"It would be time enough to promote him after my lord's recovery. But come, let me see this Itô Sôda, that I may know what manner of man he is: if he pleases me, I will consult with the other councillors, and perhaps we may grant his request."

"I will bring him in forthwith," replied Ruiten, who thereupon went out to fetch the young man.

When he returned, the priest presented Itô Sôda to the councillor, who looked at him attentively, and, being pleased with his comely and gentle appearance, said—

"So I hear that you are anxious to be permitted to mount guard in my lord's room at night. Well, I must consult with the other councillors, and we will see what can be done for you."

When the young soldier heard this he was greatly elated, and took his leave, after warmly thanking Ruiten, who had helped him to gain his object. The next day the councillors held a meeting, and sent for Itô Sôda, and told him that he might keep watch with the other retainers that very night. So he went his way in high spirits, and at nightfall, having made all his preparations, took his place among the hundred gentlemen who were on duty in the prince's bed-room.

Now the Prince slept in the centre of the room, and the hundred guards around him sat keeping themselves awake with entertaining conversation and pleasant conceits. But, as ten o'clock approached, they began to doze off as they sat; and in spite of all their endeavours to keep one another awake, by degrees they all fell asleep. Itô Sôda all this while felt an irresistible desire to sleep creeping over him, and, though he tried by all sorts of ways to rouse himself, he saw that there was no help for it, but by resorting to an extreme measure, for which he had already made his preparations. Drawing out a piece of oil paper which he had brought with him, and spreading it over the mats, he sat down upon it; then he took the small knife which he carried in the sheath of his dirk, and stuck it into his own thigh. For awhile the pain of the wound kept him awake; but as the slumber by which he was assailed was the work of sorcery, little by little he became drowsy again. Then he twisted the knife round and round in his thigh, so that the pain becoming very violent, he was proof against the feeling of sleepiness, and kept a faithful watch. Now the oil paper which he had spread under his legs was in order to prevent the blood, which might spurt from his wound, from defiling the mats.

So Itô Sôda remained awake, but the rest of the guard slept; and as he watched, suddenly the sliding-doors of the Prince's room were drawn open, and he saw a figure coming in stealthily, and, as it drew nearer, the form was that of a marvellously beautiful woman some twenty-three years of age. Cautiously she looked around her; and when she saw that all the guard were asleep, she smiled an ominous smile, and was going up to the Prince's bedside, when she perceived that in one corner of the room there was a man yet awake. This seemed to startle her, but she went up to Sôda and said—

" I am not used to seeing you here. Who are you ? "

" My name is Itô Sôda, and this is the first night that I have been on guard."

" A troublesome office, truly ! Why, here are all the rest of the guard asleep. How is it that you alone are awake? You are a trusty watchman."

" There is nothing to boast about. I'm asleep myself, fast and sound."

" What is that wound on your knee? It is all red with blood."

" Oh ! I felt very sleepy; so I stuck my knife into my thigh, and the pain of it has kept me awake."

" What wondrous loyalty ! " said the lady.

" Is it not the duty of a retainer to lay down his life for his master ? Is such a scratch as this worth thinking about ? "

Then the lady went up to the sleeping prince and said, "How fares it with my lord to-night?" But the Prince, worn out with sickness, made no reply. But Sôda was watching her eagerly, and guessed that it was O Toyo, and made up his mind that if she attempted to harass the Prince he would kill her on the spot. The goblin, however, which in the form of O Toyo had been tormenting the Prince every night, and had come again that night for no other purpose, was defeated by the watchfulness of Itô Sôda; for whenever she drew near to the sick man, thinking to put her spells upon him, she would turn and look behind her, and there she saw Itô Sôda glaring at her; so she had no help for it but to go away again, and leave the Prince undisturbed.

At last the day broke, and the other officers, when they awoke and opened their eyes, saw that Itô Sôda had kept awake by stabbing himself in the thigh; and they were greatly ashamed, and went home crestfallen.

That morning Itô Sôda went to the house of Isahaya Buzen, and told him all that had occurred the previous night. The councillors were all loud in their praise of Itô Sôda's behaviour, and ordered him to keep watch again that night. At the same hour, the false O Toyo came and looked all round the room, and all the guard were asleep, excepting Itô Sôda, who was wide awake; and so, being again frustrated, she returned to her own apartments.

Now as since Sôda had been on guard the Prince had passed quiet nights, his sickness began to get better, and there was great joy in the palace, and Sôda was promoted and rewarded with an estate. In the meanwhile O Toyo, seeing that her nightly visits bore no fruits, kept away; and from that time forth the night-guard were no longer subject to fits of drowsiness. This coincidence struck Sôda as very strange, so he went to Isahaya Buzen and told him that of a certainty this O Toyo was no other than a goblin. Isahaya Buzen reflected for a while, and said—

"Well, then, how shall we kill the foul thing?"

"I will go to the creature's room, as if nothing were the

matter, and try to kill her; but in case she should try to escape, I will beg you to order eight men to stop outside and lie in wait for her."

Having agreed upon this plan, Sôda went at nightfall to O Toyo's apartment, pretending to have been sent with a message from the Prince. When she saw him arrive, she said—

"What message have you brought me from my lord?"

"Oh! nothing in particular. Be so good as to look at this letter;" and as he spoke, he drew near to her, and suddenly drawing his dirk cut at her; but the goblin, springing back, seized a halberd, and glaring fiercely at Sôda, said—

"How dare you behave like this to one of your lord's ladies? I will have you dismissed;" and she tried to strike Sôda with the halberd. But Sôda fought desperately with his dirk; and the goblin, seeing that she was no match for him, threw away the halberd, and from a beautiful woman became suddenly transformed into a cat, which, springing up the sides of the room, jumped on to the roof. Isahaya Buzen and his eight men who were watching outside shot at the cat, but missed it, and the beast made good its escape.

So the cat fled to the mountains, and did much mischief among the surrounding people, until at last the Prince of Hizen ordered a great hunt, and the beast was killed.

But the Prince recovered from his sickness; and Itô Sôda was richly rewarded.

THE STORY OF THE FAITHFUL CAT

ABOUT sixty years ago, in the summer-time, a man went to pay a visit at a certain house at Osaka, and, in the course of conversation, said—

"I have eaten some very extraordinary cakes to-day," and on being asked what he meant, he told the following story :—

"I received the cakes from the relatives of a family who were celebrating the hundredth anniversary of the death of a cat that had belonged to their ancestors. When I asked the history of the affair, I was told that, in former days, a young girl of the family, when she was about sixteen years old, used always to be followed about by a tom-cat, who was reared in the house, so much so that the two were never separated for an instant. When her father perceived this, he was very angry, thinking that the tom-cat, forgetting the kindness with which he had been treated for years in the house, had fallen in love with his daughter, and intended to cast a spell upon her ; so he determined that he must kill the beast. As he was planning this in secret, the cat overheard him, and that night went to his pillow, and, assuming a human voice, said to him—

"'You suspect me of being in love with your daughter ; and although you might well be justified in so thinking, your suspicions are groundless. The fact is this :—There is a very large old rat who has been living for many years in your granary. Now it is this old rat who is in love with my young mistress, and this is why I dare not leave her side for a moment, for fear the old rat should carry her off. Therefore I pray you to dispel your suspicions. But as I, by myself, am no match for the rat, there is a famous cat, named Buchi, at the house of Mr. So-and-so, at Ajikawa: if you will borrow that cat, we will soon make an end of the old rat.'

"When the father awoke from his dream, he thought it so wonderful, that he told the household of it; and the following day he got up very early and went off to Ajikawa, to inquire for the house which the cat had indicated, and had no difficulty in finding it; so he called upon the master of the house, and told him what his own cat had said, and how he wished to borrow the cat Buchi for a little while.

"'That's a very easy matter to settle,' said the other: 'pray take him with you at once;' and accordingly the father went home with the cat Buchi in charge. That night he put the two cats into the granary; and after a little while, a frightful clatter was heard, and then all was still again; so the people of the house opened the door, and crowded out to see what had happened; and there they beheld the two cats and the rat all locked together, and panting for breath; so they cut the throat of the rat, which was as big as either of the cats: then they attended to the two cats; but, although they gave them ginseng[1] and other restoratives, they both got weaker and weaker, until at last they died. So the rat was thrown into the river; but the two cats were buried with all honours in a neighbouring temple."

---

[1] A restorative in high repute. The best sorts are brought from Corea.

HOW A MAN WAS BEWITCHED AND HAD HIS HEAD SHAVED BY THE FOXES

IN the village of Iwahara, in the province of Shinshiu, there dwelt a family which had acquired considerable wealth in the wine trade. On some auspicious occasion it happened that a number of guests were gathered together at their house, feasting on wine and fish; and as the wine-cup went round, the conversation turned upon foxes. Among the guests was a certain carpenter, Tokutarô by name, a man about thirty years of age, of a stubborn and obstinate turn, who said—

"Well, sirs, you've been talking for some time of men being bewitched by foxes; surely you must be under their influence yourselves, to say such things. How on earth can foxes have such power over men? At any rate, men must be great fools to be so deluded. Let's have no more of this nonsense."

Upon this a man who was sitting by him answered—

"Tokutarô little knows what goes on in the world, or he would not speak so. How many myriads of men are there who have been bewitched by foxes? Why, there have been at least twenty or thirty men tricked by the brutes on the Maki Moor alone. It's hard to disprove facts that have happened before our eyes."

"You're no better than a pack of born idiots!" said Tokutarô. "I will engage to go out to the Maki Moor this very night and prove it. There is not a fox in all Japan that can make a fool of Tokutarô."

Thus he spoke in his pride; but the others were all angry with him for boasting, and said—

"If you return without anything having happened, we will

298

pay for five measures of wine and a thousand copper cash worth of fish; and if you are bewitched, you shall do as much for us."

Tokutarô took the bet, and at nightfall set forth for the Maki Moor by himself. As he neared the moor, he saw before him a small bamboo grove, into which a fox ran; and it instantly occurred to him that the foxes of the moor would try to bewitch him. As he was yet looking, he suddenly saw the daughter of the headman of the village of Upper Horikané, who was married to the headman of the village of Maki.

"Pray, where are you going to, Master Tokutarô?" said she.

"I am going to the village hard by."

"Then, as you will have to pass my native place, if you will allow me, I will accompany you so far."

Tokutarô thought this very odd, and made up his mind that it was a fox trying to make a fool of him; he accordingly determined to turn the tables on the fox, and answered—

"It is a long time since I have had the pleasure of seeing you; and as it seems that your house is on my road, I shall be glad to escort you so far."

With this he walked behind her, thinking he should certainly see the end of a fox's tail peeping out; but, look as he might, there was nothing to be seen. At last they came to the village of Upper Horikané; and when they reached the cottage of the girl's father, the family all came out, surprised to see her.

"Oh dear! oh dear! here is our daughter come: I hope there is nothing the matter."

And so they went on, for some time, asking a string of questions.

In the meanwhile, Tokutarô went round to the kitchen door, at the back of the house, and, beckoning out the master of the house, said—

"The girl who has come with me is not really your

daughter. As I was going to the Maki Moor, when I arrived at the bamboo grove, a fox jumped up in front of me, and when it had dashed into the grove it immediately took the shape of your daughter, and offered to accompany me to the village ; so I pretended to be taken in by the brute, and came with it so far."

On hearing this, the master of the house put his head on one side, and mused a while; then, calling his wife, he repeated the story to her, in a whisper.

But she flew into a great rage with Tokutarô, and said—

"This is a pretty way of insulting people's daughters. The girl is our daughter, and there's no mistake about it. How dare you invent such lies ? "

"Well," said Tokutarô, "you are quite right to say so; but still there is no doubt that this is a case of witchcraft."

Seeing how obstinately he held to his opinion, the old folks were sorely perplexed, and said—

"What do you think of doing ? "

"Pray leave the matter to me: I'll soon strip the false skin off, and show the beast to you in its true colours. Do you two go into the store-closet, and wait there."

With this he went into the kitchen, and, seizing the girl by the back of the neck, forced her down by the hearth.

"Oh ! Master Tokutarô, what means this brutal violence ? Mother ! father ! help ! "

So the girl cried and screamed; but Tokutarô only laughed, and said—

"So you thought to bewitch me, did you ? From the moment you jumped into the wood, I was on the look-out for you to play me some trick. I'll soon make you show what you really are ; " and as he said this, he twisted her two hands behind her back, and trod upon her, and tortured her ; but she only wept, and cried—

"Oh ! it hurts, it hurts ! "

"If this is not enough to make you show your true form, I'll roast you to death ;" and he piled firewood on the hearth, and, tucking up her dress, scorched her severely.

" Oh! oh! this is more than I can bear; " and with this she expired.

The two old people then came running in from the rear of the house, and, pushing aside Tokutarô, folded their daughter in their arms, and put their hands to her mouth to feel whether she still breathed; but life was extinct, and not the sign of a fox's tail was to be seen about her. Then they seized Tokutarô by the collar, and cried—

"On pretence that our true daughter was a fox, you have roasted her to death. Murderer! Here, you there, bring ropes and cords, and secure this Tokutarô!"

So the servants obeyed, and several of them seized Tokutarô and bound him to a pillar. Then the master of the house, turning to Tokutarô, said—

"You have murdered our daughter before our very eyes. I shall report the matter to the lord of the manor, and you will assuredly pay for this with your head. Be prepared for the worst."

And as he said this, glaring fiercely at Tokutarô, they carried the corpse of his daughter into the store-closet. As they were sending to make the matter known in the village of Maki, and taking other measures, who should come up but the priest of the temple called Anrakuji, in the village of Iwahara, with an acolyte and a servant, who called out in a loud voice from the front door—

"Is all well with the honourable master of this house? I have been to say prayers to-day in a neighbouring village, and on my way back I could not pass the door without at least inquiring after your welfare. If you are at home, I would fain pay my respects to you."

As he spoke thus in a loud voice, he was heard from the back of the house; and the master got up and went out, and, after the usual compliments on meeting had been exchanged, said—

"I ought to have the honour of inviting you to step inside this evening; but really we are all in the greatest trouble, and I must beg you to excuse my impoliteness."

"Indeed! Pray, what may be the matter?" replied the priest. And when the master of the house had told the whole story, from beginning to end, he was thunderstruck, and said—

"Truly, this must be a terrible distress to you." Then the priest looked on one side, and saw Tokutarô bound, and exclaimed, "Is not that Tokutarô that I see there?"

"Oh, your reverence," replied Tokutarô, piteously, "it was this, that, and the other; and I took it into my head that the young lady was a fox, and so I killed her. But I pray your reverence to intercede for me, and save my life;" and as he spoke, the tears started from his eyes.

"To be sure," said the priest, "you may well bewail yourself; however, if I save your life, will you consent to become my disciple, and enter the priesthood?"

"Only save my life, and I'll become your disciple with all my heart."

When the priest heard this, he called out the parents, and said to them—

"It would seem that, though I am but a foolish old priest, my coming here to-day has been unusually well timed. I have a request to make of you. Your putting Tokutarô to death won't bring your daughter to life again. I have heard his story, and there certainly was no malice prepense on his part to kill your daughter. What he did, he did thinking to do a service to your family; and it would surely be better to hush the matter up. He wishes, moreover, to give himself over to me, and to become my disciple."

"It is as you say," replied the father and mother, speaking together. "Revenge will not recall our daughter. Please dispel our grief, by shaving his head and making a priest of him on the spot."

"I'll shave him at once, before your eyes," answered the priest, who immediately caused the cords which bound Tokutarô to be untied, and, putting on his priest's scarf, made him join his hands together in a posture of prayer. Then the reverend man stood up behind him, razor in hand, and, intoning a hymn, gave two or three strokes of the razor, which he then handed to his acolyte, who made a clean shave of Tokutarô's hair. When the latter had finished his obeisance to the priest, and the ceremony was over, there was a loud burst of laughter; and at the same moment the day broke, and Tokutarô found himself alone, in the middle of a large moor. At first, in his surprise, he thought that it was all a dream, and was much annoyed at having been tricked by the foxes. He then passed his hand over his head, and found that he was shaved quite bald. There was nothing for it but to get up, wrap a handkerchief round his head, and go back to the place where his friends were assembled.

"Hallo, Tokutarô! so you've come back. Well, how about the foxes?"

"Really, gentlemen," replied he, bowing, "I am quite ashamed to appear before you."

Then he told them the whole story, and, when he had finished, pulled off the kerchief, and showed his bald pate.

"What a capital joke!" shouted his listeners, and amid roars of laughter, claimed the bet of fish and wine. It was duly paid; but Tokutarô never allowed his hair to grow again, and renounced the world, and became a priest under the name of Sainen.

There are a great many stories told of men being shaved by the foxes; but this story came under the personal observation of Mr. Shôminsai, a teacher of the city of Yedo, during a holiday trip which he took to the country where the event occurred; and I [1] have recorded it in the very selfsame words in which he told it to me.

---

[1] The author of the "Kanzen-Yawa," the book from which the story is taken.

THE GRATEFUL FOXES

ONE fine spring day, two friends went out to a moor to gather fern, attended by a boy with a bottle of wine and a box of provisions. As they were straying about, they saw at the foot of a hill a fox that had brought out its cub to play; and whilst they looked on, struck by the strangeness of the sight, three children came up from a neighbouring village with baskets in their hands, on the same errand as themselves. As soon as the children saw the foxes, they picked up a bamboo stick and took the creatures stealthily in the rear; and when the old foxes took to flight, they surrounded them and beat them with the stick, so that they ran away as fast as their legs could carry them; but two of the boys held down the cub, and, seizing it by the scruff of the neck, went off in high glee.

The two friends were looking on all the while, and one of them, raising his voice, shouted out, "Hallo! you boys! what are you doing with that fox?"

The eldest of the boys replied, "We're going to take him home and sell him to a young man in our village. He'll buy him, and then he'll boil him in a pot and eat him."

"Well," replied the other, after considering the matter attentively, "I suppose it's all the same to you whom you sell him to. You'd better let me have him."

"Oh, but the young man from our village promised us a good round sum if we could find a fox, and got us to come out to the hills and catch one; and so we can't sell him to you at any price."

"Well, I suppose it cannot be helped, then; but how much would the young man give you for the cub?"

" Oh, he'll give us three hundred cash at least."

"Then I'll give you half a bu;[1] and so you'll gain five hundred cash by the transaction."

" Oh, we'll sell him for that, sir. How shall we hand him over to you?"

" Just tie him up here," said the other; and so he made fast the cub round the neck with the string of the napkin in which the luncheon-box was wrapped, and gave half a bu to the three boys, who ran away delighted.

The man's friend, upon this, said to him, " Well, certainly you have got queer tastes. What on earth are you going to keep the fox for?"

" How very unkind of you to speak of my tastes like that. If we had not interfered just now, the fox's cub would have lost its life. If we had not seen the affair, there would have been no help for it. How could I stand by and see life taken? It was but a little I spent—only half a bu—to save the cub, but had it cost a fortune I should not have grudged it. I thought you were intimate enough with me to know my heart; but to-day you have accused me of being eccentric, and I see how mistaken I have been in you. However, our friendship shall cease from this day forth."

And when he had said this with a great deal of firmness, the other, retiring backwards and bowing with his hands on his knees, replied—

" Indeed, indeed, I am filled with admiration at the goodness of your heart. When I hear you speak thus, I feel more than ever how great is the love I bear you. I thought that you might wish to use the cub as a sort of decoy to lead the old ones to you, that you might pray them to bring prosperity and virtue to your house. When I called you eccentric just now, I was but trying your heart, because I had some suspicions of you; and now I am truly ashamed of myself."

---

[1] *Bu.* This coin is generally called by foreigners "ichibu," which means "one bu." To talk of "*a hundred ichibus*" is as though a Japanese were to say "*a hundred one shillings.*" Four bus make a *riyo*, or ounce; and any sum above three bus is spoken of as so many riyos and bus—as 101 riyos and three bus equal 407 bus. The bu is worth about 1*s.* 4*d.*

And as he spoke, still bowing, the other replied, "Really! was that indeed your thought? Then I pray you to forgive me for my violent language."

When the two friends had thus become reconciled, they examined the cub, and saw that it had a slight wound in its foot, and could not walk; and while they were thinking what they should do, they spied out the herb called "Doctor's Nakasé," which was just sprouting; so they rolled up a little of it in their fingers and applied it to the part. Then they pulled out some boiled rice from their luncheon-box and offered it to the cub, but it showed no sign of wanting to eat; so they stroked it gently on the back, and petted it; and as the pain of the wound seemed to have subsided, they were admiring the properties of the herb, when, opposite to them, they saw the old foxes sitting watching them by the side of some stacks of rice straw.

"Look there! the old foxes have come back, out of fear for their cub's safety. Come, we will set it free!" And with these words they untied the string round the cub's neck, and turned its head towards the spot where the old foxes sat; and as the wounded foot was no longer painful, with one bound it dashed to its parents' side and licked them all over for joy, while they seemed to bow their thanks, looking towards the two friends. So, with peace in their hearts, the latter went off to another place, and, choosing a pretty spot, produced the wine bottle and ate their noon-day meal; and after a pleasant day, they returned to their homes, and became firmer friends than ever.

Now the man who had rescued the fox's cub was a tradesman in good circumstances: he had three or four agents and two maid-servants, besides men-servants; and altogether he lived in a liberal manner. He was married, and this union had brought him one son, who had reached his tenth year, but had been attacked by a strange disease which defied all the physician's skill and drugs. At last a famous physician prescribed the liver taken from a live fox, which, as he said, would certainly effect a cure If that were not forthcoming, the most expensive medicine in the world would not restore the boy to health. When the parents heard this, they were at their wits' end. However, they told the state of the case to a man who lived on the mountains. "Even though our child should die for it," they said, "we will not ourselves deprive other creatures of their lives; but you, who live among the hills, are sure to hear when your neighbours go out fox-hunting. We don't care what price we might have to pay for a fox's liver; pray, buy one for us at any expense." So they pressed him to exert himself on their behalf; and he, having promised faithfully to execute the commission, went his way.

In the night of the following day there came a messenger, who announced himself as coming from the person who had undertaken to procure the fox's liver; so the master of the house went out to see him.

"I have come from Mr. So-and-so. Last night the fox's liver that you required fell into his hands; so he sent me to bring it to you." With these words the messenger produced a small jar, adding, "In a few days he will let you know the price."

When he had delivered his message, the master of the house was greatly pleased, and said, "Indeed, I am deeply grateful for this kindness, which will save my son's life."

Then the goodwife came out, and received the jar with every mark of politeness.

"We must make a present to the messenger."

"Indeed, sir, I've already been paid for my trouble."

"Well, at any rate, you must stop the night here."

"Thank you, sir: I've a relation in the next village whom I have not seen for a long while, and I will pass the night with him;" and so he took his leave, and went away.

The parents lost no time in sending to let the physician know that they had procured the fox's liver. The next day the doctor came and compounded a medicine for the patient, which at once produced a good effect, and there was no little joy in the household. As luck would have it, three days after this the man whom they had commissioned to buy the fox's liver came to the house; so the goodwife hurried out to meet him and welcome him.

"How quickly you fulfilled our wishes, and how kind of you to send at once! The doctor prepared the medicine, and now our boy can get up and walk about the room; and it's all owing to your goodness."

"Wait a bit!" cried the guest, who did not know what to make of the joy of the two parents. "The commission with which you entrusted me about the fox's liver turned out to be a matter of impossibility, so I came to-day to make my excuses; and now I really can't understand what you are so grateful to me for."

"We are thanking you, sir," replied the master of the house, bowing with his hands on the ground, "for the fox's liver which we asked you to procure for us."

"I really am perfectly unaware of having sent you a fox's liver: there must be some mistake here. Pray inquire carefully into the matter."

"Well, this is very strange. Four nights ago, a man of some five or six and thirty years of age came with a verbal message from you, to the effect that you had sent him with a fox's liver, which you had just procured, and said that he would come and tell us the price another day. When we asked him to spend the night here, he answered that he would lodge with a relation in the next village, and went away."

The visitor was more and more lost in amazement, and, leaning his head on one side in deep thought, confessed that he could make nothing of it. As for the husband and wife, they felt quite out of countenance at having thanked a man so warmly for favours of which he denied all knowledge; and so the visitor took his leave, and went home.

That night there appeared at the pillow of the master of the house a woman of about one or two and thirty years of age, who said, "I am the fox that lives at such-and-such a mountain. Last spring, when I was taking out my cub to play, it was carried off by some boys, and only saved by your goodness. The desire to requite this kindness pierced me to the quick. At last, when calamity attacked your house, I thought that I might be of use to you. Your son's illness could not be cured without a liver taken from a live fox, so to repay your kindness I killed my cub and took out its liver; then its sire, disguising himself as a messenger, brought it to your house."

And as she spoke, the fox shed tears; and the master of the house, wishing to thank her, moved in bed, upon which his wife awoke and asked him what was the matter; but he too, to her great astonishment, was biting the pillow and weeping bitterly.

" Why are you weeping thus ? " asked she.

At last he sat up in bed, and said, "Last spring, when I was out on a pleasure excursion, I was the means of saving the life of a fox's cub, as I told you at the time. The other day I told Mr. So-and-so that, although my son were to die before my eyes, I would not be the means of killing a fox on purpose ; but asked him, in case he heard of any hunter killing a fox, to buy it for me. How the foxes came to hear of this I don't know; but the foxes to whom I had shown kindness killed their own cub and took out the liver ; and the old dog-fox, disguising himself as a messenger from the person to whom we had confided the commission, came here with it. His mate has just been at my pillow-side and told me all about it; hence it was that, in spite of myself, I was moved to tears."

When she heard this, the goodwife likewise was blinded by her tears, and for a while they lay lost in thought ; but at last, coming to themselves, they lighted the lamp on the shelf on which the family idol stood, and spent the night in reciting prayers and praises, and the next day they published the matter to the household and to their relations and friends. Now, although there are instances of men killing their own children to requite a favour, there is no other example of foxes having done such a thing; so the story became the talk of the whole country.

Now, the boy who had recovered through the efficacy of this medicine selected the prettiest spot on the premises to erect a shrine to Inari Sama,[1] the Fox God, and offered sacrifice to the two old foxes, for whom he purchased the highest rank at the court of the Mikado.

The passage in the tale which speaks of rank being purchased for the foxes at the court of the Mikado is, of course, a piece of nonsense. " The saints who are worshipped in Japan," writes a native authority, " are men who, in the remote ages, when the country was developing itself, were sages, and by their great and virtuous deeds having earned the gratitude of future generations, received divine honours after their death. How can the Son of Heaven, who is the father and mother of his people, turn dealer in ranks and honours ? If rank were a matter of barter, it would cease to be a reward to the virtuous."

All matters connected with the shrines of the Shintô, or indigenous religion, are confided to the superintendence of the families of Yoshida and Fushimi, Kugés or nobles of the Mikado's court at Kiyôto. The affairs of the Buddhist or imported religion are under the care of the family of Kanjuji. As it is necessary that those who as priests perform the honour-

---

[1] Inari Sama is the title under which was deified a certain mythical personage, called Uga, to whom tradition attributes the honour of having first discovered and cultivated the rice-plant. He is represented carrying a few ears of rice, and is symbolized by a snake guarding a bale of rice grain. The foxes wait upon him, and do his bidding. Inasmuch as rice is the most important and necessary product of Japan, the honours which Inari Sama receives are extraordinary. Almost every house in the country contains somewhere about the grounds a pretty little shrine in his honour ; and on a certain day of the second month of the year his feast is celebrated with much beating of drums and other noises, in which the children take a special delight. " On this day," says the Ô-Satsuyô, a Japanese cyclopædia, " at Yedo, where there are myriads upon myriads of shrines to Inari Sama, there are all sorts of ceremonies. Long banners with inscriptions are erected, lamps and lanterns are hung up, and the houses are decked with various dolls and figures ; the sound of flutes and drums is heard, and people dance and make holiday according to their fancy. In short, it is the most bustling festival of the Yedo year."

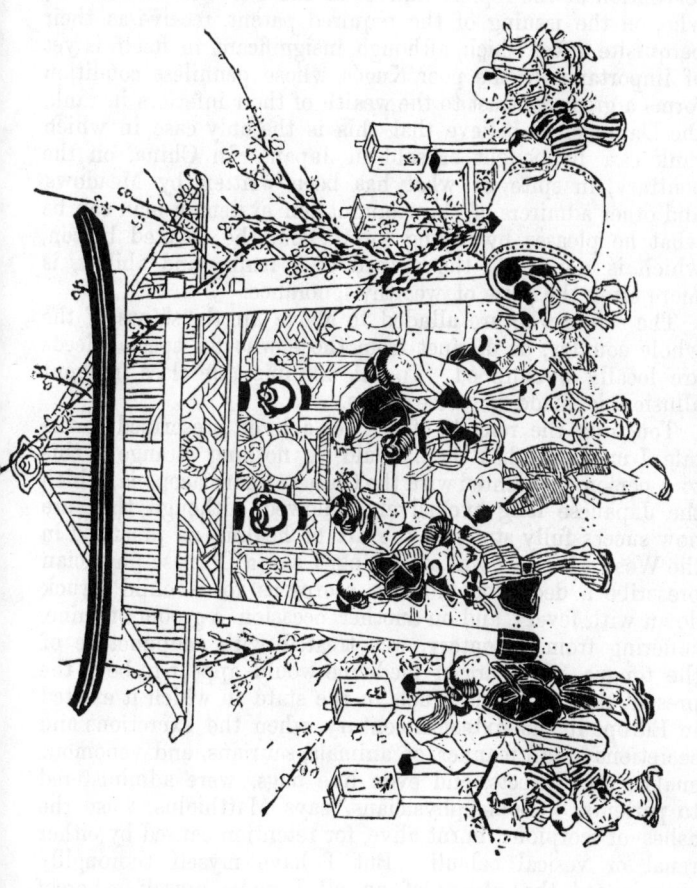

THE FEAST OF INARI SAMA

able office of serving the gods should be persons of some standing, a certain small rank is procured for them through the intervention of the representatives of the above noble families, who, on the issuing of the required patent, receive as their perquisite a fee, which, although insignificant in itself, is yet of importance to the poor Kugés, whose penniless condition forms a great contrast to the wealth of their inferiors in rank, the Daimios. I believe that this is the only case in which rank can be bought or sold in Japan. In China, on the contrary, in spite of what has been written by Meadows and other admirers of the examination system, a man can be what he pleases by paying for it; and the coveted button, which is nominally the reward of learning and ability, is more often the prize of wealthy ignorance.

The saints who are alluded to above are the saints of the whole country, as distinct from those who for special deeds are locally worshipped. To this innumerable class frequent allusion is made in these Tales.

Touching the remedy of the fox's liver, prescribed in the tale, I may add that there would be nothing strange in this to a person acquainted with the Chinese pharmacopœia, which the Japanese long exclusively followed, although they are now successfully studying the art of healing as practised in the West. When I was at Peking, I saw a Chinese physician prescribe a decoction of three scorpions for a child struck down with fever; and on another occasion a groom of mine, suffering from dysentery, was treated with acupuncture of the tongue. The art of medicine would appear to be at the present time in China much in the state in which it existed in Europe in the sixteenth century, when the excretions and secretions of all manner of animals, saurians, and venomous snakes and insects, and even live bugs, were administered to patients. "Some physicians," says Matthiolus, "use the ashes of scorpions, burnt alive, for retention caused by either renal or vesical calculi. But I have myself thoroughly experienced the utility of an oil I make myself, whereof scorpions form a very large portion of the ingredients. If only the region of the heart and all the pulses of the body be anointed with it, it will free the patients from the effects of all kinds of poisons taken by the mouth, corrosive ones excepted." Decoctions of Egyptian mummies were much commended, and often prescribed with due academical solemnity; and the bones of the human skull, pulverized and administered with oil, were used as a specific in cases of renal calculus. (See Petri Andreæ Matthioli Opera, 1574.)

These remarks were made to me by a medical gentleman to whom I mentioned the Chinese doctor's prescription of scorpion tea, and they seem to me so curious that I insert them for comparison's sake.

THE BADGER'S MONEY

It is a common saying among men, that to forget favours received is the part of a bird or a beast: an ungrateful man will be ill spoken of by all the world. And yet even birds and beasts will show gratitude; so that a man who does not requite a favour is worse even than dumb brutes. Is not this a disgrace?

Once upon a time, in a hut at a place called Namékata, in Hitachi, there lived an old priest famous neither for learning nor wisdom, but bent only on passing his days in prayer and meditation. He had not even a child to wait upon him, but prepared his food with his own hands. Night and morning he recited the prayer "Namu Amida Butsu,"[1] intent upon that alone. Although the fame of his virtue did not reach far, yet his neighbours respected and revered him, and often brought him food and raiment; and when his roof or his walls fell out of repair, they would mend them for him; so for the things of this world he took no thought.

One very cold night, when he little thought any one was outside, he heard a voice calling "Your reverence! your reverence!" So he rose and went out to see who it was, and there he beheld an old badger standing. Any ordinary man would have been greatly alarmed at the apparition; but the priest, being such as he has been described above, showed no sign of fear, but asked the creature its business. Upon this the badger respectfully bent its knees, and said—

[1] A Buddhist prayer, in which something approaching to the sounds of the original Sanscrit has been preserved. The meaning of the prayer is explained as, "Save us, eternal Buddha!" Many even of the priests who repeat it know it only as a formula, without understanding it.

" Hitherto, sir, my lair has been in the mountains, and of snow or frost I have taken no heed; but now I am growing old, and this severe cold is more than I can bear. I pray you to let me enter and warm myself at the fire of your cottage, that I may live through this bitter night."

When the priest heard what a helpless state the beast was reduced to, he was filled with pity, and said—

" That's a very slight matter : make haste and come in and warm yourself."

The badger, delighted with so good a reception, went into the hut, and squatting down by the fire began to warm itself ; and the priest, with renewed fervour, recited his prayers and struck his bell before the image of Buddha, looking straight before him.

After two hours the badger took its leave, with profuse expressions of thanks, and went out; and from that time forth it came every night to the hut. As the badger would collect and bring with it dried branches and dead leaves from the hills for firewood, the priest at last became very friendly with it, and got used to its company; so that if ever, as the night wore on, the badger did not arrive, he used to miss it, and wonder why it did not come. When the winter was over, and the spring-time came at the end of the second month, the badger gave up its visits, and was no more seen; but, on the return of the winter, the beast resumed its old habit of coming to the hut. When this practice had gone on for ten years, one day the badger said to the priest, "Through your reverence's kindness for all these years, I have been able to pass the winter nights in comfort. Your favours are such, that during all my life, and even after my death, I must remember them. What can I do to requite them? If there is anything that you wish for, pray tell me."

The priest, smiling at this speech, answered, " Being such as I am, I have no desire and no wishes. Glad as I am to hear your kind intentions, there is nothing that I can ask you to do for me. You need feel no anxiety on my account. As long as I live, when the winter comes, you shall be welcome here." The badger, on hearing this, could not conceal its admiration of the depth of the old man's benevolence; but having so much to be grateful for, it felt hurt at not being able to requite it. As this subject was often renewed between them, the priest at last, touched by the goodness of the badger's heart, said, "Since I have shaven my head, renounced the world, and forsaken the pleasures of this life, I have no desire to gratify, yet I own I should like to possess three riyos in gold. Food and raiment I receive by the favour of the villagers, so I take no heed for those things. Were I to die to-morrow, and attain my wish of being born again into the next world, the same kind folk have promised to meet and bury my body. Thus, although I have no other reason to wish for money, still if I had three riyos I would offer them up at some holy shrine, that masses and prayers might be said for me, whereby I might enter into salvation. Yet I would not get this money by violent or unlawful means; I only think of what might be if I had it. So you see, since you have expressed such kind feelings towards me, I have told you what is on my mind." When the priest had done speaking, the badger leant its head on one side with a puzzled and anxious look, so much so that the old man was sorry he had expressed a wish which seemed to give the beast trouble, and tried to retract what he had said. "Posthumous honours, after all, are the wish of ordinary men. I, who am a priest, ought not to entertain such thoughts, or to want money; so pray pay no attention to what I have said:" and the badger, feigning assent to what the priest had impressed upon it, returned to the hills as usual.

From that time forth the badger came no more to the hut. The priest thought this very strange, but imagined either that the badger stayed away because it did not like to come without the money, or that it had been killed in an attempt to steal it; and he blamed himself for having added to his sins for no purpose, repenting when it was too late: persuaded, however, that the badger must have been killed, he passed his time in putting up prayers upon prayers for it.

After three years had gone by, one night the old man heard a voice near his door calling out, "Your reverence! your reverence!"

As the voice was like that of the badger, he jumped up as soon as he heard it, and ran out to open the door; and there, sure enough, was the badger. The priest, in great delight, cried out, "And so you are safe and sound, after all! Why have you been so long without coming here? I have been expecting you anxiously this long while."

So the badger came into the hut, and said, "If the money which you required had been for unlawful purposes, I could easily have procured as much as ever you might have wanted; but when I heard that it was to be offered to a temple for masses for your soul, I thought that, if I were to steal the hidden treasure of some other man, you could not apply to a sacred purpose money which had been obtained at the expense of his sorrow. So I went to the island of Sado,[1] and gathering the sand and earth which had been cast away as worthless by the miners, fused it afresh in the fire; and at this work I spent months and days." As the badger finished speaking, the priest looked at the money which it had produced, and sure enough he saw that it was bright and new and clean; so he took the money, and received it respectfully, raising it to his head.

"And so you have had all this toil and labour on account of a foolish speech of mine? I have obtained my heart's desire, and am truly thankful."

As he was thanking the badger with great politeness and ceremony, the beast said, "In doing this I have but fulfilled my own wish; still I hope that you will tell this thing to no man."

"Indeed," replied the priest, "I cannot choose but tell this story. For if I keep this money in my poor hut, it will be stolen by thieves: I must either give it to some one to keep for me, or else at once offer it up at the temple. And when I do this, when people see a poor old priest with a sum of

---

[1] An island on the west coast of Japan, famous for its gold mines.

money quite unsuited to his station, they will think it very suspicious, and I shall have to tell the tale as it occurred; but as I shall say that the badger that gave me the money has ceased coming to my hut, you need not fear being waylaid, but can come, as of old, and shelter yourself from the cold." To this the badger nodded assent; and as long as the old priest lived, it came and spent the winter nights with him.

From this story, it is plain that even beasts have a sense of gratitude: in this quality dogs excel all other beasts. Is not the story of the dog of Totoribé Yorodzu written in the Annals of Japan? I[1] have heard that many anecdotes of this nature have been collected and printed in a book, which I have not yet seen; but as the facts which I have recorded relate to a badger, they appear to me to be passing strange.

---

[1] The author of the tale.

THE PRINCE AND THE BADGER

In days of yore there lived a forefather of the Prince of Tosa who went by the name of Yamanouchi Kadzutoyo. At the age of fourteen this prince was amazingly fond of fishing, and would often go down to the river for sport. And it came to pass one day that he had gone thither with but one retainer, and had made a great haul, that a violent shower suddenly came on. Now, the prince had no rain-coat with him, and was in so sorry a plight that he took shelter under a willow-tree and waited for the weather to clear; but the storm showed no sign of abating, and there was no help for it, so he turned to the retainer and said—

"This rain is not likely to stop for some time, so we had better hurry home."

As they trudged homeward, night fell, and it grew very dark; and their road lay over a long bank, by the side of which they found a girl, about sixteen years old, weeping bitterly. Struck with wonder, they looked stedfastly at her, and perceived that she was exceedingly comely. While Kadzutoyo stood doubting what so strange a sight could portend, his retainer, smitten with the girl's charms, stepped up to her and said—

"Little sister, tell us whose daughter you are, and how it comes that you are out by yourself at night in such a storm of rain. Surely it is passing strange."

"Sir," replied she, looking up through her tears, "I am the daughter of a poor man in the castle town. My mother died when I was seven years old, and my father has now wedded a shrew, who loathes and ill-uses me; and in the

319

midst of my grief he is gone far away on his business, so I was left alone with my stepmother; and this very night she spited and beat me till I could bear it no longer, and was on my way to my aunt's, who dwells in yonder village, when the shower came on; but as I lay waiting for the rain to stop, I was seized with a spasm, to which I am subject, and was in great pain, when I had the good luck to fall in with your worships."

As she spoke, the retainer fell deeply in love with her matchless beauty, whilst his lord Kadzutoyo, who from the outset had not uttered a word, but stood brooding over the matter, straightway drew his sword and cut off her head. But the retainer stood aghast, and cried out—

"Oh! my young lord, what wicked deed is this that you've done? The murder of a man's daughter will bring trouble upon us, for you may rely on the business not ending here."

"You don't know what you're talking about," answered Kadzutoyo: "only don't tell any one about it, that is all I ask;" and so they went home in silence.

As Kadzutoyo was very tired, he went to bed, and slept undisturbed by any sense of guilt; for he was brave and fearless. But the retainer grew very uneasy, and went to his young lord's parents and said—

"I had the honour of attending my young lord out fishing to-day, and we were driven home by the rain. And as we came back by the bank, we descried a girl with a spasm in her stomach, and her my young lord straightway slew; and although he has bidden me tell it to no one, I cannot conceal it from my lord and my lady."

Kadzutoyo's parents were sore amazed, bewailing their son's wickedness, and went at once to his room and woke him; his father shed tears and said—

"Oh! dastardly cut-throat that you are! how dare you kill another man's daughter without provocation? Such unspeakable villany is unworthy a Samurai's son. Know, that the duty of every Samurai is to keep watch over the country,

and to protect the people; and such is his daily task. For sword and dirk are given to men that they may slay rebels, and faithfully serve their prince, and not that they may go about committing sin and killing the daughters of innocent men. Whoever is fool enough not to understand this will repeat his misdeed, and will assuredly bring shame on his kindred. Grieved as I am that I should take away the life which I gave you, I cannot suffer you to bring dishonour on our house; so prepare to meet your fate!"

With these words he drew his sword; but Kadzutoyo, without a sign of fear, said to his father—

"Your anger, sir, is most just; but remember that I have studied the classics and understand the laws of right and wrong, and be sure I would never kill another man without good cause. The girl whom I slew was certainly no human being, but some foul goblin: feeling certain of this, I cut her down. To-morrow I beg you will send your retainers to look for the corpse; and if it really be that of a human being, I shall give you no further trouble, but shall disembowel myself."

Upon this the father sheathed his sword, and awaited daybreak. When the morning came, the old prince, in sad distress, bade his retainers lead him to the bank; and there he saw a huge badger, with his head cut off, lying dead by the roadside; and the prince was lost in wonder at his son's shrewdness. But the retainer did not know what to make of it, and still had his doubts. The prince, however, returned home, and sending for his son, said to him—

"It's very strange that the creature which appeared to your retainer to be a girl, should have seemed to you to be a badger."

"My lord's wonder is just," replied Kadzutoyo, smiling: "she appeared as a girl to me as well. But here was a young girl, at night, far from any inhabited place. Stranger still was her wondrous beauty; and strangest of all, that, though it was pouring with rain, there was not a sign of wet on her clothes;

and when my retainer asked how long she had been there, she said she had been on the bank in pain for some time; so I had no further doubt but that she was a goblin, and I killed her."

"But what made you think she must be a goblin because her clothes were dry?"

"The beast evidently thought that, if she could bewitch us with her beauty, she might get at the fish my retainer was carrying; but she forgot that, as it was raining, it would not do for her clothes not to be wet; so I detected and killed her."

When the old prince heard his son speak thus, he was filled with admiration for the youth's sagacity; so, conceiving that Kadzutoyo had given reliable proof of wisdom and prudence, he resolved to abdicate;[1] and Kadzutoyo was proclaimed Prince of Tosa in his stead.

[1] *Inkiyô*, abdication. The custom of abdication is common among all classes, from the Emperor down to his meanest subject. The Emperor abdicates after consultation with his ministers: the Shogun has to obtain the permission of the Emperor; the Daimios, that of the Shogun. The abdication of the Emperor was called *Sentô*; that of the Shogun, *Ogoshô*; in all other ranks it is called *Inkiyô*. It must be remembered that the princes of Japan, in becoming Inkiyô, resign the semblance and the name, but not the reality of power. Both in their own provinces and in the country at large they play a most important part. The ex-Princes of Tosa, Uwajima and Owari, are far more notable men in Japan than the actual holders of the titles.

JAPANESE SERMONS

JAPANESE SERMONS

" Sermons preached here on the 8th, 18th, and 28th days of every month." Such was the purport of a placard, which used to tempt me daily, as I passed the temple Chô-ô-ji. Having ascertained that neither the preacher nor his congregation would have any objection to my hearing one of these sermons, I made arrangements to attend the service, accompanied by two friends, my artist, and a scribe to take notes.

We were shown into an apartment adjoining a small chapel—a room opening on to a tastily arranged garden, wealthy in stone lanterns and dwarfed trees. In the portion of the room reserved for the priest stood a high table, covered with a cloth of white and scarlet silk, richly embroidered with flowers and arabesques; upon this stood a bell, a tray containing the rolls of the sacred books, and a small incense-burner of ancient Chinese porcelain. Before the table was a hanging drum, and behind it was one of those high, back-breaking arm-chairs which adorn every Buddhist temple. In one corner of the space destined for the accommodation of the faithful was a low writing-desk, at which sat, or rather squatted, a lay clerk, armed with a huge pair of horn spectacles, through which he glared, goblin-like, at the people, as they came to have their names and the amount of their offerings to the temple registered. These latter must have been small things, for the congregation seemed poor enough. It was principally composed of old women, nuns with bald shiny pates and grotesque faces, a few petty tradesmen, and half-a-dozen chubby children, perfect little

A JAPANESE SERMON

models of decorum and devoutness. One lady there was, indeed, who seemed a little better to do in the world than the rest; she was nicely dressed, and attended by a female servant; she came in with a certain little consequential rustle, and displayed some coquetry, and a very pretty bare foot, as she took her place, and, pulling out a dandy little pipe and tobacco-pouch, began to smoke. Fire-boxes and spittoons, I should mention, were freely handed about; so that half an hour which passed before the sermon began was agreeably spent. In the meanwhile, mass was being celebrated in the main hall of the temple, and the monotonous nasal drone of the plain chant was faintly heard in the distance. So soon as this was over, the lay clerk sat himself down by the hanging drum, and, to its accompaniment, began intoning the prayer, "Na Mu Miyô Hô Ren Go Kiyô," the congregation fervently joining in unison with him. These words, repeated over and over again, are the distinctive prayer of the Buddhist sect of Nichiren, to which the temple Chô-ô-ji is dedicated. They are approximations to Sanscrit sounds, and have no meaning in Japanese, nor do the worshippers in using them know their precise value.

Soon the preacher, gorgeous in red and white robes, made his appearance, following an acolyte, who carried the sacred book called *Hokké* (upon which the sect of Nichiren is founded) on a tray covered with scarlet and gold brocade. Having bowed to the sacred picture which hung over the *tokonoma*— that portion of the Japanese room which is raised a few inches above the rest of the floor, and which is regarded as the place of honour—his reverence took his seat at the table, and adjusted his robes; then, tying up the muscles of his face into a knot, expressive of utter abstraction, he struck the bell upon the table thrice, burnt a little incense, and read a passage from the sacred book, which he reverently lifted to his head. The congregation joined in chorus, devout but unintelligent; for the Word, written in ancient Chinese, is as obscure to the ordinary Japanese worshipper as are the Latin liturgies to a high-capped Norman peasant-woman.

While his flock wrapped up copper cash in paper, and threw them before the table as offerings, the priest next recited a passage alone, and the lay clerk irreverently entered into a loud dispute with one of the congregation, touching some payment or other. The preliminary ceremonies ended, a small shaven-pated boy brought in a cup of tea, thrice afterwards to be replenished, for his reverence's refreshment; and he, having untied his face, gave a broad grin, cleared his throat, swallowed his tea, and beamed down upon us, as jolly, rosy a priest as ever donned stole or scarf. His discourse, which was delivered in the most familiar and easy manner, was an *extempore* dissertation on certain passages from the sacred books. Whenever he paused or made a point, the congregation broke in with a cry of "Nammiyô!" a corruption of the first three words of the prayer cited above, to which they always contrived to give an expression or intonation in harmony with the preacher's meaning.

"It is a matter of profound satisfaction to me," began his reverence Nichirin, smiling blandly at his audience, "to see so many gentlemen and ladies gathered together here this day, in the fidelity of their hearts, to do honour to the feast of Kishimojin."[1]

"Nammiyô! nammiyô!" self-depreciatory, from the congregation.

"I feel certain that your piety cannot fail to find favour with Kishimojin. Kishimojin ever mourns over the tortures of mankind, who are dwelling in a house of fire, and she ever earnestly strives to find some means of delivering them.

"Nammiyô! nammiyô!" grateful and reverential.

"Notwithstanding this, it is useless your worshipping Kishimojin, and professing to believe in her, unless you have truth in your hearts; for she will not receive your offerings. Man, from his very birth, is a creature of requirements; he is for ever seeking and praying. Both you who listen, and I who preach, have all of us our wants and wishes. If there be any person here who flatters himself

[1] Kishimojin, a female deity of the Buddhists.

that he has no wishes and no wants, let him reflect. Does not every one wish and pray that heaven and earth may stand for ever, that his country and family may prosper, that there may be plenty in the land, and that the people may be healthy and happy? The wishes of men, however, are various and many; and these wishes, numberless as they are, are all known to the gods from the beginning. It is no use praying, unless you have truth in your heart. For instance, the prayer *Na Mu* is a prayer committing your bodies to the care of the gods; if, when you utter it, your hearts are true and single, of a surety your request will be granted. Now, this is not a mere statement made by Nichiren, the holy founder of this sect; it is the sacred teaching of Buddha himself, and may not be doubted."

"Nammiyô! nammiyô!" with profound conviction.

"The heart of man is, by nature, upright and true; but there are seven passions[1] by which it is corrupted. Buddha is alarmed when he sees the fires by which the world is being consumed. These fires are the five lusts of this sinful world; and the five lusts are, the desire for fair sights, sweet sounds, fragrant smells, dainty meats, and rich trappings. Man is no sooner endowed with a body than he is possessed by these lusts, which become his very heart; and, it being a law that every man follows the dictates of his heart, in this way the body, the lusts of the flesh, the heart, and the dictates of the heart, blaze up in the consuming fire. 'Alas! for this miserable world!' said the divine Buddha."

"Nammiyô! nammiyô!" mournful, and with much head-shaking.

"There is not so foul thing under heaven as the human body. The body exudes grease, the eyes distil gums, the nose is full of mucus, the mouth of slobbering spittle; nor are these the most impure secretions of the body. What a mistake it is to look upon this impure body as clean and perfect! Unless we listen to the teachings of Buddha, how shall we be washed and purified?"

[1] The seven passions are joy, anger, sadness, fear, love, hatred, and desire.

" Nammiyô, nammiyô!" from an impure and very miserable sinner, under ten years of age.

" The lot of man is uncertain, and for ever running out of the beaten track. Why go to look at the flowers, and take delight in their beauty? When you return home, you will see the vanity of your pleasure. Why purchase fleeting joys of loose women? How long do you retain the delicious taste of the dainties you feast upon? For ever *wishing* to do this, *wishing* to see that, *wishing* to eat rare dishes, *wishing* to wear fine clothes, you pass a lifetime in fanning the flames which consume you. What terrible matter for thought is this! In the poems of the priest Saigiyo it is written, ' Verily I have been familiar with the flowers; yet are they withered and scattered, and we are parted. How sad!' The beauty of the convolvulus, how bright it is!—and yet in one short morning it closes its petals and fades. In the book called *Rin Jo Bɩ Satsu* [1] we are told how a certain king once went to take his pleasure in his garden, and gladden his eyes with the beauty of his flowers. After a while he fell asleep; and as he slumbered, the women of his train began pulling the flowers to pieces. When the king awoke, of all the glory of his flowers there remained but a few torn and faded petals. Seeing this, the king said, ' The flowers pass away and die; so is it with mankind: we are born, we grow old, we sicken and die; we are as fleeting as the lightning's flash, as evanescent as the morning dew.' I know not whether any of you here present ever fix your thoughts upon death; yet it is a rare thing for a man to live for a hundred years. How piteous a thing it is that in this short and transient life men should consume themselves in a fire of lust! and if we think to escape from this fire, how shall we succeed save only by the teaching of the divine Buddha?"

" Nammiyô! nammiyô!" meekly and entreatingly.

" Since Buddha himself escaped from the burning flames of the lusts of the flesh, his only thought has been for the salvation of mankind. Once upon a time there was a certain

[1] One of the Buddhist classics.

heretic, called Rokutsuponji, a reader of auguries, cunning in astrology and in the healing art. It happened, one day, that this heretic, being in company with Buddha, entered a forest, which was full of dead men's skulls. Buddha, taking up one of the skulls and tapping it thus" (here the preacher tapped the reading-desk with his fan), "said, 'What manner of man was this bone when alive?—and, now that he is dead, in what part of the world has he been born again?' The heretic auguring from the sound which the skull, when struck, gave forth, began to tell its past history, and to prophesy the future. Then Buddha, tapping another skull, again asked the same questions. The heretic answered—

"'Verily, as to this skull, whether it belonged to a man or a woman, whence its owner came or whither he has gone, I know not. What think you of it?'

"'Ask me not,' answered Buddha. But the heretic pressed him, and entreated him to answer; then Buddha said, 'Verily this is the skull of one of my disciples, who forsook the lusts of the flesh.'

"Then the heretic wondered, and said—

"'Of a truth, this is a thing the like of which no man has yet seen. Here am I, who know the manner of the life and of the death even of the ants that creep. Verily, I thought that no thing could escape my ken; yet here lies one of your disciples, than whom there lives no nobler thing, and I am at fault. From this day forth I will enter your sect, praying only that I may receive your teaching.'

"Thus did this learned heretic become a disciple of Buddha. If such an one as he was converted, how much the more should after-ages of ordinary men feel that it is through Buddha alone that they can hope to overcome the sinful lusts of the flesh! These lusts are the desires which agitate our hearts: if we are free from these desires, our hearts will be bright and pure; and there is nothing, save the teaching of Buddha, which can ensure us this freedom. Following the commands of Buddha, and delivered by him from our desires, we may pass our lives in peace and happiness."

"Nammiyô! nammiyô!" with triumphant exultation.

"In the sacred books we read of conversion from a state of sin to a state of salvation. Now this salvation is not a million miles removed from us; nor need we die and be born again into another world in order to reach it. He who lays aside his carnal lusts and affections, at once and of a certainty becomes equal to Buddha. When we recite the prayer *Na Mu Miyô Hô Ren Go Kiyô*, we are praying to enter this state of peace and happiness. By what instruction, other than that of Nichiren, the holy founder of this sect, can we expect to attain this end? If we do attain it, there will be no difference between our state and that of Buddha and of Nichiren. With this view we have learnt from the pious founder of our sect that we must continually and thankfully repeat the prayer *Na Mu Miyô Hô Ren Go Kiyô*, turning our hearts away from lies, and embracing the truth."

Such were the heads of the sermon as they were taken down by my scribe. At its conclusion, the priest, looking about him smiling, as if the solemn truths he had been inculcating were nothing but a very good joke, was greeted by long and loud cries of "Nammiyô! nammiyô!" by all the congregation. Then the lay clerk sat himself down again by the hanging drum; and the service ended as it had begun, by prayer in chorus, during which the priest retired, the sacred book being carried out before him by his acolyte.

Although occasionally, as in the above instance, sermons are delivered as part of a service on special days of the month, they are more frequently preached in courses, the delivery occupying about a fortnight, during which two sermons are given each day. Frequently the preachers are itinerant priests, who go about the towns and villages lecturing in the main hall of some temple or in the guest-room of the resident priest.

There are many books of sermons published in Japan, all of which have some merit and much quaintness: none that I have seen are, however, to my taste, to be compared to the "Kiu-ô Dô-wa," of which the following three sermons compose the first volume. They are written by a priest belonging to the Shingaku sect—a sect professing to combine all that is excellent in the Buddhist, Confucian, and Shin Tô teaching. It maintains the original goodness of the human heart ; and teaches that we have only to follow the dictates of the conscience implanted in us at our birth, in order to steer in the right path. The texts are taken from the Chinese classical books, in the same way as our preachers take theirs from the Bible. Jokes, stories which are sometimes untranslatable into our more fastidious tongue, and pointed applications to members of the congregation, enliven the discourses; it being a principle with the Japanese preacher that it is not necessary to bore his audience into virtue.

SERMON I

(The Sermons of Kiu-ô, vol. i.)

Môshi [1] says, "Benevolence is the heart of man; righteousness is the path of man. How lamentable a thing is it to leave the path and go astray, to cast away the heart and not know where to seek for it!"

The text is taken from the first chapter of Kôshi (the commentator), on Môshi.

Now this quality, which we call benevolence, has been the subject of commentaries by many teachers; but as these commentaries have been difficult of comprehension, they are too hard to enter the ears of women and children. It is of this benevolence that, using examples and illustrations, I propose to treat.

A long time ago, there lived at Kiyôto a great physician, called Imaôji—I forget his other name: he was a very famous man. Once upon a time, a man from a place called Kuramaguchi advertised for sale a medicine which he had compounded against the cholera, and got Imaôji to write a puff for him. Imaôji, instead of calling the medicine in the puff a specific against the cholera, misspelt the word cholera so as to make it simpler. When the man who had employed him went and taxed him with this, and asked him why he had done so, he answered, with a smile—

"As Kuramaguchi is an approach to the capital from the

[1] Môshi, the Japanese pronunciation of the name of the Chinese philosopher Mêng Tse, whom Europeans call Mencius.

country, the passers-by are but poor peasants and woodmen from the hills : if I had written 'cholera' at length, they would have been puzzled by it; so I wrote it in a simple way, that should pass current with every one. Truth itself loses its value if people don't understand it. What does it signify how I spelt the word cholera, so long as the efficacy of the medicine is unimpaired ?"

Now, was not that delightful ? In the same way the doctrines of the sages are mere gibberish to women and children who cannot understand them. Now, my sermons are not written for the learned: I address myself to farmers and tradesmen, who, hard pressed by their daily business, have no time for study, with the wish to make known to them the teachings of the sages ; and, carrying out the ideas of my teacher, I will make my meaning pretty plain, by bringing forward examples and quaint stories. Thus, by blending together the doctrines of the Shintô, Buddhist, and other schools, we shall arrive at something near the true principle of things. Now, positively, you must not laugh if I introduce a light story now and then. Levity is not my object: I only want to put things in a plain and easy manner.

Well, then, the quality which we call benevolence is, in fact, a perfection ; and it is this perfection which Môshi spoke of as the heart of man. With this perfect heart, men, by serving their parents, attain to filial piety; by serving their masters they attain to fidelity ; and if they treat their wives, their brethren, and their friends in the same spirit, then the principles of the five relations of life will harmonize without difficulty. As for putting perfection into practice, parents have the special duties of parents; children have the special duties of children; husbands have the special duties of husbands; wives have the special duties of wives. It is when all these special duties are performed without a fault that true benevolence is reached; and that again is the true heart of man.

For example, take this fan : any one who sees it knows it to be a fan; and, knowing it to be a fan, no one would think of using it to blow his nose in. The special use of a fan is for visits of ceremony ; or else it is opened in order to raise a cooling breeze : it serves no other purpose. In the same way, this reading-desk will not do as a substitute for a shelf ; again, it will not do instead of a pillow : so you see that a reading-desk also has its special functions, for which you must use it. So, if you look at your parents in the light of your parents, and treat them with filial piety, that is the special duty of children ; that is true benevolence ; that is the heart of man. Now although you may think that, when I speak in this way, I am speaking of others, and not of yourselves, believe me that the heart of every one of you is by nature pure benevolence. I am just taking down your hearts as a shopman does goods from his shelves, and pointing out the good and bad qualities of each ; but if you will not lay what I say to your own accounts, but persist in thinking that it is all anybody's business but yours, all my labour will be lost.

Listen ! You who answer your parents rudely, and cause them to weep ; you who bring grief and trouble on your masters ; you who cause your husbands to fly into passions ; you who cause your wives to mourn ; you who hate your younger brothers, and treat your elder brothers with contempt ; you who sow sorrow broadcast over the world ;— what are you doing but blowing your noses in fans, and using reading-desks as pillows ? I don't mean to say that there are any such persons here ; still there are plenty of them to be found—say in the back streets in India, for instance. Be so good as to mind what I have said.

Consider, carefully, if a man is born with a naturally bad disposition, what a dreadful thing that is ! Happily, you and I were born with perfect hearts, which we would not change for a thousand—no, not for ten thousand pieces of gold : is not this something to be thankful for ?

This perfect heart is called in my discourses, " the original heart of man." It is true that benevolence is also called the original heart of man ; still there is a slight difference between the two. However, as the inquiry into this difference would be tedious, it is sufficient for you to look upon this original heart of man as a perfect thing, and you will fall into no error. It is true that I have not the honour of the personal acquaintance of every one of you who are present : still I know that your hearts are perfect. The proof of this, that if you say that which you ought not to say, or do that which you ought not to do, your hearts within you are, in some mysterious way, immediately conscious of wrong. When the man that has a perfect heart does that which is imperfect, it is because his heart has become warped and turned to evil. This law holds good for all mankind. What says the old song ?— " When the roaring waterfall is shivered by the night-storm, the moonlight is reflected in each scattered drop." [1] Although there is but one moon, she suffices to illuminate each little scattered drop. Wonderful are the laws of Heaven ! So the principle of benevolence, which is but one, illumines all the particles that make up mankind. Well, then, the perfection of the human heart can be calculated to a nicety. So, if we follow the impulses of our perfect heart in whatever we undertake, we shall perform our special duties, and filial piety and fidelity will come to us spontaneously. You see the doctrines of this school of philosophy are quickly learnt. If you once thoroughly understand this, there will be no difference between your conduct and that of a man who has studied a hundred years. Therefore I pray you to follow the impulses of your natural heart; place it before you as a teacher, and study its precepts. Your heart is a convenient teacher to employ too : for there is no question of paying fees ; and no need to go out in the heat of summer, or the cold of winter, to pay visits of ceremony to your master to inquire after his health. What admirable teaching this is, by means of which you can learn filial piety and fidelity so easily ! Still suspicions are apt to arise in men's minds about things that are seen to be acquired too cheaply ; but here you can buy a good thing cheap, and spare yourselves the vexation of having paid an

[1] " The moon looks on many brooks ;
The brooks see but one moon."—T. MOORE.

extravagant price for it. I repeat, follow the impulses of your hearts with all your might. In the *Chin-yo*, the second of the books of Confucius, it is certified beyond a doubt that the impulses of nature are the true path to follow ; therefore you may set to work in this direction with your minds at ease.

Righteousness, then, is the true path, and righteousness is the avoidance of all that is imperfect. If a man avoids that which is imperfect, there is no need to point out how dearly he will be beloved by all his fellows. Hence it is that the ancients have defined righteousness as that which ought to be—that which is fitting. If a man be a retainer, it is good that he should perform his service to his lord with all his might. If a woman be married, it is good that she should treat her parents-in-law with filial piety, and her husband with reverence. For the rest, whatever is good that is righteousness and the true path of man.

The duty of man has been compared by the wise men of old to a high road. If you want to go to Yedo or to Nagasaki, if you want to go out to the front of the house or to the back of the house, if you wish to go into the next room or into some closet or other, there is a right road to each of these places : if you do not follow the right road, scrambling over the roofs of houses and through ditches, crossing mountains and desert places, you will be utterly lost and bewildered. In the same way, if a man does that which is not good, he is going astray from the high road. Filial piety in children, virtue in wives, truth among friends—but why enumerate all these things, which are patent ?—all these are the right road, and good ; but to grieve parents, to anger husbands, to hate and to breed hatred in others, these are all bad things, these are all the wrong road. To follow these is to plunge into rivers, to run on to thorns, to jump into ditches, and brings thousands upon ten thousands of disasters. It is true that, if we do not pay great attention, we shall not be able to follow the right road. Fortunately, we have heard by tradition the words of the learned Nakazawa Dôni : I will tell you about that, all in good time.

It happened that, once, the learned Nakazawa went to preach at Ikéda, in the province of Sesshiu, and lodged with a rich family of the lower class. The master of the house, who was particularly fond of sermons, entertained the preacher hospitably, and summoned his daughter, a girl some fourteen or fifteen years old, to wait upon him at dinner. This young lady was not only extremely pretty, but also had charming manners ; so she arranged bouquets of flowers, and made tea, and played upon the harp, and laid herself out to please the learned man by singing songs. The preacher thanked her parents for all this, and said—

" Really it must be a very difficult thing to educate a young lady up to such a pitch as this."

The parents, carried away by their feelings, replied—

" Yes ; when she is married, she will hardly bring shame upon her husband's family. Besides what she did just now, she can weave garlands of flowers round torches, and we had her taught to paint a little ; " and as they began to show a little conceit, the preacher said—

" I am sure this is something quite out of the common run. Of course she knows how to rub the shoulders and loins, and has learnt the art of shampooing ? "

The master of the house bristled up at this and answered—

" I may be very poor, but I've not fallen so low as to let my daughter learn shampooing."

The learned man, smiling, replied, " I think you are making a mistake when you put yourself in a rage. No matter whether her family be rich or poor, when a woman is performing her duties in her husband's house, she must look upon her husband's parents as her own. If her honoured father-in-law or mother-in-law fall ill, her being able to plait flowers and paint pictures and make tea will be of no use in the sick-room. To shampoo her parents-in-law, and nurse them affectionately, without employing either shampooer or servant-maid, is the right path of a daughter-in-law. Do you mean to say that your daughter has not yet learnt shampooing, an art which is essential to her following the right path of a wife? That is what I meant to ask just now. So useful a study is very important."

At this the master of the house was ashamed, and blushing made many apologies, as I have heard. Certainly, the harp and guitar are very good things in their way; but to attend to nursing their parents is the right road of children. Lay this story to heart, and consider attentively where the right road lies. People who live near haunts of pleasure become at last so fond of pleasure, that they teach their daughters nothing but how to play on the harp and guitar, and train them up in the manners and ways of singing-girls, but teach them next to nothing of their duties as daughters; and then very often they escape from their parents' watchfulness, and elope. Nor is this the fault of the girls themselves, but the fault of the education which they have received from their parents. I do not mean to say that the harp and guitar, and songs and dramas, are useless things. If you consider them attentively, all our songs incite to virtue and condemn vice. In the song called "The Four Sleeves," for instance, there is the passage, "If people knew beforehand all the misery that it brings, there would be less going out with young ladies, to look at the flowers at night." Please give your attention to this piece of poetry. This is the meaning of it:—When a young man and a young lady set up a flirtation without the consent of their parents, they think that it will all be very delightful, and find themselves very much deceived. If they knew what a sad and cruel world this is, they would not act as they do. The quotation is from a song of remorse. This sort of thing but too often happens in the world.

When a man marries a wife, he thinks how happy he will be, and how pleasant it will be keeping house on his own account; but, before the bottom of the family kettle has been scorched black, he will be like a man learning to swim in a field, with his ideas all turned topsy-turvy, and, contrary to all his expectations, he will find the pleasures of housekeeping to be all a delusion. Look at that woman there. Haunted by her cares, she takes no heed of her hair, nor of her personal appearance. With her head all untidy, her apron tied round her as a girdle, with a baby twisted into the bosom of her dress, she carries some wretched bean sauce which she has been out to buy. What sort of creature is this? This all comes of not listening to the warnings of parents, and of not waiting for the proper time, but rushing suddenly into housekeeping. And who is to blame in the matter? Passion, which does not pause to reflect. A child of five or six years will never think of learning to play the guitar for its own pleasure. What a ten-million times miserable thing it is, when parents, making their little girls hug a great guitar, listen with pleasure to the poor little things playing on instruments big enough for them to climb upon, and squeaking out songs in their shrill treble voices! Now I must beg you to listen to me carefully. If you get confused and don't keep a sharp look-out, your children, brought up upon harp and guitar playing, will be abandoning their parents, and running away secretly. Depend upon it, from all that is licentious and meretricious something monstrous will come forth. The poet who wrote the " Four Sleeves " regarded it as the right path of instruction to convey a warning against vice. But the theatre and dramas and fashionable songs, if the moral that they convey is missed, are a very great mistake. Although you may think it very right and proper that a young lady should practise nothing but the harp and guitar until her marriage, I tell you that it is not so; for if she misses the moral of her songs and music, there is the danger of her falling in love with some man and eloping. While on this subject, I have an amusing story to tell you.

Once upon a time, a frog, who lived at Kiyôto, had long been desirous of going to see Osaka. One spring, having made up his mind, he started off to see Osaka and all its famous places. By a series of hops on all-fours he reached a temple opposite Nishi-no-oka, and thence by the western road he arrived at Yamazaki, and began to ascend the mountain called Tenôzan. Now it so happened that a frog from Osaka had determined to visit Kiyôto, and had also ascended Tenôzan; and on the summit the two frogs met, made acquaintance, and told one another their intentions. So they began to complain about all the trouble they had gone through, and had only arrived half-way after all: if they went on to Osaka and Kiyôto, their legs and loins would certainly not hold out. Here was the famous mountain of Tenôzan, from the top of which the whole of Kiyôto and Osaka could be seen: if they stood on tiptoe and stretched their backs, and looked at the view, they would save themselves from stiff legs. Having come to this conclusion, they both stood up on tiptoe, and looked about them; when the Kiyôto frog said—

"Really, looking at the famous places of Osaka, which I have heard so much about, they don't seem to me to differ a bit from Kiyôto. Instead of giving myself any further trouble to go on, I shall just return home."

The Osaka frog, blinking with his eyes, said, with a contemptuous smile, "Well, I have heard a great deal of talk about this Kiyôto being as beautiful as the flowers, but it is just Osaka over again. We had better go home."

And so the two frogs, politely bowing to one another, hopped off home with an important swagger.

Now, although this is a very funny little story, you will not understand the drift of it at once. The frogs thought that they were looking in front of them; but as, when they stood up, their eyes were in the back of their heads, each was looking at his native place, all the while that he believed himself to be looking at the place he wished to go to. The frogs stared to any amount, it is true; but then they did not take care that the object looked at was the right object, and so it was that they fell into error. Please, listen attentively. A certain poet says—

"Wonderful are the frogs! Though they go on all-fours in an attitude of humility, their eyes are always turned ambitiously upwards."

A delightful poem! Men, although they say with their

mouths, "Yes, yes, your wishes shall be obeyed,—certainly, certainly, you are perfectly right," are like frogs, with their eyes turned upwards. Vain fools! meddlers ready to undertake any job, however much above their powers! This is what is called in the text, "casting away your heart, and not knowing where to seek for it." Although these men profess to undertake any earthly thing, when it comes to the point, leave them to themselves, and they are unequal to the task; and if you tell them this, they answer—

"By the labour of our own bodies, we earn our money; and the food of our mouths is of our own getting. We are under obligation to no man. If we did not depend upon ourselves, how could we live in the world?"

There are plenty of people who use these words, *myself* and *my own*, thoughtlessly and at random. How false is this belief that they profess! If there were no system of government by superiors, but an anarchy, these people, who vaunt themselves and their own powers, would not stand for a day. In the old days, at the time of the war at Ichi-no-tani, Minamoto no Yoshitsuné[1] left Mikusa, in the province of Tamba, and attacked Settsu. Overtaken by the night among the mountains, he knew not what road to follow; so he sent for his retainer, Benkei, of the Temple called Musashi, and told him to light the big torches which they had agreed upon. Benkei received his orders and transmitted them to the troops, who immediately dispersed through all the valleys, and set fire to the houses of the inhabitants, so that one and all blazed up, and, thanks to the light of this fire, they reached Ichi-no-tani, as the story goes. If you think attentively, you will see the allusion. Those who boast about *my* warehouse, *my* house, *my* farm, *my* daughter, *my* wife, hawking about this "*my*" of theirs like pedlers, let there once come trouble and war in the world, and, for all their vaingloriousness, they will be as helpless as turtles. Let them be

[1] The younger brother of Minamoto no Yoritomo, who first established the government of the Shoguns. The battle of Ichi-no-tani took place in the year 1184 A.D.

thankful that peace is established throughout the world. The humane Government reaches to every frontier: the officials of every department keep watch night and day. When a man sleeps under his roof at night, how can he say that it is thanks to himself that he stretches his limbs in slumber? You go your rounds to see whether the shutters are closed and the front door fast, and, having taken every precaution, you lay yourself down to rest in peace: and what a precaution after all! A board, four-tenths of an inch thick, planed down front and rear until it is only two-tenths of an inch thick. A fine precaution, in very truth!—a precaution which may be blown down with a breath. Do you suppose such a thing as that would frighten a thief from breaking in? This is the state of the case. Here are men who, by the benevolence and virtue of their rulers, live in a delightful world, and yet, forgetting the mysterious providence that watches over them, keep on singing their own praises. Selfish egotists!

"My property amounts to five thousand ounces of silver. I may sleep with my eyes turned up, and eat and take my pleasure, if I live for five hundred or for seven hundred years. I have five warehouses and twenty-five houses. I hold other people's bills for fifteen hundred ounces of silver." So he dances a fling [1] for joy, and has no fear lest poverty should come upon him for fifty or a hundred years. Minds like frogs, with eyes in the middle of their backs! Foolhardy thoughts! A trusty castle of defence indeed! How little can it be depended upon! And when such men are sleeping quietly, how can they tell that they may not be turned into those big torches we were talking about just now, or that a great earthquake will not be upheaved? These are the chances of this fitful world. With regard to the danger of too great reliance, I have a little tale to tell you. Be so good as to wake up from your drowsiness, and listen attentively.

There is a certain powerful shell-fish, called the Sazayé,

[1] Literally, "a dance of the Province of Tosa."

with a very strong operculum. Now this creature, if it hears that there is any danger astir, shuts up its shell from within, with a loud noise, and thinks itself perfectly safe. One day a Tai and another fish, lost in envy at this, said—

"What a strong castle this is of yours, Mr. Sazayé! When you shut up your lid from within, nobody can so much as point a finger at you. A capital figure you make, sir."

When he heard this, the Sazayé, stroking his beard, replied—

"Well, gentlemen, although you are so good as to say so, it's nothing to boast of in the way of safety; yet I must admit that, when I shut myself up thus, I do not feel much anxiety."

And as he was speaking thus, with the pride that apes humility, there came the noise of a great splash; and the shell-fish, shutting up his lid as quickly as possible, kept quite still, and thought to himself, what in the world the noise could be. Could it be a net? Could it be a fish-hook? What a bore it was, always having to keep such a sharp look-out! Were the Tai and the other fish caught, he wondered; and he felt quite anxious about them: however, at any rate, he was safe. And so the time passed; and when he thought all was safe, he stealthily opened his shell, and slipped out his head and looked all round him, and there seemed to be something wrong—something with which he was not familiar. As he looked a little more carefully, lo and behold! there he was in a fishmonger's shop, and with a card marked "sixteen cash" on his back.

Isn't that a funny story? And so, at one fell swoop, all your boasted wealth of houses and warehouses, and cleverness and talent, and rank and power, are taken away. Poor shell-fish! I think there are some people not unlike them to be found in China and India. How little self is to be depended upon! There is a moral poem which says, "It is easier to ascend to the cloudy heaven without a ladder than to depend entirely on oneself." This is what is meant by the text, "If a man casts his heart from him, he knows not where to seek for it." Think twice upon everything that you do. To take no care for the examination of that which relates to yourself, but to look only at that which concerns others, is to cast your heart from you. Casting your heart from you, does not mean that your heart actually leaves you: what is meant is, that you do not examine your own conscience. Nor must you think that what I have said upon this point of self-confidence applies only to wealth and riches. To rely on your talents, to rely on the services you have rendered, to rely on your cleverness, to rely on your judgment, to rely on your strength, to rely on your rank, and to think yourself secure in the possession of these, is to place yourselves in the same category with the shell-fish in the story. In all things examine your own consciences: the examination of your own hearts is above all things essential.

(The preacher leaves his place.)

SERMON II

" If a man loses a fowl or a dog, he knows how to reclaim it. If he loses his soul, he knows not how to reclaim it. The true path of learning has no other function than to teach us how to reclaim lost souls." This parable has been declared to us by Môshi. If a dog, or a chicken, or a pet cat does not come home at the proper time, its master makes a great fuss about hunting for it, and wonders can it have been killed by a dog or by a snake, or can some man have stolen it ; and ransacking the three houses opposite, and his two next-door neighbours' houses, as if he were seeking for a lost child, cries, " Pray, sir, has my tortoise-shell cat been with you ? Has my pet chicken been here ?" That is the way in which men run about under such circumstances. It's a matter of the utmost importance.

And yet to lose a dog or a tame chicken is no such terrible loss after all. But the soul, which is called the lord of the body, is the master of our whole selves. If men part with this soul for the sake of other things, then they become deaf to the admonitions of their parents, and the instructions of their superiors are to them as the winds of heaven. Teaching is to them like pouring water over a frog's face ; they blink their eyes, and that is all ; they say, " Yes, yes !" with their mouths, but their hearts are gone, and, seeing, they are blind, hearing, they are deaf. Born whole and sound, by their own doing they enter the fraternity of cripples. Such are all those who lose their souls. Nor do they think of inquiring or looking for their lost soul. "It is my parents' fault; it is my master's fault; it is my husband's fault; it is my elder brother's fault; it is Hachibei who is a rogue; it is O Matsu who is a bad woman." They content themselves with looking at the faults of others, and do not examine their own consciences, nor search their own hearts. Is not this a cruel state of things? They set up a hue and cry for a lost dog or a pet chicken, but for this all-important soul of theirs they make no search. What mistaken people! For this reason the sages, mourning over such a state of things, have taught us what is the right path of man; and it is the receiving of this teaching that is called learning. The main object of learning is the examination and searching of our own hearts; therefore the text says, "The true path of learning has no other function than to teach us how to reclaim lost souls." This is an exhaustive exposition of the functions of learning. That learning has no other object, we have this gracious pledge and guarantee from the sage. As for the mere study of the antiquities and annals of China and Japan, and investigation into literature, these cannot be called learning, which is above all things an affair of the soul. All the commentaries and all the books of all the teachers in the world are but so many directories by which to find out the whereabouts of our own souls. This search after our own souls is that which I alluded to just now as the examination of our consciences. To disregard the examination of our consciences is a terrible thing, of which it is impossible to foresee the end; on the other hand, to practise it is most admirable, for by this means we can on the spot attain filial piety and fidelity to our masters. Virtue and vice are the goals to which the examination and non-examination of our consciences lead. As it has been rightly said, benevolence and malice are the two roads which man follows. Upon this subject I have a terrible and yet a very admirable story to tell you. Although I dare say you are very drowsy, I must beg you to listen to me.

In a certain part of the country there was a well-to-do farmer, whose marriage had brought him one son, whom he petted beyond all measure, as a cow licks her calf. So by degrees the child became very sly: he used to pull the horses' tails, and blow smoke into the bulls nostrils, and bully the neighbours' children in petty ways and make them cry. From a peevish child he grew to be a man, and unbearably undutiful to his parents. Priding himself on a little superior strength, he became a drunkard and a gambler, and learned to wrestle at fairs. He would fight and quarrel for a trifle, and spent his time in debauchery and riotous living. If his parents remonstrated with him, he would raise his voice and abuse them, using scurrilous language. "It's all very well your abusing me for being dissolute and disobedient. But, pray, who asked you to bring me into the world? You brought me into the world, and I have to thank you for its miseries; so now, if you hate dissolute people, you had better put me back where I came from, and I shall be all right again." This was the sort of insolent answer he would give his parents, who, at their wits' end, began to grow old in years. And as he by degrees grew more and more of a bully, unhappy as he made them, still he was their darling, and they could not find it in their hearts to turn him out of the house and disinherit him. So they let him pursue his selfish course; and he went on from worse to worse, knocking people down, breaking their arms, and getting up great disturbances. It is unnecessary to speak of his parents' feelings. Even his relations and friends felt as if nails were being hammered into their breasts. He was a thoroughly wicked man.

Now no one is from his mother's womb so wicked as this; but those who persist in selfishness lose their senses, and gradually reach this pitch of wickedness. What a terrible thing is this throwing away of our hearts!

Well, this man's relations and friends very properly urged his parents to disown him; but he was an only child, and so his parents, although they said, "To-day we really will disinherit him," or "To-morrow we really will break off all relations with him," still it was all empty talk; and the years and months passed by, until the scapegrace reached his twenty-sixth year, having heaped wickedness upon wickedness; and who can tell how much trouble he brought upon his family, who were always afraid of hearing of some new enormity? At last they held a family council, and told the parents that matters had come to such a pass that if they did not disown their son the rest of the family must needs break off all communication with them : if he were allowed to go on in his evil courses, the whole village, not to speak of his relations, would be disgraced; so either the parents, against whom, however, there was no ill-will felt, must be cut by the family, or they must disinherit their son : to this appeal they begged to have a distinct answer. The parents, reflecting that to separate themselves from their relations, even for the sake of their own son, would be an act of disrespect to their ancestors, determined to invite their relations to assemble and draw up a petition to the Government for leave to disinherit their son, to which petition the family would all affix their seals according to form ; so they begged them to come in the evening, and bring their seals with them. This was their answer.

There is an old saw which says, " The old cow licks her calf, and the tigress carries her cub in her mouth." If the instinct of beasts and birds prompt them to love their young, how much the more must it be a bitter thing for a man to have to disown his own son ! All this trouble was the consequence of this youth casting his heart from him. Had he examined his own conscience, the storm of waves and of wind would not have arisen, and all would have been calm. But as he refused to listen to his conscience, his parents, much against their will, were forced to visit him with the punishment of disinheritance, which he had brought upon himself. A sad thing indeed ! In the poems of his Reverence Tokuhon, a modern poet, there is the following passage : " Since Buddha thus winds himself round our hearts, let the man who dares to disregard him fear for his life." The allusion is to the great mercy and love of the gods. The gods wish to make men examine their consciences, and, day and night, help men to discern that which is evil; but, although they point out our desires and pleasures, our lusts and passions, as things to be avoided, men turn their backs upon their own consciences. The love of the gods is like the love of parents for their children, and men treat the gods as undutiful children treat their parents. "Men who dare to disregard the gods, let them fear for their lives." I pray you who hear me, one and all, to examine your own consciences and be saved.

To return to the story of the vagabond son. As it happened, that day he was gambling in a neighbouring village, when a friend from his own place came up and told him that his relations had met together to disinherit him; and that, fine fellow as he was, he would find it a terrible thing to be disowned. Before he had heard him half out, the other replied in a loud voice—

"What, do you mean to say that they are holding a family council to-night to disinherit me? What a good joke! I'm sure I don't want to be always seeing my father's and mother's blubbering faces; it makes me quite sick to think of them: it's quite unbearable. I'm able to take care of myself; and if I choose to go over to China, or to live in India, I should like to know who is to prevent me? This is the very thing above all others for me. I'll go off to the room where they are all assembled, and ask them why they want to disinherit me. I'll just swagger like Danjurô[1] the actor, and frighten them into giving me fifty or seventy ounces of silver to get rid of me, and put the money in my purse, and be off to Kiyôto or Osaka, where I'll set up a tea-house on my own account; and enjoy myself to my heart's content! I hope this will be a great night for me, so I'll just drink a cup of wine for luck beforehand."

And so, with a lot of young devils of his own sort, he fell

[1] A famous actor of Yedo, who lived 195 years ago. He was born at Sakura, in Shimôsa.

to drinking wine in teacups,[1] so that before nightfall they were all as drunk as mud. Well, then, on the strength of this wine, as he was setting out for his father's house, he said, "Now, then, to try my luck," and stuck a long dirk in his girdle. He reached his own village just before nightfall, thinking to burst into the place where he imagined his relations to be gathered together, turning their wisdom-pockets inside out, to shake out their small provision of intelligence in consultation; and he fancied that, if he blustered and bullied, he would certainly get a hundred ounces of silver out of them. Just as he was about to enter the house, he reflected—

"If I show my face in the room where my relations are gathered together, they will all look down on the ground and remain silent; so if I go in shouting and raging, it will be quite out of harmony; but if they abuse me, then I shall be in the right if I jump in on them and frighten them well. The best plan will be for me to step out of the bamboo grove which is behind the house, and to creep round the verandah, and I can listen to these fellows holding their consultation: they will certainly be raking up all sorts of scandal about me. It will be all in harmony, then, if I kick down the shutters and sliding-doors with a noise like thunder. And what fun it will be!"

As he thought thus to himself, he pulled off his iron-heeled sandals, and stuck them in his girdle, and, girding up his dress round his waist, left the bamboo grove at the back of the house, and, jumping over the garden wicket, went round the verandah and looked in. Peeping through a chink in the shutters, he could see his relations gathered together in council, speaking in whispers. The family were sitting in a circle, and one and all were affixing their seals to the petition of disinheritance. At last, having passed from hand to hand, the document came round to where the two parents were sitting. Their son, seeing this, said—

"Come, now, it's win or lose! My parents' signing the

---

[1] The ordinary wine-cup holding only a thimbleful, to drink wine out of teacups is a great piece of debauchery—like drinking brandy in tumblers.

paper shall be the sign for me to kick open the door and jump into the middle of them."

So, getting ready for a good kick, he held his breath and looked on.

What terrible perversion man can allow his heart to come to! Môshi has said that man by nature is good; but although not a particle of fault can be found with what he has said, when the evil we have learned becomes a second nature, men reach this fearful degree of wickedness. When men come to this pass, Kôshi [1] and Môshi themselves might preach to them for a thousand days, and they would not have strength to reform. Such hardened sinners deserve to be roasted in iron pots in the nethermost hell. Now, I am going to tell you how it came about that the vagabond son turned over a new leaf and became dutiful, and finally entered paradise. The poet says, "Although the hearts of parents are not surrounded by dark night, how often they stray from the right road in their affection for their children!"

When the petition of disinheritance came round to the place where the two parents were sitting, the mother lifted up her voice and wept aloud; and the father, clenching his toothless gums to conceal his emotion, remained with his head bent down: presently, in a husky voice, he said, "Wife, give me the seal!"

But she returned no answer, and with tears in her eyes took a leather purse, containing the seal, out of a drawer of the cupboard and placed it before her husband. All this time the vagabond son, holding his breath, was peeping in from outside the shutters. In the meanwhile, the old man slowly untied the strings of the purse, and took out the seal, and smeared on the colouring matter. Just as he was about to seal the document, his wife clutched at his hand and said, "Oh, pray wait a little."

The father replied, "Now that all our relations are looking on, you must not speak in this weak manner."

[1] Kôshi is the Japanese pronunciation of the name of the Chinese philosopher Kung Tsŭ, or Kung Fu Tsŭ, whom we call Confucius.

But she would not listen to what he said, but went on—

"Pray listen to what I have to say. It is true that if we were to give over our house to our undutiful son, in less than three years the grass would be growing in its place, for he would be ruined. Still, if we disinherit our child—the only child that we have, either in heaven or upon earth—we shall have to adopt another in his place. Although, if the adopted son turned out honest and dutiful, and inherited our property, all would be well ; still, what certainty is there of his doing so ? If, on the other hand, the adopted son turned out to be a prodigal, and laid waste our house, what unlucky parents we should be ! And who can say that this would not be the case ? If we are to be ruined for the sake of an equally wicked adopted son, I had rather lose our home for the sake of our own son, and, leaving our old familiar village as beggars, seek for our lost boy on foot. This is my fervent wish. During fifty years that we have lived together, this has been the only favour that I have ever asked of you. Pray listen to my prayer, and put a stop to this act of disinheritance. Even though I should become a beggar for my son's sake, I could feel no resentment against him."

So she spoke, sobbing aloud. The relations, who heard this, looked round at one another, and watched the father to see what he would do; and he (who knows with what thoughts in his head ?) put back the seal into the leather purse, and quickly drew the strings together, and pushed back the petition to the relations.

"Certainly," said he, "I have lost countenance, and am disgraced before all my family ; however, I think that what the good wife has just said is right and proper, and from henceforth I renounce all thoughts of disinheriting my son. Of course you will all see a weakness of purpose in what I say, and laugh at me as the cause of my son's undutiful conduct. But laugh away : it won't hurt me. Certainly, if I don't disinherit this son of mine, my house will be ruined before three years are over our heads. To lay waste the house of generations upon generations of my ancestors is a sin against those ancestors ; of this I am well aware. Further, if I don't disinherit my son, you gentlemen will all shun me. I know that I am cutting myself off from my relations. Of course you think that when I leave this place I shall be dunning you to bestow your charity upon me ; and that is why you want to break off relations with me. Pray don't make yourselves uneasy. I care no more for my duties to the world, for my impiety to my ancestors, or for my separation from my family. Our son is our only darling, and we mean to go after him, following him as beggars on foot. This is our desire. We shall trouble you for no alms and for no charity. However we may die, we have but one life to lose. For our darling son's sake, we will lay ourselves down and die by the roadside. There our bodies shall be manure for the trees of the avenue. And all this we will endure cheerfully, and not utter a complaint. Make haste and return home, therefore, all of you. From to-morrow we are no longer on speaking terms. As for what you may say to me on my son's account, I do not care."

And as his wife had done, he lifted up his voice and wept, shedding manly tears. As for her, when she heard that the act of disinheritance was not to be drawn up, her tears were changed to tears of joy. The rest of the family remained in mute astonishment at so unheard-of a thing, and could only stare at the faces of the two old people.

You see how bewildered parents must be by their love for their children, to be so merciful towards them. As a cat carrying her young in her mouth screens it from the sun at one time and brings it under the light at another, so parents act by their children, screening their bad points and bringing out in relief their good qualities. They care neither for the abuse of others, nor for their duties to their ancestors, nor for the wretched future in store for themselves. Carried away by their infatuation for their children, and intoxicated upon intoxication, the hearts of parents are to be pitied for their pitifulness. It is not only the two parents in my story who are in this plight ; the hearts of all parents of children all over the world are the same. In the poems of the late learned Ishida it is written, "When I look round me and see the hearts of parents bewildered by their love for their children, I reflect that my own father and mother must be like them." This is certainly a true saying.

To return to the story: the halo of his parents' great kindness and pity penetrated the very bowels of the prodigal son. What an admirable thing! When he heard it, terrible and sly devil as he had been, he felt as if his whole body had been squeezed in a press; and somehow or other, although the tears rose in his breast, he could not for shame lift up his voice and weep. Biting the sleeve of his dress, he lay down on the ground and shed tears in silence. What says the verse of the reverend priest Eni? "To shed tears of gratitude one knows not why." A very pretty poem indeed! So then the vagabond son, in his gratitude to his parents, could neither stand nor sit. You see the original heart of man is by nature bright virtue, but by our selfish pursuit of our own inclinations the brilliancy of our original virtue is hidden.

To continue: the prodigal was pierced to the core by the great mercy shown by his parents, and the brilliancy of his own original good heart was enticed back to him. The sunlight came forth, and what became of all the clouds of self-will and selfishness? The clouds were all dispelled, and from the bottom of his soul there sprang the desire to thank his parents for their goodness. We all know the story of the rush-cutter who saw the moon rising between the trees on a moorland hill so brightly, that he fancied it must have been scoured with the scouring-rush which grew near the spot. When a man, who has been especially wicked, repents and returns to his original heart, he becomes all the more excellent, and his brightness is as that of the rising moon scoured. What an admirable thing this is! So the son thought to enter the room at once and beg his parents' forgiveness; but he thought to himself, "Wait a bit. If I burst suddenly into the room like this, the relations will all be frightened and not know what to make of it, and this will be a trouble to my parents. I will put on an innocent face, as if I did not know what has been going on, and I'll go in by the front door, and beg the relations to intercede for me with my parents." With stealthy step he left the back of the house, and went round to the front. When he arrived there, he purposely made a great noise with his iron-heeled sandals, and gave a loud cough to clear his throat, and entered the room. The relations were all greatly alarmed; and his parents, when they saw the face of their wicked son, both shed tears. As for the son, he said not a word, but remained weeping, with his head bent down. After a while, he addressed the relations and said, "Although I have frequently been threatened with disinheritance, and although in those days I made light of it, to-night, when I heard that this family council had assembled, I somehow or other felt my heart beset by anxiety and grief. However I may have heaped wickedness upon wickedness up to the present moment, as I shall certainly now mend my ways, I pray you to delay for a while to-night's act of disinheritance. I do not venture to ask for along delay,—I ask but for thirty days; and if within that time I shall not have given proofs of repentance, disinherit me: I shall not have a word to say. I pray you, gentlemen, to intercede with my parents that they may grant this delay of thirty days, and to present them my humble apologies." With this he rubbed his head on the mat, as a humble suppliant, in a manner most foreign to his nature.

The relations, after hearing the firm and resolute answer of the parents, had shifted about in their places; but, although they were on the point of leaving the house, had remained behind, sadly out of harmony; when the son came in, and happily with a word set all in tune again. So the relations addressed the parents, and said, "Pray defer to-night's affair;" and laid the son's apologies at their feet. As for the parents, who would not have disinherited their son even had he not repented, how much the more when they heard what he said did they weep for joy; and the relations, delighted at the happy event, exhorted the son to become really dutiful; and so that night's council broke up. So this son in the turn of a hand became a pious son, and the way in which he served his parents was that of a tender and loving child. His former evil ways he extinguished utterly.

The fame of this story rose high in the world; and, before half a year had passed, it reached the ears of the lord of the manor, who, when he had put on his noble spectacles and investigated the case, appointed the son to be the head man of his village. You may judge by this what this son's filial piety effected. Three years after these events, his mother, who was on her death-bed, very sick, called for him and said, "When some time since the consultation was being held about disinheriting you, by some means or other your heart was turned, and since then you have been a dutiful son above all others. If at that time you had not repented, and I had died in the meanwhile, my soul would have gone to hell without fail, because of my foolish conduct towards you. But, now that you have repented, there is nothing that weighs upon me, and there can be no mistake about my going to paradise. So the fact of my becoming one of the saints will all be the work of your filial piety." And the story goes, that with these words the mother, lifting up her hands in prayer, died.

To be sure, by the deeds of the present life we may obtain a glimpse into the future. If a man's heart is troubled by his misdeeds in this life, it will again be tortured in the next. The troubled heart is hell. The heart at rest is paradise. The trouble or peace of parents depends upon their children. If their children are virtuous, parents are as the saints: if their children are wicked, parents suffer the tortures of the damned. If once your youthful spirits, in a fit of heedlessness, have led you to bring trouble upon your parents and cause them to weep, just consider the line of argument which I have been following. From this time forth repent and examine your own hearts. If you will become dutiful, your parents from this day will live happy as the saints. But if you will not repent, but persist in your evil ways, your parents will suffer the pains of hell. Heaven and hell are matters of repentance or non-repentance. Repentance is the finding of the lost heart, and is also the object of learning. I shall speak to you further upon this point to-morrow evening.

SERMON III

MÔSHI has said, " There is the third finger. If a man's third or nameless finger be bent, so that he cannot straighten it, although his bent finger may cause him no pain, still if he hears of some one who can cure it, he will think nothing of undertaking a long journey from *Shin* to *So*[1] to consult him upon this deformed finger ; for he knows it is to be hateful to have a finger unlike those of other men. But he cares not a jot if his heart be different to that of other men; and this is how men disregard the true order of things."

Now this is the next chapter to the one about benevolence being the true heart of man, which I expounded to you the other night. True learning has no other aim than that of reclaiming lost souls ; and, in connection with this, Môshi has thus again declared in a parable the all-importance of the human heart.

The nameless finger is that which is next to the little finger. The thumb is called the parent-finger; the first finger is called the index ; the long is called the middle finger; but the third finger has no name. It is true that it is sometimes called the finger for applying rouge ; but that is only a name given it by ladies, and is not in general use. So, having no name, it is called the nameless finger. And how comes it to have no name? Why, because it is of all the fingers the least useful. When we clutch at or grasp things, we do so by the strength of the thumb and little finger. If

[1] Ancient divisions of China.

a man scratches his head, he does it with the forefinger; if he wishes to test the heat of the wine[1] in the kettle, he uses the little finger. Thus, although each finger has its uses and duties, the nameless finger alone is of no use: it is not in our way if we have it, and we do not miss it if we lose it. Of the whole body it is the meanest member: if it be crooked so that we cannot straighten it, it neither hurts nor itches; as Môshi says in the text, it causes no pain; even if we were without it, we should be none the worse off. Hence, what though it should be bent, it would be better, since it causes no pain, to leave it as it is. Yet if a person, having such a crooked finger, hears of a clever doctor who can set it straight, no matter at how great a distance he may be, he will be off to consult this doctor. And pray why? Because he feels ashamed of having a finger a little different from the rest of the world, and so he wants to be cured, and will think nothing of travelling from Shin to So —a distance of a thousand miles—for the purpose. To be sure, men are very susceptible and keenly alive to a sense of shame; and in this they are quite right. The feeling of shame at what is wrong is the commencement of virtue. The perception of shame is inborn in men; but there are two ways of perceiving shame. There are some men who are sensible of shame for what regards their bodies, but who are ignorant of shame for what concerns their hearts; and a terrible mistake they make. There is nothing which can be compared in importance to the heart. The heart is said to be the lord of the body, which it rules as a master rules his house. Shall the lord, who is the heart, be ailing and his sickness be neglected, while his servants, who are the members only, are cared for? If the knee be lacerated, apply tinder to stop the bleeding; if the moxa should suppurate, spread a plaster; if a cold be caught, prepare medicine and garlic and gruel, and ginger wine! For a trifle, you will doctor and care for your bodies, and yet for your hearts you will take no care. Although you are born of mankind, if your

[1] Wine is almost always drunk hot.

hearts resemble those of devils, of foxes, of snakes, or of crows, rather than the hearts of men, you take no heed, caring for your bodies alone. Whence can you have fallen into such a mistake? It is a folly of old standing too, for it was to that that Môshi pointed when he said that to be cognizant of a deformed finger and ignore the deformities of the soul was to disregard the true order of things. This is what it is, not to distinguish between that which is important and that which is unimportant—to pick up a trifle and pass by something of value. The instinct of man prompts him to prefer the great to the small, the important to the unimportant.

If a man is invited out to a feast by his relations or acquaintances, when the guests are assembled and the principal part of the feast has disappeared, he looks all round him, with the eyeballs starting out of his head, and glares at his neighbours, and, comparing the little titbits of roast fowl or fish put before them, sees that they are about half an inch bigger than those set before him; then, blowing out his belly with rage, he thinks, "What on earth can the host be about? Master Tarubei is a guest, but so am I: what does the fellow mean by helping me so meanly? There must be some malice or ill-will here." And so his mind is prejudiced against the host. Just be so good as to reflect upon this. Does a man show his spite by grudging a bit of roast fowl or meat? And yet even in such trifles as these do men show how they try to obtain what is great, and show their dislike of what is small. How can men be conscious of shame for a deformed finger, and count it as no misfortune that their hearts are crooked? That is how they abandon the substance for the shadow.

Môshi severely censures the disregard of the true order of things. What mistaken and bewildered creatures men are! What says the old song? "Hidden far among the mountains, the tree which seems to be rotten, if its core be yet alive, may be made to bear flowers." What signifies it if the hand or the foot be deformed? The heart is the important thing. If the heart be awry, what though your skin be fair, your nose aquiline, your hair beautiful? All these strike the eye alone, and are utterly useless. It is as if you were to put horse-dung into a gold-lacquer luncheon-box. This is what is called a fair outside, deceptive in appearance.

There's the scullery-maid been washing out the pots at the kitchen sink, and the scullion Chokichi comes up and says to her, "You've got a lot of charcoal smut sticking to your nose," and points out to her the ugly spot. The scullery-maid is delighted to be told of this, and answers, "Really! where-abouts is it?" Then she twists a towel round her finger, and, bending her head till mouth and forehead are almost on a level, she squints at her nose, and twiddles away with her fingers as if she were the famous Gotô[1] at work, carving the ornaments of a sword-handle. "I say, Master Chokichi, is it off yet?" "Not a bit of it. You've smeared it all over your cheeks now." "Oh dear! oh dear! where can it be?" And so she uses the water-basin as a looking-glass, and washes her face clean; then she says to herself, "What a dear boy Chokichi is!" and thinks it necessary, out of gratitude, to give him relishes with his supper by the ladleful, and thanks him over and over again. But if this same Chokichi were to come up to her and say, "Now, really, how lazy you are! I wish you could manage to be rather less of a shrew," what do you think the scullery-maid would answer then? Reflect for a moment. "Drat the boy's impudence! If I were of a bad heart or an angular disposition, should I be here helping him? You go and be hung! You see if I take the trouble to wash your dirty bedclothes for you any more." And she gets to be a perfect devil, less only the horns.

There are other people besides the poor scullery-maid who are in the same way. "Excuse me, Mr. Gundabei, but the embroidered crest on your dress of ceremony seems to be a little on one side." Mr. Gundabei proceeds to adjust his dress with great precision. "Thank you, sir. I am ten million

---

[1] A famous gold and silver smith of the olden time. A Benvenuto Cellini among the Japanese. His mark on a piece of metal work enhances its value tenfold.

times obliged to you for your care. If ever there should be any matter in which I can be of service to you, I beg that you will do me the favour of letting me know;" and, with a beaming face, he expresses his gratitude. Now for the other side of the picture. "Really, Mr. Gundabei, you are very foolish; you don't seem to understand at all. I beg you to be of a frank and honest heart: it really makes me quite sad to see a man's heart warped in this way." What is his answer? He turns his sword in his girdle ready to draw, and plays the devil's tattoo upon the hilt: it looks as if it must end in a fight soon.

In fact, if you help a man in anything which has to do with a fault of the body, he takes it very kindly, and sets about mending matters. If any one helps another to rectify a fault of the heart, he has to deal with a man in the dark, who flies in a rage, and does not care to amend. How out of tune all this is! And yet there are men who are bewildered up to this point. Nor is this a special and extraordinary failing. This mistaken perception of the great and the small, of colour and of substance, is common to us all—to you and to me.

Please give me your attention. The form strikes the eye; but the heart strikes not the eye. Therefore, that the heart should be distorted and turned awry causes no pain. This all results from the want of sound judgment; and that is why we cannot afford to be careless.

The master of a certain house calls his servant Chokichi, who sits dozing in the kitchen. "Here, Chokichi! The guests are all gone; come, and clear away the wine and fish in the back room."

Chokichi rubs his eyes, and with a sulky answer goes into the back room, and, looking about him, sees all the nice things paraded on the trays and in the bowls. It's wonderful how his drowsiness passes away: no need for any one to hurry him now. His eyes glare with greed, as he says, "Hullo! here's a lot of tempting things! There's only just one help of that omelette left in the tray. What a hungry lot of guests! What's this? It looks like fish rissoles;" and with this he picks out one, and crams his mouth full; when, on one side, a mess of young cuttlefish, in a Chinese[1] porcelain bowl, catches his eyes. There the little beauties sit in a circle, like Buddhist priests in religious meditation! "Oh, goodness! how nice!" and just as he is dipping his finger and thumb in, he hears his master's footstep; and knowing that he is doing wrong, he crams his prize into the pocket of his sleeve, and stoops down to take away the wine-kettle and cups; and as he does this, out tumble the cuttlefish from his sleeve. The master sees it.

"What's that?"

Chokichi, pretending not to know what has happened, beats the mats, and keeps on saying, "Come again the day before yesterday; come again the day before yesterday."[2]

But it's no use his trying to persuade his master that the little cuttlefish are spiders, for they are not the least like them. It's no use hiding things,—they are sure to come to light; and so it is with the heart,—its purposes will out. If the heart is enraged, the dark veins stand out on the forehead; if the heart is grieved, tears rise to the eyes; if the heart is joyous, dimples appear in the cheeks; if the heart is merry, the face smiles: thus it is that the face reflects the emotions of the heart. It is not because the eyes are filled with tears that the heart is sad; nor because the veins stand out on the forehead that the heart is enraged. It is the heart which leads the way in everything. All the important sensations of the heart are apparent in the outward appearance. In the "Great Learning" of Kôshi it is written, "The truth of what is within appears upon the surface." How then is the heart a thing which can be hidden? To answer when reproved, to hum tunes when scolded, show a diseased

[1] Curiosities, such as porcelain or enamel or carved jade from China, are highly esteemed by the Japanese. A great quantity of the porcelain of Japan is stamped with counterfeit Chinese marks of the Ming dynasty.

[2] An incantation used to invite spiders, which are considered unlucky by the superstitious, to come again at the Greek Kalends.

heart; and if this disease is not quickly taken in hand, it will become chronic, and the remedy become difficult: perhaps the disease may be so virulent that even Giba and Henjaku[1] in consultation could not effect a cure. So, before the disease has gained strength, I invite you to the study of the moral essays entitled *Shin-gaku* (the Learning of the Heart). If you once arrive at the possession of your heart as it was originally by nature, what an admirable thing that will be! In that case your conscience will point out to you even the slightest wrong bias or selfishness.

While upon this subject, I may tell you a story which was related to me by a friend of mine. It is a story which the master of a certain money-changer's shop used to be very fond of telling. An important part of a money-changer's business is to distinguish between good and bad gold and silver. In the different establishments, the ways of teaching the apprentices this art vary; however, the plan adopted by the money-changer was as follows:—At first he would show them no bad silver, but would daily put before them good money only; when they had become thoroughly familiar with the sight of good money, if he stealthily put a little base coin among the good, he found that they would detect it immediately,—they saw it as plainly as you see things when you throw light on a mirror. This faculty of detecting base money at a glance was the result of having learned thoroughly to understand good money. Having once been taught in this way, the apprentices would not make a mistake about a piece of base coin during their whole lives, as I have heard. I can't vouch for the truth of this; but it is very certain that the principle, applied to moral instruction, is an excellent one,—it is a most safe mode of study. However, I was further told that if, after having thus learned to distinguish good money, a man followed some other trade for six months or a year, and gave up handling money, he would become just like any other inexperienced person, unable to distinguish the good from the base.

[1] Two famous Indian and Chinese physicians.

Please reflect upon this attentively. If you once render yourself familiar with the nature of the uncorrupted heart, from that time forth you will be immediately conscious of the slightest inclination towards bias or selfishness. And why? Because the natural heart is illumined. When a man has once learned that which is perfect, he will never consent to accept that which is imperfect; but if, after having acquired this knowledge, he again keeps his natural heart at a distance, and gradually forgets to recognize that which is perfect, he finds himself in the dark again, and that he can no longer distinguish base money from good. I beg you to take care. If a man falls into bad habits, he is no longer able to perceive the difference between the good impulses of his natural heart and the evil impulses of his corrupt heart. With this benighted heart as a starting-point, he can carry out none of his intentions, and he has to lift his shoulders sighing and sighing again. A creature much to be pitied indeed! Then he loses all self-reliance, so that, although it would be better for him to hold his tongue and say nothing about it, if he is in the slightest trouble or distress, he goes and confesses the crookedness of his heart to every man he meets. What a wretched state for a man to be in! For this reason, I beg you to learn thoroughly the true silver of the heart, in order that you may make no mistake about the base coin. I pray that you and I, during our whole lives, may never leave the path of true principles.

I have an amusing story to tell you in connection with this, if you will be so good as to listen.

Once upon a time, when the autumn nights were beginning to grow chilly, five or six tradesmen in easy circumstances had assembled together to have a chat; and, having got ready their picnic box and wine-flask, went off to a temple on the hills, where a friendly priest lived, that they might listen to the stags roaring. With this intention they went to call upon the priest, and borrowed the guests' apartments[1] of the

---

[1] All the temples in China and Japan have guests' apartments, which may be secured for a trifle, either for a long or short period. It is false to suppose

monastery; and as they were waiting to hear the deer roar, some of the party began to compose poetry. One would write a verse of Chinese poetry, and another would write a verse of seventeen syllables; and as they were passing the wine-cup the hour of sunset came, but not a deer had uttered a call; eight o'clock came, and ten o'clock came; still not a sound from the deer.

"What can this mean?" said one. "The deer surely ought to be roaring."

But, in spite of their waiting, the deer would not roar. At last the friends got sleepy, and, bored with writing songs and verses, began to yawn, and gave up twaddling about the woes and troubles of life; and as they were all silent, one of them, a man fifty years of age, stopping the circulation of the wine-cup, said—

"Well, certainly, gentlemen, thanks to you, we have spent the evening in very pleasant conversation. However, although I am enjoying myself mightily in this way, my people at home must be getting anxious, and so I begin to think that we ought to leave off drinking."

"Why so?" said the others.

"Well, I'll tell you. You know that my only son is twenty-two years of age this year, and a troublesome fellow he is, too. When I'm at home, he lends a hand sulkily enough in the shop; but as soon as he no longer sees the shadow of me, he hoists sail and is off to some bad haunt. Although our relations and connections are always preaching to him, not a word has any more effect than wind blowing into a horse's ear. When I think that I shall have to leave my property to such a fellow as that it makes my heart grow small indeed. Although, thanks to those to whom I have succeeded, I want for nothing, still, when I think of my son, I shed tears of blood night and day."

And as he said this with a sigh, a man of some forty-five or forty-six years said—

that there is any desecration of a sacred shrine in the act of using it as a hostelry; it is the custom of the country.

"No, no; although you make so much of your misfortunes, your son is but a little extravagant after all. There's no such great cause for grief there. I've got a very different story to tell. Of late years my shopmen, for one reason or another, have been running me into debt, thinking nothing of a debt of fifty or seventy ounces; and so the ledgers get all wrong. Just think of that. Here have I been keeping these fellows ever since they were little children unable to blow their own noses, and now, as soon as they come to be a little useful in the shop, they begin running up debts, and are no good whatever to their master. You see, you only have to spend your money upon your own son."

Then another gentleman said—

"Well, I think that to spend money upon your shop-people is no such great hardship after all. Now I've been in something like trouble lately. I can't get a penny out of my customers. One man owes me fifteen ounces; another owes me twenty-five ounces. Really that is enough to make a man feel as if his heart was worn away."

When he had finished speaking, an old gentleman, who was sitting opposite, playing with his fan, said—

"Certainly, gentlemen, your grievances are not without cause; still, to be perpetually asked for a little money, or to back a bill, by one's relations or friends, and to have a lot of hangers-on dependent on one, as I have, is a worse case still."

But before the old gentleman had half finished speaking, his neighbour called out—

"No, no; all you gentlemen are in luxury compared to me. Please listen to what I have to suffer. My wife and my mother can't hit it off anyhow. All day long they're like a couple of cows butting at one another with their horns. The house is as unendurable as if it were full of smoke. I often think it would be better to send my wife back to her village; but then I've got two little children. If I interfere and take my wife's part, my mother gets low-spirited. If I scold my wife, she says that I treat her so brutally because she's not of the same flesh and blood; and then she hates me. The trouble and anxiety are beyond description: I'm like a post stuck up between them."

And so they all twaddled away in chorus, each about his own troubles. At last one of the gentlemen, recollecting himself, said—

"Well, gentlemen, certainly the deer ought to be roaring; but we've been so engrossed with our conversation, that we don't know whether we have missed hearing them or not."

With this he pulled aside the sliding-door of the verandah and looked out, and, lo and behold! a great big stag was standing perfectly silent in front of the garden.

"Hullo!" said the man to the deer, "what's this? Since you've been there all the time, why did you not roar?"

Then the stag answered, with an innocent face—

"Oh, I came here to listen to the lamentations of you gentlemen."

Isn't that a funny story?

Old and young, men and women, rich and poor, never cease grumbling from morning till night. All this is the result of a diseased heart. In short, for the sake of a very trifling inclination or selfish pursuit, they will do any wrong in order to effect that which is impossible. This is want of judgment, and this brings all sorts of trouble upon the world. If once you gain possession of a perfect heart, knowing that which is impossible to be impossible, and recognizing that that which is difficult is difficult, you will not attempt to spare yourself trouble unduly. What says the Chin-Yo?[1] The wise man, whether his lot be cast amongst rich or poor, amongst barbarians or in sorrow, understands his position by his own instinct. If men do not understand this, they think that the causes of pain and pleasure are in the body Putting the heart on one side, they earnestly strive after the comforts of the body, and launch into extravagance, the end of which is miserly parsimony. Instead of pleasure

---

[1] The second book of Confucius.

they meet with grief of the heart, and pass their lives in weeping and wailing. In one way or another, everything in this world depends upon the heart. I implore every one of you to take heed that tears fall not to your lot.

APPENDICES

APPENDIX A

AN ACCOUNT OF THE HARA-KIRI

(FROM A RARE JAPANESE MS.)

SEPPUKU (*hara-kiri*) is the mode of suicide adopted amongst Samurai when they have no alternative but to die. Some there are who thus commit suicide of their own free will; others there are who, having committed some crime which does not put them outside the pale of the privileges of the Samurai class, are ordered by their superiors to put an end to their own lives. It is needless to say that it is absolutely necessary that the principal, the witnesses, and the seconds who take part in the affair should be acquainted with all the ceremonies to be observed. A long time ago, a certain Daimio invited a number of persons, versed in the various ceremonies, to call upon him to explain the different forms to be observed by the official witnesses who inspect and verify the head, &c., and then to instruct him in the ceremonies to be observed in the act of suicide; then he showed all these rites to his son and to all his retainers. Another person has said that, as the ceremonies to be gone through by principal, witnesses, and seconds are all very important matters, men should familiarize themselves with a thing which is so terrible, in order that, should the time come for them to take part in it, they may not be taken by surprise.

The witnesses go to see and certify the suicide. For

seconds, men are wanted who have distinguished themselves in the military arts. In old days, men used to bear these things in mind; but nowadays the fashion is to be ignorant of such ceremonies, and if upon rare occasions a criminal is handed over to a Daimio's charge, that he may perform *hara-kiri*, it often happens, at the time of execution, that there is no one among all the prince's retainers who is competent to act as second, in which case a man has to be engaged in a hurry from some other quarter to cut off the head of the criminal, and for that day he changes his name and becomes a retainer of the prince, either of the middle or lowest class, and the affair is entrusted to him, and so the difficulty is got over: nor is this considered to be a disgrace. It is a great breach of decorum if the second who is a most important officer, commits any mistake (such as not striking off the head at a blow) in the presence of the witnesses sent by the Government. On this account a skilful person must be employed; and, to hide the unmanliness of his own people, a prince must perform the ceremony in this imperfect manner. Every Samurai should be able to cut off a man's head: therefore, to have to employ a stranger to act as second is to incur the charge of ignorance of the arts of war, and is a bitter mortification. However, young men, trusting to their youthful ardour, are apt to be careless, and are certain to make a mistake. Some people there are who, not lacking in skill on ordinary occasions, lose their presence of mind in public, and cannot do themselves justice. It is all the more important, therefore, as the act occurs but rarely, that men who are liable to be called upon to be either principals or seconds or witnesses in the *hara-kiri* should constantly be examined in their skill as swordsmen, and should be familiar with all the rites, in order that when the time comes they may not lose their presence of mind.

According to one authority, capital punishment may be divided into two kinds—beheading and strangulation. The ceremony of *hara-kiri* was added afterwards in the case of persons belonging to the military class being condemned to death. This was first instituted in the days of the Ashikaga[1] dynasty. At that time the country was in a state of utter confusion ; and there were men who, although fighting, were neither guilty of high treason nor of infidelity to their feudal lords, but who by the chances of war were taken prisoners. To drag out such men as these, bound as criminals, and cut their heads off, was intolerably cruel; accordingly, men hit upon a ceremonious mode of suicide by disembowelling, in order to comfort the departed spirit. Even at present, where it becomes necessary to put to death a man who has been guilty of some act not unworthy of a Samurai, at the time of the execution witnesses are sent to the house ; and the criminal, having bathed and put on new clothes, in obedience to the commands of his superiors, puts an end to himself, but does not on that account forfeit his rank as a Samurai. This is a law for which, in all truth, men should be grateful.

ON THE PREPARATION OF THE PLACE OF EXECUTION

In old days the ceremony of *hara-kiri* used to be performed in a temple. In the third year of the period called Kan-yei (A.D. 1626), a certain person, having been guilty of treason, was ordered to disembowel himself, on the fourteenth day of the first month, in the temple of Kichijôji, at Komagomé, in Yedo. Eighteen years later, the retainer of a certain Daimio, having had a dispute with a sailor belonging to an Osaka coasting-ship, killed the sailor ; and, an investigation having been made into the matter by the Governor of Osaka, the retainer was ordered to perform *hara-kiri*, on the twentieth day of the sixth month, in the temple called Sokusanji, in Osaka. During the period Shôhô (middle of seventeenth century), a certain man, having been guilty of heinous misconduct, performed *hara-kiri* in the

---

[1] Ashikaga, third dynasty of Shoguns, flourished from 1336 to 1568 A.D. The practice of suicide by disembowelling is of great antiquity. This is the time when the ceremonies attending it were invented.

temple called Shimpukuji, in the Kôji-street of Yedo. On the fourth day of the fifth month of the second year of the period Meiréki (A.D. 1656), a certain man, for having avenged the death of his cousin's husband at a place called Shimidzudani, in the Kôji-street, disembowelled himself in the temple called Honseiji. On the twenty-sixth day of the sixth month of the eighth year of the period Yempô (A.D. 1680), at the funeral ceremonies in honour of the anniversary of the death of Genyuin Sama, a former Shogun, Naitô Idzumi no Kami, having a cause of hatred against Nagai Shinano no Kami, killed him at one blow with a short sword, in the main hall of the temple called Zôjôji (the burial-place of the Shoguns in Yedo). Idzumi no Kami was arrested by the officers present, and on the following day performed *hara-kiri* at Kiridôshi, in the temple called Seiriuji.

In modern times the ceremony has taken place at night, either in the palace or in the garden of a Daimio, to whom the condemned man has been given in charge. Whether it takes place in the palace or in the garden depends upon the rank of the individual. Daimios and Hatamotos, as a matter of course, and the higher retainers of the Shogun, disembowel themselves in the palace : retainers of lower rank should do so in the garden. In the case of vassals of feudatories, according to the rank of their families, those who, being above the grade of captains, carry the bâton,[1] should perform *hara-kiri* in the palace ; all others in the garden. If, when the time comes, the persons engaged in the ceremony are in any doubt as to the proper rules to be followed, they should inquire of competent persons, and settle the question. At the beginning of the eighteenth century, during the period Genroku, when Asano Takumi no Kami [2] disembowelled himself in the palace of a Daimio called Tamura, as the whole thing was sudden and unexpected, the garden was covered with

---

[1] A bâton with a tassel of paper strips, used for giving directions in war-time.

[2] See the story of the Forty-seven Rônins.

matting, and on the top of this thick mats were laid and a carpet, and the affair was concluded so ; but there are people who say that it was wrong to treat a Daimio thus, as if he had been an ordinary Samurai. But it is said that in old times it was the custom that the ceremony should take place upon a leather carpet spread in the garden ; and further, that the proper place is inside a picket fence tied together in the garden : so it is wrong for persons who are only acquainted with one form of the ceremony to accuse Tamura of having acted improperly. If, however, the object was to save the house from the pollution of blood, then the accusation of ill-will may well be brought ; for the preparation of the place is of great importance.

Formerly it was the custom that, for personages of importance, the enclosure within the picket fence should be of thirty-six feet square. An entrance was made to the south, and another to the north : the door to the south was called *Shugi-yômon* ("the door of the practice of virtue") ; that to the north was called *Umbanmon* ("the door of the warm basin "[1]). Two mats, with white binding, were arranged in the shape of a hammer, the one at right angles to the other ; six feet of white silk, four feet broad, were stretched on the mat, which was placed lengthwise ; at the four corners were erected four posts for curtains. In front of the two mats was erected a portal, eight feet high by six feet broad, in the shape of the portals in front of temples, made of a fine sort of bamboo wrapped in white[2] silk. White curtains, four feet broad, were hung at the four corners, and four flags, six feet long, on which should be inscribed four quotations from the sacred books. These flags, it is said, were immediately after the ceremony carried away to the grave. At night two lights were placed, one upon either side of the two mats. The candles were placed in saucers upon stands of bamboo, four feet high, wrapped in white silk. The person who was to

---

[1] No Japanese authority that I have been able to consult gives any explanation of this singular name.

[2] White, in China and Japan, is the colour of mourning.

disembowel himself, entering the picket fence by the north entrance, took his place upon the white silk upon the mat facing the north. Some there were, however, who said that he should sit facing the west: in that case the whole place must be prepared accordingly. The seconds enter the enclosure by the south entrance, at the same time as the principal enters by the north, and take their places on the mat that is placed crosswise, as shown in the annexed plan.

Nowadays, when the *hara-kiri* is performed inside the palace, a temporary place is made on purpose, either in the garden or in some unoccupied spot; but if the criminal is to die on the day on which he is given in charge, or on the next day, the ceremony, having to take place so quickly, is performed in the reception-room. Still, even if there is a lapse of time between the period of giving the prisoner in charge and the execution, it is better that the ceremony should take place in a decent room in the house than in a place made on purpose. If it is heard that, for fear of dirtying his house, a man has made a place expressly, he will be blamed for it. It surely can be no disgrace to the house of a soldier that he was ordered to perform the last offices towards a Samurai who died by *hara-kiri*. To slay his enemy against whom he has cause of hatred, and then to kill himself, is the part of a noble Samurai; and it is sheer nonsense to look upon the place where he has disembowelled himself as polluted. In the beginning of the eighteenth century, seventeen of the retainers of Asano Takumi no Kami performed *hara-kiri* in the garden of a palace at Shirokané, in Yedo. When it was over, the people of the palace called upon the priests of a sect named Shugenja to come and purify the place; but when the lord of the palace heard this, he ordered the place to be left as it was; for what need was there to purify a place where faithful Samurai had died by their own hand? But in other palaces to which the remainder of the retainers of Takumi no Kami were entrusted, it is said that the places of execution were purified. But the people of that day praised Kumamoto Ko (the Prince of Higo), to whom the palace at Shirokané belonged. It is a currish thing to look upon death in battle or by *hara-kiri* as a pollution: this is a thing to bear in mind. In modern times the place of *hara-kiri* is eighteen feet square in all cases; in the centre is a place to sit upon, and the condemned man is made to sit facing the witnesses; at other times he is placed with his side to the witnesses : this is according to the nature of the spot. In some cases the seconds turn their backs to the witnesses. It is open to question, however, whether this is not a breach of etiquette. The witnesses should be consulted upon these arrangements. If the witnesses have no objection, the condemned men should be placed directly opposite to them. The place where the witnesses are seated should be removed more than twelve or eighteen feet from the condemned man. The place from which the sentence is read should also be close by. The writer has been furnished with a plan of the *hara-kiri* as it is performed at present. It is annexed here. Although the ceremony is gone through in other ways also, still it is more convenient to follow the manner indicated.

If the execution takes place in a room, a kerchief of five breadths of white cotton cloth or a quilt should be laid down, and it is also said that two mats should be prepared; however, as there are already mats in the room, there is no need for special mats : two red rugs should be spread over all, sewed together, one on the top of the other; for if the white cotton cloth be used alone, the blood will soak through on to the mats; therefore it is right the rugs should be spread. On the twenty-third day of the eighth month of the fourth year of the period Yenkiyô (A.D. 1740), at the *hara-kiri* of a certain person there were laid down a white cloth, eight feet square, and on that a quilt of light green cotton, six feet square, and on that a cloth of white hemp, six feet square, and on that two rugs. On the third day of the ninth month of the ninth year of the period Tempô (A.D. 1838), at the *hara-kiri* of a certain person it is said that there were spread a large double cloth of white cotton, and on that two rugs. But, of these two occasions, the first must be commended for its careful preparation. If the execution be at night, candlesticks of white wood should be placed at each of the four corners, lest the seconds be hindered in their work. In the place where the witnesses are to sit, ordinary candlesticks should be placed, according to etiquette; but an excessive illumination is not decorous. Two screens covered with white paper should be set up, behind the shadow of which are concealed the dirk upon a tray, a bucket to hold the head after it has been cut off, an incense-burner, a pail of water, and a basin. The above rules apply equally to the ceremonies observed when the *hara-kiri* takes place in a garden. In the latter case the place is hung round with a white curtain, which need not be new for the occasion. Two mats, a white cloth, and a rug are spread. If the execution is at night, lanterns of white paper are placed on bamboo poles at the four corners. The sentence having been read inside the house, the persons engaged in the ceremony proceed to the place of execution; but, according to circumstances, the sentence may be read at the place itself. In the case of Asano Takumi no Kami, the sentence was read out in the house, and he afterwards performed *hara-kiri* in the garden. On the third day of the fourth month of the fourth year of the period Tenmei (A.D. 1784), a Hatamoto named Sano, having received his sentence in the supreme court-house, disembowelled himself in the garden in front of the prison. When the ceremony takes place in the garden, matting must be spread all the way to the place, so that sandals need not be worn. The reason for this is that some men in that position suffer from a rush of blood to the head, from nervousness, so their sandals might slip off their feet without their being aware of their loss; and as this would have a very bad appearance, it is better to spread matting. Care must be taken lest, in spreading the matting, a place be left where two mats join, against which the foot might trip. The white screens and other things are prepared as has been directed above. If any curtailment is made, it must be done as well as circumstances will permit. According to the crime of which a man who is handed over to any Daimio's

charge is guilty, it is known whether he will have to perform
hara-kiri; and the preparations should be made accordingly.
Asano Takumi no Kami was taken to the palace of Tamura
Sama at the hour of the monkey (between three and five in
the afternoon), took off his dress of ceremony, partook of a
bowl of soup and five dishes, and drank two cups of warm
water, and at the hour of the cock (between five and seven in
the evening) disembowelled himself. A case of this kind
requires much attention; for great care should be taken that
the preparations be carried on without the knowledge of the
principal. If a temporary room has been built expressly for
the occasion, to avoid pollution to the house, it should be kept
a secret. It once happened that a criminal was received in
charge at the palace of a certain nobleman, and when his
people were about to erect a temporary building for the cere-
mony, they wrote to consult some of the parties concerned;
the letter ran as follows:

"The house in which we live is very small and inconvenient
in all respects. We have ordered the guard to treat our
prisoner with all respect; but our retainers who are placed on
guard are much inconvenienced for want of space; besides,
in the event of fire breaking out or any extraordinary event
taking place, the place is so small that it would be difficult
to get out. We are thinking, therefore, of adding an apartment
to the original building, so that the guard may be able at all
times to go in and out freely, and that if, in case of fire or
otherwise, we should have to leave the house, we may do so
easily. We beg to consult you upon this point."

When a Samurai has to perform *hara-kiri* by the command
of his own feudal lord, the ceremony should take place in one
of the lesser palaces of the clan. Once upon a time, a certain
prince of the Inouyé clan, having a just cause of offence
against his steward, who was called Ishikawa Tôzayémon, and
wishing to punish him, caused him to be killed in his prin-
cipal palace at Kandabashi, in Yedo. When this matter was
reported to the Shogun, having been convicted of disrespect of
the privileges of the city, he was ordered to remove to his

lesser palace at Asakusa. Now, although the *hara-kiri* cannot be called properly an execution, still, as it only differs from an ordinary execution in that by it the honour of the Samurai is not affected, it is only a question of degree; it is a matter of ceremonial. If the principal palace[1] is a long distance from the Shogun's castle, then the *hara-kiri* may take place there; but there can be no objection whatever to its taking place in a minor palace. Nowadays, when a man is condemned to *hara-kiri* by a Daimio, the ceremony usually takes place in one of the lesser palaces; the place commonly selected is an open space near the horse-exercising ground, and the preparations which I have described above are often shortened according to circumstances.

When a retainer is suddenly ordered to perform *hara-kiri* during a journey, a temple or shrine should be hired for the occasion. On these hurried occasions, coarse mats, faced with finer matting or common mats, may be used. If the criminal is of rank to have an armour-bearer, a carpet of skin should be spread, should one be easily procurable. The straps of the skin (which are at the head) should, according to old custom, be to the front, so that the fur may point backwards. In old days, when the ceremony took place in a garden, a carpet of skin was spread. To hire a temple for the purpose of causing a man to perform *hara-kiri* was of frequent occurrence: it is doubtful whether it may be done at the present time. This sort of question should be referred beforehand to some competent person, that the course to be adopted may be clearly understood.

In the period Kambun (A.D. 1661—1673) a Prince Sakai, travelling through the Bishiu territory, hired a temple or shrine for one of his retainers to disembowel himself in; and so the affair was concluded.

---

[1] The principal yashikis (palaces) of the nobles are for the most part immediately round the Shogun's castle, in the enclosure known as the official quarter. Their proximity to the palace forbids their being made the scenes of executions.

ON THE CEREMONIES OBSERVED AT THE HARA-KIRI OF A PERSON GIVEN IN CHARGE TO A DAIMIO

When a man has been ordered by the Government to disembowel himself, the public censors, who have been appointed to act as witnesses, write to the prince who has the criminal in charge, to inform them that they will go to his palace on public business. This message is written directly to the chief, and is sent by an·assistant censor; and a suitable answer is returned to it. Before the ceremony, the witnesses send an assistant censor to see the place, and look at a plan of the house, and to take a list of the names of the persons who are to be present; he also has an interview with the *kaishaku*, or seconds, and examines them upon the way of performing the ceremonies. When all the preparations have been made, he goes to fetch the censors; and they all proceed together to the place of execution, dressed in their hempen-cloth dress of ceremony. The retainers of the palace are collected to do obeisance in the entrance-yard; and the lord, to whom the criminal has been entrusted, goes as far as the front porch to meet the censors, and conducts them to the front reception-room. The chief censor then announces to the lord of the palace that he has come to read out the sentence of such an one who has been condemned to perform *hara-kiri*, and that the second censor has come to witness the execution of the sentence. The lord of the palace then inquires whether he is expected to attend the execution in person, and, if any of the relations or family of the criminal should beg to receive his remains, whether their request should be complied with; after this he announces that he will order everything to be made ready, and leaves the room. Tea, a fire-box for smoking, and sweetmeats are set before the censors; but they decline to accept any hospitality until their business shall have been concluded. The minor officials follow the same rule. If the censors express a wish to see the place of execution, the retainers of the palace show the way, and their lord accompanies them; in this, however, he may be replaced by one of his *karô* or councillors. They then return, and take their seats in the reception-room. After this, when all the preparations have been made, the master of the house leads the censors to the place where the sentence is to be read; and it is etiquette that they should wear both sword and dirk.[1] The lord of the palace takes his place on one side; the inferior censors sit on either side in a lower place. The councillors and other officers of the palace also take their places. One of the councillors present, addressing the censors without moving from his place, asks whether he shall bring forth the prisoner.

Previously to this, the retainers of the palace, going to the room where the prisoner is confined, inform him that, as the censors have arrived, he should change his dress, and the attendants bring out a change of clothes upon a large tray: it is when he has finished his toilet that the witnesses go forth and take their places in the appointed order, and the principal is then introduced. He is preceded by one man, who should be of the rank of *Mono-gashira* (retainer of the fourth rank), who wears a dirk, but no sword. Six men act as attendants; they should be of the fifth or sixth rank; they walk on either side of the principal. They are followed by one man who should be of the rank of *Yônin* (councillor of the second class). When they reach the place, the leading man draws on one side and sits down, and the six attendants sit down on either side of the principal. The officer who follows him sits down behind him, and the chief censor reads the sentence.

When the reading of the sentence is finished, the principal leaves the room and again changes his clothes, and the chief censor immediately leaves the palace; but the lord of the palace does not conduct him to the door. The second censor returns to the reception-room until the principal has changed his clothes. When the principal has taken his seat

[1] A Japanese removes his sword on entering a house, retaining only his dirk.

at the place of execution, the councillors of the palace announce to the second censor that all is ready; he then proceeds to the place, wearing his sword and dirk. The lord of the palace, also wearing his sword and dirk, takes his seat on one side. The inferior censors and councillors sit in front of the censor: they wear the dirk only. The assistant second brings a dirk upon a tray, and, having placed it in front of the principal, withdraws on one side: when the principal leans his head forward, his chief second strikes off his head, which is immediately shown to the censor, who identifies it, and tells the master of the palace that he is satisfied, and thanks him for all his trouble. The corpse, as it lies, is hidden by a white screen which is set up around it, and incense is brought out. The witnesses leave the place. The lord of the palace accompanies them as far as the porch, and the retainers prostrate themselves in the yard as before. The retainers who should be present at the place of execution are one or two councillors (*Karô*), two or three second councillors (*Yônin*), two or three *Monogashira*, one chief of the palace (*Rusui*), six attendants, one chief second, two assistant seconds, one man to carry incense, who need not be a person of rank—any Samurai will do. They attend to the setting up of the white screen.

The duty of burying the corpse and of setting the place in order again devolves upon four men; these are selected from Samurai of the middle or lower class; during the performances of their duties, they hitch up their trousers and wear neither sword nor dirk. Their names are previously sent in to the censor, who acts as witness; and to the junior censors, should they desire it. Before the arrival of the chief censor, the requisite utensils for extinguishing a fire are prepared, firemen are engaged,[1] and officers constantly go the rounds to watch against fire. From the time when the chief censor comes into the house until he leaves it, no one is allowed to enter the premises. The servants on guard at the entrance porch should wear their hempen dresses of ceremony. Every-

---

[1] In Japan, where fires are of daily occurrence, the fire-buckets and other utensils form part of the gala dress of the house of a person of rank.

thing in the palace should be conducted with decorum, and the strictest attention paid in all things.

When any one is condemned to *hara-kiri*, it would be well that people should go to the palace of the Prince of Higo, and learn what transpired at the execution of the Rônins of Asano Takumi no Kami. It is my intention to annex a plan of the event. A curtain was hung round the garden in front of the reception-room; three mats were laid down, and upon these was placed a white cloth. The condemned men were kept in the reception-room, and summoned, one by one; two men, one on each side, accompanied them; the second followed behind; and they proceeded together to the place of execution. When the execution was concluded in each case, the corpse was hidden from the sight of the chief witness by a white screen, folded up in white cloth, placed on a mat, and carried off to the rear by two foot-soldiers; it was then placed in a coffin. The blood-stained ground was sprinkled with sand, and swept clean; fresh mats were laid down, and the place prepared anew; after which the next man was summoned to come forth.

ON CERTAIN THINGS TO BE BORNE IN MIND BY THE WITNESSES

When a clansman is ordered by his feudal lord to perform *hara-kiri*, the sentence must be read out by the censor of the clan, who also acts as witness. He should take his place in front of the criminal, at a distance of twelve feet; according to some books, the distance should be eighteen feet, and he should sit obliquely, not facing the criminal; he should lay his sword down by his side, but, if he pleases, he may wear it in his girdle; he must read out the sentence distinctly. If the sentence be a long document, to begin reading in a very loud voice and afterwards drop into a whisper has an appearance of faint-heartedness; but to read it throughout in a low voice is worse still: it should be delivered clearly from beginning to end. It is the duty of the chief witness to set an example of fortitude to the other persons who are to take part in the execution. When the second has finished his work, he carries the head to the chief witness, who, after inspecting it, must declare that he has identified it; he then should take his sword, and leave his place. It is sufficient, however, that the head should be struck off without being carried to the chief witness; in that case, the second receives his instructions beforehand. On rising, the chief witness should step out with his left foot and turn to the left. If the ceremony takes place out of doors, the chief witness, wearing his sword and dirk, should sit upon a box; he must wear his hempen dress of ceremony; he may hitch his trousers up slightly; according to his rank, he may wear his full dress—that is, wings over his full dress. It is the part of the chief witness to instruct the seconds and others in the duties which they have to perform, and also to preconcert measures in the event of any mishap occurring.

If whilst the various persons to be engaged in the ceremony are rubbing up their military lore, and preparing themselves for the event, any other person should come in, they should immediately turn the conversation. Persons of the rank of Samurai should be familiar with all the details of the *hara-kiri*; and to be seen discussing what should be done in case anything went wrong, and so forth, would have an appearance of ignorance. If, however, an intimate friend should go to the place, rather than have any painful concealment, he may be consulted upon the whole affair.

When the sentence has been read, it is probable that the condemned man will have some last words to say to the chief witness. It must depend on the nature of what he has to say whether it will be received or not. If he speaks in a confused or bewildered manner, no attention is paid to it: his second should lead him away, of his own accord or at a sign from the chief witness.

If the condemned man be a person who has been given in charge to a prince by the Government, the prince, after the reading of the sentence, should send his retainers to the prisoner with a message to say that the decrees of the Government are not to be eluded, but that if he has any last wishes to express, they are ordered by their lord to receive them. If the prisoner is a man of high rank, the lord of the palace should go in person to hear his last wishes.

The condemned man should answer in the following way:—

"Sir, I thank you for your careful consideration, but I have nothing that I wish to say. I am greatly indebted to you for the great kindness which I have received since I have been under your charge. I beg you to take my respects to your lord and to the gentlemen of your clan who have treated me so well." Or he may say, "Sirs, I have nothing to say; yet, since you are so kind as to think of me, I should be obliged if you would deliver such and such a message to such an one." This is the proper and becoming sort of speech for the occasion. If the prisoner entrusts them with any message, the retainers should receive it in such a manner as to set his mind at rest. Should he ask for writing materials in order to write a letter, as this is forbidden by the law, they should tell him so, and not grant his request. Still they must feel that it is painful to refuse the request of a dying man, and must do their best to assist him. They must exhaust every available kindness and civility, as was done in the period Genroku, in the case of the Rônins of Asano Takumi no Kami. The Prince of Higo, after the sentence had been read, caused paper and writing-materials to be taken to their room. If the prisoner is light-headed from excitement, it is no use furnishing him with writing-materials. It must depend upon circumstances; but when a man has murdered another, having made up his mind to abide by the consequences, then that man's execution should be carried through with all honour. When a man kills another on the spot, in a fit of ungovernable passion, and then is bewildered and dazed by his own act, the same pains need not be taken to conduct matters punctiliously. If the prisoner be a careful man, he will take an early opportunity after he has been given in charge to express his wishes. To carry kindness so far as to supply writing-materials and the like is not obligatory. If any doubt exists upon the point, the chief witness may be consulted.

After the Rônins of Asano Takumi no Kami had heard their sentence in the palace of Matsudaira Oki no Kami, that Daimio in person went and took leave of them, and calling Oishi Chikara,[1] the son of their chief, to him, said, " I have heard that your mother is at home in your own country ; how she will grieve when she hears of your death and that of your father, I can well imagine. If you have any message that you wish to leave for her, tell me, without standing upon ceremony, and I will transmit it without delay." For a while Chikara kept his head bent down towards the ground ; at last he drew back a little, and, lifting his head, said, " I humbly thank your lordship for what you have been pleased to say. My father warned me from the first that our crime was so great that, even were we to be pardoned by a gracious judgment upon one count, I must not forget that there would be a hundred million counts against us for which we must commit suicide ; and that if I disregarded his words his hatred would pursue me after death. My father impressed this upon me at the temple called Sengakuji, and again when I was separated from him to be taken to the palace of Prince Sengoku. Now my father and myself have been condemned to perform *hara-kiri*, according to the wish of our hearts. Still I cannot forget to think of my mother. When we parted at Kiyôto, she told me that our separation would be for long, and she bade me not to play the coward when I thought of her. As I took a long leave of her then, I have no message to send to her now." When he spoke thus, Oki no Kami and all his retainers, who were drawn up around him, were moved to tears in admiration of his heroism.

Although it is right that the condemned man should bathe and partake of wine and food, these details should be cur-

[1] Oishi Chikara was separated from his father, who was one of the seventeen delivered over to the charge of the Prince of Higo.

tailed. Even should he desire these favours, it must depend
upon his conduct whether they be granted or refused. He
should be caused to die as quickly as possible. Should he
wish for some water to drink, it should be given to him. If
in his talk he should express himself like a noble Samurai,
all pains should be exhausted in carrying out his execution.
Yet however careful a man he may be, as he nears his death
his usual demeanour will undergo a change. If the execution
is delayed, in all probability it will cause the prisoner's
courage to fail him; therefore, as soon as the sentence shall
have been passed, the execution should be brought to a con-
clusion. This, again, is a point for the chief witness to
remember.

CONCERNING SECONDS (KAISHAKU)

When the condemned man is one who has been given in
charge for execution, six attendants are employed; when the
execution is within the clan, then two or three attendants
will suffice; the number, however, must depend upon the
rank of the principal. Men of great nerve and strength must
be selected for the office; they must wear their hempen
dress of ceremony, and tuck up their trousers; they must
on no account wear either sword or dirk, but have a small
poniard hidden in their bosom: these are the officers who
attend upon the condemned man when he changes his dress,
and who sit by him on the right hand and on the left hand
to guard him whilst the sentence is being read. In the event
of any mistake occurring (such as the prisoner attempting to
escape), they knock him down; and should he be unable to
stand or to walk, they help to support him. The attendants
accompanying the principal to the place of execution, if they
are six in number, four of them take their seats some way off
and mount guard, while the other two should sit close behind
the principal. They must understand that should there be
any mistake they must throw the condemned man, and,
holding him down, cut off his head with their poniard, or

stab him to death. If the second bungles in cutting off the head and the principal attempts to rise, it is the duty of the attendants to kill him. They must help him to take off his upper garments and bare his body. In recent times, however, there have been cases where the upper garments have not been removed: this depends upon circumstances. The setting up of the white screen, and the laying the corpse in the coffin, are duties which, although they may be performed by other officers, originally devolved upon the six attendants. When a common man is executed, he is bound with cords, and so made to take his place; but a Samurai wears his dress of ceremony, is presented with a dagger, and dies thus. There ought to be no anxiety lest such a man should attempt to escape; still, as there is no knowing what these six attendants may be called upon to do, men should be selected who thoroughly understand their business.

The seconds are three in number—the chief second, the assistant second, and the inferior second. When the execution is carried out with proper solemnity, three men are employed; still a second and assistant second are sufficient. If three men serve as seconds, their several duties are as follows :— The chief second strikes off the head; that is his duty: he is the most important officer in the execution by *hara-kiri*. The assistant second brings forward the tray, on which is placed the dirk; that is his duty: he must perform his part in such a manner that the principal second is not hindered in his work. The assistant second is the officer of second importance in the execution. The third or inferior second carries the head to the chief witness for identification; and in the event of something suddenly occurring to hinder either of the other two seconds, he should bear in mind that he must be ready to act as his substitute: his is an office of great importance, and a proper person must be selected to fill it.

Although there can be no such thing as a *kaishaku* (second) in any case except in one of *hara-kiri*, still in old times guardians and persons who assisted others were also called *kaishaku*: the reason for this is because the *kaishaku*, or second, comes to the assistance of the principal. If the principal were to make any mistake at the fatal moment, it would be a disgrace to his dead body : it is in order to prevent such mistakes that the *kaishaku*, or second, is employed. It is the duty of the *kaishaku* to consider this as his first duty.

When a man is appointed to act as second to another, what shall be said of him if he accepts the office with a smiling face? Yet must he not put on a face of distress. It is as well to attempt to excuse oneself from performing the duty. There is no heroism in cutting a man's head off well, and it is a disgrace to do it in a bungling manner ; yet must not a man allege lack of skill as a pretext for evading the office, for it is an unworthy thing that a Samurai should want the skill required to behead a man. If there are any that advocate employing young men as seconds, it should rather be said that their hands are inexpert. To play the coward and yield up the office to another man is out of the question. When a man is called upon to perform the office, he should express his readiness to use his sword (the dirk may be employed, but the sword is the proper weapon). As regards the sword, the second should borrow that of the principal: if there is any objection to this, he should receive a sword from his lord ; he should not use his own sword. When the assistant seconds have been appointed, the three should take counsel together about the details of the place of execution, when they have been carefully instructed by their superiors in all the ceremonies ; and having made careful inquiry, should there be anything wrong, they should appeal to their superiors for instruction. The seconds wear their dresses of ceremony when the criminal is a man given in charge by the Government: when he is one of their own clan, they need only wear the trousers of the Samurai. In old days it is said that they were dressed in the same way as the principal ; and some authorities assert that at the *hara-kiri* of a nobleman of high rank the seconds should wear white clothes, and that the handle of the sword should be wrapped in white silk. If the execution takes place in the house, they should partially tuck up their trousers; if in the garden, they should tuck them up entirely.

The seconds should address the principal, and say, " Sir, we have been appointed to act as your seconds; we pray you to set your mind at rest," and so forth; but this must depend upon the rank of the criminal. At this time, too, if the principal has any last wish to express, the second should receive it, and should treat him with every consideration in order to relieve his anxiety. If the second has been selected by the principal on account of old friendship between them, or if the latter, during the time that he has been in charge, has begged some special retainer of the palace to act as his second in the event of his being condemned to death, the person so selected should thank the principal for choosing so unworthy a person, and promise to beg his lord to allow him to act as second : so he should answer, and comfort him, and having reported the matter to his lord, should act as second. He should take that opportunity to borrow his principal's sword in some such terms as the following: " As I am to have the honour of being your second, I would fain borrow your sword for the occasion. It may be a consolation to you to perish by your own sword, with which you are familiar." If, however, the principal declines, and prefers to be executed with the second's sword, his wish must be complied with. If the second should make an awkward cut with his own sword, it is a disgrace to him; therefore he should borrow some one else's sword, so that the blame may rest with the sword, and not with the swordsman. Although this is the rule, and although every Samurai should wear a sword fit to cut off a man's head, still if the principal has begged to be executed with the second's own sword, it must be done as he desires.

It is probable that the condemned man will inquire of his second about the arrangements which have been made : he must attend therefore to rendering himself capable of answering all such questions. Once upon a time, when the condemned man inquired of his second whether his head would be cut off at the moment when he received the tray with the dirk upon it, "No," replied the second; "at the moment when you stab yourself with the dirk your head will be cut off." At the execution of one Sanô, he told his second that, when he had stabbed himself in the belly, he would utter a cry; and begged him to be cool when he cut off his head. The second replied that he would do as he wished, but begged him in the meantime to take the tray with the dirk, according to proper form. When Sanô reached out his hand to take the tray, the second cut off his head immediately. Now, although this was not exactly right, still as the second acted so in order to save a Samurai from the disgrace of performing the *hara-kiri* improperly (by crying out), it can never be wrong for a second to act kindly. If the principal urgently requests to be allowed really to disembowel himself, his wish may, according to circumstances, be granted; but in this case care must be taken that no time be lost in striking off the head. The custom of striking off the head, the prisoner only going through the semblance of disembowelling himself, dates from the period Yempô (about 190 years ago).

When the principal has taken his place, the second strips his right shoulder of the dress of ceremony, which he allows to fall behind his sleeve, and, drawing his sword, lays down the scabbard, taking care that his weapon is not seen by the principal; then he takes his place on the left of the principal and close behind him. The principal should sit facing the west, and the second facing the north, and in that position should he strike the blow. When the second perceives the assistant second bring out the tray on which is laid the dirk, he must brace up his nerves and settle his heart beneath his navel: when the tray is laid down, he must put himself in position to strike the blow. He should step out first with the left foot, and then change so as to bring his right foot forward: this is the position which he should assume to strike; he may, however, reverse the position of his feet. When the principal removes his upper garments, the second must poise his sword: when the principal reaches out his hand to draw the tray towards him, as he leans his head forward a little, is the exact moment for the second to strike. There are all sorts of traditions about this. Some say that the principal should take the tray and raise it respectfully to his head, and set it down; and that this is the moment to strike. There are three rules for the time of cutting off the head: the first is when the dirk is laid on the tray; the second is when the principal looks at the left side of his belly before inserting the dirk; the third is when he inserts the dirk. If these three moments are allowed to pass, it becomes a difficult matter to cut off the head: so says tradition. However, four moments for cutting are also recorded: first, when the assistant second retires after having laid down the stand on which is the dirk; second, when the principal draws the stand towards him; third, when he takes the dirk in his hand; fourth, when he makes the incision into the belly. Although all four ways are approved, still the first is too soon; the last three are right and proper. In short, the blow should be struck without delay. If he has struck off the head at a blow without failure, the second, taking care not to raise his sword, but holding it point downwards, should retire backward a little and wipe his weapon kneeling; he should have plenty of white paper ready in his girdle or in his bosom to wipe away the blood and rub up his sword; having replaced his sword in its scabbard, he should readjust his upper garments and take his seat to the rear. When the head has fallen, the junior second should enter, and, taking up the head, present it to the witness for inspection. When he has identified it, the ceremony is concluded. If there is no assistant or junior second, the second, as soon as he has cut off the head, carrying his sword reversed in his left hand, should take the head in his right hand, holding it by the top-knot of hair, should advance towards the witness, passing on the right side of the corpse, and show the right profile of the head to the witness, resting the chin of the head upon the hilt of his sword, and kneeling on his left knee; then return-ing again round by the left of the corpse, kneeling on his left knee, and carrying the head in his left hand and resting it on the edge of his sword, he should again show the left profile to the witness. It is also laid down as another rule, that the second, laying down his sword, should take out paper from the bosom of his dress, and placing the head in the palm of his left hand, and taking the top-knot of hair in his right hand, should lay the head upon the paper, and so submit it for inspection. Either way may be said to be right.

NOTE.—To lay down thick paper, and place the head on it, shows a disposition to pay respect to the head; to place it on the edge of the sword is insulting: the course pursued must depend upon the rank of the person. If the ceremony is to be curtailed, it may end with the cutting off of the head: that must be settled beforehand, in consultation with the witness. In the event of the second making a false cut, so as not to strike off the head at a blow, the second must take the head by the top-knot, and, pressing it down, cut it off. Should he take bad aim and cut the shoulder by mistake, and should the principal rise and cry out, before he has time to writhe, he should hold him down and stab him to death, and then cut off his head, or the assistant seconds, who are sitting behind, should come forward and hold him down, while the chief second cuts off his head. It may be necessary for the second, after he has cut off the head, to push down the body, and then take up the head for inspection. If the body does not fall at once, which is said to be sometimes the case, the second should pull the feet to make it fall.

There are some who say that the perfect way for the second to cut off the head is not to cut right through the neck at a blow, but to leave a little uncut, and, as the head hangs by the skin, to seize the top-knot and slice it off, and then submit it for inspection. The reason of this is, lest, the head being struck off at a blow, the ceremony should be confounded with an ordinary execution. According to the old authorities, this is the proper and respectful manner. After the head is cut off, the eyes are apt to blink, and the mouth to move, and to bite the pebbles and sand. This being hateful to see, at what amongst Samurai is so important an occasion, and being a shameful thing, it is held to be best not to let the head fall, but to hold back a little in delivering the blow. Perhaps this may be right; yet it is a very difficult matter to cut so as to leave the head hanging by a little flesh, and there is the danger of missing the cut ; and as any mistake in the cut is most horrible to see, it is better to strike a fair blow at once. Others say that, even when the head is struck off at a blow, the semblance of slicing it off should be gone through afterwards ; yet be it borne in mind that this is unnecessary.

Three methods of carrying the sword are recognized amongst those skilled in swordmanship. If the rank of the principal be high, the sword is raised aloft ; if the principal and second are of equal rank, the sword is carried at the centre of the body ; if the principal be of inferior rank, the sword is allowed to hang downwards. The proper position for the second to strike from is kneeling on one knee, but there is no harm in his standing up : others say that, if the execution takes place inside the house, the second should kneel ; if in the garden, he shonld stand. These are not points upon which to insist obstinately : a man should strike in whatever position is most convenient to him.

The chief duty for the assistant second to bear in mind is the bringing in of the tray with the dirk, which should be produced very quietly when the principal takes his place : it should be placed so that the condemned man may have to tretch his hand well out in order to reach it.[1] The assistant second then returns to his own place ; but if the condemned man shows any signs of agitation, the assistant second must lend his assistance, so that the head may be properly cut off. It once happened that the condemned man, having received the tray from the assistant second, held it up for a long time without putting it down, until those near him had over and over again urged him to set it down. It also happens that after the tray has been set down, and the assistant second has retired, the condemned man does not put out his hand to take it ; then must the assistant second press him to take it. Also the principal may ask that the tray be placed a little nearer to him, in which case his wish must be granted. The tray may also be placed in such a way that the assistant

---

[1] It should be placed about three feet away from him.

second, holding it in his left hand, may reach the dirk to the condemned man, who leans forward to take it. Which is the best of all these ways is uncertain. The object to aim at is, that the condemned man should lean forward to receive the blow. Whether the assistant second retires, or not, must depend upon the attitude assumed by the condemned man.

If the prisoner be an unruly, violent man, a fan, instead of a dirk, should be placed upon the tray; and should he object to this, he should be told, in answer, that the substitution of the fan is an ancient custom. This may occur sometimes. It is said that once upon a time, in one of the palaces of the Daimios, a certain brave matron murdered a man, and having been allowed to die with all the honours of the *hara-kiri*, a fan was placed upon the tray, and her head was cut off. This may be considered right and proper. If the condemned man appears inclined to be turbulent, the seconds, without showing any sign of alarm, should hurry to his side, and, urging him to get ready, quickly cause him to make all his preparations with speed, and to sit down in his place; the chief second, then drawing his sword, should get ready to strike, and, ordering him to proceed as fast as possible with the ceremony of receiving the tray, should perform his duty without appearing to be afraid.

A certain Prince Katô, having condemned one of his councillors to death, assisted at the ceremony behind a curtain of slips of bamboo. The councillor, whose name was Katayama, was bound, and during that time glared fiercely at the curtain, and showed no signs of fear. The chief second was a man named Jihei, who had always been used to treat Katayama with great respect. So Jihei, sword in hand, said to Katayama, " Sir, your last moment has arrived : be so good as to turn your cheek so that your head may be straight." When Katayama heard this, he replied, " Fellow, you are insolent;" and as he was looking round, Jihei struck the fatal blow. The lord Katô afterwards inquired of Jihei what was the reason of this; and he replied that, as he saw that the prisoner was meditating treason, he determined to kill him at once, and put a stop to this rebellious spirit. This is a pattern for other seconds to bear in mind.

When the head has been struck off, it becomes the duty of the junior second to take it up by the top-knot, and, placing it upon some thick paper laid over the palm of his hand, to carry it for inspection by the witness. This ceremony has been explained above. If the head be bald, he should pierce the left ear with the stiletto carried in the scabbard of his dirk, and so carry it to be identified. He must carry thick paper in the bosom of his dress. Inside the paper he shall place a bag with rice bran and ashes, in order that he may carry the head without being sullied by the blood. When the identification of the head is concluded, the junior second's duty is to place it in a bucket.

If anything should occur to hinder the chief second, the assistant second must take his place. It happened on one occasion that before the execution took place the chief second lost his nerve, yet he cut off the head without any difficulty; but when it came to taking up the head for inspection, his nervousness so far got the better of him as to be extremely inconvenient. This is a thing against which persons acting as seconds have to guard.

As a corollary to the above elaborate statement of the ceremonies proper to be observed at the *hara-kiri*, I may here describe an instance of such an execution which I was sent officially to witness. The condemned man was Taki Zenza-burô, an officer of the Prince of Bizen, who gave the order to fire upon the foreign settlement at Hiogo in the month of February 1868,—an attack to which I have alluded in the preamble to the story of the Eta Maiden and the Hatamoto. Up to that time no foreigner had witnessed such an execution, which was rather looked upon as a traveller's fable.

The ceremony, which was ordered by the Mikado himself, took place at 10.30 at night in the temple of Seifukuji, the head-quarters of the Satsuma troops at Hiogo. A witness was sent from each of the foreign legations. We were seven foreigners in all.

We were conducted to the temple by officers of the Princes of Satsuma and Choshiu. Although the ceremony was to be conducted in the most private manner, the casual remarks which we overheard in the streets, and a crowd lining the principal entrance to the temple, showed that it was a matter of no little interest to the public. The courtyard of the temple presented a most picturesque sight; it was crowded with soldiers standing about in knots round large fires, which threw a dim flickering light over the heavy eaves and quaint gable-ends of the sacred buildings. We were shown into an inner room, where we were to wait until the preparation for the ceremony was completed : in the next room to us were the high Japanese officers. After a long interval, which seemed doubly long from the silence which prevailed, Itô Shunské, the provisional Governor of Hiogo, came and took down our names, and informed us that seven *kenshi*, sheriffs or witnesses, would attend on the part of the Japanese. He and another officer represented the Mikado; two captains of Satsuma's infantry, and two of Choshiu's, with a representative of the Prince of Bizen, the clan of the condemned man, completed the number, which was probably arranged in order to tally with that of the foreigners. Itô Shunské further inquired whether we wished to put any questions to the prisoner. We replied in the negative.

A further delay then ensued, after which we were invited to follow the Japanese witnesses into the *hondo* or main hall of the temple, where the ceremony was to be performed. It was an imposing scene. A large hall with a high roof supported by dark pillars of wood. From the ceiling hung a profusion of those huge gilt lamps and ornaments peculiar to Buddhist temples. In front of the high altar, where the floor, covered with beautiful white mats, is raised some three or four inches from the ground, was laid a rug of scarlet felt. Tall candles placed at regular intervals gave out a dim mysterious light, just sufficient to let all the proceedings be seen. The seven Japanese took their places on the left of the raised floor, the seven foreigners on the right. No other person was present.

After an interval of a few minutes of anxious suspense, Taki Zenzaburô, a stalwart man, thirty-two years of age, with a noble air, walked into the hall attired in his dress of ceremony, with the peculiar hempen-cloth wings which are worn on great occasions. He was accompanied by a *kaishaku* and three officers, who wore the *jimbaori* or war surcoat with gold-tissue facings. The word *kaishaku*, it should be observed, is one to which our word *executioner* is no equivalent term. The office is that of a gentleman : in many cases it is performed by a kinsman or friend of the condemned, and the relation between them is rather that of principal and second than that of victim and executioner. In this instance the *kaishaku* was a pupil of Taki Zenzaburô, and was selected by the friends of the latter from among their own number for his skill in swordsmanship.

With the *kaishaku* on his left hand, Taki Zenzaburô advanced slowly towards the Japanese witnesses, and the two bowed before them, then drawing near to the foreigners they saluted us in the same way, perhaps even with more deference : in each case the salutation was ceremoniously returned. Slowly, and with great dignity, the condemned man mounted on to the raised floor, prostrated himself before the high altar twice, and seated[1] himself on the felt carpet with his back to the high altar, the *kaishaku* crouching on his left-hand side. One of the three attendant officers then came forward, bearing a stand of the kind used in temples for offerings, on which, wrapped in paper, lay the *wakizashi*, the short sword or dirk of the Japanese, nine inches and a half in length, with a point and an edge as sharp as a razor's. This he handed, prostrating himself, to the condemned man, who received it

---

[1] Seated himself—that is, in the Japanese fashion, his knees and toes touching the ground, and his body resting on his heels. In this position, which is one of respect, he remained until his death.

reverently, raising it to his head with both hands, and placed it in front of himself.

After another profound obeisance, Taki Zenzaburô, in a voice which betrayed just so much emotion and hesitation as might be expected from a man who is making a painful confession, but with no sign of either in his face or manner, spoke as follows :—

"I, and I alone, unwarrantably gave the order to fire on the foreigners at Kôbé, and again as they tried to escape. For this crime I disembowel myself, and I beg you who are present to do me the honour of witnessing the act."

Bowing once more, the speaker allowed his upper garments to slip down to his girdle, and remained naked to the waist. Carefully, according to custom, he tucked his sleeves under his knees to prevent himself from falling backwards; for a noble Japanese gentleman should die falling forwards. Deliberately, with a steady hand, he took the dirk that lay before him ; he looked at it wistfully, almost affectionately; for a moment he seemed to collect his thoughts for the last time, and then stabbing himself deeply below the waist on the left-hand side, he drew the dirk slowly across to the right side, and, turning it in the wound, gave a slight cut upwards. During this sickeningly painful operation he never moved a muscle of his face. When he drew out the dirk, he leaned forward and stretched out his neck ; an expression of pain for the first time crossed his face, but he uttered no sound. At that moment the *kaishaku*, who, still crouching by his side, had been keenly watching his every movement, sprang to his feet, poised his sword for a second in the air ; there was a flash, a heavy, ugly thud, a crashing fall; with one blow the head had been severed from the body.

A dead silence followed, broken only by the hideous noise of the blood throbbing out of the inert heap before us, which but a moment before had been a brave and chivalrous man. It was horrible.

The *kaishaku* made a low bow, wiped his sword with a piece of paper which he had ready for the purpose, and retired from the raised floor; and the stained dirk was solemnly borne away, a bloody proof of the execution.

The two representatives of the Mikado then left their places, and, crossing over to where the foreign witnesses sat, called us to witness that the sentence of death upon Taki Zenzaburô had been faithfully carried out. The ceremony being at an end, we left the temple.

The ceremony, to which the place and the hour gave an additional solemnity, was characterized throughout by that extreme dignity and punctiliousness which are the distinctive marks of the proceedings of Japanese gentlemen of rank; and it is important to note this fact, because it carries with it the conviction that the dead man was indeed the officer who had committed the crime, and no substitute. While profoundly impressed by the terrible scene, it was impossible at the same time not to be filled with admiration of the firm and manly bearing of the sufferer, and of the nerve with which the *kaishaku* performed his last duty to his master. Nothing could more strongly show the force of education. The Samurai, or gentleman of the military class, from his earliest years learns to look upon the *hara-kiri* as a ceremony in which some day he may be called upon to play a part as principal or second. In old-fashioned families, which hold to the traditions of ancient chivalry, the child is instructed in the rite and familiarized with the idea as an honourable expiation of crime or blotting out of disgrace. If the hour comes, he is prepared for it, and bravely faces an ordeal which early training has robbed of half its horrors. In what other country in the world does a man learn that the last tribute of affection which he may have to pay to his best friend may be to act as his executioner?

Since I wrote the above, we have heard that, before his entry into the fatal hall, Taki Zenzaburô called round him all those of his own clan who were present, many of whom had carried out his order to fire, and, addressing them in a short speech, acknowledged the heinousness of his crime and the justice of his sentence, and warned them solemnly to avoid any repetition of attacks upon foreigners. They were also addressed by the officers of the Mikado, who urged them to bear no ill-will against us on account of the fate of their fellow-clansman. They declared that they entertained no such feeling.

The opinion has been expressed that it would have been politic for the foreign representatives at the last moment to have interceded for the life of Taki Zenzaburô. The question is believed to have been debated among the representatives themselves. My own belief is that mercy, although it might have produced the desired effect among the more civilized clans, would have been mistaken for weakness and fear by those wilder people who have not yet a personal knowledge of foreigners. The offence—an attack upon the flags and subjects of all the Treaty Powers, which lack of skill, not of will, alone prevented from ending in a universal massacre— was the gravest that has been committed upon foreigners since their residence in Japan. Death was undoubtedly deserved, and the form chosen was in Japanese eyes merciful and yet judicial. The crime might have involved a war and cost hundreds of lives; it was wiped out by one death. I believe that, in the interest of Japan as well as in our own, the course pursued was wise, and it was very satisfactory to me to find that one of the ablest Japanese ministers, with whom I had a discussion upon the subject, was quite of my opinion.

The ceremonies observed at the *hara-kiri* appear to vary slightly in detail in different parts of Japan; but the following memorandum upon the subject of the rite, as it used to be practised at Yedo during the rule of the Tycoon, clearly establishes its judicial character. I translated it from a paper drawn up for me by a Japanese who was able to speak of what he had seen himself. Three different ceremonies are described:—

1st. *Ceremonies observed at the "hara-kiri" of a Hatamoto (petty noble of the Tycoon's court) in prison.*—This is conducted with great secrecy. Six mats are spread in a large courtyard of the prison; an *ometsuké* (officer whose duties appear to consist in the surveillance of other officers), assisted by two other *ometsukés* of the second and third class, acts as *kenshi* (sheriff or witness), and sits in front of the mats. The condemned man, attired in his dress of ceremony, and wearing his wings of hempen cloth, sits in the centre of the mats. At each of the four corners of the mats sits a prison official. Two officers of the Governor of the city act as *kaishaku* (executioners or seconds), and take their place, one on the right hand and the other on the left hand of the condemned. The *kaishaku* on the left side, announcing his name and surname, says, bowing, "I have the honour to act as *kaishaku* to you; have you any last wishes to confide to me?" The condemned man thanks him and accepts the offer or not, as the case may be. He then bows to the sheriff, and a wooden dirk nine and a half inches long is placed before him at a distance of three feet, wrapped in paper, and lying on a stand such as is used for offerings in temples. As he reaches forward to take the wooden sword, and stretches out his neck, the *kaishaku* on his left-hand side draws his sword and strikes off his head. The *kaishaku* on the right-hand side takes up the head and shows it to the sheriff. The body is given to the relations of the deceased for burial. His property is confiscated.

2nd. *The ceremonies observed at the "hara-kiri" of a Daimio's retainer.*—When the retainer of a Daimio is condemned to perform the *hara-kiri*, four mats are placed in the yard of the *yashiki* or palace. The condemned man, dressed in his robes of ceremony, and wearing his wings of hempen cloth, sits in the centre. An officer acts as chief witness, with a second witness under him. Two officers, who act as *kaishaku*, are on the right and left of the condemned man; four officers are placed at the corners of the mats. The *kaishaku*, as in the former case, offers to execute the last wishes of the condemned. A dirk nine and a half inches long is placed before him on a stand. In this case the dirk is a real dirk, which the man takes and stabs himself with on the left side, below the navel, drawing it across to the right side. At this moment, when he leans forward in pain, the *kaishaku* on the left-hand side cuts off the head. The *kaishaku* on the right-hand side takes up the head, and shows it to the sheriff. The body is given to the relations for burial. In most cases the property of the deceased is confiscated.

3rd. *Self-immolation of a Daimio on account of disgrace.*— When a Daimio had been guilty of treason or offended against the Tycoon, inasmuch as the family was disgraced, and an apology could neither be offered nor accepted, the offending Daimio was condemned to *hara-kiri*. Calling his councillors around him, he confided to them his last will and testament for transmission to the Tycoon. Then, clothing himself in his court dress, he disembowelled himself, and cut his own throat. His councillors then reported the matter to the Government, and a coroner was sent to investigate it. To him the retainers handed the last will and testament of their lord, and he took it to the Gorôjiu (first council), who transmitted it to the Tycoon. If the offence was heinous, such as would involve the ruin of the whole family, by the clemency of the Tycoon, half the property might be confiscated, and half returned to the heir; if the offence was trivial, the property was inherited intact by the heir, and the family did not suffer.

In all cases where the criminal disembowels himself of his own accord without condemnation and without investigation, inasmuch as he is no longer able to defend himself, the offence is considered as non-proven, and the property is not confiscated. In the year 1869, a motion was brought forward in the Japanese parliament by one Ono Seigorô, clerk of the house, advocating the abolition of the practice of *hara-kiri*. Two hundred members out of a house of 209 voted against the motion, which was supported by only three speakers, six members not voting on either side. In this debate the *seppuku*, or *hara-kiri*, was called " the very shrine of the Japanese national spirit, and the embodiment in practice of devotion to principle," " a great ornament to the empire," " a pillar of the constitution," "a valuable institution, tending to the honour of the nobles, and based on a compassionate feeling towards the official caste," "a pillar of religion and a spur to virtue." The whole debate (which is well worth reading, and an able translation of which by Mr. Aston has appeared in a recent Blue Book) shows the affection with which the Japanese cling to the traditions of a chivalrous past. It is worthy of notice that the proposer, Ono Seigorô, who on more than one occasion rendered himself conspicuous by introducing motions based upon an admiration of our Western civilization, was murdered not long after this debate took place.

There are many stories on record of extraordinary heroism being displayed in the *hara-kiri*. The case of a young fellow, only twenty years old, of the Choshiu clan, which was told me the other day by an eye-witness, deserves mention as a marvellous instance of determination. Not content with giving himself the one necessary cut, he slashed himself thrice horizontally and twice vertically. Then he stabbed himself in the throat until the dirk protruded on the other side, with its sharp edge to the front; setting his teeth in one supreme effort, he drove the knife forward with both hands through his throat, and fell dead.

One more story and I have done. During the revolution, when the Tycoon, beaten on every side, fled ignominiously to Yedo, he is said to have determined to fight no more, but to yield everything. A member of his second council went to him and said, "Sir, the only way for you now to retrieve the honour of the family of Tokugawa is to disembowel yourself; and to prove to you that I am sincere and disinterested in what I say, I am here ready to disembowel myself with you." The Tycoon flew into a great rage, saying that he would listen to no such nonsense, and left the room. His faithful retainer, to prove his honesty, retired to another part of the castle, and solemnly performed the *hara-kiri*.

APPENDIX B

THE MARRIAGE CEREMONY

(From the "Sho-rei Hikki"—Record of Ceremonies.)

THE ceremonies observed at marriages are various, and it is not right for a man, exceeding the bounds of his condition in life, to transgress against the rules which are laid down. When the middle-man has arranged the preliminaries of the marriage between the two parties, he carries the complimentary present, which is made at the time of betrothal, from the future bridegroom to his destined bride; and if this present is accepted, the lady's family can no longer retract their promise. This is the beginning of the contract. The usual betrothal presents are as follows. Persons of the higher classes send a robe of white silk; a piece of gold embroidery for a girdle; a piece of silk stuff; a piece of white silk, with a lozenge pattern, and other silk stuffs (these are made up into a pile of three layers); fourteen barrels of wine, and seven sorts of condiments. Persons of the middle class send a piece of white silk stuff; a piece of gold embroidery for a girdle; a piece of white silk, with a lozenge pattern, and other silk stuffs (these are made up into a pile of two layers); ten barrels of wine, and five sorts of condiments. The lower classes send a robe of white silk, a robe of coloured silk, in a pile of one layer, together with six barrels of wine and three sorts of condiments. To the future father-in-law is sent a sword, with a scabbard for slinging, such as is worn in war-time, together with a list of the presents; to the mother-in-law, a silk robe, with wine and condiments. Although all these presents are right and proper for the occasion, still they must be regulated according to the means of the persons concerned. The future father-in-law sends a present of equal value in return to his son-in-law, but the bride elect sends no return present to her future husband; the present from the father-in-law must by no means be omitted, but according to his position, if he be poor, he need only send wine and condiments.

In sending the presents care must be taken not to fold the silk robe. The two silk robes that are sent on the marriage night must be placed with the collars stitched together in a peculiar fashion.

The ceremonies of sending the litter to fetch the bride on the wedding night are as follows. In families of good position, one of the principal retainers on either side is deputed to accompany the bride and to receive her. Matting is spread before the entrance-door, upon which the bride's litter is placed, while the two principal retainers congratulate one another, and the officers of the bridegroom receive the litter. If a bucket containing clams, to make the wedding broth, has been sent with the bride, it is carried and received by a person of distinction. Close by the entrance-door a fire is lighted on the right hand and on the left. These fires are called garden-torches. In front of the corridor along which the litter passes, on the right hand and on the left, two men and two women, in pairs, place two mortars, right and left, in which they pound rice; as the litter passes, the pounded rice from the left-hand side is moved across to the right, and the two are mixed together into one. This is called the blending of the rice-meal.[1] Two candles are lighted, the one on the right hand and the other on the left of the corridor; and after the litter has passed, the

---

[1] Cf. Gibbon on Roman Marriages, "Decline and Fall of the Roman Empire," vol. iv. p. 345 : "The contracting parties were seated on the same sheepskin; they tasted a salt cake of *far*, or rice; and this *confarreation*, which denoted the ancient food of Italy, served as an emblem of their mystic union of mind and body."

candle on the left is passed over to the right, and, the two wicks being brought together, the candles are extinguished. These last three ceremonies are only performed at the weddings of persons of high rank; they are not observed at the weddings of ordinary persons. The bride takes with her to her husband's house, as presents, two silken robes sewed together in a peculiar manner, a dress of ceremony with wings of hempen cloth, an upper girdle and an under girdle, a fan, either five or seven pocket-books, and a sword: these seven presents are placed on a long tray, and their value must depend upon the means of the family.

The dress of the bride is a white silk robe with a lozenge pattern, over an under-robe, also of white silk. Over her head she wears a veil of white silk, which, when she sits down, she allows to fall about her as a mantle.

The bride's furniture and effects are all arranged for her by female attendants from her own house on a day previous to the wedding; and the bridegroom's effects are in like manner arranged by the women of his own house.

When the bride meets her husband in the room where the relations are assembled, she takes her seat for this once in the place of honour, her husband sitting in a lower place, not directly opposite to her, but diagonally, and discreetly avoiding her glance.

On the raised part of the floor are laid out beforehand two trays, the preparations for a feast, a table on which are two wagtails,[1] a second table with a representation of Elysium,

---

[1] The god who created Japan is called Kunitokodachi no Mikoto. Seven generations of gods after his time existed Izanagi no Mikoto and Izanami no Mikoto—the first a god, the second a goddess. As these two divine beings were standing upon the floating bridge of heaven, two wagtails came; and the gods, watching the amorous dalliance of the two birds, invented the art of love. From their union thus inaugurated sprang the mountains, the rivers, the grass, the trees, the remainder of the gods, and mankind. Another fable is, that as the two gods were standing on the floating bridge of heaven, Izanagi no Mikoto, taking the heavenly jewelled spear, stirred up the sea,

fowls, fish, two wine-bottles, three wine-cups, and two sorts of kettles for warming wine. The ladies go out to meet the bride, and invite her into a dressing-room, and, when she has smoothed her dress, bring her into the room, and she and the bridegroom take their seats in the places appointed for them. The two trays are then brought out, and the ladies-in-waiting, with complimentary speeches, hand dried fish and seaweed, such as accompany presents, and dried chestnuts to the couple. Two married ladies then each take one of the wine-bottles which have been prepared, and place them in the lower part of the room. Then two handmaids, who act as wine-pourers, bring the kettles and place them in the lower part of the room. The two wine-bottles have respectively a male and female butterfly, made of paper, attached to them. The female butterfly is laid on its back, and the wine is poured from the bottle into the kettle. The male butterfly is then taken and laid on the female butterfly, and the wine from the bottle is poured into the same kettle, and the whole is transferred with due ceremony to another kettle of different shape, which the wine-pourers place in front of themselves. Little low dining-tables are laid, one for each person, before the bride and bridegroom, and before the bride's ladies-in-waiting ; the woman deputed to pour the wine takes the three wine-cups and places them one on the top of the other before the bridegroom, who drinks two cups [1] from the upper cup, and pours a little wine from the full kettle into the empty kettle. The pouring together of the wine on the wedding night is symbolical of the union that is being contracted. The bridegroom next pours out a third cup of wine and drinks it, and the cup is carried by the ladies to the bride, who drinks three cups, and pours a little wine from one kettle into the other, as the bridegroom did. A cup is then set down and put on the other two, and they are carried back to

and the drops which fell from the point of it congealed and became an island, which was called *Onokoro-jima*, on which the two gods, descending from heaven, took up their abode.

[1] Each cup contains but a sip.

the raised floor and arranged as before. After this, condiments are set out on the right-hand side of a little table, and the wine-pourers place the three cups before the bride, who drinks three cups from the second cup, which is passed to the bridegroom; he also drinks three cups as before, and the cups are piled up and arranged in their original place, by the wine-pourers. A different sort of condiment is next served on the left-hand side; and the three cups are again placed before the bridegroom, who drinks three cups from the third cup, and the bride does the same. When the cups and tables have been put back in their places, the bridegroom, rising from his seat, rests himself for a while. During this time soup of fishes' fins and wine are served to the bride's ladies-in-waiting and to the serving-women. They are served with a single wine-cup of earthenware, placed upon a small square tray, and this again is set upon a long tray, and a wine-kettle with all sorts of condiments is brought from the kitchen. When this part of the feast is over, the room is put in order, and the bride and bridegroom take their seats again. Soups and a preparation of rice are now served, and two earthenware cups, gilt and silvered, are placed on a tray, on which there is a representation of the island of Takasago.[1] This time butterflies of gold and silver paper are attached to the wine-kettles. The bridegroom drinks a cup or two, and the ladies-in-waiting offer more condiments to the couple. Rice, with hot water poured over it, according to custom, and carp soup are brought in, and, the wine having been heated, cups of lacquer ware are produced; and it is at this time that the feast commences. (Up to now the eating and drinking has been merely a form.) Twelve plates of sweetmeats and tea are served; and the dinner consists of three courses, one course of seven dishes,

---

[1] In the island of Takasago, in the province of Harima, stands a pine-tree, called the "pine of mutual old age." At the root the tree is single, but towards the centre it springs into two stems—an old, old pine, models of which are used at weddings as a symbol that the happy pair shall reach old age together. Its evergreen leaves are an emblem of the unchanging constancy of the heart. Figures of an old man and woman under the tree are the spirits of the old pine.

one of five dishes, and one of three dishes, or else two courses of five dishes and one of three dishes, according to the means of the family. The above ceremonies are those which are proper only in families of the highest rank, and are by no means fitting for the lower classes, who must not step out of the proper bounds of their position.

There is a popular tradition that, in the ceremony of drinking wine on the wedding night, the bride should drink first, and then hand the cup to the bridegroom ; but although there are some authorities upon ceremonies who are in favour of this course, it is undoubtedly a very great mistake. In the " Record of Rites," by Confucius, it is written, " The man stands in importance before the woman : it is the right of the strong over the weak. Heaven ranks before earth ; the prince ranks before his minister. This law of honour is one." Again, in the " Book of History," by Confucius, it is written, " The hen that crows in the morning brings misfortune." In our own literature in the Jusho (Book of the Gods), " When the goddesses saw the gods for the first time, they were the first to cry out, ' Oh ! what beautiful males ! ' But the gods were greatly displeased, and said, ' We, who are so strong and powerful, should by rights have been the first to speak ; how is it that, on the contrary, these females speak first ? This is indeed vulgar.' " Again it is written, " When the gods brought forth the cripple Hiruko, the Lord of Heaven, answering, said that his misfortune was a punishment upon the goddesses who had presumed to speak first." The same rule therefore exists in China and in Japan, and it is held to be unlucky that the wife should take precedence : with this warning people should be careful how they commit a breach of etiquette, although it may be sanctioned by the vulgar.

At the wedding of the lower classes, the bride and her ladies and friends have a feast, but the bridegroom has no feast ; and when the bride's feast is over, the bridegroom is called in and is presented with the bride's wine-cup ; but as the forms observed are very vulgar, it is not worth while to point out the rules which guide them. As this night is essentially of importance to the married couple only, there are some writers on ceremonies who have laid down that no feast need be prepared for the bride's ladies, and in my opinion they are right: for the husband and wife at the beginning of their intercourse to be separated, and for the bride alone to be feasted like an ordinary guest, appears to be an inauspicious opening. I have thus pointed out two ill-omened customs which are to be avoided.

The ceremonies observed at the weddings of persons of ordinary rank are as follows:—The feast which is prepared is in proportion to the means of the individuals. There must be three wine-cups set out upon a tray. The ceremony of drinking wine three times is gone through, as described above, after which the bride changes her dress, and a feast of three courses is produced—two courses of five dishes and one of three dishes, or one course of five dishes, one of three, and one of two, according to the means of the family. A tray, with a representation of the island of Takasago, is brought out, and the wine is heated; sweetmeats of five or seven sorts are also served in boxes or trays; and when the tea comes in, the bridegroom gets up, and goes to rest himself. If the wine-kettles are of tin, they must not be set out in the room: they must be brought in from the kitchen; and in that case the paper butterflies are not attached to them.

In old times the bride and bridegroom used to change their dress three or five times during the ceremony; but at the present time, after the nine cups of wine have been drunk, in the manner recorded above, the change of dress takes place once. The bride puts on the silk robe which she has received from the bridegroom, while he dons the dress of ceremony which has been brought by the bride.

When these ceremonies have been observed, the bride's ladies conduct her to the apartments of her parents-in-law. The bride carries with her silk robes, as presents for her parents and brothers and sisters-in-law. A tray is brought out, with three wine-cups, which are set before the parents-in-law and the bride. The father-in-law drinks three cups and hands the cup to the bride, who, after she has drunk two cups, receives a present from her father-in-law; she then drinks a third cup, and returns the cup to her father-in-law, who again drinks three cups. Fish is then brought in, and, in the houses of ordinary persons, a preparation of rice. Upon this the mother-in-law, taking the second cup, drinks three cups and passes the cup to the bride, who drinks two cups and receives a present from her mother-in-law; she then drinks a third cup and gives back the cup to the mother-in-law, who drinks three cups again. Condiments are served, and, in ordinary houses, soup; after which the bride drinks once from the third cup and hands it to her father-in-law, who drinks thrice from it; the bride again drinks twice from it, and after her the mother-in-law drinks thrice. The parents-in-law and the bride thus have drunk in all nine times. If there are any brothers or sisters-in-law, soup and condiments are served, and a single porcelain wine-cup is placed before them on a tray, and they drink at the word of command of the father-in-law. It is not indispensable that soup should be served upon this occasion. If the parents of the bridegroom are dead, instead of the above ceremony, he leads his bride to make her obeisances before the tablets on which their names are inscribed.

In old days, after the ceremonies recorded above had been gone through, the bridegroom used to pay a visit of ceremony to the bride's parents; but at the present time the visit is paid before the wedding, and although the forms observed on the occasion resemble those of the ancient times, still they are different, and it would be well that we should resume the old fashion. The two trays which had been used at the wedding feast, loaded with fowl and fish and condiments neatly arranged, used to be put into a long box and sent to the father-in-law's house. Five hundred and eighty cakes of rice, in lacquer boxes were also sent. The modern practice of sending the rice cakes in a bucket is quite contrary to etiquette: no matter how many lacquer boxes may be required for the purpose, they are the proper utensils for sending the cakes in. Three, five, seven, or ten men's loads of presents, according to the means of the family, are also offered.   The son-in-law gives a sword and a silk robe to his father-in-law, and a silk robe to his mother-in-law, and also gives presents to his brothers and sisters-in-law.   (The ceremony of drinking wine is the same as that which takes place between the bride and her parents-in-law, with a very slight deviation : the bridegroom receives no presents from his mother-in-law, and when the third cup is drunk the son-in-law drinks before the father-in-law.)   A return visit is paid by the bride's parents to the bridegroom, at which similar forms are observed.

At the weddings of the great, the bridal chamber is composed of three rooms thrown into one,[1] and newly decorated. If there are only two rooms available, a third room is built for the occasion.   The presents, which have been mentioned above, are set out on two trays.   Besides these, the bridegroom's clothes are hung up upon clothes-racks.   The mattrass and bedclothes are placed in a closet.   The bride's effects must all be arranged by the women who are sent on a previous day for the purpose, or it may be done whilst the bride is changing her clothes.   The shrine for the image of the family god is placed on a shelf adjoining the sleeping-place.   There is a proper place for the various articles of furniture.   The *kaioké*[2] is placed on the raised floor ; but if there be no raised floor, it is placed in a closet with the door open, so that it may be conspicuously seen.   The books are arranged on a book-shelf or on a cabinet ; if there be neither shelf nor cabinet, they are placed on the raised floor.   The bride's clothes are set out on a clothes-rack ; in families of high rank, seven robes are hung up on the rack ; five of these are taken away and replaced by others and again three are taken away and replaced by others ; and there are either two or three clothes-racks : the towel-rack is set up in a place of more honour than the clothes-racks.

---

[1] The partitions of a Japanese suite of apartments being merely composed of paper sliding-screens, any number of rooms, according to the size of the house, can be thrown into one at a moment's notice.

[2] A *kaioké* is a kind of lacquer basin for washing the hands and face.

If there is no dressing-room, the bride's bedclothes and dressing furniture are placed in the sleeping-room. No screens are put up on the bridal night, but a fitting place is chosen for them on the following day. All these ceremonies must be in proportion to the means of the family.

NOTE

The author of the "Sho-rei Hikki" makes no allusion to the custom of shaving the eyebrows and blackening the teeth of married women, in token of fidelity to their lords. In the upper classes, young ladies usually blacken their teeth before leaving their father's house to enter that of their husbands, and complete the ceremony by shaving their eyebrows immediately after the wedding, or, at any rate, not later than upon the occasion of their first pregnancy.

The origin of the fashion is lost in antiquity. As a proof that it existed before the eleventh century, A.D., a curious book called "Teijô Zakki," or the Miscellaneous Writings of Teijô, cites the diary of Murasaki Shikibu, the daughter of one Tamésoki, a retainer of the house of Echizen, a lady of the court and famous poetess, the authoress of a book called "Genji-mono-gatari," and other works. In her diary it is written that on the last night of the fifth year of the period Kankô (A.D. 1008), in order that she might appear to advantage on New Year's-day, she retired to the privacy of her own apartment, and repaired the deficiencies of her personal appearance, by reblackening her teeth, and otherwise adorning herself. Allusion is also made to the custom in the "Yeiga-mono-gatari," an ancient book by the same authoress.

The Emperor and nobles of his court are also in the habit of blackening their teeth; but the custom is gradually dying out in their case. It is said to have originated with one Hanazono Arishito, who held the high rank of *Sa-Daijin*, or "minister of the left," at the commencement of the twelfth century, in the reign of the Emperor Toba. Being a man of refined and sensual tastes, this minister plucked out his eyebrows, shaved his beard, blackened his teeth, powdered his face white, and rouged his lips in order to render himself as like a woman as possible. In the middle of the twelfth century, the nobles of the court, who went to the wars, all blackened their teeth; and from this time forth the practice became a fashion of the court. The followers of the chiefs of the Hôjô dynasty also blackened their teeth, as an emblem of their fidelity; and this was called the Odawara fashion, after the castle town of the family. Thus a custom, which had its origin in a love of sensuality and pleasure, became mistaken for the sign of a good and faithful spirit.

The fashion of blackening the teeth entails no little trouble upon its followers, for the colour must be renewed every day, or at least every other day. Strange and repelling as the custom appears at first, the eye soon learns to look without aversion upon a well-blacked and polished set of teeth; but when the colour begins to wear away, and turns to a dullish grey, streaked with black, the mouth certainly becomes most hideous. Although no one who reads this is likely to put a recipe for blackening the teeth to a practical test, I append one furnished to me by a fashionable chemist and druggist in Yedo:—

"Take three pints of water, and, having warmed it, add half a teacupful of wine. Put into this mixture a quantity of red-hot iron; allow it to stand for five or six days, when there will be a scum on the top of the mixture, which should then be poured into a small teacup and placed near a fire. When it is warm, powdered gall-nuts and iron filings should be added to it, and the whole should be warmed again. The liquid is then painted on to the teeth by means of a soft feather brush, with more powdered gall-nuts and iron, and, after several applications, the desired colour will be obtained."

The process is said to be a preservative of the teeth, and I have known men who were habitual sufferers from toothache to prefer the martyrdom of ugliness to that of pain, and apply the black colouring when the paroxysms were severe. One man told me that he experienced immediate relief by the application, and that so long as he blackened his teeth he was quite free from pain.

ON THE BIRTH AND REARING OF CHILDREN

(From the "Sho-rei Hikki.")

In the fifth month of a woman's pregnancy, a very lucky day is selected for the ceremony of putting on a girdle, which is of white and red silk, folded, and eight feet in length. The husband produces it from the left sleeve of his dress; and the wife receives it in the right sleeve of her dress, and girds it on for the first time. This ceremony is only performed once. When the child is born, the white part of the girdle is dyed sky-blue, with a peculiar mark on it, and is made into clothes for the child. These, however, are not the first clothes which it wears. The dyer is presented with wine and condiments when the girdle is entrusted to him. It is also customary to beg some matron, who has herself had an easy confinement, for the girdle which she wore during her pregnancy; and this lady is called the girdle-mother. The borrowed girdle is tied on with that given by the husband, and the girdle-mother at this time gives and receives a present.

The furniture of the lying-in chamber is as follows:—Two tubs for placing under-petticoats in; two tubs to hold the placenta; a piece of furniture like an arm-chair, without legs, for the mother to lean against;[1] a stool, which is used

[1] Women in Japan are delivered in a kneeling position, and after the birth of the child they remain night and day in a squatting position, leaning back against a support, for twenty-one days, after which they are allowed to recline. Up to tha time the recumbent position is supposed to produce a dangerous rush of blood to the head.

by the lady who embraces the loins of the woman in labour to support her, and which is afterwards used by the midwife in washing the child; several pillows of various sizes, that the woman in child-bed may ease her head at her pleasure; new buckets, basins, and ladles of various sizes. Twenty-four baby-robes, twelve of silk and twelve of cotton, must be prepared; the hems must be dyed saffron-colour. There must be an apron for the midwife, if the infant is of high rank, in order that, when she washes it, she may not place it immediately on her own knees: this apron should be made of a kerchief of cotton. When the child is taken out of the warm water, its body must be dried with a kerchief of fine cotton, unhemmed.

On the seventy-fifth or hundred and twentieth day after its birth, the baby leaves off its baby-linen; and this day is kept as a holiday. Although it is the practice generally to dress up children in various kinds of silk, this is very wrong, as the two principles of life being thereby injured, the child contracts disease; and on this account the ancients strictly forbade the practice. In modern times the child is dressed up in beautiful clothes; but to put a cap on its head, thinking to make much of it, when, on the contrary, it is hurtful to the child, should be avoided. It would be an excellent thing if rich people, out of care for the health of their children, would put a stop to a practice to which fashion clings.

On the hundred and twentieth day after their birth children, whether male or female, are weaned.[1] This day is fixed, and there is no need to choose a lucky day. If the child be a boy, it is fed by a gentleman of the family; if a girl, by a lady. The ceremony is as follows:—The child is brought out and given to the weaning father or sponsor. He takes it on his left knee. A small table is prepared. The sponsor who is to feed the child, taking some rice which has

---

[1] This is only a nominal weaning. Japanese children are not really weaned until far later than is ordinary in Europe; and it is by no means uncommon to see a mother in the poorer classes suckling a hulking child of from five to seven years old. One reason given for this practice is, that by this means the danger of having to provide for large families is lessened.

been offered to the gods, places it on the corner of the little table which is by him ; he dips his chop-sticks thrice in this rice, and very quietly places them in the mouth of the child, pretending to give it some of the juice of the rice. Five cakes of rice meal are also placed on the left side of the little table, and with these he again pretends to feed the child three times. When this ceremony is over, the child is handed back to its guardian, and three wine-cups are produced on a tray. The sponsor drinks three cups, and presents the cup to the child. When the child has been made to pretend to drink two cups, it receives a present from its sponsor, after which the child is supposed to drink a third time. Dried fish is then brought in, and the baby, having drunk thrice, passes the cup to its sponsor, who drinks thrice. More fish of a different kind is brought in. The drinking is repeated, and the weaning father receives a present from the child. The guardian, according to rules of propriety, should be near the child. A feast should be prepared, according to the means of the family. If the child be a girl, a weaning mother performs this ceremony, and suitable presents must be offered on either side. The wine-drinking is gone through as above.

On the fifteenth day of the eleventh month of the child's third year, be the child boy or girl, its hair is allowed to grow. (Up to this time the whole head has been shaven: now three patches are allowed to grow, one on each side and one at the back of the head.) On this occasion also a sponsor is selected. A large tray, on which are a comb, scissors, paper string, a piece of string for tying the hair in a knot, cotton wool, and the bit of dried fish or seaweed which accompanies presents, one of each, and seven rice straws—these seven articles must be prepared.[1]

The child is placed facing the point of the compass which is auspicious for that year, and the sponsor, if the child be a boy, takes the scissors and gives three snips at the hair on the left temple, three on the right, and three in the centre.

[1] For a few days previous to the ceremony the child's head is not shaved.

He then takes the piece of cotton wool and spreads it over the child's head, from the forehead, so as to make it hang down behind his neck, and he places the bit of dried fish or seaweed and the seven straws at the bottom of the piece of cotton wool, attaching them to the wool, and ties them in two loops, like a man's hair, with a piece of paper string; he then makes a woman's knot with two pieces of string. The ceremony of drinking wine is the same as that gone through at the weaning. If the child is a girl, a lady acts as sponsor; the hair-cutting is begun from the right temple instead of from the left. There is no difference in the rest of the ceremony.

On the fifth day of the eleventh month of the child's fourth year he is invested with the *hakama*, or loose trousers worn by the Samurai. On this occasion again a sponsor is called in. The child receives from the sponsor a dress of ceremony, on which are embroidered storks and tortoises (emblems of longevity—the stork is said to live a thousand years, the tortoise ten thousand), fir-trees (which, being evergreen, and not changing their colour, are emblematic of an unchangingly virtuous heart), and bamboos (emblematic of an upright and straight mind). The child is placed upright on a chequer-board, facing the auspicious point of the compass, and invested with the dress of ceremony. It also receives a sham sword and dirk. The usual ceremony of drinking wine is observed.

NOTE.—In order to understand the following ceremony, it is necessary to recollect that the child at three years of age is allowed to grow its hair in three patches. By degrees the hair is allowed to grow, the crown alone being shaved, and a forelock left. At ten or eleven years of age the boy's head is dressed like a man's, with the exception of this forelock.

The ceremony of cutting off the forelock used in old days to include the ceremony of putting on the noble's cap; but as this has gone out of fashion, there is no need to treat of it.

Any time after the youth has reached the age of fifteen, according to the cleverness and ability which he shows, a lucky day is chosen for this most important ceremony, after which the boy takes his place amongst full-grown men. A person of virtuous character is chosen as sponsor or "cap-father." Although the man's real name (that name which is only known to his intimate relations and friends, not the one by which he usually goes in society) is usually determined before this date, if it be not so, he receives his real name from his sponsor on this day. In old days there used to be a previous ceremony of cutting the hair off the forehead in a straight line, so as to make two angles : up to this time the youth wore long sleeves like a woman, and from that day he wore short sleeves. This was called the "half cutting." The poorer classes have a habit of shortening the sleeves before this period; but that is contrary to all rule, and is an evil custom.

A common tray is produced, on which is placed an earthenware wine-cup. The sponsor drinks thrice, and hands the cup to the young man, who, having also drunk thrice, gives back the cup to the sponsor, who again drinks thrice, and then proceeds to tie up the young man's hair.

There are three ways of tying the hair, and there is also a particular fashion of letting the forelock grow long; and when this is the case, the forelock is only clipped. (This is especially the fashion among the nobles of the Mikado's court.) This applies only to persons who wear the court cap, and not to gentlemen of lower grade. Still, these latter persons, if they wish to go through the ceremony in its entirety, may do so without impropriety. Gentlemen of the Samurai or military class cut off the whole of the forelock. The sponsor either ties up the hair of the young man, or else placing the forelock on a willow board cuts it off with a knife, or else, amongst persons of very high rank, he only pretends to do so, and goes into another room whilst the real cutting is going on, and then returns to the same room. The sponsor then, without letting the young man see what he is doing, places the lock which has been cut into the pocket of his left sleeve, and, leaving the room, gives it to the young man's guardians, who wrap it in paper and offer it up at the shrine of the family gods. But this is wrong. The locks should be well wrapped up in paper and kept in the house until the man's death, to serve as a reminder of the favours which a man receives from his father and mother in his childhood; when he dies, it should be placed in his coffin and buried with him. The wine-drinking and presents are as before.

In the "Shorei Hikki," the book from which the above is translated, there is no notice of the ceremony of naming the child: the following is a translation from a Japanese MS.:—

"On the seventh day after its birth, the child receives its name; the ceremony is called the congratulations of the seventh night. On this day some one of the relations of the family, who holds an exalted position, either from his rank or virtues, selects a name for the child, which name he keeps until the time of the cutting of the forelock, when he takes the name which he is to bear as a man. This second name is called *Yeboshina*,[1] the cap-name, which is compounded of syllables taken from an old name of the family and from the name of the sponsor. If the sponsor afterwards change his name, his name-child must also change his name. For instance, Minamoto no Yoshitsuné, the famous warrior, as a child was called Ushiwakamaru; when he grew up to be a man, he was called Kurô; and his real name was Yoshitsuné."

[1] From *Yeboshi*, a court cap, and *Na*, a name.

FUNERAL RITES

(From the "Shorei Hikki.")

On the death of a parent, the mourning clothes worn are made of coarse hempen cloth, and during the whole period of mourning these must be worn night and day. As the burial of his parents is the most important ceremony which a man has to go through during his whole life, when the occasion comes, in order that there be no confusion, he must employ some person to teach him the usual and proper rites. Above all things to be reprehended is the burning of the dead: they should be interred without burning.[1] The ceremonies to be observed at a funeral should by rights have been learned before there is occasion to put them in practice. If a man have no father or mother, he is sure to have to bury other relations; and so he should not disregard this study. There are some authorities who select lucky days and hours and lucky places for burying the dead, but this is wrong; and when they talk about curses being brought upon posterity by not observing these auspicious seasons and places, they make a great mistake. It is a matter of course that an auspicious day must be chosen so far as avoiding wind and rain is concerned, that men may bury their dead without their minds being distracted; and it is important to choose a fitting cemetery, lest in after-days the tomb should be damaged by rain, or by men walking over it, or by the place being turned

[1] On the subject of burning the dead, see a note to the story of Chôbei of Bandzuin.

into a field, or built upon. When invited to a friend's or neighbour's funeral, a man should avoid putting on smart clothes and dresses of ceremony; and when he follows the coffin, he should not speak in a loud voice to the person next him, for that is very rude; and even should he have occasion to do so, he should avoid entering wine-shops or tea-houses on his return from the funeral.

The list of persons present at a funeral should be written on slips of paper, and firmly bound together. It may be written as any other list, only it must not be written beginning at the right hand, as is usually the case, but from the left hand (as is the case in European books).

On the day of burial, during the funeral service, incense is burned in the temple before the tablet on which is inscribed the name under which the dead person enters salvation.[1] The incense-burners, having washed their hands, one by one, enter the room where the tablet is exposed, and advance half-way up to the tablet, facing it; producing incense wrapped in paper from their bosoms, they hold it in their left hands, and, taking a pinch with the right hand, they place the packet in their left sleeve. If the table on which the tablet is placed be high, the person offering incense half raises himself from his crouching position; if the table be low, he remains crouching to burn the incense, after which he takes three steps backwards, with bows and reverences, and retires six feet, when he again crouches down to watch the incense-burning, and bows to the priests who are sitting in a row with their chief at their head, after which he rises and leaves the room. Up to the time of burning the incense no notice is taken of the priest. At the ceremony of burning incense before the grave, the priests are not saluted. The packet of incense is made of fine paper folded in three, both ways.

[1] After death, a person receives a new name. For instance, the famous Prince Tokugawa Iyéyasu entered salvation as Gongen Sama. This name is called *okurina*, or the accompanying name.

NOTE

The reason why the author of the "Shorei Hikki" has treated so briefly of the funeral ceremonies is probably that these rites, being invariably entrusted to the Buddhist priesthood, vary according to the sect of the latter; and, as there are no less than fifteen sects of Buddhism in Japan, it would be a long matter to enter into the ceremonies practised by each. Should Buddhism be swept out of Japan, as seems likely to be the case, men will probably return to the old rites which obtained before its introduction in the sixth century of our era. What those rites were I have been unable to learn.

THE END